LOOK BACK TO GLORY

LOOK BACK TO GLORY

Herbert Ravenel Sass

With a new introduction by
Barbara L. Bellows

the
History
CHARLESTON PRESS LONDON

Published by The History Press
18 Percy Street
Charleston, SC 29403
866.223.5778
www.historypress.net

Copyright © (new material) 2005 by Barbara L. Bellows
All rights reserved
First published 1933
The History Press edition 2005

Front Cover Image: Boone Hall, Mt. Pleasaant, South Carolina. *Courtesy of the Library of Congress*

Manufactured in the United Kingdom
ISBN 1-59629-032-3

Library of Congress Cataloging-in-Publication Data

Sass, Herbert Ravenel, 1884-1958.
  Look back to glory / Herbert Ravenel Sass ; with new introduction by Barbara L. Bellows.
     p. cm.
  ISBN 1-59629-032-3 (alk. paper)
  1. South Carolina--History--Civil War, 1861-1865--Fiction. 2. Charleston (S.C.)--Fiction. 3. Diplomats--Fiction. I. Title.
  PS3537.A842L66 2005
  813'.52--dc22
                                       2005007566

From the Publisher:
This new edition contains the full text from the Charleston edition of Herbert Ravenel Sass's *Look Back to Glory*, published in 1933 by The Bobbs-Merrill Company. All efforts have been made to maintain the integrity of the original work, including spelling, dialect and punctuation.

Notice: The information in this book is true and complete to the best of our knowledge. It is offered without guarantee on the part of the author or The History Press. The author and The History Press disclaim all liability in connection with the use of this book.

All rights reserved. No part of this book may be reproduced or transmitted in any form whatsoever without prior written permission from the publisher except in the case of brief quotations embodied in critical articles and reviews.

Contents

Introduction by Barbara L. Bellows … 7

Look Back to Glory

    Part One: Avalon … 49

    Part Two: Notteley … 191

    Part Three: Charleston … 335

INTRODUCTION
by Barbara L. Bellows

HERBERT RAVENEL SASS'S *LOOK BACK to Glory* may be read and enjoyed simply as a romantic tale that captures both the charm and the tragedy of the Old South at the end of its Golden Age. Human passions and emotions are set against the backdrop of historical events. Days on the opulent plantations of the Carolina Lowcountry are filled with activities pursued at a leisurely pace. The highly structured, mannered society is governed by a code of behavior that crystallized during the eighteenth century when America was evolving into an agrarian republic. In the novel, a love triangle forms and plays out against the drama of the coming of the Civil War, and is resolved in 1863 during the Confederacy's dramatic struggle against the Federal ironclads trying to retake Fort Sumter. But the reader who probes more deeply will be rewarded with a rich analysis of South Carolina's history and contemporary politics that Sass inserted "between the lines."

Herbert Ravenel Sass was born on November 2, 1884, at a time when Charleston was still bowed by postwar poverty. He grew up in the Sass family home at 23 Legaré Street, a stately brick house that was filled not only with a wistfulness about the past, but also a passion to keep alive the memory of all that had been and now was lost. Sass's aunts kept a school for girls in a rear building. His father, George Herbert Sass, was a Charlestonian of German extraction whose family had been in South Carolina since the American Revolution. In 1883, George Sass married Anna Eliza Ravenel, who belonged to an old Huguenot family—plantation aristocrats whose ancestors were among the earliest settlers of the colony. Anna's mother Harriott Horry Rutledge Ravenel wrote biographies of both her own famous great-grandmother Eliza Lucas Pinckney and her kinsman, South Carolina Congressman William Lowndes, as well as *Charleston: The Place and the People* (1906). Her father, St. Julien Ravenel, was the inventor of the first "submersible" vessel, a prototype of the submarine.

George Herbert Sass trained as a lawyer and spent most of his career as the city's master-in-equity of the Court of Common Pleas, but his real love was literature. Even though times were hard, he scrimped and sacrificed to buy books to expand his notable private library. Had the Civil War not intervened and broken up the literary circle of writers and poets that was making Charleston a literary center of note during the 1850s, Sass (who was born in 1845) would likely have joined Charleston's small cluster of professional men of letters. As a young man he had won the praise of novelist William Gilmore Simms. Writing under the name of "Barton Grey" and cultivating a classical

INTRODUCTION

Herbert Ravenel Sass, 19xx.

style, Sass won prizes for his patriotic poetry during the war and was widely considered the successor to South Carolina's Henry Timrod, poet laureate of the Confederacy. For many years, Sass tried to encourage interest in the arts among Charlestonians through a weekly column in the Charleston *News and Courier*. He reviewed books, commented on current plays and gave notice of public lectures. In 1904, the New York firm of George P. Putnam published his collected poetry as *The Heart's Quest*. George Herbert Sass died in 1908.

As a young man, Herbert Ravenel Sass was also fascinated by literature and science. He pursued both these fields at the College of Charleston, where he edited the school's literary magazine. He stayed on at the college after graduation in 1905, and received his MA in biology the next year. Years later, the College of Charleston awarded Sass an honorary doctorate in literature. After working for a time with the struggling Charleston Museum, Sass took a position at the Charleston *News and Courier* in 1908. Developing a distinct and graceful writing style, he moved swiftly from reporter to assistant editor with chief responsibility for editorial writing. At every opportunity, though, Sass slipped away from his desk to explore the expansive beaches or black-water cypress swamps that beckoned just outside the city. He found his most profound literary inspiration in nature, and continued the tradition of writing about the Lowcountry that had established the reputation of nineteenth-century writer William Elliott in *Carolina Sports by Land and Water* (1846, 1859).

While still in his twenties, Sass earned a national reputation as an expert on the birds and other fauna of the Carolina Lowcountry. In addition to his newspaper column "Woods and Waters," he wrote articles for *Nature* magazine and short stories, such as "Lynx Lucifer" (1924), for popular magazines including *The Saturday Evening Post*, *Harpers*, *Colliers* and *Good Housekeeping*.

Sass was the first among the modern Charleston writers to win national attention. When his collection of nature essays *The Way of the Wild* was released in 1925 (on the same day as DuBose Heyward's first novel *Porgy*), many compared him to John Burroughs, America's most beloved nature writer who had died a few years earlier. Like Burroughs, Sass distained the

INTRODUCTION

Herbert Ravenel Sass, 19xx.

"nature fakers" who sacrificed accuracy for a sentimental animal story. He was always "darn careful not to do violence to the known facts of natural history" in his own writing. Sass crafted delightful tales of his encounters with nature that echoed Burroughs's own philosophy, "What is knowledge without enjoyment, without love?"

In fact, love of the Carolina Lowcountry—its natural environment, its people and its history—was the animating emotion that defined Sass as a man and as a writer. In 1920, Sass admitted to *Atlantic Monthly* editor Ellery Sedgwick, "I am so much in love with this Low Country that I expect (rather unreasonably, perhaps) everyone else to fall in love with it, too." And after reading Sass's articles, many people did.

After World War I, when reunion was more or less complete and even southerners spoke of *the* United States instead of *these*, Charleston was becoming a popular tourist destination. Americans anxious to escape northern cities transformed by the demands of industry and commerce took enormous pleasure in the town's old world charm and the natural beauty of its surrounding area. Sass's magazine pieces transcended sectional issues by focusing upon the universal appeal of nature. He wrote about beauty, not politics. His South was the inviting land of pink- and lavender-hued spring and "broom-grass golden in the November sunlight," a place teeming with life, not the black crepe-draped place of mourning for a Lost Cause that visitors such as Henry James had reported years before.

Among all the writers and artists associated with Charleston's cultural "renaissance" after World War I, Herbert Ravenel Sass most fully embodied the wide range of interests, intellectual curiosity, grounding in science and literature and history that the term implies. Sass never traveled widely, focusing his prodigious intellectual energies on understanding all aspects of the Carolina Lowcountry, but he possessed the sort of mind that could perceive "a universe in a grain of sand." His historical research provided him perspective on the past, his scientific training and nature study grounded him very much in the present moment, and his half-century of work as a newspaperman and editor forced him to always be anticipating future events. Herbert Ravenel Sass chose to be a "regional" writer so that he might express his "feeling for this Carolinian country—its natural beauty, its mystical fascination and its fine and too often misunderstood past."

With his growing success as a freelancer and the encouragement of Charles Livingston Bull (a noted nature artist who had illustrated Sass's stories), Sass began to glimpse the possibility of achieving his father's dream of making a living exclusively from writing, liberated from his workaday job. He left his position at the newspaper in 1925. An engaging companion who possessed an unaffected natural chivalry in his interactions with others, Sass displayed such a lack of interest in the acquisition of material goods that his friends dubbed him "Hobo."

In 1918, Sass married Marion Hutson, a young Charleston woman who was as outgoing and vivacious as Sass was reserved. They had three children, Elizabeth Elliott, Herbert Ravenel Jr. ("Sparrow") and Marion Hutson ("Chick"). The "astonishingly shy" and modest Sass sought no society except that of his large extended family and close friends and was happiest when they were all gathered for long days of fishing and crabbing at "Curlew Town," his Edisto Island retreat.

As his fame increased, Sass eluded reporters and curious folk with the same skill as the woodland creatures he loved, but he always welcomed the serious writers, such Sinclair Lewis and John P. Marquand, who sought him out when they visited Charleston. A man of "unshakable integrity," Sass resembled the type of nineteenth-century South Carolinian identified by Joseph Hergeshemier in his book *Sword and Roses* (1929) who "held themselves more dearly than they held their possessions." Or, to use another formulation, Sass sought "to be" rather than "to have."

At the time Sass began working on *Look Back to Glory* around 1932, he was approaching the height of his literary powers. He had written four books: *The Way of the Wild* (1925), *Adventures in Green Places* (1926), *Grey Eagle* (1927), *On the Wings of a Bird* (1929) and a novel, *War Drums* (1928). In 1931, he wrote the lead article and helped edit *The Carolina Lowcountry*, a volume of articles and songs published by the Society for the Preservation of Spirituals, an organization dedicated to preserving Gullah culture, which was of special interest to Sass's wife.

By the 1930s, a larger "southern renaissance" had expanded from its modest beginnings in Charleston. William Faulkner's violent frontier Mississippi and Erskine Caldwell's decadent Georgia began superseding the genteel Lowcountry in the American imagination. The growing popularity of the "sneering or satirical" approach to writing about the region promoted the persistent image of the "benighted South" that South Carolina's writers had tried so hard to dispel. Ever since 1865, almost all elements of southern life and thought were tarred with the brush of intellectual and moral inferiority. Sass was disturbed by the growing prominence of this "bloody head and bones" school of literature (as Ellen Glasgow called it). He rejected the notion that "realism" perforce meant "ugliness" or perversion.

In the evenings after supper, Sass would retire to his back steps where he listened for whirring wings as birds swooped down to roost in his oasis. In rebellion against the Charleston formal garden with its sterile snipped privet, Sass (a bit of contrarian) had let the rear of his property on Legaré Street revert to a state of nature, a jungle of bamboo, trees and berried vines. Sitting alone during the dark days of the Great Depression, Sass began to brood not just about the reputation of the South, but also about the fate of the nation. How had things gone so terribly wrong? Banks had locked their doors; depositors lost their savings. The city of Charleston was broke, its workers paid in script. Bonds were worthless, stocks depleted of value. Farmers burned worthless crops while urban dwellers went hungry. Unemployment lines grew longer. Southern factories cut costs with cheap child labor. Against this background of despair, Sass began to turn over in his mind the idea for a novel with a contemporary message. He believed he knew where the nation had taken a "wrong turn" and resolved to share it in his tale that cast the South in the unusual role of the redeemer.

To win the war, Sass would argue, Lincoln had accelerated the transformation of the American economy away from its traditional agricultural base and turned too much discretion over to northern financiers and industrialists. Through various banking acts and tariffs of the one-sided type that never would have passed before secession, the government subsidized the creation of an industrialized belt from Chicago to Boston that came to dominate all sectors of the national economy. Creating a northeastern monopoly of the essential elements of transportation, finance and manufacturing destroyed the equilibrium between rural and urban life that had been at the heart of the founding principles of the republic. The Great Depression was born out of this disequilibrium.

By the 1930s, with slavery "a dead issue" and industrial capitalism faltering, Sass believed that the historical pendulum had reached its apogee and was going to swing back. The time was right to reconsider the lost wisdom of the antebellum South. Sass's goal, in this novel and for the rest of his life actually, was to assert a Southern Tradition that he believed had existed quite apart from slavery and white supremacy. This southern ethic, as Sass and other southern intellectuals were reconceiving it, embraced the ideals of republicanism, Western Christian Civilization, the model of English law and constitutionalism and understood social hierarchy as natural and inevitable. The Southern Tradition also assumed a transcendent order was at work in the world and often described political problems in moral terms. Sass wanted to encourage all Americans living on the edge of crisis to sift through the charred ruins of the world that was lost at Appomattox and to take a second look at the "essential principles" of the Old South "in the light that a chastened experience has brought us." Southern principles had been "crushed," but not discredited, and only became obsolete, he argued, because "the North became hostile to its own past."

The "real and very great glory" that Sass memorializes in his Civil War novel is not the expected exaltation of blind bravery and slashing sabers of cavaliers charging into the valley of death. Instead, Sass seeks to relate the never-before-told story of thirty years of South Carolina's statecraft during the period from about 1828, when the first sustained arguments over the tariffs and nullification began, to secession in 1860. At that time the Palmetto State wielded influence vastly disproportionate to its size and "typified the philosophy of the South." South Carolina "had established here the most successful agrarian society known in American history, a society which had attained maturity and stability and had begun to flower," he wrote to his perspective editor at Bobbs-Merrill, an Indiana-based publishing house. South Carolina represented the "most compact and successful application of principles to which, in large degree, we are going to have to return and return pretty quickly."

The Carolina Lowcountry, enriched first by indigo, then rice and sea-island cotton, showered its blessings on a small fraction of the population. The established families intermarried with one another to form an agrarian aristocracy. Suggestive of how closely Sass identified personally with the story of South Carolina, he populates the plantation district with characters bearing names of his family and those of his wife, such as Ravenel, Waight, Hutson and Elliott. These lucky few live charmed lives on plantations with the authentic Lowcountry names of Wantoot, Crowfield and Lewisfield. Anticipating the criticism of class-conscious reviewers during the 1930s, Sass describes South Carolina and the "city-state" of Charleston as being run by an oligarchy, a ruling class open to all men of talent. Sass makes sure Langdon Cheves, James Henry Hammond, William Gilmore Simms and James Louis Petigru, who were self-made

17

or one generation removed, mingle socially at the plantation parties with the scions of old families.

Sass personally admired John C. Calhoun, the "Marx of the Master Class," whom he held up as a prime example of the permeability of the Carolina clique. Calhoun had turned to the ancient Greeks for his model of government. The underlying premise was the "realistic" assumption that within human society, a natural hierarchy of talents and abilities exists. By using the Greek example, Calhoun moved the discussion away from race to class. In the Greek model, the inferiors serve their superiors, but those at the top of the hierarchy also have responsibilities to the bottom rung. The northern free-market economy, in contrast, was based upon the "root, hog or die" philosophy of the emerging radical bourgeois individualism.

The editors at Bobbs-Merrill Publishing Company immediately recognized Sass's manuscript as possessing the power of authenticity and being far superior to the common run of historical novels that flooded the market during the 1930s. This "intelligently, even brilliantly conceived" novel, one reader observed, was "written by a gentleman about gentlemen," and was further distinguished by "the charm of good manners." Another reader pronounced Sass's passages describing the Carolina Lowcountry as "exquisitely beautiful" and praised his "most unusual and lovely gift for translating to the reader his own delicate and comprehensive appreciation of nature—the woods, the rice lands, the river, the wild life, all are here set down in their own grace and beauty."

INTRODUCTION

Look Back to Glory begins with a sense of impending doom. One of the alternative titles had been "High Noon." In 1859, after a dozen years in the diplomatic service, Richard Acton returns home to Avalon, his family's Lowcountry home. He rides through a mist of "fateful foreboding" hanging over the shadow-darkened pine woods and moss-draped live oaks. World weary from his travels that included time in Czarist Russia and in Paris, Acton is shocked to find the quiet beauty of the Lowcountry shattered by wild talk of secession. John Brown's recent raid upon Harpers Ferry, the fruit of the northern abolitionist's "incitement to bloody insurrection," has given new life to the frenzy for disunion. Acton's boyhood friends can speak of nothing else but the need to avenge the South's honor; they had been stirred up by rabid editorials in the *Charleston Mercury*. Acton sees the leader of the "Fire eaters," Barnwell Rhett, as "a primary menace to the South's safety."

After his years abroad, Acton understands that slavery, a reviled feudal system, had been a "trap" for the South that had isolated the region from the rest of the world. He is clear in his mind that the institution "must go" and had hoped that southerners would have been allowed to work out their own solution to this intractable problem. Possibly anticipating the argument of historian Bertram Wyatt Brown in *Southern Honor: Ethics and Behavior in the Old South* (1982), Sass blames the prevalent Southern Code with the failure to resolve sectional differences, as much as the threatening overblown attacks of the abolitionists. The Southern Code of Honor, an almost medieval set of rules of behavior, endowed Carolina's young men, who were often more brave than wise, with a hypersensitivity to arcane points of honor that made it impossible for them to live in the harried modern world grown "careless of manners and contemptuous of the old punctilio." When the war comes, Acton considers it a "folly of fanaticisms" on both sides.

By 1859, older South Carolinians no longer recognized the agrarian republic of their youth. They felt that industrial capitalism had thrust the northern states into a different universe. As northerners left their farms for factories, their culture changed as well. Cooperation gave way to competition. The organic family unit succumbed to individualism. Many in the plantation communities of the Lowcountry viewed the triumphalism of the market-oriented North, the expansion of the federal government, the secularization of society and the blind faith in material progress with the same sense of impending disastrous fate that traditional societies now view globalization. The assertion of states' rights was about preserving chattel slavery against the imposition of a wage labor system, but it was also about opposing concepts of the Union, holding onto local autonomy and preserving southern "individualities" against the tidal wave of standardization. The South stood alone as the last "non-materialistic" society among the Western nations, a society that valued character more than wealth.

Ever polite, Sass made many concessions to the wishes of his editors (too many, he later thought), but he warned them, "I'll fight with ferocity when I'm sure I'm right." One scene that Sass fought for was the tilting tournament, as elaborately crafted a scene as may be found in Sir Walter Scott's *Ivanhoe*. Sass's editors thought the whole thing too unbelievable, too "utopian," but Sass, hackles up, asserted he could cite the date of a column in the *Charleston Mercury* of an account very much like the one he described. He wanted to illustrate the dramatic time vacuum in which the "Carolina civilization" existed. Indeed, in late March 1859, the *Mercury* gave extensive coverage to a "tilting and ring contest" staged by the Charleston Light Dragoons, a "kid glove" home guard that had been organized in the early eighteenth century. The *Mercury*, mouthpiece for secessionist Robert Barnwell Rhett, was subtly suggesting southern preparedness for war. The reader, of course, knows that the young centaurs dashing furiously about with sabers whirling at wooden posts, and pistols blazing at fixed targets were preparing for the wrong war. In the impending conflict, they would be riding not against the black knight, but against well-aimed, fire-tempered artillery. Southern chivalry would be exploded upon a field of slaughter.

Richard Acton (like Sass) takes up the unrewarding role of truth-teller. "Behold the effect of the unpalatable truth," quips Acton when he warns his hotheaded friends that Dixie would not prevail in a contest with the North. After his time in Europe, Acton understands that the power of the liberal "dream" had become more powerful than the value of southern cotton. "Good God, nobody here realizes what Mrs. Stowe's done with her book," Acton exclaims. "A false picture but with enough truth in it to make the whole thing believed.... The Europeans believe it because they want to and would never stand still for their government's supporting the slave South."

Acton quickly runs afoul of James Hail, the personification of all "the fire and ardor of the South," by inadvertently wounding the young man's "fine spun sense of honor." Hail is reminiscent of those "prehistoric" southern men such as Faulkner's John Satorious, the South Carolina native from *Flags in the Dust*, who was "too grandly conceived and executed either to exist very long or to vanish utterly when dead." Quick to take offense, Hail, like South Carolina's Preston Brooks, who had thrashed the insulting Charles Sumner of Massachusetts on the floor of the Senate, can only see the compelling obligation of honor, "not the lamentable practical results."

Inevitably, in this age of "pistols for two and coffee for one," Hail and Acton meet on the field of honor. Their differences are not only political; they have become rivals for the beautiful Diane Rowland, Hail's fiancée with whom Acton has fallen in love. As Acton rides through the dawn, he catches phrases from eerie Gullah spirituals coming from the slave cabins like a Greek chorus: "Eb'rybody who is libin' got to die/De rich en de po', de great en de small,/All got to meet at Jedgement hall." Acton and Hail, as well as their obsolete world, it seems, are moving toward their denouement.

Throughout the novel, James Hail remains a "marble man," high minded and never doubting the archaic ideas of honor that cause him to push the South toward war. The narcissistic Diane Rowland complains that Hail loves South

Carolina more than her. She is probably right. Sass modeled Hail after his boyhood friend, Edward L. Wells, who was "in his salient characteristics James Hail exactly." Wells, Sass and DuBose Heyward had all been members of the "Galahads," a young men's club in Charleston. Wells died a hero's death in the Meuse-Argonne Offensive during World War I. Raised on tales of the Charleston Light Dragoons' daredevil bravery, told by his father, a Confederate veteran who wrote romantic Civil War stories, Wells was killed during an exceptional act of personal bravery. He won a posthumous oak-leaf cluster for moving alone against a nest of machine-gun emplacements that blocked the American advance against the Germans. Sass perhaps had sensed Wells's determination to distinguish himself in the headlong Confederate manner, for in his last letter Sass had warned his friend, "Take care of yourself, old man, and don't be unnecessarily rash in going after the Hun."

DuBose Heyward, whose physical infirmities from polio kept him out of the war, dedicated "Aftermath," a poem in *Skylines and Horizons*, "to Edward L. Wells. Killed in Action." Heyward wrote, "Almost I envy you your rich, young death." *Look Back to Glory* was Sass's tribute. The tall, painfully thin Sass had been rejected when he volunteered because of his "deficiency in weight," and chafed at being left behind. Sass's editorial praising of Wells's heroism so affected the soldier's family that they gave him the silver flatware that Wells would have inherited.

After winning a reputation for his novels of African American life, DuBose Heyward had also turned to historical fiction, a genre that was extraordinarily popular during the Depression and had the potential of catching Hollywood's eye for a costume drama. In 1932, Heyward's Civil War novel *Peter Ashley* was published. His story shares a common element with Sass's, the Charleston scene on the eve of secession viewed through the critical eyes of a native son returned home from Europe. Born only a year apart, Sass and Heyward both had a perspective on both sides of the cultural divide that separated the old heartbroken Lost Cause literature and modernism. World War I, its devastation and complicated aftermath, and the ultimate sectional reunion influenced both of these authors as they wrote about the Civil War. Their stories are sober and paint the Confederate War as the angel of misery and death, destroying all that southerners held dear. Neither one of their protagonists want to fight, although both ultimately do. Their discussions of the coming of the war owe nothing to the old "devil" school of causation. Both seek a balanced approach. Unionist James Louis Petigru, the savvy old Charleston lawyer, is a prescient Cassandra in both novels. In 1938, Heyward and Sass would collaborate on a book about Fort Sumter.

Peter Ashley moves along more smoothly than does Sass's novel, but to a less satisfying conclusion. Sass was more intellectually daring than Heyward, taking more risks, doing more research and striving to "enlighten" as well as entertain his readers. John Bennett, the elder statesman of the Charleston Renaissance who had mentored Heyward a decade earlier, thought *Look Back to Glory* compared favorably with Heyward's novel. Sass discussed his novel at regular Monday evening meetings with Bennett, his Legaré Street neighbor, Peter Gething, a British veteran who found some success writing tales of the horrors of World War I, and nationally recognized ornithologist Alexander Sprunt, whose own nature stories had been collected into a book, *Dwellers of the Silences* (1931).

Determined to win a national audience for his ideas, Sass realized that his portrait of South Carolina and its people had to reveal the full range of human valor and vainglory, fineness and frailty. Sass unequivocally repudiated slavery, but in his novel makes the case that on the wealthy plantations of the Lowcountry the fate of the slave was relatively better than those on the frontiers of the Old Southwest, such as Mississippi or Alabama. He also punctures the widespread argument that slavery had been a "Godsend" for uncivilized Africans. When Diane Rowland reflects upon the popular ironic concept of slavery as a "school" for the primitive, she notes sardonically, "no method was provided for the graduation of pupils who had completed the course." Illustrative of her point, the restive Big Sam flings himself in to the river and drowns rather than receive another whipping. Sass's portrayal of slaves endows them with humanity and individual personalities, suggesting that slaves dealt with their dilemma in their own unique ways.

Sass knew he must also "grasp the nettle" and deal with the "poison" of miscegenation, a topic that Heyward breezed over. After the Civil War, a veil had dropped upon this subject that was once a common topic of gossip. In her famous diary,

Mary Boykin Chesnut had observed that everyone whispered about the paternity of house servants except, of course, those waiting tables in their own homes. In his 1837 *Memoir on Slavery*, Chancellor William Harper claimed that miscegenation, like slavery itself, was a positive good because it elevated the social position of all white women and freed the South of the odious class of prostitutes that haunted northern cities.

At the Rowland's Notteley plantation, Richard Acton observes the lithe slave Vienna, a golden-skinned quadroon, parading in a red headdress before the leering young gentlemen like "a leopardess languid after sleep." A master exercising his droit was a brutal aspect of the system that abolitionists had seized upon, accusing slaveholders of operating brothels, but the worldly Richard Acton, who had himself been enamored with a high-class French courtesan, discerns that Vienna was making an economic calculation of her own. If she could win the attention, and perhaps the affections, of one of the young plantation hot bloods, "it might even lead to a little house of one's own and a life of agreeable indolence instead of work in the fields." The poor workingwomen of the North had the alternatives of factory labor, domestic service or prostitution, choices that inevitably lead to disease, degradation and death. "What a damned twisted mess the abolitionists were making of the truth!" Acton thought.

Southern plantation mistresses stoically accepted what they could not change and used their husband's weaknesses to their own advantage. Their tacit acceptance of miscegenation endowed plantation wives with moral power and social virtue. When Diane Rowland accidentally discovers that the stain of miscegenation had worked its way into her own family, she is horrified. Her mother Adèle Chantilly Rowland counsels her to be philosophical, "We have to speak of facts." Miscegenation, she explains, is an inevitable consequence of slavery, the institution that made possible the plantation system from which they all benefited. Any man from any region would react in the same way if provided with the unique enticements offered by their peculiar institution. "Our Notteley magnolias have grown out of black muck. You have just seen the muck."

When Sass shared his manuscript with Josephine Pinckney, who was beginning her own historical novel *Hilton Head*, she praised him for mounting the "courage it takes in a community like ours to ignore the established tabus." She also cautioned him that he was putting himself between "two fires," the old conservative Charlestonians and the New York critics of the new southern literature who were especially keen to detect signs of the old atavistic romance, local color, filiopiety or special pleading.

Sass sent copies of *Look Back to Glory* to two local newspaper editors, William Watts Ball and Thomas R. Waring. Both were gentlemen of the old school for whom Sass felt a great deal of admiration and affection. He explained that he could not do a "full-length picture of our people's past," throwing light upon their achievements "for the first time in fiction, without also dealing explicitly with the shadows which of course existed." It would never do, Sass asserted, for a Charlestonian "to set forth on a printed page what is actually in his heart about his city."

Sass wanted to transcend "the petty meannesses of the Southern sentimentalists" in laying out the life and record of the Lowcountry's people. If he were to bow to local pressure and filter history through "rose-tinted lights only," Sass wrote Waring, he would never find a publisher and "our whole great achievement here should be rendered practically unavailable as literary material....We have nothing to fear from a candid exposition of the facts." Sass believed "it is our policy of dignified evasion of these matters that gives the so-called realists their chance to paint as black, unmitigated shame what was in reality only the inevitable reaction of human nature to the pre-civil war Southern environment."

Both editors supported Sass. Waring generously agreed that a candid discussion of the Lowcountry's past "cried to be done" and that Sass, with his knowledge and insight, was the man to do what an earlier generation could not. "We who are so deeply rooted in the soil of our traditions and are so near to the fires that burned these to the ground," Waring wrote, "find it hard to resist the urge to emotion when we hark back, or to resent what—perhaps unjustly—seems to us assault upon things cherished."

Ball wrote a review for the Charleston *News and Courier*, comparing the fast-paced action of *Look Back to Glory* with its "thud of hoofs, the clash and crackle of arms," with the popular *Prisoner of Zenda*. But it was the historical representation of the

South that most concerned Ball. He praised Sass not only for his originality in being the first to outline why South Carolinians went to war, but for the graceful and readable way in which he presented his research in novel form. Although not a school text, Ball encouraged all the schoolteachers "who cherish the Old South" to direct their students to this novel because "history as Mr. Sass has written it is true."

Sass was equally as honest with his publisher as he had been with his Charleston mentors. "I am very much an unreconstructed rebel," he confessed. By this he meant that he rejected the consensus view that defeat of the Confederacy had been "a blessing" for the nation. In fact, he thought removing the voice of the agrarian South from the national conversation had been "disastrous" for the republic. The "underlying thesis" of *Look Back to Glory* was that the Civil War destroyed "a civilization, more realistic, sounder and saner than the one that supplanted it." Sass later admitted to a "savage pleasure" in refuting the misconceptions about the South. He hoped to explode the stereotypes of southerners as decadent and lazy, and embracing such a "childishly romantic and essentially sinister philosophy" that all they had suffered during and after the Civil War was "merited retribution."

At a time when most scholars dismissed the political writings of William Gilmore Simms, Chancellor William Harper, Paul Hamilton Hayne and James Henry Hammond as merely self-serving defenses of an exploitative labor system, Sass took the southern intellectual critique of industrial capitalism seriously, as have later historians. He also believed that southerners had a unique agrarian way of life (outside of slaveholding) that they were willing to defend. The great architects of South Carolina's agrarian ideology all make appearances in the novel, often interrupting the flow of the narrative with their expositions. At one point, Simms explains the circle of responsibility for slavery, the nation's original sin.

> *The Northern States never in any true sense freed their slaves. What they really did was this: having found that Negro labor was not profitable in their climate, which gave their slave-owners plenty of time to sell their slaves in the South. Then, after selling their Negroes to us and taking our cash for them, they announced grandly that they had ended slavery within their borders. So they had, and they had made money by it.*

Sass contends that the political thought of South Carolina was not merely pro-slavery, but part of the larger history of modern conservative thought that coalesced in opposition to what were considered irresponsible egalitarian claims of the French Enlightenment and the later violence and bloodshed accompanying both the French and Industrial Revolutions. Sass includes a quotation from Irish-born British statesman Edmund Burke, the fountainhead of modern conservatism, in the opening of the novel and later has a character reading from his works. Burke's writings, particularly those upholding the rights of the landed aristocracy against the encroachments of the rising urban merchant class, enjoyed honored places in Lowcountry libraries.

One of Burke's most devoted followers was political philosopher Lord John Acton, from whom Sass draws the name of his protagonist, Richard Acton. (Richard was the name of Lord John's father.) Lord Acton, who is best remembered for his famous quotation, "Power corrupts and absolute power corrupts absolutely," denounced all forms of arbitrary power and absolutism. Sass agreed with Lord Acton, who hypothesized in his essay "Political Causes of the American Civil War" (1860) that the Civil War was caused by the agricultural South's resistance to encroachments on their autonomy by a northern majority manipulated by industrialists, capitalists, fanatics and those favoring a more powerful central government.

Sass blamed Francophile Thomas Jefferson for setting America, the world really, on a search for a democratic utopia where everyone was equal. Sass believed that the same ideas of "perfectionism" that spawned the radical abolitionist movement had imbedded within it a dangerous element of intolerance of difference. The rise of the totalitarian governments, "Caesarism and Socialism," in Europe during the 1930s further confirmed his belief.

John C. Calhoun, in contrast to the romantic Jefferson, tried to "save democracy from itself." Fearful of the "despotism of the majority," Calhoun, the most original political thinker of his generation, had kept the problem of minority rights foremost in the political discussion. He had provided the only viable solution to secession by arguing for the establishment of a "concurrent minority." Another tragedy of the defeat of the Confederacy, in Sass's opinion, had been the silencing of Calhoun's voice in the modern political forum.

In the same way that Sass thought it important to place the political thought of South Carolina in a historical continuum, so too is it valuable to locate Sass within his own intellectual tradition. Sass was not a solitary voice alone on his piazza raging at the world. He belongs to a southern tradition of agrarian thinkers whose American origins can be traced back to eighteenth-century Virginia. The writings of John Randolph of Roanoke and John Taylor of Caroline reflect their concern that individual liberties could be crushed by the mass will and that republican values were suppressed to meet the demands of commerce and industry. Sass, however, is more closely connected to the 1930s expression of agrarianism that actually coalesced in response to the materialism of the previous decade, when Americans first began to see their common identity as consumers instead of citizens.

Sass joined a chorus of Americans expressing their concerns about the "Frankenstein" of industrialization, with its attendant trends toward consolidation, centralization and standardization. In *Look Back to Glory*, a book that Sass declared was in "rebellion" against the modern liberal state, he mounts a critique of industrial capitalism that was in harmony with the main thesis of *I'll Take My Stand* (1930), the magnum opus of southern agrarianism. John Crowe Ransom, Allen Tate, Donald Davidson and Robert Penn Warren were among the "Twelve Southerners" who wrote the essays for this symposium. The agrarian *cri de coeur* in its most succinct formulation was that the economy should serve man, not the other way around. Sass met both Ransom and Davidson during their visits to Charleston. Ransom spoke to the Poetry Society in 1928. Davidson also gave a lecture in 1927, and returned in 1932 for a meeting of southern writers held in Charleston that Sass helped organize.

In December 1933, Sass delivered a radio address under the auspices of the South Carolina Economic Association. As he explained the relationship between *Look Back to Glory* and the contemporary problems of Depression America, he endorsed the ideas of the agrarians and remarked that "thoughtful men are coming more and more into agreement that the only solution, outside of a rigidly and permanently managed national existence, lies in the effective restoration of the equilibrium between urban and rural life." "They believe that the Machine Age has not entirely destroyed the human spirit and sense of individualism," but warn that "the overwhelming dominance of the great industrial cities must be ended; that there must be a decentralization of money, of power; that the surplus masses in the cities must be distributed upon the land; that a prosperous rural life must be restored." Sass contended that instead of being unsound, the South had been on its way to a mixed economy with agriculture dominant. Although economic historians continue to be divided on this point, Sass argued that the South's agrarian economy had been viable, and "when we contemplate the pass to which the Northern economics have brought us today," the contention that an industrial economy was superior "loses about all the weight it ever had."

In Sass's thought, as in the agrarians', there lingered a subtle shade of Southern Nationalism, the belief that southerners actually were a different people with a unique heritage. Henry Timrod's *Ethnogenesis*, proclaiming the birth of the Southern nation in 1860, had been a staple of Sass's childhood, and indeed every southern schoolboy's education. Lying beneath the talk of a different civilization, however, was a yearning shared by many southern traditionalists for a mythical lost moral community bound by a common faith. Southern agrarianism, it should be noted, was a movement carried forward by poets and writers rather than economists. Thinking they were perpetuating the southern tradition, they actually generated a new mythology for the modern age, since so much of the past had already faded away.

Much to Sass's delight, the publication of *Look Back to Glory* became part of the debate sparked by *I'll Take My Stand*, and was discussed on editorial pages as well as book review columns. One of the leading voices for industrialization as a cure for southern poverty, North Carolina editor Jonathan Daniels, took up Sass's critique in the Raleigh *Times-Observer*. In "Lavender and Old Lace," Daniels advised southerners to give up their nostalgia for the past and realize that the New South, with its cities and factories, is "the bed in which we were born and the one in which we must die."

Sass has been accused of being an Old South romantic, but what he most mourned about the modern age, a sadness we might all share, was the separation, even alienation, of man from nature. If James Hail stands for southern honor, and Richard Acton for southern political realism, it is Diane Rowland whom Sass endows with a profound connection to the untamed wildness of the South. Unlike most of the Lowcountry women of her class, she is oblivious to politics and careless of the rules of the Code. Bored with the local society along the river and jaded with the earnest swain vying for her attention, her only real joy is found among the wild things in the green world. Consequently, she is the character most alive to the full mystical experience of nature. The shimmering iridescent waves of shore birds taking flight in the late afternoon sun could still inspire her with awe. She experiences a mystical kinship with the natural world that pulsates with life, and she felt, *knew* "that somehow in some incomprehensible way she was part of it and it a part of her." Driven by an irresistible compulsion, she writes down her profound experiences with nature, but then locks them away.

Rejecting Christian pieties, Diane Rowland is "pretty thoroughly pagan." Nature, she concludes, is "beyond good and evil; there couldn't be evil where beauty was." Ultimately, through Diane, Sass expresses the core of his belief. He argues for the redemptive power of beauty, the transcendence of nature. The Carolina Lowcountry was a flawed society, but also a graceful and dignified one. Its sins were the sins of human weakness. Its justification was its beauty and intimacy with nature.

At least one of the readers at Bobbs-Merrill understood Sass. After evaluating his manuscript, she declared a change of heart about the region she had always found "incomprehensible and indefensible." "Well, to know all is to forgive all!" she wrote. But ultimately, Sass was deeply disappointed, even embittered, by his publisher's dismissal of his novel as a "southern book," doing little to promote it in the North where readers were passionately interested in an alternative vision of American life. Nevertheless, with little more than word of mouth, the book sold well in northern cities, even hitting the "best seller" list in San Francisco. Sass's efforts to produce a balanced story were rewarded by endorsements from both the United Daughters of the Confederacy and a relative of Harriet Beecher Stowe. Lyman Beecher Stowe, as reported in the Emporia Gazette (Kansas), said that his grandmother would have agreed with much that Richard Acton said, not only about slavery being an anachronistic institution that had brought down the South, but also that the "doomed civilization had in it the elements of real beauty, true culture, chivalric idealism, and knightly nobility." Stowe also noted that more animosity still festered in the South over Uncle Tom's Cabin and the Civil War than it did in Europe after the much more recent Great War.

Charlestonians flocked to buy Look Back to Glory, and one local bookstore exhibited the book against a backdrop of the Stars and Bars and South Carolina's palmetto flag. Sales surpassed those of Peter Ashley. His novel's "endorsement by its own people, in spite of the frank treatment of the miscegenation matter, far exceeded that given any other Charleston book," Sass reported. He judged his efforts "worthwhile," and would always consider this his most important book, but found himself at the conclusion of his long struggle still "as poor as ever in the world's goods." He was particularly pleased when Look Back to Glory was selected for the White House Library along with Heyward's Peter Ashley and Julia Peterkin's Bright Skin.

Sass followed an exhausting writing regime for over thirty years after publication of *Look Back to Glory*. In 1935, Sass collaborated with Charleston watercolorist Alice Ravenel Huger Smith by writing the text for her renderings of life along the rice coast in *A Carolina Rice Plantation of the Fifties*. Sass then returned to one of his early and abiding interests, the North American Indians, whose environmental ethic and appreciation of nature so closely resembled his own. *Hear Me My Chiefs* (1940) is a fascinating and moving account of the resistance of Nez Perce Chief Joseph and other Indian leaders to the encroachment of the white man and the modern world upon their traditional ways of life. *Emperor Brims* (1941) tells the story of the Yamassee War and the "virile" role of Charlestonians in exploring the western frontier during the eighteenth century. Later Sass completed *Charleston Grows* (1949), *Outspoken: 150 Years of the* News and Courier (1953) and *The Story of the South Carolina Lowcountry* (1956).

Sass rode the waves of changing popular taste and continued his prodigious output of magazine articles. In 1951, his short story "Anne of the Indies," about a young woman who is taught to be a pirate by Blackbeard himself, was made into a feature

Herbert Ravenel Sass, 19xx.

movie, as was "The Raid," which is based on Sass's account of the Confederate raid on a bank in St. Albans, Vermont, an act committed to avenge the burning of Atlanta. He was always disheartened that a Hollywood production studio did not option *Look Back to Glory*, a disappointment made all the more poignant by the success of Margaret Mitchell's *Gone with the Wind* a few years later in 1936. Even today, grumblings may be heard in certain quarters of Charleston over the similarities between the two novels.

Sass never enjoyed the financial bonanzas that many southern authors reaped from their popular works, but his fiction and non-fiction ranks among the best written during the Charleston Literary Renaissance. He worked hard at his craft until illness prevented him from going up to his book-lined study on the second story of 23 Legaré Street. He faced this last battle with "antique courage," and died on February 18, 1958, the same day that in 1865 Old Charleston had died when Union troops invaded the city.

This new edition of *Look Back to Glory* provides contemporary readers an opportunity to appreciate Sass's penetrating insights into the southern past. Many of his arguments and warnings have been vindicated by new historical research and the passage of time.

Material for this essay was drawn from interviews with Betty Sass Phillips and Marion H. Sass, the Herbert Ravenel Sass Papers and the Edward L. Wells Papers housed at the South Carolina Historical Society; the Bobbs-Merrill Papers, at the Lilly Library, University of Indiana; and Eugene D. Genovese, *The Southern Tradition: The Achievement and Limitations of an American Conservatism* (Cambridge, Massachusetts: Harvard University Press, 1994).

Barbara L. Bellows

LOOK BACK TO GLORY

For ELIZABETH ELLIOTT,
HERBERT RAVENEL
AND THE TWO MARION HUTSONS

Senator James H. Hammond of South Carolina is speaking in the United States Senate:

"The Senator from New York says that you intend to take the Government from us, that it will pass from our hands into yours. Perhaps what he says is true. But do not forget—it can never be forgotten—it is written on the brightest page of human history—that we, the slave-holders of the South, took our country in her infancy and, after ruling her for sixty out of the seventy years of her existence, we shall surrender her to you without a stain upon her honour, boundless in prosperity, incalculable in her strength, the wonder and the admiration of the world."

Sheba, a negro slave, is speaking to her lover Sharpio, as he knocks on the door of her cabin one April night:

"Is dat you, Sharpio? Come in, black boy; I'se waitin' for you."

Former Senator Robert Barnwell Rhett, leader of the Secession party in South Carolina, is speaking through the columns of the *Charleston Mercury*:

"...Eight millions of the white race, raised to the use of arms and constituting one of the most military people of the world, are unconquerable by any power upon earth. Why, then, should we not be independent in Government, as we are in all our resources for national power, wealth and prosperity? Why should we still continue vexed tributaries to the North—harassed dependencies—despised underlings—to be eternally scourged from tariff to slavery and from slavery to tariff—only at last to be trampled out of existence in blood?

> *"Break from the North and give us a Southern Confederacy as you value honor, prosperity, even life itself."*

James Louis Petigru of Charleston, a famous lawyer and for many years a leader of the Union party in South Carolina, is writing to his friend, John Acton of Avalon Plantation, in the South Carolina Low-Country, near Charleston:

> *"Nobody can tell what the end of this movement is to be, but it can not be for good. It is formed on the shallow conceit that all nations will pay tribute to King Cotton and that our new reading of 'The Whole Duty of Man' will be accepted by Christendom."*

Chancellor Harper, of the Supreme Court of South Carolina, is speaking before the South Carolina Society for the Advancement of Learning:

> *"...South Carolina is an aristocracy, as all the great and successful republics of the world have been aristocracies. It is an aristocracy, but it has this advantage, that the privileged class is larger in proportion to the whole society—the advantage of rank is conferred on a greater number—than in any civilized community that has heretofore existed."*

Vienna, a quadroon girl, keeping an appointment in a deserted cabin, is talking to herself:

> *"...He's coming; I hear his horse. Maybe if he likes me, he'll buy me. Maybe I'll live in a little **house in** Charleston——"*

Preston Brooks, a Representative from South Carolina, is speaking to Senator Charles Sumner of Massachusetts, a leading abolitionist, in the Senate Chamber:

"Mr. Sumner, I have read your speech. I have read it carefully, with as much consideration and forbearance and fairness as I could. But, sir, I have came to punish you now for the contents of that speech, which is a libel on my State and on a gray-haired relative."

Mazÿck Marion, of Deer Hall Plantation in the South Carolina Low-Country, is reading in his library; he has come by chance upon the following quotation from the speeches of Edmund Burke:

"There is, however, a circumstance attending these (Southern) colonies which...makes the spirit of liberty still more high and haughty than in those to the Northward. It is, that in Virginia and Carolina they have a vast multitude of slaves. Where this is the case, in any part of the world, those who are free are by far the most proud and jealous of their freedom. Freedom with them is not only an enjoyment, but a kind of rank and privilege."

The *New York Independent*, an abolitionist organ, is paying its respects to the people of the South:

"...The mass of the population of the Atlantic Coast of the slave region of the South are descended from the transported convicts and outcasts of Great Britain. Oh, glorious chivalry and hereditary aristocracy of the South! Peerless first families of Virginia and Carolina! Progeny of the highwaymen and horse-thieves and sheep-stealers and pick-pockets of Old England."

Daniel Webster of New England is speaking in the United States Senate:

> "...Then, sir, there are the Abolition societies, of which I am unwilling to speak, but in regard to which I have very clear notions and opinions. I do not think them useful. I think their operations for the last twenty years have produced nothing good or valuable...I can not but see what mischief their interference with the South has caused."

William Lloyd Garrison, abolitionist agitator, is speaking in Boston:

> "...He [the southern slave-holder] is a man who is grievously and wickedly trampling upon the rights of his fellow man...he is a sinner before God—a great sinner."

Abraham Lincoln, a rising political leader of the West, is speaking at Peoria, Illinois:

> "...When the Southern people tell us they are no more responsible for slavery than we are, I acknowledge the fact. When it is said that the institution exists, and that it is very difficult to get rid of it, in any satisfactory way, I can understand and appreciate the saying. I surely do not blame them for not doing what I would not know how to do myself."

Richard Acton, until recently attaché at the American Legation in Paris, is writing from France to his brother, John Acton of Avalon Plantation, at present residing in his town-house in Charleston:

"...Your letters and the newspapers—especially the Mercury, which I read with mingled pride and apprehension—tell the same story. There is going to come, I am more than ever afraid, an end of our Golden Age—that Golden Age of many things in which you people are living in Carolina on the great plantations like Avalon, and in too-proud, too-confident, ever-beloved Charleston.

"The world's going one way, John, and we're trying to go another. Ours may be the better way, but that won't save us. We can't fight the world; and that practically is what we shall have to do if we let the abolitionists of Massachusetts and the hotspurs of South Carolina lash us to madness.

"Well, if our Golden Age is to end, I want to share the years of it that are still to run. It was golden when we were boys at Avalon; it will be golden for some years yet. Perhaps that is one reason why I am coming home. You might tell Lowndes Fenwick, if you see him, but nobody else. Next to you and Elizabeth and Lowndes, it's the live-oaks of Avalon I want to see—"

The *Charleston Mercury*, organ of Barnwell Rhett, the secessionist leader, and one of the most influential of southern newspapers, is commenting upon the "irrepressible conflict" speech of Senator Seward of New York:

"...It is not merely slavery which makes the sectional issue between the North and South. Sectional ambition and sectional interests to be enforced through the tariff throw them also into collision. The two sections of the Union have to face each other in the Union—and the South will have to leave it or be overmastered and provincialized by the superior power of the North."

Senator Jefferson Davis of Mississippi is delivering his farewell speech in the United States Senate:

"...Then, Senators, we recur to the compact which binds us together. We recur to the principles upon which this government was founded; and when you deny them, and when you deny to us the right to withdraw from a Union which, thus perverted, threatens to be destructive of our rights, we but tread in the path of our fathers when we proclaim our independence and take the hazard."

Jeremiah S. Black, Secretary of State in the Cabinet of President Buchanan, is speaking to his assistant secretary, William Henry Trescot of South Carolina:

"...There, your little State, no bigger than the palm of my hand, has broken up this mighty empire. Like Athens, you control Greece. You have made and you will control this revolution by your indomitable spirit. Up to this time you have played your part with great wisdom—unequalled—but now you are going wrong."

Major Stephen Elliott of the Confederate Army, holding the battered ruin of Fort Sumter in Charleston harbor against the Federal Army and fleet, is answering the Union admiral's demand for surrender:

"Inform Admiral Dahlgren that he may have Fort Sumter when he can take and hold it."

A mockingbird is singing in the moonlight in a magnolia tree at Notteley Plantation. No man knows what the bird is saying; but the enchantment of a woman pours through Richard Acton like a tide.

Part One: Avalon

> In seeds of laurel in the earth
> > The blossom of your fame is blown,
> And somewhere, waiting for its birth,
> > The shaft is in the stone.
> > > —*Henry Timrod*

Chapter I

Two young women and a young man descended the wide steps leading down from the piazza of Notteley Plantation house and stood talking in the warm November sunlight.

One of the young women, slender and of middle height, was altogether fair. She was wearing a dark-blue riding habit; her hair, barely visible under her dark beaver, was a pale gold and her eyes were blue. The other, in a close-fitting white basque and full silk skirt, was pale with only a faint tinge of color in her cheeks; her hair was a rich red-brown and her eyes, less animated than those of the fair girl, were a darker brown than her hair. She wore a small black felt hat with a white cock's feather, and over her arm she carried a blue barcelona. The young man was tall and rather dark, his clean-shaven face was thin and decisive, he dominated easily the brilliance of the crimson vest beneath his blue riding-coat.

A barouche, drawn by two handsome bays, an exceedingly black negro coachman in the driver's seat, halted in front of the steps. Behind the barouche another negro appeared, leading two spirited riding horses. The fair-haired girl ran quickly up the steps and called, "Mother, we're all ready." A very small old lady, in black silk with a small black bonnet, came out of .the front door and descended the steps, her hand on the girl's arm.

The young man assisted her into the barouche. "I don't want to be out long," she said. "The old road through the Avalon pine-lands, then home by way of Crane Pond."

The young man nodded. He extended his hand to the dark-haired girl. She placed her hand, which was very small, in his, and he said with a whimsical smile, "Confound that headache."

She smiled at him as she seated herself in the barouche. "Never mind," she replied. "It won't last long."

The young man turned away. The fair-haired girl in the riding habit was standing beside one of the saddle-horses. He helped her to mount and himself mounted the horse. They rode, ahead of the barouche, around the circle in front of the house and along the lane, under magnolia trees, toward the gate.

A light wind blew through the Avalon pine-lands, making a low unceasing music in the high green boughs. Richard Acton heard the sound; it was sweet to his ears with a sweetness that was not of the present but was rather a remembered sweetness—something that came to him faintly from days long past.

He smiled. It was all like that: the mare between his knees, the gun in the hollow of his arm, the long misty-purple corridors of the pine-wood, the hawk screaming in the distance, the smell of woods-smoke, the unending sea of golden grass through which he was riding under the pines. These things, perceptible around him and before him, did not really belong to the day, the moment; they had all come from a time long ago and were like a picture or a fragrance for many years forgotten and now reborn in memory.

He rode on slowly, sitting relaxed in his saddle. A week had passed since his return to Avalon, but the spell of the place was as strong upon him now as it had been on the day of his home-coming. Richard Acton wondered whether there was anywhere on earth another country like this Low-Country of Carolina, a land whose brooding mystery and fateful foreboding loveliness became part of one's very soul. It was strange, this enchantment of the land. He had believed himself no longer capable of any strong emotion except those that had their springs in bitterness; yet now he was shaken, possessed, by an exaltation at once tender and fierce and indescribably sweet.

He thought of Jacqueline Fleur, of all that she had been and still was to him. He was guilty, he knew, of no treason to her memory when he confessed the power of the feeling gripped him now. This was not like the love that grew between a man and a woman. It came out of the soil, the pines, the broom-grass golden in the November sunlight; out of the sunlit air, the song of the wind in the treetops, the smell of broom and myrtle and pine and the thin woods-smoke that was like a lilac mist; out of the gray moss hanging from the trees, the great glossy-green magnolia leaves, the huge stalwart trunks of live-oaks, the wide sweeps of marsh and river, the still cypress-shadowed lagoons.

It was the song of the pines that now possessed him, a music out of the happy past. It had meant little to him in those days, for it had been one of the commonplace, accustomed sounds of life. Certainly he had not missed it, had never consciously recalled it during his years in Europe; amid the excitements and preoccupations of the life that he had lived there, Avalon and Carolina had seemed very far away. Yet now, hearing this song of the pines again after twelve years, he was lifted out of himself, swept upward by a force that he could not control.

He frowned, striving deliberately to beat down his soaring spirit. It must not soar thus; he could see Jacqueline's reproachful eyes. He told himself that it was only a thing of the moment, that after a little the intensity of his feeling would diminish and he would be himself again. That was how it had affected him during this week of his home-coming; the emotion that possessed him came in waves, each wave produced by some remembered sight or sound or odor; presently this wave would pass.

Suddenly his gray eyes narrowed. Amid the pine-trunks ahead of him something had moved, brown, indeterminate, stealthy. The mare stopped instantly in response to his tightened rein. She was a small shaggy sorrel of the native breed, in appearance a pariah among the Avalon thoroughbreds, but she had a genius for woodcraft which gave her a high value in a country devoted to deer hunting. Richard Acton lifted the gun quickly to his shoulder. A low growth of myrtle bushes intercepted his view and he stood erect in his stirrups.

Beyond the myrtles there was a flash of white, the uplifted tail of a fleeing buck that had slunk out of the thicket and was now bounding away in full flight. Instantaneously, as though that flash of white were a signal to his brain, the impression of unreality returned. Again what was happening was not an actuality but a memory; a hundred times when he was a boy he had seen those white flags of the deer go rocking away through the woods.

He fired. The mare stood rigid under him; her steadiness under fire was one of the boasts of the plantation stables. Standing in his stirrups, Acton peered through the thick smoke. He knew that he had missed, but there was a pleasure at once sweet and piercing in the sight of that white flag undulating amid the pine-trunks. He wanted another glimpse of it before it disappeared.

What he saw through the smoke surprised him. Far away under the pines something moved across the line of his vision. Intervening tree-trunks constantly interrupted view, but he could see that it was a carriage moving rapidly and that on the high driver's seat a man was struggling to control his horses. Immediately behind it were two other persons, on horseback and also moving fast. Acton realized at once what was happening. Evidently there was a road through the wood and this was a runaway along that road. He understood, too, that he was responsible, that his shot at the fleeing deer had caused the runaway.

He reached the road—a narrow track through the pineland—as quickly as possible and swung the mare to the right in the direction in which the carriage and the two persons on horseback had disappeared.

He saw them three hundred yards away. The carriage, a barouche, had stopped; it was half out of the road and had evidently collided with a pine sapling. The negro driver had jumped from his seat and was clinging to the rein of one of the plunging horses. Of the two riders, one, a young man in close-fitting dark-blue coat and riding breeches, had dismounted and was running to assist the driver; the other, a young woman in riding habit, had stopped her horse beside the barouche and, leaning from her saddle, was speaking to its occupants. Richard Acton, galloping toward the scene, perceived that a dangerous accident had been averted. The combined efforts of the driver and the young man who had gone to his assistance were quieting the horses attached to the barouche.

The thick carpet of pine-straw covering the road dulled the sounds of the mare's hoofs; Acton's approach was not noticed until he was less than a dozen yards distant. The young woman sitting her horse beside the barouche turned her head, met his eyes and nodded slightly in response to his bow. In the barouche, which apparently had not been damaged, two other ladies were seated, one of them elderly and wearing black, the other a young woman in white. Acton's bow was prolonged to include these also. The older of the two acknowledged his salutation. The young woman looked at him steadily; her lips were parted slightly; he was aware momentarily of the intentness of her gaze.

Acton was about to dismount when the young man who had been engaged with the negro driver in quieting the horses turned and moved toward him. He was tall and well built, and Acton perceived at once that his thin, somewhat swarthy face was flushed with anger.

"You have," he said, "nearly caused a serious accident. The deer you shot at crossed the road in front of the horses and they bolted. May I ask with whose permission you are hunting on these lands?"

Richard Acton hesitated. Plainly the young man in the riding suit was unaware that he was addressing one of his own social station, a gentleman. He was not to be blamed for that, perhaps; Acton had put on that morning an old and exceedingly battered hunting jacket of his brother's which he had found at Avalon. His appearance, no doubt, like his mare's, was not prepossessing; scarcely above that of the poor-whites or crackers who lived in their little frame or log-houses here and there about the edges of the great plantations. Obviously, he understood with a momentary amusement, he had been mistaken for a poor-white poaching on the Acton lands. Probably the young man was a friend and neighbor of John Acton and would naturally take it upon himself to deal with any undesirable trespasser whom he found in the Avalon woods.

"Answer me," he said sharply. "By what right are you hunting on Avalon?"

Richard Acton was conscious of a sudden resentment. It became all at once impossible to follow the course that he had been about to follow—explain politely that he was John Acton's brother.

He turned his shoulder to the young man and addressed the ladies. The girl on horseback and the old lady in the barouche were looking at him, but the girl in the barouche was looking down at her hands. She seemed not to be listening. She was wearing, he perceived, a small felt hat with a white cock's feather, and her face—he saw it only for an instant, for she turned and looked away into the pine-wood—was pale. It was, he thought, as fine, as highly bred, as any face that he had ever seen. Its reticent fineness fitted perfectly into what was now occurring and somehow served to tighten his resolve. He ignored the young man completely.

"I am sorry," he said to the ladies, "that I have caused this annoyance. I did not know that you were coming on the road; in fact, I didn't know that there was a road. Your carriage is not damaged and I see that I can be of no service to you. I hope you will accept my regrets and apologies."

He bowed with a careful courtesy, which, however, took no account of the young man standing at his right, and, turning the mare, rode slowly away.

Richard Acton was at once amused and interested by what had happened. Who were these people, he wondered. He ran over in his mind the plantations near Avalon. Despite his long absence, he could name every house on the middle stretch of the river and the family that lived in it: the Fenwicks of Haddon

Hill, the Nesbits of Wisboo, the Colcocks of Mowbray, the Dwights of Indian Town, the McPhersons of Tranquil Vale, the Treveses of Fair Spring, the Pinckneys of Chetsworth, the St. Juliens of Craneflield, the Chantillys of Montauban.

The party he had encountered belonged to none of these places, he concluded. By a process of elimination he decided finally that they must have come from either Laurel Bluff or Notteley. He remembered suddenly that Notteley had changed hands within the past several years; his brother had written to him in Paris that a Beaufort district planter had bought the place. He could not now recall the name, though it was that of one of the prominent Low-Country families. It seemed altogether likely that these people belonged to Notteley, since the lonely and little-used road through the pine-land led in that general direction.

The question, however, was unimportant; it engaged Richard Acton only temporarily. Riding back through the woods toward Avalon house, he was concerned, quite impersonally, with two things: the fineness of the face of the young woman in the barouche and the manner of the young man who had questioned him. These two things—that face, that manner—became, as he thought about them, increasingly significant.

It was hard to say precisely why. You could see faces as fine as that one in drawing-rooms in Philadelphia or New York; the young man's manner had been little different from that in which a Boston gentleman, strolling down Summer Street, might address some newly-arrived Irish immigrant whom he had occasion to reprove. Yet Acton realized that there was a difference. It arose somehow out of the environment, the whole scene and establishment that lay about him here in Carolina: the great land-holdings like baronial estates, some of them still known as baronies as in the time of the old Carolinian Landgraves; the spacious manor houses along the river each the center of a wide domain; the little houses of the poor-whites here and there in the pine-lands; the hundreds of negroes idling in the cabins or working in the fields.

Richard Acton was vaguely disturbed by what had just happened. It seemed to him, fantastically perhaps, to have subtle implications that carried far. It brought back into his mind again, subtly yet very surely, a question that had taken form there during his years abroad, assuming more and more definite shape as he watched the course of American affairs. For him it came down to this: How long would Avalon last—Avalon with its master and mistress, its thousands of unused acres surrounding its cultivated rice-lands, its hundreds of black bondsmen, its traditions of conduct and of manners, its paneled rooms and its portraits, its beauty and its opulence, as far beyond reach of the poor-whites in the pine-lands as the stars in heaven?

These thoughts trailed off gradually into nothingness. He realized, with a smile at his fondness for far-leaping conclusions, that there was no adequate basis for these in the fineness of a young woman's face, the authority of a young man's voice. Presently he was submerged again in the familiar loveliness of his surroundings. The pine forest became a mixed growth of broad-leafed trees; the great rough-barked hickories were a bright amber in the late sunlight, the black gums a deep rich red. Passing a small pond, he was startled by a gigantic gray heron that rose suddenly from the nearer margin and flapped away with long legs trailing; and two minutes later a covey of partridges burst into whirring flight almost under his mare's hoofs. It was here, he remembered, that Marion the Swamp Fox and Colonel Wade Hampton of the Revolution had fought a stiff skirmish with the British dragoons; you could still see, when he was a boy, the mounds where the dead had been buried.

Mockingbirds and Carolina wrens were singing now over those lost graves; cardinals glowed blood-red in the dark-green hollies; he heard the musical whistle of doves' wings as they left their roosts in the tail willow-oaks. Five deer, led by a splendid buck with branching antlers, broke from a fringe of myrtles and went bounding away in single file across an open glade, their white flags flying. He watched them with an observant, unmixed pleasure, though they were too far off for a shot. Suddenly it all became again a picture out of the past; and suddenly, as though it had been only yesterday, he recalled a morning when Black Samson, the negro hunter who had been one of the most constant companions of his boyhood, had brought down a running buck at ninety-three and a half yards.

At the entrance of Avalon avenue four black children raced from the gatekeeper's cabin to open the gate for him. He tossed them some small coins as he rode through, and they scrambled frantically in the dust. Ahead, the white portico of Avalon house was visible: he saw it through a long vista, a tunnel formed by the thick trunks and over-arching branches of great evergreen live-oaks lining the straight wide road on either side. They had been planted by William Acton, of Croxton Manor in Leicestershire, who settled in Carolina in 1693; now, in the time of his grandchildren's great-grandchildren, they had attained the stateliness that he had perhaps foreseen.

It was a noble approach, perfect in its dignity. The short trunks of the double line of trees were huge and gnarled; their wide-spreading boughs met and mingled overhead, forming a long arched canopy of dark-green foliage, from which graceful streamers of silvery-gray Spanish moss hung like a tapestry; the groining of stout branches supporting this wide arched roof was massive and strong. Richard Acton was filled with a sense of security, of permanence. He had been afraid, and the fear had grown upon him of late, that danger hung over Avalon; now, in the presence of Avalon's bearded oaks, that fear became fantastic.

Riding slowly, he reached the end of the avenue. Before him, across a wide lawn of close-cropped gray-green grass, he saw Avalon house. The house that the first William had built had been burned, the family tradition said, in the Indian wars; this, the third to stand upon the site, had been built by another William thirty years before the Revolution.

It was a square house and of brick, two stories on a high base—an ample house and, Richard Acton said to himself, of a kindly rather than an austere dignity. Beyond it, under its flanking elms and sycamores, he could see the sheen of the river and the flooded rice-fields. At the right, bordered by crêpe-myrtle, wild orange and opoponax shrubs, was the garden, while at the left, shaded by willow-oaks and tall pecans, lay the plantation yard with its brick outbuildings; past these again, half-hidden by Chinese mulberry and Pride-of-India trees, the stable and carriage house were partly visible, and, still farther to the left, the first cabins of the negro Quarters. He heard, thin and high, the voice of a negro woman singing a slow monotonous song.

Avalon house, directly ahead of him, was bathed in the late afternoon light; its weathered brick front glowed a soft warm red above the dark-green shrubbery massed below. The road led straight across the lawn to a box-bordered circle in front of wide iron-railed steps ascending to the columned piazza; in the middle of this circle a copper sun-dial flashed back the slanting rays. It was one of his earliest recollections, that sun-dial; in the gray stone of its base an aide of Lord Cornwallis had etched with his sword-point a silhouette of his chief. Cornwallis had gone, but the sun-dial with his effigy, still stood where it had stood then. Kept brightly polished by black hands, it had recorded for generations of Actons the march of long unhurried days.

Richard Acton's sense of permanence increased. Avalon house was as enduring as its everlasting oaks; its stout pillars, white against the mellow background of its high façade, were proof against time and change.

Chapter II

He slept later than usual the next morning; the negro boy who had come in early to light the fire for him had accomplished this duty without waking him. Opening his eyes to find the bright sun shining through the east windows, Acton sleepily blamed the French brandy of which he had allowed himself a fairly liberal portion the night before. He had sat late reading in the library, and Chance had put the bottle beside him. His brother, of course, had given him the key to the Avalon wine closet. He wondered whether John Acton would not have contrived to forget this detail if he had been aware of certain episodes in Paris and St. Petersburg.

However, all that—all except the memory of one woman— was definitely behind Richard Acton now; he had no misgivings on that score. He dressed quickly, again selecting his brother's dingy hunting suit and boots. Nevertheless, he would hardly go hunting to-day or spend much time idly roaming through the woods or along the rice-field banks. John and Elizabeth Acton and their two children, with the servants that they had taken with them to the city, would arrive some time in the afternoon. The first frosts of autumn had come; the river plantations were wholesome and safe again for the white man no less than for the black whom the summer fevers seldom touched. Most of the other houses on the river were already re-occupied by the families that owned them; but the annual anabasis of John and Elizabeth Acton from their town-house in Charleston to their plantation home had been delayed until to-day because of a business trip which had taken John to Savannah.

It was this that had made it possible for Richard Acton to spend a week by himself at Avalon. He had resigned his post in the American Legation in Paris in the late summer and had sailed immediately for the United States. After a brief stay in Boston with Philips Cordray, who had been his classmate at Oxford, he bad come on by steamer to Charleston where he had been made welcome at his brother's town-house. There, for the first time, he had seen Elizabeth Acton, his sister-in-law now for more than six years. She had been a Granville of the French Huguenot family of St. Denis's Parish, and he had found her on the whole a more than satisfactory confirmation of the photograph that John had sent to him in Paris. He had remained several days in Charleston, but his eagerness to see Avalon again had been obvious, and, as soon as the first black frost came, John had suggested that he go up at once.

His week at Avalon had been the happiest—though that could not be in his case exactly the right word—since Jacqueline's death. He had passed out of drab actuality into a world of dreams. He had not thought about anything; he had simply lived, lived again the life that he had lived on the plantation as a boy and as a very young man while his father and mother were alive. Until yesterday he had seen no white face except that of Murson Janvers, his brother's overseer; but he hadn't been lonely, he hadn't been really alone.

The memory of Jacqueline had been with him. He had left Paris telling himself grimly that the time had come when he must escape from that memory. Thank heaven, he told himself now, standing before the mirror in his room, that hadn't happened, could never happen; Jacqueline would be with him always wherever he went. There was a tap on his door; a servant girl asked softly whether he was ready for breakfast. He slipped into John Acton's brown hunting coat and stepped out of the room.

The house, he found, was alive with servants, principally women, sweeping, dusting, rearranging curtains, coverlets and bed linen, carrying pails of water to the bedrooms. They grinned at him even more expansively than usual as he passed down the stairs and through the lower hall, where the portraits of General Stuart Acton of the Continental Army and of another Richard Acton who had been President Monroe's minister to Russia regarded him with an immeasurable calm. An air of cheerful expectancy pervaded the whole house, and in the dining-room Chance's smile was wide enough, as Richard remarked, to swallow the table and all that was on it. "'Tis a great day, Mas' Richard," Chance said in reply, "when Mas' John en Missis comes home."

That was a tribute more convincing in its simplicity, he told Chance, than a hundred orations by impassioned southerners in the Senate. He wished that some of the people he had met in Boston at Philips Cordray's could be with him at Avalon today. He found himself wishing, too—he had been aware of a courteous but quite discernible complacency in Boston—that some of them could have been with him the afternoon before in the pine-wood so that they might have seen the profile of the young woman in the barouche. He could not recall her features in detail, but there lingered in his mind an impression of something rare—a certain sensitiveness that Boston, some of the Bostonians at any rate, would not readily attribute to a civilization that rested, as one of their pamphleteers had expressed it, upon the whip-scarred shoulders of cringing blacks. Over his breakfast, cold teal with hominy and corn muffins, Richard Acton decided that he would hunt up young Ephraim at the stables and, with him as paddler, explore the upper backwater for black bass. First, however, the last of the muffins having been disposed of, he went out on the west piazza overlooking the river to smoke a cigar.

Outside, he observed that the terraces leading down to the river had been freshly swept that morning so that there was scarcely a fallen leaf on the smooth grass. Below the terraces and to the right, Janvers the overseer and a force of hands were busy at the landing fitting a new hand-rail and repairing the plank walk. Acton's gaze lifted above the group of men at the landing, crossed the river and swept the wide expanse of the flooded rice-lands beyond. The harvest was over, the crop had long since been gathered, the rice-fields lay submerged except for the narrow dikes separating one field from another. Wherever his eyes roamed over the watery plain he saw fleets and squadrons wild ducks resting on the surface: mallards, teal, gadwalls, pintails, a dozen different kinds.

In spite of the crispness of the November morning, a mockingbird was singing enthusiastically in a wild-orange bush close to the piazza; the shaggy-barked pecan trees and tall willow-oaks in the plantation yard were alive with noisy blackbirds and yellowhammers. The yard was being raked and swept by half a dozen negro women; they worked deliberately, their skirts tucked up behind, revealing their thick, strong calves. Daddy Marony, who had charge of the yard, appeared from behind the kitchen and stood for a moment surveying the activities of his underlings; he spoke to a mulatto girl sitting on the kitchen step and pointed to a flower-bed near the house where crimson poinsettias were in bloom.

The girl looked up at him, said something and laughed; then she walked slowly to the shed where the garden tools were kept and emerged with a trowel and a small hoe. On her way to the poinsettia bed she stopped to talk with three old women who were moving toward the kitchen from the direction of the Quarters. She stood relaxed, one hand on her hip, the other holding the hoe. She was graceful as a leopard, Richard Acton perceived, and the red handkerchief around her head shone like a flame.

The three old women were all of them smoking pipes. Their head-cloths, too, were brilliant—yellow and red—and they wore hoops of bright metal in their ears, though their skirts were drab. One of them carried a large wooden bucket; another was burdened with fowls tied by the feet, while the third, taller than the others, bore upon her head a flat fanner basket heaped with yellow and white chrysanthemums.

These were gift-bearers, Acton understood; butter and fowls and flowers for the mistress who was coming home. He recognized the tall woman with the chrysanthemums. She was Cornelia, the widow of Black Samson; he had gone to see her in her cabin immediately upon his return to the plantation. Suddenly she saw him sitting on the piazza and dropped him a curtsy, the wide flower-heaped basket remaining perfectly balanced. The two other old women also curtsied. But the yellow girl stood in her leopard-like grace and did not turn her head.

Richard Acton, watching her idly, wondered who she was. Her name, Chance had informed him, was Vienna, but that meant nothing. He had noticed her the day after his arrival at Avalon; there was something about her, something more subtle than her gracefulness, that compelled attention. She was a yard servant, evidently; her duties seemed to be confined chiefly to the flower-beds and the garden; she wasn't out of place, he said to himself, among the crimson poinsettias.

Vienna. A queer name, but in fairly common use among the plantation negroes. She was probably a quadroon, he decided, with more than a trace of Indian; her skin was almost a bright orange and her straight hair, under the red handkerchief, was black. He wondered what strange conflicts took place within her between her white and her negro blood. At any rate, it wasn't hard to understand why curtsying didn't come as easily to her as to the old black women.

His gaze shifted to Daddy Marony hobbling away toward the kitchen. Acton's eyes followed the old man regretfully; Marony was still tall and straight, despite his rheumatism, but twenty years ago he had been a black Hercules. There was a story, Richard recalled, that Marony used to tell about his grandfather. His grandfather, he said, had been a king in Africa and one day he took some of his people down to the coast and sold them to the white men. The slavers invited him on board their ship and then sail away with him. Marony used to laugh so uproariously when he told the tale that sometimes he rolled helplessly on the ground.

The old man disappeared behind the kitchen and Acton turned his chair so that he could look out over the river and the sweep of the rice-fields beyond. A sloop was passing loaded to the gunwales with rice for the Charleston mills; down-stream, a schooner was beating up against a slow tide. The flooded rice-fields were still thronged with ducks; there must be twenty thousand of them, he estimated within range of his vision, while the surrounding uplands were full of wild turkey and deer. There was none to molest them. Almost as far as his eyes could see, these fields and the hazy blue woods beyond were Acton lands and no man could lift a finger on them unless an Acton willed it.

It was a paradise, he said to himself, this Carolina Low-Country—a paradise for those who were privileged to enjoy the blessings it afforded; and it was, his thoughts took a familiar turn, just now the most important district upon the continent of North America. It was here really that the long controversy between North and South focused. South Carolina, supplanting Virginia, had been for a quarter-century or more the political leader of the South; and in the main the leadership of South Carolina came from the Low-Country where Charleston and the great rice and cotton plantations round-about it formed what was really a city-state unlike any other community in the world. It was, he saw clearly, essentially a feudal society directed and controlled by an accepted upper class whose power remained unchallenged. It couldn't last, he believed; it must change or be destroyed. But for many years it had fixed the thought and action of the South as effectually as Athens had controlled Greece; and while it lasted, the land where it flowered was, for its rulers at any rate, perhaps the most delightful land under the sun.

Well, he reflected, he could enjoy it—in so far as he could enjoy anything since Jacqueline's death—in his own right. He had a foothold in it; he could be one of the landed country gentlemen, chiefly of English or French Huguenot blood, whose manor houses dotted the parishes around Charleston and whose authority was not less absolute than that which the Carolina Landgraves of the early Colonial days had exercised upon their vast baronies. Above Avalon lay Sherborne which his father had willed to him, knowing somehow that soon or late he would give up the diplomatic career that he chosen and come home. Yet that foot-hold might have been precarious but for his brother John. Below Avalon, though not fronting on the river, were Oak Hill, Greentree and Content, plantations which John Acton had bought within the past few years. They made, with Avalon and Sherborne, an impressive holding.

Richard Acton's thoughts gathered more particularly around his brother. John was three years his senior, a larger, heavier man—undoubtedly, Richard admitted, a solider man. Certainly he had kept his feet upon the solid earth. He had never been troubled, as Richard had been, with a desire for a broader life than Carolina afforded. At the time of Colonel Acton's death, John was already, a four years at the South Carolina College, a rice planter of proved ability, while Richard was a dilettante student of life, in love with many things but wedded to none, roaming more or less aimlessly over Europe after two not very satisfactory years at Oxford. After his parents' death (they had died suddenly and within a few days of each other) Richard had had no desire to return home; he had accepted finally a minor diplomatic post, secured through brother's influence, and was successively in St. Petersburg, London and Paris.

Meanwhile, in Carolina, John had prospered; he had bought more land and more negroes, had married Elizabeth Granville, herself an heiress, and had had two children. Yes, Richard said to himself, John had done well. Despite his abstention so far from public life, he had amply sustained the honorable place that the Acton name had held in Carolina from the beginning. He had added largely to the Acton holdings, and in Carolina prestige rested upon land. His plantations were among the most successful in the Low-Country and Avalon house was still one of the finest on Berkeley River. His town-house, overlooking the sea-wall promenade in Charleston, was not only an establishment worthy of one of the principal families of the South but also, during the period of the year when John Acton and his wife occupied it, the seat of a graceful, even a lordly, hospitality.

Richard Acton's teeth were clamped tightly on his cigar, his gray eyes had grown somber. The solidity of John Acton's achievement made all the more tragic his own failure, own collapse. What had he to show for his twelve years abroad? A not discreditable record, so far as the public knew, in the diplomatic service of the United States, which, however, for reasons which were nobody's fault if not his own, had brought him no post of real authority or distinction. Now, at home at last on the plantation where he had been born, he realized more poignantly than ever how great a mistake those years abroad had been.

And yet he could not say that, for they had brought him Jacqueline. She was a part of those years, the only really important thing in them; and though she was now only a secret memory, the existence of which none must ever know, that memory meant more to him than anything in his life. But it, too, was, after all, a waste, a loss, a dead weight upon him, fettering his spirit and his mind. It would have been better in every reasonable sense if he had remained in Carolina, a planter at Sherborne or a lawyer in Charleston. He could have done fairly well, he believed, in either sphere. And he would not have been, at thirty-one, a man already dead.

He turned, away suddenly, from the piazza banister and reentered the house through one of the French doors leading into the drawing-room. The house-cleaning here had been completed, the cypress-paneled walls of the room were fleckless, the Sheraton chairs and tables shone, the central chandelier with its glass hurricane-guards glittered like crystal, no vestige of a cobweb marred the carved cornices. Acton passed into the hail with its portraits and its tall gilt-framed mirror and thence into the small room devoted to guns and fishing equipment. Having found the fishing pole and spoon that he desired, he looked about for his hat, and, not seeing it where he had left it the night before, he called for Chance, whose step he heard in the hall. Chance appeared in the doorway and said:

"Two gen'lemens comin' up de abby-new, Mas' Richard. Mus' I ask dem in or is you gwine to see dem on de eas' pyazza?"

Chapter III

He would meet them, he told Chance, on the east piazza. "See that a boy is ready to take their horses," he added. "I'll be right out." Richard Acton walked directly to the east piazza, wondering with more than a little irritation who his visitors could be. He had had, fortunately, no visitors at all during his solitary week at Avalon.

From the east piazza he looked across the lawn straight down the vista of the double line of oaks forming the avenue. The two gentlemen, he perceived, were just emerging from the avenue. They were young men wearing riding clothes, one of them with a wild turkey feather jauntily in his gray felt hat. They were well mounted, one on a black horse, the other on a bay. Richard Acton failed to recognize either, but that was not surprising after more than a decade in Europe. "Probably they're from Wisboo or Cranefield," he said to himself. "Young Nesbits or St. Juliens grown up since my time. It won't be my fault if they stay too long."

Nevertheless, he received them with a completely engaging courtesy, with the extraordinary charm of manner, adaptable to any circumstances, which had been his principal asset during his diplomatic service abroad. Chance had already arranged chairs and a small table with decanter and cigars. Acton met his visitors at the head of the stone steps leading up from the lawn.

"I am Richard Acton," he said, "John's brother. I suppose I ought to know both of you, but I don't. I have been away from Carolina for twelve years."

"Then let us welcome you to the river," the shorter of the two replied. "I am Louis Treves of Fair Spring and this is Charles Gough of Wickenham. We are both of us house-guests at Notteley and we rode over from there. Charles is almost as much a stranger as you, since Wickenham has the misfortune to be situated not on *the* river but on Combahee in Beaufort district."

"Beaufort, Mr. Acton," Gough said, smiling, "has been able to open Louis's eyes. In fact, I am afraid it has spoiled his young life, but that's a delicate subject. Though I am not of *the* river, it is a pleasure to welcome you back to Carolina."

"Louis," Richard Acton said, "I remember you now. You were about ten years old when I was fifteen and I saw you at Fair Spring with other little Treveses. Besides, you are certainly my cousin, for if you will go back far enough, you will find that an Acton married a Treves."

Charles Gough swore gently. "You people of *the* river," he complained, "are worse than we are on the Combahee! You are all related. I can't say anything about anybody without getting into devilish hot water."

"Good discipline for you, Charles," Treves said, smiling, and Richard remarked that he also would have to remember to be careful. Treves and Gough were seated at Acton's invitation and Gough accepted a cigar. At any rate, he remarked when he had lighted it, they knew good cigars along the river; or perhaps Mr. Acton had brought these from Europe. He was older than Treves, strongly built and fair-skinned, and his features, positive and perhaps a little heavy, were entirely English. Plainly there was no French Huguenot blood in him as there was in Louis Treves, whose eyes and thick hair were black. Acton mentioned this apparent fact, and Treves seized upon it humorously as another illustration of the superiority of Berkeley River and its adjacent parishes. The Huguenots, he declaimed, had supplied most of the brains and all of the wit in Carolina. It was a great pity, and Gough was a living demonstration of its result, that none of the Huguenots had chosen to settle in Beaufort.

Louis was wrong, as usual, Charles Gough interrupted. There were Huguenots in Beaufort district; not many but the best. The Ravignacs, for instance. "James Hail's mother," he added, looking at Treves, "was a Ravignac."

There was a momentary pause. Richard Acton perceived that Charles Gough was gazing steadily at Treves; he saw Treves shake his head almost imperceptibly and observed that he led the conversation quickly into another channel. It became immediately clear to Acton that the visit had some other than a purely social purpose. He waited, with a lively but a completely concealed curiosity, for the moment which Louis Treves would consider the right one; evidently the matter, whatever it was, was in his hands.

Richard received the impression that Treves was taking especial pains to make the occasion pleasant; Gough, on the other hand, he thought, was not particularly concerned. After the first few minutes, Gough said comparatively little. A faint sense of something antagonistic in Gough grew in Richard Acton; not actively hostile, perhaps, but cold, formal, as if there existed some necessity for formality.

Louis Treves, naturally quick and vivacious, spoke enthusiastically of the charms of Avalon, of his admiration for the abilities of John Acton as a planter. He declared that Elizabeth Acton was the most gracious matron on Berkeley River; he was delighted to learn that he was her cousin by marriage, though he feared the cousinship must be somewhat remote since no one had ever mentioned it to him before. After a quarter of an hour of this and of neighborhood talk and of inquiry about European affairs, Charles Gough grew obviously restive.

"I think, Louis," he said decisively, "we might now tell Mr. Acton how this very pleasant visit came about."

Louis Treves was evidently disturbed. "Damn it, Charles," he said, "there's no hurry. I'll come to that in a minute. But, since you've brought it up, I suppose I'd better come to it now. The fact is, Richard, —you're older than I am, but it seems you're my kinsman, so I'll call you Richard,—the fact is I find I like you very much and I hope you'll see the position I'm in. I wouldn't have come if I had known about the relationship. I hope you under stand."

"Partly," Richard replied pleasantly. "I understand that you wouldn't have come if you had known that I was your cousin. But why not, Louis?"

"You'll see in a minute," Treves said quickly. "Now let me tell you about James Hail. He is a splendid fellow. You'll like him when you know him. But he's particular as the very devil—damned if I don't think the northerners are right when they say we're too infernally particular. It isn't James's Huguenot blood that makes him so sensitive. Huguenots are reasonable people; it must be his Scotch blood, I think. And in this case there were aggravating—er—unfortunate circumstances. It all happened before the eyes of the girl he's in love with. I think you'll admit that was a trifle hard."

"I haven't any idea what you are talking about, Louis," Acton answered, "and I have never heard of Mr. James Hail."

Charles Gough leaned forward in his chair.

"Louis is in an embarrassing position, Mr. Acton," he said, "since discovering that you are his relative. Mr. Hail asked him to take the lead in approaching you because he is of this parish, while both Hail and I are Beaufort men. In the circumstances I think I ought to relieve Louis."

He glanced inquiringly at Treves and the latter nodded. Gough was silent for a moment, chewing his cigar. Plainly he was considering his words.

"I think I ought to say," he began, "that I don't altogether agree with Louis as to James Hail's sensitiveness. I can't follow Louis either in commending the North's dislike of us because we are careful about personal honor. I am compelled to regret also that a young lady has been mentioned. Her presence at the time had nothing to do with what happened."

Gough turned to Treves. "I'm sorry to have to state these exceptions, Louis," he said gravely, "but I feel that I must do so, since the affair now rests with me. I'm sure you will see that."

Treves's face had reddened, but he nodded, and Gough, addressing Richard Acton, proceeded:

"Mr. Hail, like Louis and myself, is a house-guest of the Lowlands at Notteley Plantation. Yesterday he was escorting some ladies of the Rowland household who were driving; since Louis has mentioned one of the ladies, I had better be explicit. Mrs. Rowland and one of her daughters were in the barouche; another daughter and Hail were following on horseback. Suddenly they heard a shot in the woods, a deer dashed across the road in front of the barouche, the horses bolted, and for some minutes Mrs. Rowland and her daughter were in great danger. The horses were finally brought to a stand after the barouche had collided with a small tree, and Hail was helping to quiet them when, as you will recall, you rode up in your hunting clothes and with your gun across your pommel."

Gough paused, and Richard nodded. Gough lifted his shoulders.

"It's hardly necessary to go over the rest of what happened," he continued. "You will remember it perfectly. Hail, of course, didn't know who you were. He learned later from some negroes whom he met in the road that you were staying at Avalon and they identified you from his description."

"And Mr. Hail," Richard Acton said, has asked you to present his regrets?"

Gough looked up quickly. "No," he replied, "I'm afraid not. Louis and I suggested something like that, but Hail can't see it in that light. He feels that, if he was a little abrupt in addressing you, the reason must have been plain: he had no means of identifying you; your costume, your horse—well, to be perfectly frank, his mistake perhaps, only natural. He feels that you could have cleared it up with a word and that the courteous—or, let me say, the friendly—thing on your part would have been to speak that word. But what particularly weighs upon him is what followed, and perhaps the fact that it took p. the presence of the ladies *is* important. Mr. Hail feels you ignored him to an extent which had the appearance of a deliberate discourtesy. I am using the words that he asked us to use in order to make his position perfectly clear."

Gough ceased speaking. Richard Acton, gazing across the lawn at the live-oaks of Avalon, offered no comment. The silence lengthened until it became awkward. Louis Treves cleared his throat and was evidently about to say something when Gough resumed:

"Of course, this whole proceeding is irregular, Mr. Acton, but we hoped that a friendly conference with you might avoid the necessity of carrying the matter further. Hail's request isn't difficult; at least, I hope you won't find it difficult. He feels that he must have your assurance that your behavior yesterday was not intentionally insulting. If this assurance is given, the matter will remain entirely confidential except that the ladies who were witnesses of incident are to be informed."

Richard Acton seemed unwilling to withdraw his gaze from the oaks at the entrance of the avenue. His eyes were thoughtful. He was thinking again of those great trees as symbols of Avalon, of all that surrounded him, the whole order of life to which he had come home. His thoughts had taken this turn at the moment when he realized that he was confronted with the preliminaries of a challenge, a duel. He approved of Hail's attitude completely. It was astonishing, almost fantastic, but he found it wholly admirable. It was the proud, the knightly South, and Richard Acton loved it.

Yes, he said to himself, knightly was the right word. But wasn't using it only in the sense in which professional panegyrists of the South were fond of using it. It was a word that belonged really to the past; it had come down from a time that was over and done; with all the handsome qualities that it connoted, it implied also a long outdated medievalism. But because a thing was archaic, obsolescent, it wasn't necessarily bad. Richard Acton admired many things that seemed to be becoming obsolete. He admired for instance, this thing with which he was now confronted, this antique conception of the obligation of a gentleman. James Hail had become at once a shining image in

Acton's mind; but he feared that the James Hails were among the obsolescent things—that they were Don Quixotes, gallant and handsome Don Quixotes, tilting not at windmills but at a huge and immovable rock mountain. And they were Carolina, the South. They didn't exist anywhere else; the rest of America, for better or for worse, had become different. Not only different but hostile, hostile to the traditions, the institutions to which the South still clung. The South where men who were gentlemen still thought it, necessary to fight duels over inconsequential points of honor. Because they believed that no point of honor could be inconsequential.

He spoke to Charles Gough:

"Please say to Mr. Hail that I understand his feeling exactly. You can assure him that if I appeared to be discourteous yesterday, I regret it sincerely and I will be obliged to him if he will inform the ladies of this fact.

Louis Treves jumped to his feet. "That's magnificent, Richard!" he exclaimed.

Charles Gough also rose. "I'm delighted, Acton," he said warmly; there was no trace now of his formal manner. "I was afraid you might not see James's position—especially when you spoke of his making an apology. I must say I think something is due you from him. But, as Louis you are sure to like him. He is one of my closest friends."

"If I can like him," Treves said mournfully, "you certainly can. I may as well tell you, Richard, before somebody else does: I've been desperately in love for months with Diane Rowland only to discover that she has been practically engaged for years to this damned James Hail."

Gough laughed. "Behold an outrage!" he cried. "A scion of *the* river rejected in favor of a mere person from the barbaric Combahee! Poor Louis never had a chance, Acton. This thing started long before the Rowlands moved from Beaufort district to Notteley. Another case of propinquity. James and Diane were neighbors on the Combahee since childhood."

"Curses on thee, cruel Propinquity!" Louis Treves murmured. Richard confessed his curiosity as to which of the two young ladies he had seen was *la femme fatale*. Presumably Diane Rowland was the girl on horseback with Hail. Gough, however, informed him to the contrary: the lady on horseback was Sally Rowland: Diane had had a slight headache that morning and was with her mother in barouche.

"I don't blame you for feeling cut-up, Louis," Acton remarked. "I saw the young lady in the barouche only for a minute and I couldn't tell you now whether her hair was black or gold. But I was struck by something in her face."

"Good lord, man," Treves groaned, "don't rub salt in my wounds! She is the most divine creature on the face of the earth. I am destroyed forever."

Gough picked up his hat from the table. "You must ride over to Notteley, Acton," he said cordially. "Hail and I will be there a few days longer and I want you to know James. And you'll like the Rowlands; Sinkler and Ash are as fine as their sisters."

Richard Acton assured them that he would pay his respects at Notteley as soon as John and Elizabeth were settled at Avalon; he would bring Elizabeth with him to be his sponsor. Charles Gough's blue eyes suddenly narrowed. He was looking at something on the lawn. A servant, the quadroon girl, Vienna, was walking across the grass. She had in her hand a piece of red flannel; it was as bright in the bright sun as the red handkerchief around her head. She was walking toward the sun-dial evidently with the intention of rubbing it down with the cloth. She moved slowly, and again to Richard Acton she was like a leopard, a leopardess languid after sleep, as unhurried and as lithe.

Charles Gough gave a low whistle. "Look at that," he exclaimed. "She knows devilish well we're watching her. Delilah—no, Lais parading before the Athenians. And the damned holy abolitionists blame us because we're only human! Well! *I'm* human. I could find a place for that wench—"

Richard interrupted him. "It has been a pleasant visit, gentlemen," he said, "and I have enjoyed it—most of it. You'll excuse me if I don't see you to your horses. I have some duties—"

He bowed and waited until they were half-way down the steps; then he reentered the house. His thoughts returned suddenly to Paris, to Jacqueline. But now she was curiously vague in his memory, a lovely but indistinct image, like a blurred water-color.

Chapter IV

THIS STRANGE VAGUENESS OF HER image persisted. He became suddenly and sharply aware of it, and it puzzled and disturbed him, filling his mind so completely that the events of the past hour were forgotten. He gave up his plan to go fishing with Ephraim and, wandering restlessly, found himself again on the piazza facing the river. Dragging a chair to the end of the piazza overlooking the plantation yard, he sat there frowning, his teeth clamped upon his unlighted cigar.

He called Chance presently in an imperative loud tone and ordered brandy. The liquor—he had poured himself a generous portion—helped him; his mind seemed now to respond less reluctantly to his will. He was trying consciously to see across time and space the face of the woman had loved, and now that face was coming back to him more clearly.

Richard Acton felt, suddenly, relieved. For a few moments he had been in the grip of a fantastic fear, the fear that, for some reason that he could not fathom, Jacqueline was slipping away from him. His thoughts swung gradually back to the two visitors who had just left him. Louis Treves he had liked immediately; Gough, too, when once he had unbent, had been not unattractive: engaging types of Carolinian plantation youth, the kind of men with whom he would now be thrown. Provincial, perhaps—a little countryfied, thank heaven, compared with Paris—but with a certain urban finish too.

That, he reflected, was one good result of the fact that the climate of the Low-Country plantations was inhospitable in summer, it sent the plantation people to Charleston or at least to the smaller towns for almost half the year. The threatened duel obviously was absurd and yet he could see that the incident in the pine-wood wasn't trivial from James Hail's view-point. He must know this James Hail; a man whose sense of honor was so fine-spun would be worth knowing.

That, of course, his thoughts ran on, was another of the South's difficulties: it was too confoundedly, too medievally, sensitive to get along well with an age that was growing careless of manners and contemptuous of the old punctilio. The famous Brooks-Sumner affair in the Senate came to his mind as a case in point. Sumner's speech had been so outrageous that it would have defeated its own ends; but Preston Brooks of South Carolina, conceiving that the honor of his state and of his family had been impugned, had chastised the Massachusetts Senator in the Senate chamber, and the resulting furor had been unfortunate for the whole South. Brooks, a kindly man and a gentleman, and physically no match for Sumner, had been pictured in flaming northern editorials as a "southern ruffian" and a "bully," and the South as the home of ruffians. James Hail, Richard Acton said to himself, would have done exactly what Preston Brooks did: he would have seen only the obligation of honor, immediate and compelling, and not the lamentable practical results.

Yes, undoubtedly he would like James Hail. But, equally of course, Hail would be—he was sure to be—an ardent secessionist: he was obviously too completely southern to be anything else. Probably, Acton's thoughts continued, Hail was a supporter of Barnwell Rhett, the most extreme of the States' Rights leaders, whose separatist propaganda in his organ, the *Charleston Mercury*, was, in Richard's judgment, a primary menace to the South's safety.

The trouble with Barnwell Rhett, he reflected, was his obvious sincerity—he had resigned his seat in the United States Senate because South Carolina hadn't seceded when he thought it ought to; and the trouble with the *Mercury* was the fact that it was so exceedingly able, undoubtedly one of the ablest newspapers in America. That was why both were dangerous. Their arguments were often unanswerable, yet the course which they advocated—South Carolina's withdrawal from the Union—would be, he believed, fatal.

He returned to the visit of Louis Treves and Charles Gough. Gough's remark about the quadroon girl, Vienna, had been significant; a certain amount of that went on, had always gone on, he remembered; under the conditions it was inevitable. He couldn't blame the girl, being what she was, for parading before Gough and Treves. But, he said to himself, with a trace of a frown, how different the truth was from the familiar abolitionist picture of innocent and modest colored maidens forced to become the unwilling mistresses of arrogant and brutal young plantation bloods. Nine-tenths of the time, of course, the girls invited it, precisely as Vienna had, and for very practical reasons: it might even lead to a little house of one's own and a life of agreeable indolence instead of work in the fields.

What a damned twisted mess the abolitionists were making of the truth! He didn't like slavery—Europe had done that to him—any more than they did. But, whatever its defects, it had been for the negro not only a necessity but a godsend, bringing him up from barbarism more swiftly than any other race in the world's history; and when he read the abolitionists' fulminations, their frenzied misrepresentations of the South, he was ready momentarily, to support even Barnwell Rhett. And yet, he understood, they meant well, most of them, though sometimes, remembering their incitements to bloody insurrection, this was hard to believe: and underneath all their outrageous slander of the South and disastrous meddling with an almost hopelessly difficult problem which was not their problem and about which they were abysmally ignorant, lay one truth—that slavery had to end.

It might have ended, he said to himself, or it might now have been well on the way to extinction but for their meddling: it wasn't only cotton, it was equally Garrison's mad campaign of incendiarism and slander that had stopped the emancipation movement in the South. The worst disaster—since it threatened the very existence of the Union—that America had sustained; a tragic lesson for all the generations on the folly of fanaticisms.

His thoughts lingered on the girl Vienna; there, he reflected, was the more subtle poison of slavery. Well, the same system that had produced her had produced that girl in the barouche—what was her name—Diane? A striking face but, like all women's faces since Jacqueline, already indistinct in his memory; he couldn't ever remember the color of her hair, though, as a rule, he bad an eye for color. What, momentarily, he had been aware of in her was something quite apart from beauty—a certain fineness.

James Hail, however, he recalled clearly, had been handsome: a dark, rather thin, forceful face. He hadn't been arrogant; he had simply been conscious of what he was—a gentleman and therefore the superior of the supposed poor-white whom he was reproving. The South's philosophy, Acton said to himself, the philosophy of the South's ruling class, wasn't, as so many supposed, romantic; it was fundamentally realistic. When South Carolina had supplanted Virginia, he pursued the thought further, the realism of John C. Calhoun had supplanted the sentimentalism of Thomas Jefferson. The South's social system, its whole practise of government, was based on a complete recognition of the fact that all men, and women, were not equal.

But that was becoming, he went on in his thoughts, an increasingly unpopular doctrine in the United States of America and not only in America but in practically the whole civilized world. The new democracy, the new humanitarianism, were sweeping on. He had little enough faith in either of them—

already the expanding industrialism of the North was shaping them to its own ends—but he had a comprehension of their power; he saw that the South, trapped by the enormous fact of slavery, which in itself compelled a feudalistic system, had been forced into a position opposed at many points to the most powerful tides of world opinion. This, he believed, would be fatal to it if the political conflict which had raged for thirty years between North and South should develop into actual war. In such a war, he was convinced—and his years in Europe had confirmed the conviction—the South would be not merely defeated but destroyed.

He considered this, chewing moodily on his cigar, in terms of Avalon and of the southern people, the southern society, that he knew. Whatever might be the defects of the South's civilization, he reflected, here in the Low-Country it had borne handsome fruit. It had produced a society as truly civilized as any that America could boast; a society prosperous and happy—he excepted mentally the poorer whites of the pine barrens and the free negroes; a society which from the beginning of the Union had demonstrated its vigor by its influence upon national affairs.

South Carolina's success, he said to himself, had been astonishing. She had wielded a power in the nation out of all proportion to her size. Not only had she shaped the thought of the South and directed its policy; it wasn't too much to say,—and he didn't forget that Calhoun had been born an up-countryman,—that the plantations of the Low-Country, the city-state of Charleston, had to a great extent directed the later course of the Republic. Certainly, Richard Acton concluded with a certain pride, no other single unit of the Union, except Tidewater Virginia in the early days, had played so commanding a role. And Avalon was typical of the Low-Country; Avalon's master, John Acton, was typical of it. It was primarily the vision and the character of men like John Acton—planters of rice and of long-staple Cotton, of which commodities South Carolina produced the finest grades in the world—that had made the Low-Country what it was.

What it was was a handsome thing, the large and generous plantation civilization of the South at its best. But it couldn't last, he repeated to himself; it had to change with the changing times or perish. And yet, he realized, he didn't want it to change. His thoughts went back to his early years at Avalon. His childhood there had been supremely happy; as a boy he had lived on horseback with a gun on his shoulder; there hadn't been, so far as he could recall, a single feature of his boyhood on the plantation that he could reasonably have wished to alter. Yet he had left Carolina in response to some vague but potent longing for a larger life. What actually he had sought he had never been able to decide—certainly the life he had lived in Europe had not been his intended goal—and now he had come back to Avalon with nothing gained except the memory of Jacqueline.

That, however, was a very great thing. Jacqueline had been a part of, and yet she was distinct from, the life he had led in Paris and St. Petersburg. He loved her but now he hated that life; he had begun consciously to hate it soon after death had taken her from him. He was aware, too, of a stranger paradox: he loved Jacqueline, loved her still; but what above all else he valued and looked forward to in Carolina was the tradition of womanhood that prevailed there, a tradition that was the antithesis of Jacqueline.

In Europe, for a time, that Carolinian tradition had seemed to him archaic, even absurd, a mere narrow provincialism expressing a shallow and one-sided morality; but later it had taken on in his mind an indescribable beauty, a profound importance. Its beauty wasn't sensibly diminished now by the implications of Charles Gough's remark about the quadroon girl, Vienna. Long ago he had recognized that condition as an inevitable result of the South's bi-racial population. The fact remained that southern men drew a line between white and all the shades of color and held their white women sacred to a degree perhaps unparalleled anywhere else in the world. Whatever lay behind that fact, the fact itself was fortunate. A womanhood that couldn't be soiled. Yes, somehow that was, after all, one of the fundamental necessities, an indispensable ideal. Mankind needed it, couldn't get on permanently without it. He knew that now—in spite of Jacqueline.

Well, he would find it here. Carolina, thank God, hadn't changed in that respect; the old ideal of woman remained impregnable. His thoughts returned momentarily to the girl in the barouche: her profile (his impression of its fineness persisted, though beyond this he was wholly vague about her) might serve, he said to himself, as a picture of that ideal. A creed, a code that had come down, like so much else that was the South, from the simpler past. Yes, the past had its wisdom, deeper than the contemptuous sophistication of callow revolutionaries imagining themselves the liberators of human thought. Again concerned with the past, his reflections widened, lingering upon many aspects of the life of Avalon as he remembered it.

It hadn't been a lonely life. The plantations were measured more often in thousands than in hundreds of acres, but the houses, built on bluffs overlooking the river, were fairly near one another. Mr. Frederick Fenwick's big barge, rowed by six hands, could come from Haddon Hill, the Fenwick plantation, to Avalon in fifteen minutes with the flood-tide. It came often in those days and in it came Lowndes Fenwick, Richard Acton's chum, and Mary and Constance and Eliza Fenwick, his first flame, and sometimes house-guests from Charleston or from other plantations of the neighborhood. The Wisboo Nesbits and the Marions of Deer Hall were as frequent visitors—Mazÿck Marion had been, next to Lowndes Fenwick, his most intimate friend. Motte Nesbit's long cypress canoes in which he took special pride were the fastest things on the river. He had six of them, besides bateaux and punts used in the rice-fields, and occasionally eight or ten of these would come down-stream in a squadron.

Richard Acton recalled an April evening when a gay house-party at Wisboo had transferred itself without warning to Avalon. Suddenly, as he sat with the family on the front piazza, the river beyond the landing became alive with lights: in a dozen boats, invisible until that moment, pine torches had been lighted, and simultaneously banjoes, fiddles, flutes and twenty hilarious voices began *A Life on the Ocean Wave*.

The surprise was complete, Avalon was captured with out a struggle. His father, he remembered, had hurried down to the landing and surrendered the plantation formally to Mr. Motte Nesbit, Admiral of the invading flotilla, and to Mrs. Nesbit, his "sovereign lady." There were distinguished guests, or at least strangers, on board; visitors from Charleston and Captain Robert Anderson and Lieutenant William Tecumseh Sherman from the Fort Moultrie garrison. A rum punch had been hastily prepared; Mrs. Acton, with two or three servants hurriedly summoned from the Quarters, had caused the plantation pantry to produce an amazing variety of cakes and other delicacies. There had been dancing in the big room until after midnight; and Richard Acton recalled—he must have been about sixteen years of age at the time—that Eliza Fenwick was on that evening summarily dethroned as queen of his affections by a beautiful black-haired girl from Charleston whose name he now found himself entirely unable to recall.

All that was more than fifteen years ago; it was before he had begun his studies at Oxford University; but life on the river had certainly not changed for the worse. On the contrary, new houses had been built, roads had been improved, and there was now, besides the Rail Road, regular communication by steamer with Charleston and with the other river plantations. Richard Acton realized with a shadow of a frown that his quiet enjoyment of

Avalon was over. With the return of John and Elizabeth and their children, there would be interruptions of his seclusion. Visitors would be coming and going; there would be cousins and friends from Charleston and the parishes; hunts and parties and perhaps dances from time to time. John Acton was a prodigious worker, but he welcomed occasional relaxation; and Elizabeth enjoyed society—she was so attractive that she was naturally a favorite.

Well, if he found existence at Avalon irksome or if he conceived himself to be a nuisance there, he could at any time remove to Sherborne, his own place. He intended to do this in any event some time during the winter, for he planned to begin at once his new career as a planter. The house at Sherborne had been unoccupied for years; it would need certain repairs and some interior furbishing up. But the plantation itself was in fine shape. John had been operating it successfully during Richard's residence abroad; its rice-lands were in every way equal to those of Avalon, and John would make it easy for him to take over the necessary number of hands until such time as he could conveniently pay for them. He would be lonely at Sherborne, perhaps, having with him only his memories of Jacqueline. But Avalon would be near; he could ride there whenever his spirit needed it.

Jacqueline—Jacqueline Fleur. How different she was from all this that was around him now, the life upon which he was now entering! Jacqueline of the Chaussée d'Antin, the Boulevard Saint-Michel. He could never have brought her here; she would have hated Carolina as much as Carolina would have hated her and condemned her. And yet she must go with him to Sherborne and live with him there; she must be with him at Sherborne as she had been with him ever since her death, a vital presence in his mind, so real that often she seemed physically visible.

He could see her now before him He could see every detail of her face, the golden flecks in her hazel eyes, the flame-lights in her copper hair, the symmetry of her hands, the silken whiteness of her body. Her body. It had belonged to him for three years and he had worshiped it because it was to him the utter perfection of beauty. Losing it and losing her, he had lost forever a loveliness that had satisfied the most passionate yearnings of his spirit. But he had not lost it wholly, after it had perished, gone back to dust, it lived on in his memory.

Thank God, it still lived on there. For a few moments that morning he had been afraid that it was dying there also. It had become suddenly so vague that there had been born in him the terrible conception that even in his memory Jacqueline was fading, that after a while she would be gone from his thoughts even as she was gone from his arms. The impact of that fear had shaken him, it had compelled him to call for brandy—brandy at eleven o'clock in the morning! He straightened suddenly in his chair, frowning at the empty glass on the table beside him. He had never before needed brandy to bring her before him. Was she fading after all? Would it require hereafter the stimulation of liquor to make his memory recreate her for him as a vital element in his being?

The thought dismayed him, overwhelmed him with a kind of panic. He reached for the decanter, refilled the glass and swallowed the contents at once; and, within a few minutes, scarcely aware, in his absorption, of what he was doing, he filled the glass again...

Presently came reassurance, a renewed and stronger confidence that all was well. Jacqueline would never fade. There would be no need of drink to bring her back to him. Drink had all but ruined him in Europe; it would never again get its grip upon him. Drink and Jacqueline Fleur. Yes, those two had destroyed him: the liquor that had made a slave of him for a while; the woman, the light woman of Paris, whom he had loved and who had loved him so much that she could not give him up though his passion for her was wrecking his career.

Well, Acton told himself, that didn't matter now. It was all over and past. If he could begin again at the beginning, he would do just what he had done. He would not give up one hour of Jacqueline for all the glory in the world; he would not exchange what she had given him for an ambassadorship. His cigar dropped to the floor and he did not trouble to pick it up. His eyes were heavy, but his mind was intensely awake, abnormally alive, and he was happy, happier than he had been since he had put liquor behind him. It was the same happiness that he had known when he and Jacqueline had been living life together.

Reclining languidly in his chair, Richard Acton was four thousand miles from Avalon, from Carolina. He was dancing with Jacqueline in the Moulin de la Galette. He was sitting beside her in a coach; they were beginning that ecstatic tour which they had made together through the Midi, stopping often to gather flowers by the way and sleeping in the uncomfortable little inns. He was with her—she was a Queen of Babylon—in that incredible house of bacchanalian splendor in St. Petersburg, the palace of a Grand Duke known as the most prodigal libertine in Europe. He was with her in her house in the Rue Percival; she was in his arms, her eyes were half-closed, her red hair was an aureole of dusky light against the white pillow.

Richard Acton did not hear the plantation bell that rang at twelve o'clock; he was asleep in his chair on the east piazza. He woke at about half-past twelve and sat for some minutes staring straight in front of him. Presently he called Chance, told him to remove the decanter and glass, and informed him that there would be no need of dinner. Then he walked, perfectly steadily, to his room, where he slept for three hours.

He rose in mid-afternoon, dressed and sat reading in the library until Chance rushed in to tell him that the Acton carriage was coming up the avenue. He was standing with Janvers, the overseer, at the foot of the steps, backed by a small army of voluble and grinning blacks, when the carriage stopped and Elizabeth Acton, too excited to wait for her husband to help her alight, flung open the door, leaped out and kissed him first on one cheek and then on the other.

Chapter V

IN THE LIBRARY, AFTER SUPPER, when the excitement of the home-coming had died down and the house servants had gone to their Quarters, he recounted, half humorously, to John Acton the incident in the pine-wood and the consequent visit of Charles Gough and Louis Treves that morning.

Elizabeth was up-stairs with the nurse, seeing that the children were properly put to bed. John listened attentively and gravely, his large frame filling one of the big wing-chairs in front of the fire; and before Richard had finished, Elizabeth returned so that he had to repeat most of his story. "So you see," he concluded, "though I am no longer in the diplomatic service, I still know how to be diplomatic. Having got myself into hot water with this belligerent Mr. Hail, I have got myself out again."

There was a pause. Elizabeth glanced at her husband, who was gazing thoughtfully into the fire. "Of course," John began in his deep deliberate voice, "what you have done amounts practically to an apology. And that's not the best way to begin a residence in Carolina. But I'm not blaming you, Richard. A meeting would have been infinitely worse, especially a meeting over so small a matter."

"I thought so," Richard said dryly.

"It isn't very important," his brother continued, "but, frankly, I'm sorry it happened. However, we can be reasonably sure that it won't go any further, won't become generally known, I mean. James Hail is to be trusted absolutely. I don't quite approve of his politics—he is a leader of the extreme States' Rights party, and perhaps he is too extreme,—but he is very completely a gentleman. Louis Treves is naturally talkative, but he knows what not to talk about. Gough I don't know personally, but he is James Hail's friend and that's sufficient. As for the three women, we're quite safe there, I think."

"I see," Richard said, "that the matter is important, more important than I had supposed. You mean that it would be damaging to me if the fact should become known that I had expressed my regrets to Mr. Hail?"

"Not if the circumstances were understood," John explained. "But they wouldn't be, they never are. The story, once started, would assume all kinds of twisted forms. People would only know that Hail had sent a friend with a demand for an apology and that you had apologized. With a great many that wouldn't hurt you, but on the whole it wouldn't be helpful. The code is losing ground, but its implications are still strong. As a practical matter, it's always best to avoid putting yourself in a position where an apology may be demanded of you. That's more or less true everywhere, I suppose, but perhaps it's more essential here than in most of the states."

Richard nodded thoughtfully. "I ought to have remembered that," he said. "I ought to have remembered that in some ways we haven't changed in the last hundred years. I'm not sure I'm sorry—I think I like the old ways best—but it worries me. It makes me wonder whether the South can survive. We're a queer people, John. We don't realize, we people here in the Low-Country, that we're among the most fortunate people on the face of the earth. We may be able to go on being prosperous and happy for a long while yet if only we'll keep our heads and move with the tide. Instead, we listen to Barnwell Rhett and the editor of the *Mercury*—both of whom I admire exceedingly. They persuade me that we can do the impossible, sweep back the ocean. Then I wake up."

John smiled. "You haven't changed, Richard," he said, "since those letters you used to write me from Paris. You're with Petigru and against Rhett. Well, you're partly right and Barnwell Rhett is partly right. He's Calhoun's disciple and Calhoun saw pretty clearly."

"Too clearly," Richard replied. "He saw so clearly that he saw the impossibility of a dream the world's dreaming: the dream of a universal democracy with everybody equal. He saw the folly of that, of Tom Jefferson's Utopia, and he offered a substitute for it. He went back to the Greeks and proposed a democracy on the Greek plan—one that would recognize the fact of human inequality, the fact that there will always be an inferior class to be taken care of or made use of by the others. He proposed both to use them and to take care of them and his idea was to rear his democracy upon them as a foundation. A sound idea, John; we'll all come to it some day. But the world hasn't come to it yet and won't come to it in our time. The world's dreaming its dream of universal equality and freedom…"

He paused, his forehead wrinkled. "Confound it, John," he went on, "they call us romantics here in the South, when actually we're the realists. John, that's the greatest thing South Carolina has done—and it's South Carolina that did it. South Carolina pointed out to America the only kind of democracy that can succeed. That's why South Carolina is going to be destroyed. Because the truth we've pointed out is unpalatable, because it's contrary to the world's dream, to America's dream."

"Part of the way," John said, "I can follow you. But I think you go too far. Its dream, as you call it, isn't as important to the world, to England especially, as its cotton. You'll find, if it comes to that, the English mill owners more influential than the English dreamers."

"You won't!" Richard told him. "Good God, nobody here realizes what Mrs. Stowe's done with her book. A false picture but with enough truth in it to make the whole thing believed. John, hundreds of thousands of people, millions, in Europe believe it. It's their conception of the South. They believe it because they want to; it's in accord with their dream. John, I tell you there isn't a European government that would dare support a slaveholding South. Uncle Tom's ten times mightier than Calhoun, and between them they've ruined us."

"Richard," Elizabeth put in, "I'll have you know, sir, that Calhoun is my idol and Barnwell Rhett my prophet, and that comparisons between Mr. Calhoun and Uncle Tom are odious. If you go on talking like this, I won't give you any battercakes for breakfast."

Richard smiled. "Behold," he said, "the effect of the unpalatable truth. No battercakes for the truth-teller. Well, there won't be any battercakes for Mr. Calhoun, either; not even in the South. We'll abuse him some day as loudly as we praise him now—because he will have led us into trouble. Then, after a while, we'll be praising him again. But that's a long way off, I'm afraid. It won't come until the world discovers that Calhoun was right and Barnwell Rhett was right and South Carolina was right. And by the time it discovers that, there won't be any South Carolina—not the South Carolina we've known.

"By jove, John, I'm proud of her—and I'm scared to death for her. She's not the kind to bend to the storm. She has made a political philosophy—a good one—and she's given it to the South, and she will fight for it. Of course she has made it because she needs it; with the negro fastened on us, the only kind of democracy we can even think of is one frankly based on an inferior class. But we've been too frank about it—too realistic. The world doesn't want realism—the masses of the world. They want to go on dreaming their dream. The wage-slaves of England and New England want to dream that some day they'll be free. And we've made one mistake—one enormous and fatal mistake. We saw that there must always be slaves, but we didn't see that we mustn't call them slaves: we saw that there must always be slavery, because the strong will always rule the weak, but we didn't see that the time for our kind of slavery had passed. That's where Calhoun went wrong…"

Elizabeth interrupted him. "Richard," she said, "I give you fair warning: the prospect of battercakes for you is diminishing every minute."

"*Fiat justitia*—"Richard Acton announced. "Elizabeth, you're a tyrant of the worst kind. I'll have to propitiate you. If I thought secession could succeed, I'd be for it. Barnwell Rhett's right when he says that if we don't secede we'll be the North's vassals. He's right when he says that the North is aiming at a consolidated government which will ignore and override the rights of the Southern States. He's right in pretty much everything except the most important thing of all—his belief that we can beat the North.

"We can't. They're so much stronger than we are that our only chance would be Europe—England and France; and if you knew Europe as well as I do—John, you can talk yourself black in the face about the rights of the states, about the guarantees of the Constitution, about local self-government as the corner-stone of liberty, about the tariff that robs us for the North's benefit, about the African savage transformed into a civilized being under our system of slavery, about the crazy abolition program that would mean financial ruin and social suicide for the South—and all those things, the sum of them all, don't mean as much in Europe as Little Eva and Simon Legree..."

He broke off suddenly. His frown dissolved in a smile.

"John," he said, don't ever let me talk about politics again. Elizabeth's a secessionist and you're a half-secessionist and the peace of Avalon is more important than the peace of the Union. And my battercakes are most important of all. What were we talking about before I began that oration? Oh, yes, my apology, as you called it. If I was rude to Hail, he brought it on himself. I suppose I could have challenged him if I had wanted to—for mistaking me for a poor-white, a pine-land cracker. But that would have been ridiculous. Besides, I don't want to shoot Hail, even if he is in favor of secession; I want to know him."

"You are going to know him," Elizabeth put in. "Evidently John hasn't told you what's in store and I've been so excited over getting home to Avalon that I forgot to tell you. We are all going to a party at Notteley tomorrow. Mrs. Rowland wrote to me about it in Charleston some days ago, and this afternoon, soon after we arrived, one of the Rowland negroes brought another note from her in which she particularly mentioned you, Richard. So that's one happy result of your apology, as John calls it. If you and James Hail had been getting ready to fight a duel, you couldn't have been invited."

She turned quickly to her husband. "John, you have always admired Diane Rowland. You may as well abandon any hopes you may have entertained of her in case of my taking-off. I'm perfectly sure now that at this party tomorrow her engagement to James Hail will be announced."

"Is that just feminine intuition," John asked, "or have you official information?"

"Oh, everything points to it," she continued. "Of course, he has been devoted for years; I don't see how she has resisted him so long. And it's plain from Mrs. Rowland's note that this is to be no ordinary affair. She expects several notables: Barnwell Rhett and Mr. Petigru and possibly Senator Hammond. John Chesnut and Singleton Manning and Gaillard Cantey are coming— she mentioned them as special friends of yours—and Wade Hampton, from Columbia, and Stephen Elliott of Beaufort. So many of them wouldn't come from so far away unless this were a special occasion. Besides, I heard rumors in Charleston of an interesting announcement from Notteley soon. I'm confident it will be Diane's engagement."

"Diane Rowland," Richard said, "was the girl in the barouche with her mother when Mr. Hail was addressing his remarks to me. I only saw her for a moment, but there was something in her face. Tell me about her, Elizabeth."

"She's rather a hard person to tell about," Elizabeth Acton replied thoughtfully. "She isn't quite like the rest of us. I can't say I—"she paused and considered. "No, I think I won't do that, Richard. It will be more interesting to leave you in the dark about her so that you can meet her without any preconceived notions. Then you can tell me later how she impresses you. I've said enough to whet your curiosity."

John smiled. "I wouldn't have the slightest difficulty," he said, "in telling you about Diane Rowland. But I wouldn't dare do it in this presence, and, besides, it wouldn't be fair now. It would spoil Elizabeth's experiment."

"I'm afraid," Richard remarked, "that the experiment won't be very successful. I'm free to confess, and I'm not trying to appear blasé, that the only woman I am interested in is my fascinating sister-in-law. I won't care if I don't meet Miss Rowland, though, of course, I'll have to. You're going to find me a terrible burden socially, Elizabeth. I'll have a better time at the Notteley party if you'll leave me entirely to the men. Lowndes Fenwick and Mazÿck Marion and Hutson Waight and the others I used to know. I'll get along better with them than with the women."

"That sounds," Elizabeth Acton said, "as though there might be some secret chapter of your European life that you haven't yet told us about. Don't tell me, Richard, that you've come home with a broken heart, the victim of some foreign charmer whom you can't forget."

For a moment he was speechless. His experience of the morning, his agony over Jacqueline, must have left, he surmised fantastically, some sign upon his face, some sign that Elizabeth had read. But in another instant he saw the absurdity of this. Her remark, he realized, had been wholly innocent, mere badinage suggested by what he had just said about his lack of interest in women. He leaned over and took Elizabeth's hand.

"If my heart were broken," he said, "Avalon would make me forget, Avalon and its delightful mistress. You know, Elizabeth,

John didn't prepare me for you at all. Of course, all that he said in his letters was most enthusiastic. But the picture he sent me didn't do you justice; it couldn't show those hazel eyes and that lovely chestnut hair."

He rose. "That's a nice speech," he said, "and I'm quite proud of it. I hope I've made John jealous. Well, I'm going to bed. You're both of you tired after your long drive, and I'm sleepy too and I suppose we'll be up until the small hours tomorrow."

He went up-stairs in a cold perspiration. He was trying to see Jacqueline in his mind and, again, he could not see her clearly. "Avalon would make me forget," he repeated, standing beside his bed. "Good God! Is that what's happening?"

Chapter VI

THE RIVER FOR TWO MILES or more below Avalon had been shimmering silver, but when they turned toward the sunset into Notteley reach, their watery path became a sinuous lane of polished gold. That was why, Elizabeth explained, she had insisted upon coming by water instead of driving over; it was a longer journey but, in the late afternoon, more beautiful; she wanted to see the late lights on the river and the ducks streaming overhead. She sat, more silent than usual, beside her husband in the stern sheets. Richard Acton sat opposite. Manigo, the foreman responsible for the plantation boats, managed the tiller. The four younger negroes at the oars pulled steadily, keeping time with their slow song.

Richard Acton roused himself from a state of profound abstraction into which he had been sinking more and more completely. It was the first time since his return to Avalon that he had been on the river at sunset; again there had swept over him that sense of a panorama remembered rather than actually perceived. The shining, placid stream, the rush-grown banks shutting off the rice-fields from the tide, the crimson sky above the distant woods, the swirl of a rockfish just ahead of the boat's bow, the harsh croak of a startled heron, the keen sibilance of wings as the duck squadrons swept over, the incessant chant of the black oarsmen singing *Old Egypt*—all this was a memory, a dream.

He had actually to persuade himself that it was real. It was the past come to life again, and he couldn't quite believe it. He was on the river with his father, with John, with Lowndes Fenwick of Haddon Hill, with Mazÿck Marion of Deer Hall, with Black Samson the hunter, with Penny or Isam or Twis'foot Toby or some other of the little black boys of Avalon who had been as truly his chums as Lowndes Fenwick was. It was Twis'foot Toby who was with him when he had caught the twenty-pound rockfish. Penny had helped him rob the eagle nest on Ragged Island. On just such an evening as this, with the water golden and the duck squadrons swishing overhead, he had confessed to Lowndes Fenwick, in a sudden inexplicable burst of sentimental eloquence, his undying love for Lowndes's fourteen-year-old sister, Eliza.

"You've been dreaming, Richard," Elizabeth Acton said suddenly, "all the way from Avalon. I don't wonder. It must be almost unbelievable to come back to this after Napoleon the Third's Paris. But you must wake up now. Notteley is just around the next bend and I want my new and handsome brother-in-law to make a successful debut in plantation society."

"He won't," John remarked with his rather solemn smile, unless he gets rid of that expression. I've been watching you all the way down, Richard, and you haven't heard a word that's been spoken. You've been in a 'strance,' as the darkies would say."

Richard Acton admitted that he had been in a kind of trance. "So would you be, John, if you were spending your first evening on the river after a dozen years. I can't describe to you what it means to come back. I seem never to have been away. All those years in Europe seem to have been blotted out."

He had no sooner uttered the words than their essential falseness struck him. They were true in a superficial sense, but he told himself that fundamentally they were utterly false and he would never have spoken them if he had stopped to consider. He had thought it all out the previous night, lying awake for hours after his conversation in the library, and he had convinced himself that the truth was simple and sure. Avalon could not in a million years make him forget. After the first emotional reactions of his home-coming were over, say in another week or so, Jacqueline would resume her accustomed place in his memory. There would be no more of those ghastly moments when she seemed to be fading. In the peace of Avalon and the solitude of Sherborne, when he had established himself there, she would be more real than ever.

They were rounding the bend now. Suddenly he saw the landing and, on the rising ground beyond it, Notteley house, white against its dark background of magnolias. It appeared, he thought, as handsome as Avalon and fully as large. The Rowlands were among the wealthiest families in the Low-Country, and he remembered Elizabeth's telling him that they had added extensively to the house not long before Mr. Rowland's death. There were people at the landing and a number of boats;

Chinese lanterns had been strung across the lawn on slender ropes attached to the trees, and the front piazza had been enclosed in canvas. Beyond, under the magnolias, saddle horses were tethered, and negro hostlers and drivers moved amid an imposing array of waiting carriages and buggies.

The lanterns on the lawn had not yet been lighted, but lamps glowed in the upper windows of the house, for now dusk was coming fast. A group of men and women came down the front steps and stood talking.

"There's Louis Treves," Elizabeth told Richard, "and Ralph Cain and young Ash Rowland and Doctor Roupell, and Stephen Elliott and Mary Ball and Stuart Chantilly. Gilmore Simms the novelist, is at the foot of the steps and Jane Laurens—you remember her—and Mr. Petigru, who's delightful even if he is a Unionist, and Paul Hayne the poet. And there's Barnwell Rhett, Richard,—the tall, fine-looking, baldish man with gray hair. I think that's Julie Chardon in the blue dress and I know Harriott Keating by her walk. Sinkler Rowland's at the end of the wharf with Alfred Rhett, Mr. Barnwell Rhett's son, and just behind him is your beloved Lowndes Fenwick—he told me in Charleston the other day that he was dying to see you."

She waved gaily to the group at the landing and John Acton raised his hand. Manigo spoke a brief word and the rowers shipped their oars. "Hello, Avalon!" Sinkler Rowland's voice came across the narrowing space of water. "Welcome to Notteley!"

Lowndes Fenwick, in a gale of exuberant spirits, took charge of Richard Acton. "Leave him to me, Elizabeth," he said. "You've had him all day and I haven't seen him for countless centuries. We're going to celebrate with a barrel of Madeira." They moved, Richard and Lowndes arm in arm, in a straggling group across the lawn, where servants carrying long rush tapers were lighting the Chinese lanterns.

Lowndes hadn't changed much, Richard Acton remarked; he had filled out and grown a mustache but not a gray hair. "That's because I'm still a bachelor like yourself," Fenwick replied. "No life like the single life if you want to keep your youthful bloom. Look at John, now: solemn as a judge, though he has the prettiest wife on the river." Sinkler Rowland guided them toward the group around the piazza steps. "You all know Mr. and Mrs. Acton of Avalon," he announced, "but Mr. Acton has with him a long-lost brother. This is he and Richard Acton is his name."

"He's my cousin," said Louis Treves, "but don't hold that against him. He's really very nice. He's been in Europe for a dozen years safe from my demoralizing influence."

Ralph Cain, a slender middle-aged man, held out his hand. "You must remember me, Acton, and the rest of us at Somerset. We used to see you now and then and twelve years isn't such a long time."

Richard Acton assented. "The biggest turkey I ever saw flew over me in Somerset swamp just where the creek crosses. You saw me miss it, Mr. Cain, and I'll never forget the look on your face."

Ralph Cain smiled. He had seen many men miss turkeys in Somerset swamp, he remarked. "I had an impression, though, Acton," he added, "that you were an especially good shot. Didn't you have quite a reputation?"

Richard nodded. "That was the trouble," he said. "I used to think I couldn't miss."

Elizabeth Acton, her hand on Richard's arm, propelled him gently toward a slight, erect, elderly man whose close-cropped gray beard emphasized a mouth at once sensitive and firm. "Hold your breath, Richard," she whispered. "You're about to meet the head-devil of the awful secessionists—Barnwell Rhett. Can't you smell the brimstone?" A tall girl in a gay barcelona, who had been talking with Rhett, turned toward them expectantly.

"Harriott," Elizabeth Acton said, "let me present John's brother, Richard. Miss Keating, Mr. Acton." She turned with a smile to Harriott Keating's companion. "Mr. Rhett, this is my brother-in-law, Richard Acton. He has just come home after twelve years in Europe and I have been specially anxious for him to meet you. Then, to be perfectly impartial, I'm going to introduce him to Mr. Petigru and see whether he goes for secession or the Union."

Barnwell Rhett laughed. Richard Acton had immediately a sense of Rhett's frankness, genuineness, and of his high breeding; of strength, too, in the clear-cut, rather ruddy face, disfigured by a white patch on the cheek, and the blue-gray eyes. Strength and courage, he said to himself, that wouldn't count odds. Rhett hadn't counted them, the thought flashed through Richard's mind, when he had stood unawed in the United States Senate, a proud solitary figure, and reaffirmed his belief in South Carolina's right and duty to secede. His eyes, however, as they met Acton's, were extraordinarily gentle. Barnwell Rhett, he realized suddenly, was an old man, older than his years, whose scars were so deep that his pride was at pains to cover them.

"That's apt to be fatal, Mrs. Acton." Rhett's smile was as engaging as his laugh. "You know I can't prevail against Petigru.

He's probably the greatest lawyer in America. But I think we're safe even from him. If, with so charming a sister-in-law, this young gentleman goes against us..."

He bowed to Elizabeth, leaving his sentence unfinished. Richard Acton was momentarily at a loss; it hadn't been he thought, quite tactful of Elizabeth to put him in this position. He felt a hand on his shoulder and turned. It was Lowndes Fenwick. Lowndes bowed—a little stiffly, Richard noticed—to Barnwell Rhett.

"Richard," he said, "I hope I'm not intruding, but you must meet your hostess, Mrs. Rowland." Acton, making his acknowledgments to Rhett and Miss Keating, turned away. Moving toward the piazza steps, Lowndes whispered: "I thought perhaps you wouldn't mind being rescued; unless you've changed since the last time you wrote me from Paris, you don't like the Rhett kind of secessionism."

Richard nodded. "I like the man, though," he declared. "I want to talk with him again, find out what's inside of him. By the way, Lowndes, there's another man I want to meet; Hail, James Hail."

Fenwick smiled. "You seem to be going in for all the red-hot secessionists," he said, "and I thought you were the other way. I'm not a Rhett man, Richard, but I'm no Unionist; you'll find damned few Unionists in the Low-Country, especially among the younger men...Well, you'll like Hail. He's here, of course. It's an open secret that he's engaged to Diane Rowland."

He led the way up the steps and across the piazza into the hall. "Why didn't you Avalonians come over earlier?" he continued. "We've had a big deer hunt and a dinner in the woods with all the girls in fine spirits. Most of them are upstairs now dressing for the reception and dance." From the hall, decorated with holly and evergreen cassina, they passed into the ballroom where long sprays of smilax hid the carved cornices and pennons of Spanish moss hung from the chandeliers. "Duty before pleasure," Lowndes Fenwick whispered. "I'll present you to Mrs. Rowland; then we'll look for the champagne or whatever we can find."

Richard Acton bent over Mrs. Rowland's hand. She was very small, in a handsome black evening dress, and she appeared younger than when he had seen her in the barouche—a delicate, aquiline, exceedingly alert face, lit by unusually bright black eyes. She leaned toward him holding up her large feather fan.

I thought you behaved very sensibly," she whispered, "and I gave James Hail a piece of my mind...Mrs. Seabrook, Mr. Lesesne, Miss St. Julien," she added aloud to those around her, "this is Mr. Richard Acton, a brother of our neighbor at Avalon. He has been away from South Carolina for a long time, but he has had the good sense to come back."

Richard Acton had a feeling, a strange insistent consciousness, that some one was looking at him intently. Miss St. Julien had engaged him in conversation; he could not immediately turn his head. The feeling persisted and, yielding to it, he contrived presently to shift his position. At the other end of the room a young woman in white with a white rose in her hair was disappearing through a door leading to the rear of the house. He saw her only momentarily, a fleeting glimpse of her back—dark hair with a white rose and shoulders as white. He wondered who she was.

Chapter VII

Lowndes Fenwick's search for spirituous refreshment could not at the moment be prosecuted successfully. Returning to the hall, they were met by several young women, all in evening dress, descending the stairs; before they could escape from these, half a dozen men who had been strolling outside entered. Some of them Richard Acton knew and recognized; twelve years was not, after all, as Ralph Cain had remarked, so long a time. Motte Nesbit of Wisboo greeted him cordially; Nesbit was considerably his senior, but he had been one of Richard's boyhood heroes because he was the best shot on the river. Peter Delamott of Mattesaw, Huger Simons of Lewisfield, Rutledge Ravenel of Wantoot, William Colcock of Mowbray, Mazÿck Marion of Deer Hall, Paul Middleton of Crowfield, Hutson Waight of Cypress Hall—he had enthusiastic reunions with all of these.

All of them except Delamott, he learned somewhat to his dismay, were now married and settled on plantations of their own; most of the girls whom he had known on the river, he discovered with equal surprise, were also married. Of course John's letters had informed him of many of these matches, but he hadn't been able to keep them all in his head. He had forgotten entirely, for instance, that Sophronia Izard of The Elms was now Smith Prioleau's wife. Recognizing her as she descended the stairs and addressing her as Miss Izard—he had never known her very well—he was formally and promptly corrected by a severe-looking aunt who was with her. He had the same experience with Margaret Porcher, though in this case it was her husband Heyward Drayton, who good-humoredly set him straight. "Well anyhow," he told Eliza Fenwick, who came running to greet him just after his mistake about Margaret, "I know who you married. You're just as pretty as ever, Eliza, and I can't believe you've been Mrs. Granville Stoney for seven years."

"Only six, Richard," she corrected him. "And I'm not so pretty as I used to be. My, but it's splendid to see you! You look older, but not much older, and it's very becoming to you; you're much handsomer than you were in the old romantic days."

She told him to tell her all about himself, but he had scarcely begun when Ball Moultrie came up. Moultrie had been one of his classmates at Oxford and was now planting rice at the old Moultrie place, Windsor Hill. Then came Elizabeth with a rather stout, somewhat red-faced gentleman of seventy or thereabouts.

"This is Mr. Petigru, Richard," she said, "the sweetest man and the cleverest lawyer in the South. Of course you know all about him, how we all love him in spite of his perfectly horrid political views. Don't let him contaminate you; you're inclined too much that way already."

Acton studied the older man with keen interest. Petigru had been the real head of the Union party in the Nullification crisis, the ablest brain opposed to the intellect of Calhoun; thereafter he had continued, throughout the political struggle between Unionism and States' Rights, an uncompromising Unionist in the hotbed of secessionism. "I want you to tell me some time," he said in a queer falsetto voice, "how the real undercurrents are now running on the other side of the water. You must have had in your diplomatic experience first-rate opportunities for observation. They say here that opinion is changing favorably to South. Is that true?"

"I can answer that now, sir," Acton replied immediately. You mean England principally, of course. They prefer us to the North, but they won't lift a finger for us. Because of slavery, the South is alone in the world."

Petigru nodded. His quizzical eyes examined Acton's face with close attention. "An excellent compact statement of essentials," he said. "Well, you can't make our people believe it. They'd rather ride to ruin with Barnwell Rhett and my young friend James Hail in the Southern Rights parade."

He was silent for a moment, his hand tugging at his chin, his eyes roving here and there about the crowded hall.

"A pity," he said as though talking to himself. "Lovely women and strong warm-hearted men. And silks and satins and rich jewels and broad lands and a beautiful proud city; wealth and happiness and greater things to come. Paul Hayne writing his poems, and Simms his novels, and Trescot's fine prose, and Timrod—a southern literature getting ready to flower. What a pity to risk it all!"

Suddenly he laughed, laying his hand impulsively on Acton's arm.

"I'm an old croaker," he said. "A confounded old pessimist. Because I don't believe South Carolina can whip the Union and I don't want to see her burnt with fire. I'd like to talk with you again, young man." He nodded and moved off, to be appropriated immediately by a handsome, black-eyed girl in violet moire, who seized his hands in hers and, laughing, shook a finger in his face. "But I wasn't preaching Unionism," Acton heard him say. "I was telling him how irresistible you secessionists are—"

In a moment he was lost in the throng.

Richard Acton, attempting to rejoin Elizabeth, found that progress had become difficult. More and more women, some simply, some elaborately dressed, came down the stairs to be joined by their waiting escorts. Additional guests arrived from other plantations; carriages dispatched to the railway station returned with another contingent that had come up from Charleston by train.

"It's one of the largest parties ever given on the river," Elizabeth whispered, when at last he reached her. "There are people here from all over the parishes and even from Savannah. And I'm surer than ever now about what I told you—the engagement, I mean. In fact, everybody expects it. You notice that James Hail and Diane haven't yet appeared. Probably Mrs. Rowland has planned some dramatic way of making the announcement. She's nothing if not original."

There was a general drift toward the ballroom where on a table at one end of the room, a punch bowl had become a center of interest, while negro girls, in neat blue uniforms and white turbans, moved here and there carrying silver trays laden with sandwiches and cakes. John Acton carried off Elizabeth to meet the bride of an old friend of his, Townsend Jenkins of Edisto Island. Charles Gough caught Richard's eye, smiled and made his way through the throng, bringing with him a graceful blonde girl in Brussels net over white silk, whose animated face was vaguely familiar. "This young lady," he said, "has seen you before, but she doesn't yet know you officially. She was the lady on horseback—Miss Sally Rowland of Notteley. Sally, may I have the distinguished honor of presenting Sir Richard Acton, the haughty cavalier of the pine-wood?"

Gough had had, Acton suspected, a little too much punch; his rather stern features were animated, almost excited. Too much punch, or else, Acton surmised, too much Sally Rowland. She gave him her hand with a wicked gleam in her vivacious eyes. "I've been dying to meet you, Acton," she said, "ever since—" and passed on at once with an eloquent yet enigmatical smile.

Richard Acton's eyes followed her. There was something, a singular quality, in her face that seemed to remind him of something else. His mind groped for it and it came to him: the glimpse he had had of her sister, the girl in the barouche. He was mildly surprised; it was odd that his impression of the sister had persisted so clearly. Yet even now it was the mere ghost of an impression. Was Diane Rowland fair like her sister or dark? He couldn't remember. All that remained with him was a certain singularity of feature and expression recalled to memory by something in Sally Rowland's face.

The subject occupied him only for a moment. His interest in Diane Rowland lay principally in the fact that James Hail was apparently going to marry her. Hail's appearance, however, he awaited with lively anticipation, not because of what had passed between them but because he thought of Hail as the type of much that he loved and, at same time, lamented in Carolina. Even more than Barnwell Rhett, Hail personified the fire and ardor of the South, for Rhett was an old man now—Acton had been surprised to see how old the maker of so many fiery speeches actually appeared.

His mind went back to Petigru's words, his prophecy. Petigru saw the situation clearly, but, after all, a negative policy couldn't solve the South's problem. It was well enough to preach moderation, but moderation had accomplished less than nothing. It had simply meant, as Calhoun had foreseen years ago, the steady strengthening of the North's advantage, its sure, relentless march toward complete political ascendency. And the continuous flow of immigration from abroad meant a progressive increase of the North's preponderance. Yes, it was a hard choice for the South. Petigru's policy was safer, but

Barnwell Rhett's was braver: if he could persuade himself that secession could succeed he would be with Rhett.

Lost in these thoughts, he did not immediately observe that Lowndes Fenwick had rejoined him and was standing at his elbow.

"James Hail and Diane have just come in;" Fenwick said. "There they are near the window; the tall man and the girl in white. They slipped in through the door just behind them. Now for the excitement."

Richard Acton could see James Hail's dark thin face above the throng. He studied it with an eager curiosity which absorbed him so completely that he did not for a moment glance at Diane Rowland; when finally his eyes sought her, she was hidden from him by Mazÿck Marion, who was bowing over her hand. At the other end of the room some one rapped loudly for attention. The clatter of voices died quickly away. Acton saw Barnwell Rhett standing beside the punch bowl, his glass lifted.

"My friends," Rhett's high voice was clear and far-carrying, "our hostess, Mrs. Rowland, has conferred upon me a rare distinction. She has chosen me, among so many more eloquent men, to make an announcement of interest to all this company. She has, however, left nothing to my discretion, knowing only too well that I have none; and she has instructed me to be both brief and dignified; a command which I am highly resolved to carry out, though I perish in the effort. I ask you, therefore, to fill your glasses. I ask you to lift them high. I ask you to drink to the health and happiness of Mistress Diane Rowland of Notteley and James Hail of Beaufort. And I ask you to look upon them where they stand and praise God that South Carolina has sons and daughters like these two to keep her name clean and bright in the dangerous days to come."

He made with his left hand a graceful gesture toward the opposite end of the room where Hail and Diane Rowland were standing and lowered his uplifted glass to his lips. Amid an excited murmur of voices every one turned to face the couple. A moment of silence followed as the glasses were drained.

Richard Acton stood motionless, his glass still lifted. He held it thus for an instant. Then his hand sank slowly to his side, the liquid in the glass running over and falling, unnoticed by any one, in an amber stream to the floor.

Richard's eyes were fixed upon Diane Rowland's face. He was aware of nothing except her face and there swept over him suddenly, like a wave, a sense of complete fulfilment.

He was conscious of nothing else during that first moment—only this calm sense of fulfilment. It was as definite, as sure, as though it were mathematically demonstrable; something, he knew at once, had happened for which he had been waiting all his life.

Presently he was moving forward with the others about him; Lowndes Fenwick's hand was clasped lightly on his upper arm. It was a slow progress; the crowd around Hail and Diane Rowland was dense. The empty glass dropped from Acton's fingers; in the clatter of excited voices the tinkling crash was all but inaudible.

An absurd thought came to him; the thought, the spectacle, of all these people crowding forward to felicitate Diane Rowland

and James Hail upon their engagement. They believed that Diane Rowland was going to be James Hail's wife. He laughed—so precisely like a man who is a little drunk that Fenwick glanced quickly at him and took a firmer grip on his arm.

"I'm not drunk," he told Fenwick; "I'm insane." Fenwick could not hear him in the babel of talk, but the act of speaking seemed to waken Richard Acton to reality. Suddenly the immensity of what had happened to him crashed into his brain. Strangely, even after the impact of that realization, his thoughts remained for an interval perfectly ordered and cool. Why had this happened now? Why hadn't it happened the first time he saw Diane Rowland, in the barouche in the pine forest? He dropped the question impatiently. Why was a man struck by lightning on Thursday when he hadn't been struck on Wednesday? This was lightning, the lightning of the gods. His eyes, as he moved forward beside Fenwick, had never left her face. Her hair, he realized, was dark and in it she was wearing a white rose.

Suddenly he was standing before her and Lowndes Fenwick was presenting him. He knew only vaguely that Fenwick was speaking. He himself said nothing to her; he bowed and his lips moved inaudibly. He saw in her eyes, as they met his, what seemed to him a light and then a shadow; for a moment she looked at him steadily; he was aware again of a strange intentness in her gaze. She turned quickly away from him to be kissed by Margaret Drayton, and he felt Lowndes Fenwick's hand on his arm and realized dimly that he was being introduced to James Hail. He bowed mechanically in response to Hail's greeting.

Lowndes's firm hand on his elbow guided him skilfully toward one of the French doors opening on the piazza.

"Let's get some air, Richard," Fenwick said. "It's stifling in this room." Then, as they passed outside, he added: "What the devil, man! That baby punch couldn't have sewn you up like this. You must have found that barrel of Madeira we were looking for."

Richard Acton did not answer. Fenwick's grip tightened on his arm. With an enormous effort Richard forced himself to speak.

"Lowndes," he heard himself saying, "I haven't touched a drop. I am very tired. I am going out and rest under the trees."

Chapter VIII

He descended the piazza steps. Before him lay the moon drenched lawn where the red and green Chinese lanterns swung in the faint wind. To the right a syringa hedge extended from the corner of the house to the forest flanking the lawn. He walked slowly in the shadow of this hedge and in a few moments found himself under the trees.

They were magnolias and willow-oaks still holding their leaves. The moonlight, splintered into separate shafts by their boughs, lay upon the ground in pale pools of many shapes. He walked aimlessly amid these pools of delicate light. He walked by touch rather than by sight, seeing nothing of what was around him.

He paced back and forth under the trees at the edge of the lawn, his gaze fixed upon the ground, his hands behind him.

He was completely calm. This was all unreal, he told himself coolly, a kind of mental vertigo, a species of hallucination. There was nothing mystical about the thing that people called love, nothing mystical about its origin, at any rate. It began usually with physical attraction: out of this sometimes something deeper developed. It was a perfectly natural growth, the result of natural process. And this process required time; it needed, too, something to stimulate it—contact, association. Love, full-formed, couldn't be born in an instant out of nothing. Jacqueline had always insisted that it could, that she had loved him completely at first sight, but that was mere fantasy...

He paced back and forth under the trees, sometimes in moonlight, sometimes in shadow. Diane, Diane, Diane—a dozen times he repeated the name. Why was he doing this? What did the name mean to him? Why was he whispering it thus over and over again? It had been something like this years ago when he had imagined himself in love with Eliza Fenwick. But he was a boy then. He wasn't a boy now. He had been through the fires. Life had burnt him; it had left him nothing but a shell. Diane! Diane Rowland! What was there in her face—what incredible magic?

Born out of nothing? Who could be sure of that? Who could say what existed, invisible, intangible; what forces, what realities? Here, for instance, was an extraordinary, an astounding, thing: he felt that he had known Diane Rowland all his life, that all his life he had expected what had now happened. How explain this feeling? It was so strong that for him it was complete conviction. There must be some reason for it, some truth in it. Never having seen her, yet he had known her. That was nonsense, yet it was true.

He walked for nearly an hour, back and forth, back and forth, under the heedless trees. From the house a sound of fiddles floated across the lawn. He realized that the reception was over, the dancing about to begin. He must go back to the house, he said to himself; he couldn't stay out here all night; people would begin to wonder where he was.

Perhaps five minutes after this a twig snapped behind him and he turned. Diane Rowland, a luminous, almost a ghostly figure in her filmy white dress, was standing in one of the pools of moonlight.

He stood motionless, staring, and she came slowly toward him. The white rose in her hair gleamed with a silver radiance; over her bare shoulders she had thrown a silver-fringed shawl. When she was very near he saw that her lips were parted slightly. She stopped in front of him and gazed steadily into his eyes. Her eyes were bright with the same absorbed intentness that he had seen in them twice before. Yet, they were calm; they appeared tranquil, happy, with a serene and indestructible certitude.

He saw this—this certitude of her eyes—and a swift excitement surged in him. She said nothing; she remained motionless, gazing at him. He spoke to her quietly:

"This is serious," he said. "Do you realize how serious it is?"

She nodded. "It is the most serious thing that has ever happened to me." Her tone was as quiet as his. "It is the most terrible thing I have ever done."

"Why have you done it?" His voice trembled.

"Because it was now or never. If I had waited, my courage would have gone."

There was no wind under the trees, yet he had a sense of wind; he was caught up and driven through space, a dust-mote riding a hurricane. She turned her head, looking out across the lawn toward the house.

"We can't stay here," she said. She took his hand in hers guiding him with a gentle assured pressure along a path winding amid the black magnolia trunks.

The moonlight grew dim. They had turned sharply to the right and were walking now along a straight tunnel like way formed by a double row of smaller evergreen trees planted under the magnolias. He remembered the place with an astonishing clearness. This was the Holly Walk. He had strolled there one afternoon with his mother years ago during a visit to Notteley, and at the end of the avenue of hollies they had found a summerhouse where they had rested for a while—a small rustic pavilion at the edge of a shallow pond fringed with purple wampee blooms.

Diane Rowland's hand released itself from his clasp. She took hold of his upper arm with a firm grip. It was almost pitch-black under the hollies, but her steady hand guided him confidently. The darkness about them lightened; they were approaching the end of the Holly Walk; just ahead he saw the summer-house and a glint of moonlit water beyond it.

They mounted the low wooden steps. The interior of the summer-house, roofed over but open at the sides, was bathed in a silvery diffusion of moonlight. There were chairs and couches piled with cushions and in the center a small table with a vase of crimson poinsettia blooms.

She stopped beside one of the couches and removed her hand from his arm. In a thicket near by a mockingbird burst suddenly into song; from the direction of Notteley house floated a musical tinkling of fiddles. She looked at him steadily, smiling a little. She swayed toward him.

An overwhelming emotion engulfed him. He took her into his arms, gently at first, as though fearing that she would vanish at his touch. She lifted her face and he kissed her.

Suddenly she was trembling violently. Her arms enclosed him, pressing him tightly to her. She became limp as though she had fainted, her weight lay heavily against him. Holding her close, he kissed her again and again. There was a moment of utter breathlessness. Then the words came from her in a broken, tumultuous torrent:

"It happened the moment I saw you...on your horse in the pinewood...I fought against it...it was incredible...but to-night..."

Her breath failed her. He opened his lips to speak, but she checked him:

"I want you to understand. I had to do it—this way...before I had time to think. If I had waited, I couldn't...Don't you see it had to be at once or never? I had to give you at once, to-night, so much of me..."

She stopped, breathless. He could not speak. In the thicket the mockingbird was still singing.

"I must go now," she whispered. "I must have time—before anything is done—about James and what I must do now that the world has changed. Please let me go."

He stared down at her. "Good God!" he cried. "I can't... so soon."

She nodded gravely.

"I know," she said gently. "But this is only the beginning."

She waited, passive, unresisting, in his arms. He was aware of an inexpressible dignity in her. He pressed her to him again; then, with a low cry, he released her, turned and stumbled down the steps of the summer-house. He groped blindly through the blackness of the Holly Walk and found himself almost at once under the magnolias flanking the moonlit lawn.

The brightly lighted house, the louder music of the fiddles, brought sudden realization of the practical necessity confronting him. He must face people, must talk naturally, quietly, as though nothing had happened. They were dancing now in the large down-stairs rooms and on the enclosed front piazza. He would have to join the dancers, fulfill his obligations as a guest. He realized that a similar necessity confronted her, Diane. She would certainly return to the house at once, and he would see her there. Probably she would be dancing with James Hail. His lips tightened; he started swiftly across the lawn.

The fiddles were playing Donizetti's *Salut à la France*. The music beat in upon his exaltation and at last penetrated to his consciousness so that he recognized the air. Richard Acton's tight lips relaxed. "Jacqueline used to sing that," he said to himself, "long, long ago."

Chapter IX

The words repeated themselves in his brain. "Long, long ago," he whispered audibly, "and far, far away." He was lost suddenly in amazement and under this a deep calm happiness swelled in him. "Now that the world has changed," Diane had said. It had changed for him also; its darkness had become light. By God, it was incredible! But he knew that it was true.

His thoughts became all at once ordered and clear, as though his brain, superseded until this instant by emotion, had now resumed its function. He walked more slowly, striving consciously to realize, to understand, the tremendous thing that had happened. That, however, was impossible, and at once his excitement, his exaltation returned. He could think only of Diane, Diane in his arms.

Diane! His whole being flew to her, enwrapped her in an ecstasy. He was aware suddenly of a white spot on the lapel of his coat. He plucked it away in his hand and saw that it was a rose petal, a petal of the white rose that she had worn in her hair. It was there, against his breast, that her head had rested. He stood, in a fresh transport of emotion, gazing at the rose petal in his hand; then he placed it carefully in a pocket of his waistcoat and at a swifter pace walked onward.

He was close to the house now; the necessity of calmness, of self-control, forced itself again into his consciousness. The clamor of the fiddles filled his ears. Abruptly they ceased, and in the sudden stillness he heard a mockingbird singing in the woods behind him. The mockingbird of the summer-house! The silver thread of sound snapped, obliterated by a storm of hand-clapping. In a moment the fiddles began again—the *Carnival of Venice*. Richard Acton walked slowly up the broad front steps of Notteley house and at once found himself among the dancers.

He danced first, to her evident pleasure, with Eliza Stoney, and, in answer to her question as to where he had been, informed her that he had been walking under the trees. "You mustn't, Richard," she said. "Every woman here wants to dance with you and that will keep you busy all night. You're not only remarkably handsome but you're a romantic figure with your air of ennui and your experience of European embassies. I want to hear all about Paris when you have time."

He would tell her, he replied, but not quite all. There were aspects of Paris that Carolina wouldn't approve. He was now, in spite of the surging happiness within him, outwardly self-possessed. He talked easily and well, with a gaiety unknown to him in years. A Mrs. de Lansac of Charleston, who, he learned afterward, was a married daughter of Mrs. Rowland, informed him, when he was leaving her, that he was the wittiest man in the room. Harriott Keating was his next partner in a lively schottische, then Mary Ball in a leisurely Boulanger, and then the girl whom he had known in his boyhood as Margaret Porcher but who was now Mrs. Heyward Drayton.

"Where is Diane?" Louis Treves asked Margaret as they passed him: "Isn't she dancing?" Diane had gone to her room for a few minutes, Margaret replied; the excitement of the announcement had been too much for her. But it wasn't serious; she would soon be down.

"This is a bad night for Louis;" Margaret whispered to Richard Acton. "He was really hard hit. And I think Mazÿck Marion—" She stopped abruptly.

"There she is now," she exclaimed a few moments later. "She is pale, but I never saw her look lovelier."

Diane Rowland had come into the ballroom through a doorway opening from a room at the rear. Richard saw her clearly only for an instant. She was white with the delicate whiteness of a white pearl; the color in her cheeks was faint, a barely discernible flush of rose; her hair, brushed smoothly back, was, in the bright light of the chandeliers, a dark and lustrous red-brown. The white flower, he saw, was no longer in her hair; it had been crushed, he realized, against his breast, and he had saved one petal of it, only one. Only one petal! And the rose was crushed, destroyed.

Richard Acton knew that his limbs were quivering. She was the most beautiful woman that he had ever seen, but he did not know how or why. It was, if that were possible, something that transcended beauty, something wholly incomprehensible and inexpressible.

"Yes," he heard himself replying stupidly to Margaret Drayton, "she is very lovely."

He did not see her again immediately; presumably she was dancing in one of the other rooms or on the enclosed piazza and he wondered whether she was purposely keeping out of his sight. He knew that he could not trust himself to dance with her or even to speak to her. He danced a quadrille with Jane Laurens and later he was with various other young women, some of them friends of his boyhood days on the river, others girls from more distant plantations or from Charleston or Beaufort. He bowed before Sally Rowland, conscious again of that elusive quality in her which earlier in the evening had brought Diane to his mind.

"I haven't seen you dancing with Diane," Sally said. "You must, you know. This is *her* evening. But I'm glad you chose me first. You don't realize how excited we all are over you. With your continental manner and your look of secret sorrow, you've fluttered all our hearts." Later she told him that his look of secret sorrow had vanished. There was a light in his eyes, she said. "Either you've had too much wine," she added, "or else you've become terribly interested in some one. I hope I'm the one."

Sitting through the next dance with Elizabeth Acton, he tried deliberately to give an impression of weariness, of polite boredom; he was afraid that she, too, might see what Sally Rowland had seen.

"You're a fraud, Richard," his sister-in-law remarked. "You told me I would find you a burden socially and that you didn't like female society. I was really afraid you might be something of a problem. And, instead, you've been having the time of your life and all the women are raving about you. I heard Louise de Lansac say that you were as charming as James Hail."

The name startled him. It seemed to touch a spring in his mind that released vaguely disturbing thoughts. The fact came to him definitely for the first time that he had injured Hail unforgivably. "That's a real compliment," Elizabeth was saying. "James Hail is one of the most attractive men I've ever known. I don't understand Diane Rowland; it has taken her years to make up her mind to marry him and I don't like these long-drawn-out courtships. I always feel that when the girl yields at last it's due to exhaustion rather than real love. It didn't take me ten minutes to decide about John."

Richard's blood quickened. He had not until this moment thought about anything that had preceded the lightning flash that had changed his life; but now Elizabeth's words flung his mind back to the relation between Diane and Hail, the fact of their engagement. Elizabeth glanced at him curiously.

"You don't seem to find me very interesting, Richard," she said. "You aren't paying the slightest attention to what I'm saying." He woke from his absorption with a start and insisted solemnly that he was hanging on her words, silently assimilating her wisdom. "What do you think of Diane?" she continued. "I haven't seen you dancing with her yet, but at any rate you've seen her. Do you agree with me that she's rather too—"

She was interrupted by the arrival of Louis Treves. "I was asking Richard what he thought of Diane," Elizabeth said mischievously, "but now that you're here, Louis, suppose we had better talk about something else."

Treves wiped away a hypothetical tear.

"My heart's broken," he declared, "but while there's life there's hope. Perhaps James Hail will break his neck or be drowned in the cursed Combahee or something. Come dance with me, cousin, and help me forget my woe."

Richard Acton, left to himself, wandered aimlessly across the room and presently found himself standing beside Sinkler Rowland.

A large, robustly-built man talking volubly to Rowland was introduced by the latter as Gilmore Simms and Acton acknowledged—adequately, he hoped, though his thoughts were elsewhere—his pleasure at meeting a novelist and poet whose fame had spread to Europe. "I read the new edition of *The Partisan* in Paris, Mr. Simms," he said. You are well-known there." That, Simms declared with unaffected delight, was gratifying and surprising. He hadn't supposed the French would be interested in tales of Revolutionary Carolina. He returned quickly, however, to the subject that he had been discussing with Rowland.

"Of course, Sinkler," he asserted, "the Northern States never in any true sense freed their slaves. What they really did was this: having found that negro labor was not profitable in their climate, they adopted systems of gradual emancipation, so called, which gave their slave-owners plenty of time to sell their slaves in the South. Then, after selling their negroes to us and taking our cash for them, they announced grandly that they had ended slavery within their borders. So they had, and they had made money by it."

Sinkler Rowland laughed. "And now," he said, "they don't want us to keep the negroes they sold to us." He caught the sleeve of a younger man who was passing. "Have you met my brother Ash, Mr. Acton?" he asked.

Acton perceived that Ash Rowland was strikingly like Diane; the resemblance was so marked that it startled and momentarily disconcerted him. Sinkler Rowland continued:

"Acton, I want you to meet Wade Hampton, the son of Colonel Hampton of Millwood, who, I suppose, was the greatest planter in the South. I wish you could see Wade ride. He hunted with us today and I never saw such riding."

Hampton, tall and broad-shouldered, with blond beard and fair sun-tanned skin, seemed almost embarrassed by the compliment. "I hear you're fresh from Europe, Mr. Acton," he said quickly. "Perhaps you can tell us how they really feel about us over there. I hope the British statesmen are more liberal than *Punch* and *The Spectator*."

Sinkler Rowland grasped Hampton's arm. "No more politics, Wade," he exclaimed. "You'll start Simms off again. Let's talk about something harmless. The rice crop or deer hunting or literature. Paul Hayne's article in Russell's, or Tennyson's latest. 'Come into the garden, Maud, For the black bat, night, has flown.' What do you think of that metaphor, Simms? By jove, I could listen better if I had a drink."

They moved toward the punch bowl where a number of men were gathered. A general and animated discussion was proceeding. Peter Delamott, his arm on Mazÿck Marion's shoulder, acknowledged the virtue of all conceivable whiskeys, but West Indian Shrub, compounded rum, orange juice and French brandy, was undoubted the Grand Seigneur of drinks. It was, in fact, the *crème de la crème*, the crowning achievement of the Caucasian race. He challenged Marion to deny the assertion, but Marion, standing with an empty glass in his hand, was silent, with a somber face. His expression caught Richard Acton's attention; Margaret Porcher, Acton remembered had started to say something about Mazÿck, something in connection with Diane. Charles Gough's deep, and metallic voice interrupted Delamott.

It was politics again, Richard discovered; Gough was denouncing an abolitionist pamphlet that had recently come to his attention. "The most infernal lies!" he declared. "Those damned fanatics stop at nothing. According to this one, most southern plantations are nothing but vast seraglios where the virtuous and high-minded ladies from Africa are forced to take turns at being their master's concubines. You'd think they were all Lucretias and of course we're all Simon Legrees. We've heard all that before and we can stand it. But that's not the worst. I won't tell you what this scoundrel says about our southern women. How long is the South going to stand these insults, gentlemen?"

"Not much longer, Gough," Mazÿck Marion told him, his dark Huguenot face stern, his black eyes narrowed. Not much longer, by God!" Peter Delamott in a louder tone repeated the phrase: "Not much longer, by the Eternal! When they dare insult our women. The Goddamned lying sons of bitches!" He looked about him in increasing indignation. "Hampton," he exclaimed, "you're against secession. Damned if I see how you can be when the North insults our women."

Wade Hampton replied quietly that the North wasn't insulting southern women. "The abolitionists aren't the North," he said. "They're a crew of irresponsible fanatics. They aren't believed even in Massachusetts nor in Illinois, Lincoln's own state. Garrison and his crowd are so extravagant they are defeating their own aims."

Gilmore Simms turned to Richard Acton.

"How about Europe, Mr. Acton?" he asked. "Are these fantastic tales about us believed over there?"

"Many people believe them," Acton replied. "They are doing the South a certain amount of harm. Especially since Mrs. Stowe's book. And it doesn't help us much to deny details when we can't, of course, deny the fact of slavery. That's our great weakness. It's the thing that's likely to destroy us in the end."

He had spoken without reflection, for he was thinking of Diane, merely putting mechanically into words the opinion that he had long held. It was followed by a complete silence.

Charles Gough was frowning; Peter Delamott, lost in a foggy and incredulous amazement, swore unintelligibly.

Mazÿck Marion took a step forward. "Good God, Richard!" he exclaimed. "Do you mean to say you think we ought to free the negroes?"

After a pause, Richard Acton answered coolly: "Yes—if we could find a way to do it. But, of course, it can't be done now safely either for us or for them. We've got to go on, but if we want to survive, we'd better keep our fire-eaters under control."

Marion, his forehead flushed, started to reply but checked himself and walked away; Sinkler Rowland began quickly to give an account of a new method of constructing field sluice gates with which he was experimenting, Lowndes Fenwick, who had just joined the group, drew Richard a little aside.

"You'll find," he said, "that politics is a hot subject South Carolina, especially among the active States' Rights men. Naturally Mazÿck's on edge tonight; I'll tell you why later. Gough is a close friend of James Hail, and Hail is one of Barnwell Rhett's supporters. I suppose you'd call him a fire-eater, though he isn't."

He smiled and moved away to join a slim girl in pale pink. Acton's eyes followed him. Lowndes was still the Lowndes Fenwick of the old days when they had been inseparable—gay, buoyant, quick-witted. He wasn't however, Lowndes Fenwick of Haddon Hill now, and that was a pity since Haddon Hill was almost opposite Sherborne on the river. He had moved, so Elizabeth had said, to another place, Elm Hill, and he was a lawyer as well as a planter, dividing his time between an office in Charleston and his plantation. Acton's thoughts lingered affectionately on Fenwick, speculatively on Marion. There had always been, he recalled, a smoldering fire in Mazÿck. Evidently it was still there, and he seemed to have grown more grave, more silent. But Lowndes hadn't changed a particle; after twelve years the old comradeship between them had been instantly renewed. What would Lowndes think if he knew about Diane? What would he think if he knew what he, Richard Acton, was doing to James Hail?

This thought, occurring to him abruptly, immediately filled his mind. What ought he to do about Hail? He had as yet hardly seen Hail, had had no speech with him, yet from the first Hail had stirred his imagination powerfully. He hoped that, for this evening at any rate, they would not be thrown together; it wouldn't be easy to look Hail in the eye. Easy! By God, it wouldn't be possible! How could he, even for a day or an hour, deliberately conceal from Hail what he was doing to him behind his back? Yet Diane evidently expected him to be silent. She had said that she wanted time before anything was done.

He was standing at the moment a little apart from the group around the punch bowl. The fiddlers, hidden behind a screen of holly branches in the hall outside the ballroom door, were playing *La Belle Catherine*. Sally Rowland, at the head of the dancers, had called for the figure and the floor was thronged. Suddenly, amid the dancers, Richard saw and James Hall moving directly toward him.

He knew at once that a crisis was at hand. It was evident that Diane was coming to speak to him, that she was bringing Hail with her, that he would have to face them both. He was conscious of a profound shock, a feeling of outrage. How could she do this thing? How could she stand there smiling, calm, lovely as some celestial lily, between Hail and himself? Her eyes, as they met his, were serene; the faint color of her cheeks was still as delicate, as cool, as the pink flush of some pearly seashell; her voice, low and clear, was entirely controlled.

"James insisted on coming to talk to you," she said, "and he wouldn't come without me. I think he wants to smoke a pipe of peace with you about that ridiculous affair in the pine-wood when you first saw each other. I'll leave you to talk about it. I promised this dance to Paul Middleton and he's in the other room."

She moved away with a nod that included them both. James Hail smiled; Richard was immediately conscious of a singularly winning quality in Hail's dark thin face; it, was something quite apart from the rather stern aloofness of his features in repose.

"No," Hail said, "I wouldn't have brought that up, Mr. Acton, if Diane hadn't mentioned it. But, now that she has, let me say I'm sorry I bothered you by putting Charles Gough and Treves on your trail. They brought back such pleasant accounts of you that I've been eager to have the pleasure of knowing you."

He extended his hand. "I hope we'll see a great of deal of each other, Acton," he said, "and some time when you feel inclined, I'd like to ask you some questions about Europe's attitude toward the South's problems."

Richard Acton's throat contracted. Something rose in him and threatened to choke him. James Hail's smile, his eyes, his voice, the whole person and personality of the man, exerted an extraordinary charm. It seemed to Acton that Hail's fineness, his complete integrity, were actually visible upon him; that if he clasped Hail's proffered hand and remained silent about Diane, his own hand would wither, his treachery would burn his soul to black ashes. With a sudden sense of relief, he realized that there was only one thing to do. He grasped Hail's hand.

"I shall be glad to talk with you, sir," he said. "Perhaps we can find a quiet corner of the piazza." He added in a lower tone: "Will you please come with me now? There is a matter of immediate importance."

Outside on the piazza, he wondered whether Diane had seen him the leave room with Hail. James Hail was talking easily as they walked along:

"I ought to tell you, Acton, if you don't know it already, that I'm an out-and-out secessionist. I don't see any hope for South Carolina in the Union and I think we shall have to get out of it, the sooner the better. I don't know what your own views are, but I feel I ought to tell you mine before I begin to pump you about Europe's attitude."

Richard replied absently that he was not in favor of secession. It might become necessary, but it should be a last resort. "Probably," he concluded, "I am what you would call a submissionist. I think we should submit to a great deal rather than secede."

Hail laughed pleasantly. "Sorry," he said, "I had hoped we might think alike. But no matter. I'll hope you'll be converted before long."

A number of men were on the piazza smoking and talking: Mazÿck Marion, Hutson Waight, Alfred Rhett and several others. "Here comes the bridegroom," Waight said, as Hail and Acton moved toward the steps. "Where are you two going?"

"Outside to talk politics," Hail answered with a smile. "I'm going to try to make a good secessionist out of Mr. Acton."

They descended the steps and walked on across the lawn in the moonlight.

"You said there was something immediate?" Hail asked presently.

"Yes," Richard Acton replied.

He stopped. A mockingbird was singing some distance away beyond the tall magnolias flanking the lawn. The bird's voice was a thin, bright, silver thread running through the softened music of the fiddles—a silver thread running undulantly on and on through an obscurity of overarching hollies to a summerhouse bathed in moonlight.

"Yes," Richard repeated. "There is something immediate, James. I'd like to go on calling you that, but I'm not sure you will want me to. I was glad to shake your hand just now, but it's likely you won't want to hands with me again. I am in love with Diane."

At once he realized that he had not said enough. He had no right to speak for Diane—her secret was her own—but his position, above all his purpose, must be made entirely clear, clear beyond the shadow of a doubt.

"I want you to understand, Hail," he added, "that I love Diane and that I am going to take her from you."

Chapter X

There followed a blank interval—a period of silence, of absolute stillness. It lasted so long, Hail's face remained so immobile, so composed, that Acton began to believe that the other had not heard him. Then Hail fell back a step, his face changed; in the bright moonlight Acton could see in Hail's face the onrush of the several emotions that followed one another in swift waves: amazement, bewilderment, anger, changing to bewilderment again. Hail's arms hung rigidly at his sides, his hands opened and closed, his black eyes, intense and penetrating, were incredulous rather than angry. His voice, however, quivered.

"God, Acton!" The words came rapidly in a harsh whisper. "What do you mean? What in hell's the meaning of this?"

Richard Acton considered carefully what he should say. His mind had been full of the necessity, the unescapable duty, of telling Hail what he had now told him; he had not considered the question of what would follow. He realized now that almost anything might follow, and there arose in him suddenly a profound concern for Hail, a fear that Hail might lose his self-control. There remained, however, the necessity for complete clearness. There could be no qualification of what had been said; at any cost, Hail must be made to understand.

"There's nothing to add," Acton answered steadily. "I have discovered to-night that I love Diane. I've told you because it was the only decent thing to do. I couldn't take her from you like a thief."

"Take her from me! Take her from me!" Hail repeated incredulously, his voice rising. "Damn it, man, are you crazy? Or is this some idiotic joke? You don't know Diane. You never spoke to her until to-night."

"Hail," Richard Acton said earnestly, "it struck me like lightning. I wouldn't have believed it could happen. But it did... Hail, you've got to believe me. I love her."

Hail's hand went to his forehead; he pushed his fingers through his thick black hair. He was frowning; his eyes were like black gems, but his face still revealed amazement rather than anger.

"Wait a minute; wait a minute," he said hoarsely. "Let me try to understand this thing. You're sober, aren't you? You know that Diane Rowland is engaged to me? Do you mean to tell me that you are in love with her and that you are going to try to make her love you? Is that what I am to understand?"

"Yes," Acton replied. "That is it. I'm sorry, but it can't be helped."

Hail's hands, held rigidly at his sides, again opened and closed convulsively. Suddenly his eyes were glittering points of black metal in a contorted furious face. He stepped swiftly forward.

"You damned infernal hound! What do you think Diane is? Do you think you can come here and play with her as I suppose you've played with the gutter-women of Paris? Do you think she is like those sluts—one lover to-day, another lover to-morrow? Do you think you can come to me and insult her like this?"

His open right hand jerked back, then whipped forward. It struck Richard's left cheek, pivoting his head around on his shoulders. Acton had been standing with his back toward the house: in the instant following the blow, he saw over his shoulder men running down the piazza steps.

"Why did you have to shout?" he asked Hail hoarsely. "They've heard you. They're coming."

He grew suddenly cold. His cheek was stinging, but he wasn't thinking about the blow. Diane and the "gutter-women" of Paris! That was hard, hideous to listen to, but he couldn't blame Hail; he realized instantly how inevitable it was that Hail should see the thing in that light—as a shocking insult to Diane. It was natural, too, that Hail's temper should blaze, and it took nothing from him, but it was a pity he had shouted.

This was a damnable mess now. The men on the piazza were coming. They couldn't have heard what had been said, but they had heard angry words, had probably seen the blow, for the moonlight was bright. They mustn't that Diane was the cause; his sudden realization of that necessity obliterated every other thought.

"Hail, we must keep Diane..." he began, but the other interrupted him.

"Charles Gough will act for me," Hail said. "He'll see you at once, as soon as I've spoken to him. I struck you, Acton, but I claim the right of challenge—for the filthy you've offered her." Outwardly Hail's anger had passed from him; his voice was low, even, with a chill deadliness; his eyes were fixed on the forms hurrying forward across the moonlit lawn.

"We must keep Diane out of it," he continued rapidly. "They mustn't know..." He paused, his hand tugging at his chin.

The approaching figures were still some yards away. James Hail standing in front of Acton, his hands clenched at his sides, leaned closer to him:

"We quarreled over politics," he whispered. "We came out here to discuss politics, the question of secession. We quarreled over that."

He stepped back and turned to face the others who were now at hand.

There were a half a dozen of them: Alfred Rhett, Mazÿck Marion, Motte Nesbit, Hutson Waight, Stuart Chantilly and another man whom Acton did not know.

"What's this, gentlemen?" Alfred Rhett exclaimed. "We heard loud words, and we saw you strike him, James."

Motte Nesbit said hurriedly: "Nonsense, Alfred. You imagined that. There's no trouble..."

Richard Acton interrupted him. "Mr. Hail and I have been talking politics," he said. "We haven't been able to agree as to the right course for South Carolina. We became quite earnest about it and we shall have to pursue the matter further."

"What the devil do you mean?" Stuart Chantilly broke in.

Mazÿck Marion grasped James Hail's arm. "James," he exclaimed, "we won't have that...to-night of all nights! If you struck him in the heat of anger, you've cooled down now. You'll know what to do."

James Hail shook his head. "No, Mazÿck," he replied "This goes deep. It's deeper than the blow you saw struck. The cartel will come from me."

Motte Nesbit turned furiously on Richard Acton.

"What in hell did you say to him to bring this on?" he cried. "Can't you tell him now that you didn't mean it?"

Acton made no reply. "Nesbit," James Hail said quietly, "Mr. Acton and I are in perfect agreement as to what is necessary and we alone are able to decide that. We'll ask you not to get excited."

"Excited!" Nesbit exclaimed. "If this goes on, you two aren't worth getting excited about. You're a couple of damned fools. You can't discuss a political question without getting into a fight. Go ahead and shoot each other full of holes. What the hell difference will it make to South Carolina or secession or—" His voice trailed off impotently.

"James," Mazÿck Marion said earnestly, "can't you think of Diane? Can't you remember that your engagement to her was announced not an hour ago? Can't you consider what this might do to her?"

There was a pause. James Hail was gazing steadily at Marion. He shook his head.

"Thank you, Mazÿck" he said, "but it's useless." He addressed the group generally: "Hutson, Stuart, Mr. Acton and I consider that all of you are pledged to absolute silence. There's nothing that any of you can do, and any effort to interfere would do great harm. You know me well enough to accept my statement that this must go on; I, personally, will resent any attempt to hinder it. I hope that's understood. I ask you all to go back quietly to the house and I ask you, Alfred, to find Charles Gough and tell him that I want to see him here as soon as possible. Probably one of you can perform a like service for Mr. Acton."

The sound of his name brought Richard Acton back to the present and to the spot where he was standing amid stern unsmiling faces. A mockingbird was singing again in the woods beyond the lawn where the Holly Walk led down to the summerhouse. How long it had been singing he did not know. Suddenly, as the fiddles ceased, he had become aware of the song, and now for some moments he had been listening to it—it was so much more important than what was happening around him. He had never heard anything more beautiful. So long as he lived a mockingbird singing in the night would mean Diane, the loveliness of Diane against his breast.

Hearing his name spoken, he came back, with a sudden quick pain, a swift foreboding, to the ugly present. James Hail repeated his suggestion; Acton glanced quickly from one to another of the men about him. Most of them were, or had been years ago, his friends, but that was a long way back. They were closer now to James Hail than to him. As they stood silently regarding him, he had a sharp momentary consciousness of isolation, loneliness.

"If I can do anything, Richard—" Mazÿck Marion volunteered.

"Thank you, Mazÿck," he replied. "I'll be glad if you'll ask Lowndes Fenwick to come out here for a minute."

Marion and the others walked slowly toward the house, leaving Acton and Hail on the lawn. Hail suggested in a matter-of-fact tone that they had better wait for Gough and Fenwick in the shadow of an oak where they would be less conspicuous, and they walked there side by side but a little apart. Waiting in the shadow, Hail said carefully:

"I think it is understood between us that Miss Rowland isn't to know the cause of this meeting. It will be best if she never knows."

Acton replied immediately, "Yes, that's understood."

Hail turned and moved some distance away, and presently Charles Gough descended the piazza steps and, at Hail's call, joined him in the oak's shadow. Lowndes Fenwick came down the steps a few moments later; Acton called to him and he hurried toward the oak.

"Lowndes," Acton said, when Fenwick had joined him, "this will be a shock to you. James Hail and I have quarreled and I am asking you to act for me."

Diane possessed him, she pervaded his whole being; her eyes as he had seen them in the summer-house were before him as he spoke, and all the while he heard the mockingbird's song. Yet his thoughts were clear and he dealt decisively with the business before him.

"We were discussing secession," he told Fenwick, "and I didn't remember your warning about politics being a dangerous subject in certain quarters. I was rather frank about our fire-eaters, and a blow was struck by Hail. The first offense came from me, and I grant him the right of challenge. No accommodation is possible, and I want you to agree at once to whatever arrangements he proposes."

With an enormous relief Richard Acton returned to the mockingbird's song—to the summer-house—to Diane.

Chapter XI

Lowndes Fenwick's home, Elm Hill, where for the present he was living alone, lay some five miles distant from Notteley. Richard Acton, on a horse borrowed from the Rowlands, rode there with Fenwick between two and three o'clock in the morning; their departure followed a series of consultations between Fenwick and Charles Gough under the Notteley oaks. It was Lowndes Fenwick's idea that Acton might get a little sleep at Elm Hill; although, upon reflection, he was undecided whether Richard had better sleep or not, since the time was so short before the dawn.

They spoke seldom during the ride along the shadowy woodland road. Acton seemed lost in his own thoughts and Fenwick, too, was sunk in a kind of mental numbness the result of his present maddening futility. Remembering Acton's colloquy with Mazÿck Marion, he blamed himself bitterly for not having warned him more urgently against too emphatic an expression of his opinions. It wasn't hard, in view of what Richard had said to Marion, to see how the quarrel with Hail had come about, but the suddenness of the catastrophe had stunned him. What he had been able to do had amounted to exactly nothing. His function and Gough's also had, in fact, been reduced to a mere routine. Richard had insisted that Hail's wishes be met in every particular; and those wishes, presented formally and privately to Fenwick by Charles Gough, had been specific.

There should be, Gough had proposed, no preliminary exchanges looking to an adjustment of the quarrel since an adjustment was admittedly impossible; and the meeting should be held on the coming morning as soon as there was sufficient light. Fenwick had protested vehemently against both these proposals, pointing out that they were unusual and irregular, depriving the seconds of all power to negotiate; and Gough had replied that he was simply and regretfully transmitting his principal's desires. Protesting with equal vehemence to Acton, Fenwick had been met with the calm statement that if he felt unable to act, some other friend would have to be called in; and Lowndes had returned heavily to the spot where Gough waited for him a little apart.

Gough had handed him then a formal challenge addressed to Acton, written in pencil on a scrap of paper torn from a letter and signed by Hail. Acton had written on this same scrap of paper the two words: "I accept," and under this affixed his signature. At Gough's suggestion the time had been fixed definitely for seven o'clock, the place an oak avenue about midway between Notteley and Elm Hill, the conditions those which customarily obtained.

It had been simple and swift; the remaining practical details, too, had been arranged with an appalling ease. These had been managed chiefly by Charles Gough, who, it appeared, had had experience in these matters.

Since neither Hail nor Acton had weapons, it would be necessary, Gough had remarked, to borrow a set. He could do this, he thought, without difficulty and would bring them with him to the ground. The question of surgical attendance need present no obstacle. In strict compliance with the code, each principal should be attended by a surgeon, but it could be agreed, Gough had pointed out, that one surgeon would suffice; and Dr. Christopher Roupell was a guest of the Rowlands and could be called upon to serve. He was the neighborhood physician and a competent man, and, since he lived at Pineland village; only four miles away, his case of instruments could easily be obtained.

These matters disposed of, there had remained only the problem of providing some plausible reason why Richard should not return with John and Elizabeth to Avalon that night; Richard, after a moment's thought, had decided to say nothing to John about the challenge. The conferences with Gough over, Acton and Fenwick had returned to the house where they found John and Elizabeth preparing to leave.

Richard wasn't going with them, Lowndes informed them. He was going instead to Elm Hill for the rest of the night to have a quiet talk about old times.

"I see," Elizabeth had remarked. "A bachelor party after this party. And plenty of the scuppernong wine for which Elm Hill is famous. Well, Lowndes, bring him back to Avalon to-morrow in time for dinner."

They reached Elm Hill about three o'clock, greeted by a tumultuous chorus from Fenwick's hounds as they rode into the dark, oak-shaded yard. A sleepy stable-boy was waiting to take the horses, and Fenwick, calling him back, gave him certain directions before entering the house. In the hall, where one swinging globe-lamp was burning, the question whether Acton should sleep or not became of immediate practical importance.

"We ought to start soon after daylight," Lowndes pointed out. "It's hardly worthwhile undressing, but you could have a nap on the sofa in the library. Do you think that would help you? The fire there is laid and we can have the room warm in a few minutes."

"I'll lie down," Richard told him, "but I'll probably not sleep. There's a great deal to think about and not much time to think about it. It's good of you, Lowndes, to take all this trouble."

Fenwick turned away; I hope I haven't overlooked anything." He couldn't prevent his voice from shaking a little. "If only I had had some experience, but I haven't. I've never acted for any one or had any part in a duel. I wasn't in Charleston at the time or Will Taber would probably have asked me; he was one of my closest friends."

He had no sooner uttered the words than he regretted them. More than once on the ride from Notteley he had thought about Will Taber, and now unguardedly he had spoken the name. "Taber," Richard Acton said absently. "Oh, yes, my brother wrote to me about that and of course I saw the accounts in the newspapers. Magrath killed him at the second fire, didn't he?"

"The third," Fenwick said. "But for God's sake, Richard, don't let's talk about that now."

He walked quickly into the library and Acton heard him strike a match and start the fire there. He went then into a smaller room opening from the hall and returned in a few moments with a pistol in his hands, a heavy weapon of the old flintlock type.

"This isn't the right kind, Richard," he said. "I don't own a dueling set. But it's better than nothing. I don't know why I didn't think of it before, but you'd better spend what little time we've got practicing instead of sleeping. We'll light three or four lanterns in the barn and set up a target there."

Acton shook his head. "I don't need practice, Lowndes," he replied. "I've never fought a duel, but I'm a good pistol shot. It's a hobby of mine. I used to win prizes in the shooting halls in Paris."

Fenwick glanced at him quickly. "Thank God for that!" he exclaimed. "I remember what a crank you used to be about shooting, but that was with shotguns and rifles, sporting weapons. I didn't know you had gone in for pistols." Pistols, Acton explained, were the only firearms he could practice with in Europe, since he had lived there always in cities and had had few opportunities to hunt. Lowndes was silent for a moment.

"I think I ought to tell you," he said gravely, "that James Hail is a good shot, too, and the coolest man I know. He'll be as steady as though he were sitting at dinner. He is in deadly earnest and he is going to kill you if you don't kill him. That seems the devil of a thing to tell you now, but I think you ought to know it."

Acton nodded and Fenwick went on quickly: "I sent, word to Jonas to have the horses at the door at daylight. We'll have coffee and something stronger if you like and a bite to eat. The distance is about three miles and we ought to ride slowly." He hesitated. "If there are any private matters, Richard," he continued, probably now's the time..."

Richard Acton was taking off his coat. "There's nothing, Lowndes," he said. "I haven't much to leave except Sherborne. And my will's made; if anything happens, they'll find it among my things. I think I'll lie down now."

He moved with his coat over his arm toward the door leading to the library.

Chapter XII

Diane! Stretched on the sofa in the stillness and the semidarkness of the library, he returned to her at once. Going back to her thus, he was for a time profoundly content; and, wrapped in a vague happiness, as of a dream in which Diane was not so much a definite being as a pervading presence, he fell asleep. Sleeping, he was dimly aware that a word, a name, was tapping, tapping for admittance; it was tapping at his brain as a woodpecker taps at a tree. The tapping became louder, and suddenly he woke. He remembered the name at once. It was Taber.

He was fully awake in a moment—he had slept no more than a few minutes—but now he could not go back wholly to Diane; or, rather, he could not now forget all else in his consciousness of her. Taber! The details came back to him with complete clearness; the affair had taken place two years before and the newspapers, which usually passed over such encounters in silence or with the briefest possible mention, had discussed it at great length. Will Taber had been one of the editors of the *Charleston*

Mercury, a brilliant and popular young man. He had been challenged because of certain articles by a contributor and he had accepted the responsibility and the challenge. At the second fire—no, Lowndes had said it was the third—Taber had fallen. He had been buried, Acton recalled, in St. Philip's churchyard in Charleston. John Acton, who knew Taber well, had described the funeral with much feeling in one of his letters.

Well, that had been the end of Will Taber, a brave man and a gentleman. Richard Acton wondered, with an odd leisureliness, whether anything had been settled, anything accomplished by his death. A certain tradition had been maintained; an obligation of honor had been met. The code, it was argued, saved more lives than it sacrificed, since it prevented unregulated encounters and, as a rule, provided time and opportunity for the peaceful settlement of differences. That was largely true; and while, dueling might be in practice an evil, the traditions of conduct that led up to it were sound. It was a gentleman's device, in the old, perhaps the proper, meaning of a gentleman. Nevertheless, the duel, like slavery, was another thing the South would have to get rid of. Even in Carolina opposition to it was growing. It was, like the South itself, a survival from a simpler, more rigorous age; it didn't suit the new times.

Yet, Acton reflected, there was something to be said in its favor beyond the more obvious arguments of its champions. There were obligations that could be discharged in no other way; his present obligation was conspicuously one of these. He was going to take Diane Rowland from James Hail. That was, he told himself, an act which called for the fullest recognition of the responsibility which it involved. He had known instantly that he would have to accept Hail's challenge. Later, riding with Lowndes from Notteley to Elm Hill, he had seen vaguely the inadequacy of this—perceived, without fully realizing the implications of the fact, that a sterner necessity confronted him.

He couldn't, however, think of that now, couldn't dwell upon what it might mean. He could think only of Diane. His mind went back to those first moments of realization when, having escaped from the ballroom, he had paced back and forth under the magnolias whispering her name. He hadn't known then that what had happened to him with such astounding swiftness and completeness had happened to her also. That was the miracle. But it didn't now seem miraculous; rather, it was wholly natural, familiar...an event long-awaited, pre-ordained.

What would he have done, he wondered, if she had not come to him? Would he have been able to strangle his love for her because she was promised to another man? But she had come, and suddenly he knew that she loved him, and that amazing fact hadn't amazed him; he seemed really to have known it all along. She had come; and from that moment the obligation of honor which forbade him to take her from Hail had been superseded by a stronger obligation, one that transcended everything else.

He was perfectly clear as to that: what she had done bound him to her forever. This light that had burst upon them both had come almost too late. But for her courage, it would have been too late. She, acting instantly, had saved them. If she had not come to him at once, their lives would never have been joined. She couldn't, if she had hesitated, have done what she had done to James Hail, have faced deliberately all that must follow. She herself had realized this; it had to be at once or never, she had said, and, knowing this, she had come to him.

How had she found him, he wondered, when she came to him under the magnolias? She had pretended—he remembered Margaret Drayton's remark—that she was going to her room to rest. Instead, she had come, by some circuitous way, to the spot where he was pacing back and forth under the trees. Had she seen him from the piazza? Or had she known mysteriously that he was there, drunk with the magic of her, whispering her name? Some day he would ask her about this, he said to himself, some day when they were together.

They would have long days together—long perfect days at Sherborne when he had established himself there. Suddenly, as he lay with closed eyes, her beauty blazed before him, quickening his breath.

He lay, completely, rapturously happy, seeing her plainly, rejoicing in her. He had known many beautiful women—in Paris, in Russia, in Vienna, in Spain, in London Diane's beauty was totally unlike anything that he had ever known. There was something in Diane's beauty that he couldn't account for as he could account for the beauty of other lovely women. He was filled with wonder that neither John nor Elizabeth, in speaking of Diane, had mentioned this—this magic of hers. Was it possible that they weren't aware of the magic of her, that they didn't feel it as he did?

Well, for him it was everything; it was the justification of the universe. And he had never suspected its existence! He had never before encountered beauty informed with, this transcendent, this inexplicable, power. Of course, Jacqueline had been beautiful and he had loved her—he sat up suddenly on the sofa, his hands clenched at his sides.

Jacqueline! Jacqueline Fleur! Good God! Good God! Jacqueline had gone from him! He realized this, knew it, instantly, completely. Jacqueline, Jacqueline Fleur, the woman he had loved, the woman whose memory had dwelt with him, whose image he had cherished! In a blinding flash the truth came to him. Diane Rowland had annihilated the past; in an instant she had obliterated everything that had preceded her; she had annihilated Jacqueline!

That fact—it smote him like a physical blow—left him shaken, bewildered, his thoughts a whirling chaos. In the midst of it, though, he still saw Diane, saw her smiling up at him in the summer-house. Slowly his mind grew calmer; he was able presently to consider with comparative steadiness the revelation that had burst upon him. His thoughts shaped themselves slowly, inexorably. Jacqueline Fleur and the Richard Acton who had loved her had become parts of another existence. They were ghosts of a time irrevocably and happily dead.

This shocked him even as the thought took form. Happily dead? Good God, could he say that? Could he say that about Jacqueline? Yes, happily dead. Slowly, with dry lips, he whispered the words. She had gone from him, and it was well that she had gone. If this was treason to Jacqueline, he could not help it; he was in the grip of a thing mightier than his will. He realized now that she had not gone from him suddenly; she had been fading, receding, slowly, gradually, ever since his return to Carolina. That was why she had seemed less real to him, why her image had grown dim. Even then she was slipping away. There was something in the land, perhaps, something in Carolina, that had been fatal to her.

And now she had gone. She would be henceforth not a vital presence but only a ghost. She would no longer rule his life. Her hold upon him had been destroyed. Diane had destroyed it, dealt it the final blow. Yet he had loved her so much that when she had died he would not let her die, keeping her alive in his heart. He had lived thus with the dead and his own spirit had died. And then Diane! The miracle of his love for Diane, Diane's love for him. Rebirth. The rebirth of his dead soul.

It was nothing less than that. He had been dead and now he was reborn. Diane had done it, done it in an instant. She had quickened him, after a period of death, into a new life. Lying again relaxed, his eyes closed, he gave himself wholly to her. He was filled with an aching longing to hold her again in his arms as he had held her in the summer-house. He couldn't believe now that he had held her thus; it was wholly impossible. He had hoped for one last glimpse of her before leaving Notteley to ride to Elm Hill with Fenwick, but this had been denied him. He had looked for her vainly in the ballroom after bidding the other Rowlands goodbye, and then Lowndes Fenwick had hurried him away.

A sudden anger swelled in him. James Hail! Hail stood between Diane and himself. If he had been drowsy, he was now completely alert again. That swift surge of anger, it seemed, had roused him like a dash of cold water in the face. For the first time he saw clearly, nakedly, the alternatives that he faced. Riding with Lowndes from Notteley to Elm Hill, he had decided simply to receive Hail's fire. There had seemed to be nothing else to do; he had felt—he hadn't even questioned his instinct—that to kill Hail would be fatal. He couldn't in that way win Diane, for he would win her only to lose her. It had been clear to him then, clear as day, that if he added murder to the deeper injury already done the man, he couldn't go on living with himself.

But he hadn't realized then what would follow if he didn't kill Hail; drugged by his dreams of Diane, his mind hadn't dealt with facts. They rose before him now, merciless, unescapable. Lying rigid upon the sofa, his forehead wet with sweat, he stared at the ceiling with unseeing eyes.

James Hail was a good shot, Lowndes had told him. Well, there wasn't one chance in a hundred that Hail's skill equaled his own. He was better even with pistols than he had been with sporting weapons; in the Tir au Pistolet in Paris he had had no superior. He could kill James Hail at the first fire, could shoot him anywhere he chose, in the heart, in the lung, in the brain. Then he would have Diane. He would have her forever and completely. She would be his wife. There would be those days at Sherborne that he had dreamed of.

Yes, the heart or lung would be best; to aim at the brain might involve some possibility of failure. It would be, after all, very simple. Every one would believe, of course, that the quarrel had grown out of a difference about politics. It was fortunate, he reflected, that he had had his colloquy over slavery with Mazÿck Marion; a dozen men had witnessed that and it had happened just before the quarrel with Hail. The thought occurred to him that he would be doing service to South Carolina in killing James Hail because Hail and the other secessionists were leading the South to disaster.

He lay for a long while thinking of Diane. They were together at Sherborne; he realized without surprise that the days he had dreamed of had begun. There was a lilac haze over the rice-fields and the river was burnished silver. He was sitting with Diane on the piazza; he was riding with her through the pine-woods looking for deer; they were in a punt on Sherborne backwater moving slowly amid yellow lotus blooms and under moss-draped cypress boughs. The punt began to rock violently; he became gradually aware that someone was shaking him. He opened his eyes and saw Lowndes Fenwick standing beside the sofa.

"It's daylight, Richard," Fenwick said, and Jonas is ready with the horses. We'll have something to eat and then we'd better start."

Chapter XIII

COFFEE AWAITED THEM IN THE dining-room, and, as they sat down, a colored girl appeared from the pantry with a dish of cold sliced duck. Lowndes proposed brandy, but, after a moment's thought, Richard Acton declined; they might take a little with them, he suggested, and Fenwick filled a flask. Outside, where Jonas waited with the horses, the great oaks and sycamores in the plantation yard were barely visible in the beginning light. The air was still and cold; the horses, a gray and a roan, fidgeted and Jonas admonished them soothingly. Acton didn't recognize the man; if he had been a Fenwick stable-boy in the old days at Haddon Hill, his features had faded from memory. The negro's face was solemn, his eyes unnaturally wide. "For God's sake Cap'n," he whispered, as Acton mounted the gray, "don't let nobody hurt Mr. Lowndes."

"It isn't Mr. Lowndes, Jonas," Acton replied; "I'm the victim." He smiled grimly at the immediate relief in the negro's face. They rode, Fenwick in the lead, through the yard under the moss-bannered oaks toward the back gate. Lowndes opened it and it swung shut behind them. To the right, just off the road, stretched a long, double row of cabins, the Quarters. The smoke from the chimneys mingled with the morning mists and here and there in the "street" between the rows of little houses dim figures moved. Suddenly from one of the nearer cabins a wailing voice was lifted:

> *"Eb'rybody who is libin' got to die,*
> *Eb'rybody who is libin' got to die,*
> *De rich en de po', de great en de small,*
> *All got to meet at Jedgement hall,*
> *Eb'rybody who is libin' got to die."*

Lowndes Fenwick swore under his breath. "Good God!" he muttered. "Think of singing at this time of the morning." His voice was harsh, unnatural. He turned to Richard with a forced laugh. "And such a damned cheerful song," he continued. "I could choke that black wench." There was an odd contraction of Richard Acton's throat which, for a moment, prevented him from replying. In a dozen years he had not heard that song or any other like it; it was a plantation spiritual, probably unknown outside of Carolina. "Lowndes," he said presently, that was perfect. If you'd been away from home as long as I have..."

He did not finish the sentence and Fenwick offered no comment. They rode on in silence—a long straight reach across open fields lying vast and empty under the lifting mists. Thence they passed into tall pine-woods, fragrant and full of a low continuous music, where partridges ran through the brown fern and big gray fox squirrels bounded out of their path. "A good place for deer," Lowndes remarked. "I killed a fine buck just over yonder three or four days ago with Mazÿck, and last week I saw twenty turkeys feeding along the edge of that little slash. We'll have some great hunts, Richard…"

He stopped abruptly. The light was growing stronger, but the air was, if anything, colder in the pine-wood, and Fenwick was busy for a moment buttoning his coat close around his throat. "Damn it, Richard!" he exclaimed, his voice husky, "I can't go on talking about deer and turkeys. I've got to tell you again what I told you last night: Hail's going to kill you unless you kill him. That's the only thing you and I can afford to think of now."

Acton nodded slowly and Fenwick, in a more controlled voice, continued:

"God knows I'm sorry, but I'm responsible for you, Richard, and if you spare Hail, it will probably cost you your life. I won't mention that again, but don't let anything make you forget it. There are one or two details I want to consult you about. I think the shortest distance allowed by the code is ten paces and Hail will probably prefer that. If you are good at a longer range, say fifteen, there's no reason why we shouldn't…"

Acton interrupted him. "No, Lowndes," he said, "I'd rather let Hail fix the distance."

Fenwick glanced at him quickly. "By jove," he exclaimed, "you're cool. Well, thank heaven for that…And a good shot…It will probably be ten paces then. My God, I wish it were a thousand. And Hail will insist on a second fire if necessary; Gough told me he had never seen him so intense about anything."

He leaned over in his saddle and placed his hand on Acton's shoulder.

"Richard, he said, "I can't realize this thing, this thing we're riding into. A quarrel over the secession question—good lord, man, it's not worth it. You and James Hail—" He broke off. "Richard," he continued, "you haven't even let me try to arrange this matter. You've tied my hands so far. Won't you let me make an effort before it's too late?"

Acton shook his head gravely. "It's a peculiar case, Lowndes," he answered. "It's been good of you to act for me, with your hands tied. You'd have been justified in refusing. But it can't be helped. A suggestion could come only from them. And it won't come."

Lowndes looked at him steadily, but made no reply. They rode for some moments in silence. Fenwick's shoulders straightened suddenly. "We can't afford to be late," he said hoarsely. "We'd better make these nags travel a little faster."

Richard Acton perceived that the increasing light was filling the forest with color. He had never fully realized before how much color there was in a pine-wood. The straight trunks, soaring sixty feet without a branch, were rich with orange-tawny, purple and lavender. Above, the high roof of the forest was a dark lustrous green washed here and there with gold, the Spanish moss, trailing from branches and wreathing the upper parts of the pine trunks, was often a clear, delicate silver-gray tinted with lilac. He never grew weary of the moss; it was why, he thought, these Carolina woods were more beautiful to him than any others he had ever seen. And yet there was some thing tragic and fateful in the moss, in its effect upon the mind. It was somehow like that song, the spiritual the negro woman had been singing.

The comparison struck him as fantastic, yet it was true. And Carolina itself was like that, all this plantation country. It was lovely beyond all imagining, but it wasn't a pastoral loveliness; it didn't suggest shepherds or the notes of Pan's pipes. It, too, was tragic, tragic in the Greek sense, fateful; over it all an ancient spirit, a brooding mystery, hung. Lowndes Fenwick, riding in the lead, kept his eyes upon the ground ahead of him, but Acton's eyes roamed ceaselessly. Fifty yards in front of Fenwick three deer crossed the road, bounding high, their white flags flying. Lowndes, his chin sunk upon his chest, did not see them, but Richard saw all three vividly in the moment while they were visible—three shapes of misty sunlight, slim, swift, graceful as birds.

He was filled with an overwhelming realization of beauty all around him, beauty which had never been so clearly visible to him before. Mixed with this sense of newly discovered beauty was a vague feeling that time was escaping from him, but this did not sensibly annoy him; it was inevitable, he had accepted it. The road dipped into a hollow dark with magnolia and bay; to the left, under magnolia boughs, he saw the shimmer of water and, as the horses clattered past, a snow-white heron rose from the pool and, lifting into the brighter sunlight, sailed slowly away.

Beyond the low ground the way led through open forest; oaks and hickories festooned with moss and interspersed with thickets of myrtle and holly and tangles of jessamine and Cherokee rose. Here the trees and thickets were alive with birds; two Carolina wrens were singing, answering each other; all about sounded the mellow calls of swamp robins; blood-red against the dark-green foliage of a holly bush, a splendid male cardinal fronted the morning sun.

Lowndes Fenwick checked the roan's stride, so that Acton came abreast of him. "We have half an hour," Fenwick said. "That will just about put us there in time." Some part of Acton's mind that had been asleep woke suddenly. "Half an hour, half an hour;" the words were reiterated in his brain. That was all that was left, then—all that was left of his new life, his life with Diane.

He hadn't, in a sense, thought definitely of Diane since leaving Elm Hill, but all the while she had been with him; there had not been a moment when he was not conscious of her. She underlay everything, was fused with everything; all his thoughts, it seemed, had their springs in her. She was a part, the essential element, of all this beauty around him of which he was so poignantly aware. Without her, without the consciousness of her, he could not love it as he now loved it, for without her it would all be meaningless, blank—lacking a soul.

A flash of comprehension came to him. That was the secret; that was why all this around him had taken on a new and more vital loveliness. She had become for him the life, the soul, of this country that he had always loved, this Carolina that had never ceased calling to him even when his world had been the world of the Boulevard Saint-Michel and Jacqueline. He had always been in reality a stranger there. Jacqueline had held him for a time; she had made him a part of that world; she had held him until death had taken her and she had clung to him even after that. But he saw clearly now that she must have gone from him in the even if Diane had not come, that sooner or later her empire over him must have ended. The land had him; it had claimed him again—this land, this life, these people; and Jacqueline of Paris, of the Rue Percival and the Chausée d'Antin, could not have become for him, as Diane had become, the soul, the very spirit of this land.

God, how he loved it, how he loved her—Diane, who was the soul of it! "Half an hour, half an hour!" The horses' hoofs beat a grim tattoo on the hard sand of the road. Half an hour, half an hour: less than that now, much less. In less than half an hour he would reach the spot where James Hail would be waiting.

James Hail and the pistols. Lying on the sofa at Elm Hill, he had made up his mind to kill Hail. Why, then, did he have the feeling that only a little time was left to him? After he had killed Hail there would be plenty of time. It was a pity he had to kill Hail. Hail believed that he was avenging an insult to Diane, defending her honor. He, Acton, also would be there because of honor—because honor required him to meet Hail; and that, in turn, was necessary because an obligation of honor bound him to Diane. Honor: a difficult, a perplexing word. What about honor here—now?

His thoughts were hurrying desperately, keeping pace with the horses' hoofs. Honor! A damned, cruel, merciless, fatal word. Suddenly he hated it. But a handsome, word...handsome... handsome. It was one reason why he loved Carolina. Honor was esteemed there; men were careful, particular, about it, precise in their conceptions of it. Especially in all that concerned their women. Well, what was his conception of it? He had, although Hail didn't know it, already robbed him of Diane. What did honor require of him now?

He had to answer that quickly; there couldn't be more than a few minutes left before they would reach the place. He had intended—it had seemed both an obligation and a necessity—to receive Hail's fire and, on his part, to fire wide. Then, later, realizing that Hail would probably kill him, he had abandoned that plan, had decided instead to shoot Hail through the heart. Why had he decided to kill Hail? If he killed James Hail, he would have Diane. But would he have her? Wouldn't the bullet that killed James Hail send him, Richard Acton, stripped of honor, to hell? Wouldn't it—

His racing thoughts stopped suddenly, cut short by Lowndes Fenwick's voice.

"There's the place, Richard," he heard Fenwick say, "and they're waiting for us."

Chapter XIV

THE ROAD, NOW NO MORE than a faint track, had emerged from the woods. To the right, in the middle of an abandoned field deep in broom-grass, Richard Acton saw a grove of live-oaks surrounding the ruined walls and tall brick chimneys of what had once been a large house. The scene was vaguely familiar to him, but he couldn't place it exactly. The morning light had a mellow glow like that of evening; the rounded, dome-like oaks rising out of the expanse of golden grass were themselves tinged with gold.

At the edge of the grove, two saddled horses were tethered; near them, in charge of a negro slouched in the driver's seat, a carriage waited. No other human figures were visible. Lowndes Fenwick turned to the right out of the road and Acton followed, the horses moving at a walk through the breast-high broom.

The negro saluted them as they halted near the carriage, staring at them with scared, yellow-white eyes. They dismounted, fastened the horses to a low oak limb, and walked on under the trees toward the ruined house.

"You remember this, don't you?" Lowndes said. "It's the old Gillon place; the house burned about a dozen years ago." Without waiting for an answer, he continued: "This was the yard. The avenue's on the other side. We'll probably find them there. That was Doctor Roupell's carriage."

He stopped and, half-turning, placed his hand on Acton's shoulder. "Richard," he began, his face white, haggard, "I'd give all I have..."

He turned away, and Acton said in a low steady tone, "Thank you, old fellow, for what you've done." They walked on around the wrecked house and saw, at the entrance of the avenue beyond, James Hail with his back toward them and, a little beyond Hail, Charles Gough and two other men whom Acton did not know.

Charles Gough moved toward them at once. Passing Hail, Gough spoke a brief word to him, and Hail turned glanced quickly at them, then looked away. He was bareheaded, in a close-fitting, dark blue riding suit; he held an unlighted cigar in his fingers.

"Good morning, gentlemen," Gough said briskly. "You're prompt; we haven't been here ten minutes. We were looking over the ground..."

The two other men had come forward and one of them, elderly and rather stout, shook hands with Fenwick.

"Lowndes," he said, "I hate this. Wouldn't be here if I could have helped it, but felt it my duty—possibly can be of service—hope not, though—hope there'll be no need."

He turned abruptly to Acton and bowed. "Saw you at Notteley," he said, "but didn't meet you, sir. I'm Roupell, Doctor Roupell. And this is Skene of Charleston. You're lucky in having him; he's the best in the state."

Acton bowed silently. Charles Gough addressed Fenwick. "Mr. Fenwick,"—his manner was formal,—"Doctor Skene is here at my request. We agreed last night that one surgeon would suffice, but the code prefers that each principal be attended by a surgeon. When Doctor Roupell told me that Doctor Skene was visiting him in Pineland, I took the liberty of asking him to serve. I hope you approve."

"Entirely," Lowndes Fenwick replied. "I am grateful Doctor Skene."

Skene, slight and dark, with black mustache and alert dark eyes, inclined his head. Doctor Roupell walked to where James Hail was standing and Fenwick drew Gough aside. "For God's sake, Gough," Acton heard him say; the rest was lost. Gough shook his head and spread his hands helplessly; Acton caught the word "useless."

Fenwick and Gough walked together to the foot of an oak where two small black satchels—the surgeons' instrument bags—and a rectangular mahogany box had been placed upon the ground. Gough stooped, opened the box and took from it first one pistol and then another. Richard Acton saw that they were handsome silver-mounted weapons of the approved percussion type, the weight and size to which he was accustomed. Gough conferred briefly with Fenwick; then, holding a pistol in each hand, he turned to face the others.

"Gentlemen," he said, "we are indebted to Mr. Peter Delamott for the use of these pistols. It was necessary to borrow a set and Mr. Delamott was able, regretfully, to provide these. They are by Happoldt of Charleston and, therefore, the best, and they are identical; Mr. Delamott has assured me that there is no choice between them. Mr. Fenwick has asked me to load them both, and I am about to do so in his presence."

He was busy for some moments with this task. Richard Acton heard a hawk screaming in the distance above a confused clamor of crows. Doctor Skene, standing a little to his right, was kicking at a tuft of weed. James Hail was talking with Doctor Roupell; he was smiling; Richard Acton was conscious again of Hail's extraordinary charm. Beyond Hail and Roupell the long vista of the avenue, under the trailing banners of the moss, was suffused with a faint golden haze. It was as fine, he thought, as the avenue at Avalon, the oaks nearly or quite as large. They couldn't have chosen a lovelier spot, he reflected calmly, for what was coming. He heard Charles Gough's voice.

"Mr. Fenwick and I have tossed a coin," Gough announced, "and Mr. Fenwick has won the toss. This entitles him either to select the position or to give the word. He has chosen to select the position, and he will post his man in a moment. The distance of ten paces has been agreed upon. The principals are to face each other. If the first fire is ineffective, the challenger has the right to demand another fire and so on until one or the other principal has been hit."

He turned to Fenwick, spoke to him in a low tone, and Fenwick selected one of the pistols. Together they walked to a point midway between the first two oaks of the avenue. Fenwick halted there and Gough stepped ten paces, each step covering about three feet. He stooped and pushed into the soft ground a small wooden peg which he had been carrying in his left hand.

"The principals will please take their positions," he said, "Mr. Fenwick has chosen to place his principal on the spot where he is standing—facing down the avenue."

Richard Acton walked to where Lowndes had driven a similar peg; simultaneously James Hail took his place at Gough's side. Skene and Roupell moved quickly toward the oak where their instrument bags were lying. Gough nodded to Fenwick and Lowndes cocked the pistol that he was holding and sprung the hair-trigger. He handed the weapon to Acton and stood looking at him for a moment, his lips quivering slightly. Then, without a word, he moved away.

Charles Gough handed Hail his pistol, spoke to him briefly, then walked quickly to a spot midway between Hail and Acton and a little to the side.

"Gentlemen," he addressed them both, "I beg your careful attention. It has fallen to me to give the word. I shall ask whether you are ready. Then I shall pronounce the words 'Fire, one, two, three, stop.' Until the word 'Fire'—this is important, gentlemen,—your pistols must be held with the muzzles pointing straight downward. They may then be raised and discharged, but you must not fire after the word 'stop.' Mr. Fenwick, is this clear to you and to your principal?"

Acton inclined his head slightly and Fenwick nodded. Gough stepped farther back. Richard Acton, his lowered pistol grasped in his right hand, looked at James Hail. Hail stood facing him, his weapon similarly pointing downward. In his left hand he still held his unlighted cigar. His tall straight form was sharply outlined against the golden haze filling the vista of the avenue behind him.

Richard scarcely saw Hail. He was thinking about something else—a white rose-petal in a pocket of his vest. In the swift onrush of events he had forgotten that it was there, but now, strangely, he remembered it. One petal! He had saved it, but the rose was crushed, destroyed. One petal, one moment in a summer-house, then—nothing. He heard a mockingbird faintly, far off; he wasn't sure whether or not the sound was real. Charles Gough's voice, vibrant, deliberate, ended it:

"Gentlemen, are you ready?"

Hail replied in a loud clear tone, "Yes," and Acton answered "Ready."

Again he heard Gough:

"Fire—one—"

Richard raised his arm slowly, giving Hail plenty of time.

"Two!"

Twelve inches from Hail's foot there was a small tussock of grass, a spot of bright green against the dead leaves covering the ground. Aiming at this spot, Acton pressed the trigger; he saw the dirt fly precisely where he had aimed. He heard a sharp report, felt a crashing blow, a stab of pain in his right side. He staggered backward, sinking into darkness, blackness.

Chapter XV

This passed, however, almost at once; for a moment he believed that he had not, after all, been badly hit. He was on the ground and Skene was bending over him, unbuttoning his vest. Roupell was standing behind Skene, looking down: if they spoke, their words were lost in a rushing sound that filled Richard's ears. This became quickly a tremendous roar like that of a train of cars. A curtain of blackness fell, and at once—he was aware of no lapse of time—he was in his bed at Avalon.

He recognized his room immediately. They had got him home, then; he realized that he must have been a long while unconscious. There was a pulsing pain in his chest, a worse pain in his head, he breathed rapidly and with difficulty. Doctor Skene and Elizabeth Acton were standing near the door; some one else was with them; he saw presently that it was Lowndes Fenwick. Skene and Fenwick disappeared and Elizabeth returned toward the bed. Coming toward him, she grew suddenly dim, fading into a deepening darkness.

When, much later, he awoke, a woman was standing in the doorway. Her face was pale, troubled, with only a tinge of color in the cheeks; her lips were parted slightly. She was wearing—he remembered vaguely that he had seen her like this before—a small felt hat with a white cock's feather. His mind groped vainly for a moment and then he knew that she was Diane.

Diane had come to him! A hammer was pounding in his head, the pain there was intolerable, each blow of the hammer a new torture. Yet his brain was clear, his senses little blurred. He saw Diane come into the room; Elizabeth was talking with her at the foot of the bed. He heard, quite distinctly, Elizabeth say: "He's been sleeping for hours, but his fever is still high. Stay with him while I run to the pantry..." He could not hear the rest of what she said. Elizabeth left the room and Diane moved swiftly to the side of the bed. She took his hand in hers, bent over him and kissed his lips.

There were streaks of fire before his eyes, the hammer strokes in his head were redoubled, a black curtain shut her from him, then lifted. She was still bending over him, but now the mounting fever possessed his brain; he did not know her. In a flash it came to him. He had been ill once for a long while in Paris and Jacqueline had nursed him. A hundred times she had bent over his bed and kissed him. Yes, this was Jacqueline. She had been away it seemed, but she had come back. Suddenly, in a clearly audible whisper, he spoke her name:

"Jacqueline!"

Diane Rowland walked slowly down the stairs. She had left the room as soon as Elizabeth had returned. She could not in any case have remained there; it was doubly impossible now. She wanted to be, as quickly as possible, back at Notteley, in her room, alone.

In the hall below she saw, with a numb surprise, Mazÿck Marion. He was standing, in riding clothes, at the foot of the stairs, looking up at her as she descended. She knew without glancing at it how his face looked; she had seen it like that so often. At the bottom stair he took her hands in his. His voice was low, hurried:

"I rode over with Motte Nesbit to see if I could help John. He told me you were here."

He raised her hands to his lips, held them there a long moment. She drew away, without haste, and, passing him silently, walked slowly toward the door leading to the east piazza. He followed her.

"You aren't angry, Diane?" he asked miserably. "That was my farewell...The first time and the last."

"It's all right, Mazÿck," she answered listlessly. "But don't come with me now."

John Acton and Motte Nesbit were on the east piazza. At the foot of the steps the chaise in which Diane had driven over from Notteley was waiting, the negro driver in his place. John Acton helped her into the chaise. "It was good of you to come so quickly," he said. "But you mustn't feel badly, Diane, because James Hail did it; you aren't married to him yet. Thank heaven,

Skene's here. But I'm afraid Richard hasn't a chance."

She nodded, picking up her shawl from the seat. "I've told Elizabeth to send for me if she needs help," she replied in a low tone. "Good-by."

As the chaise swung around the circle and headed toward the avenue, she looked up at the windows of the room in which Richard Acton was lying. It was unlikely, she realized dully, that she would see him again alive. He might live for some days, Doctor Skene had said, but there wasn't much doubt about the end. The November air was cold; she shivered and drew the shawl around her shoulders. Richard Acton, she told herself over and over again, was dying in that room thinking about a woman named Jacqueline.

Part Two: Notteley

> I say that, in a country like this, in which land is so abundant as to render the evils of a general monopoly impossible, a landed gentry is precisely what is most needed for the higher order of civilization, including manners, tastes, and the minor principles, and is the very class which, if reasonably maintained and properly regarded, would do the most good at the least risk of any social caste known.
>
> —*James Fenimore Cooper.*

Chapter I

ON A SUNDAY MORNING NEAR the middle of April, when wild wistaria was still blooming and buds were swelling on the tall magnolias around Notteley house, a sanguillah singing in a wild-orange tree close to her window woke Diane Rowland from a sound sleep. She lay with closed eyes for some minutes thinking only of the sanguillah; it was beautiful name for a graceful and melodious bird, and she it all the more because it was in a sense her own.

No one else, so far as she knew, called those slim black and russet troubadours sanguillahs; generally they were known as orchard orioles. Sanguillah was an antique name for them, long ago forgotten; she had come across it in an old book on Carolina and, attracted at once by its beauty, she had decided that thenceforward orchard orioles would be sanguillahs to her.

It was amazing, she thought sleepily, the volume of sound pouring from that small throat. The first sanguillahs that arrived in spring always sang with a rapture that few other birds could rival; they were the happiest of all birds except the Carolina wrens, yet no poet had ever celebrated their great joy. This seemed to her now a lamentable omission; to repair it, she stole a stanza from Michael Bruce addressed to the cuckoo and, her eyes still closed, bestowed upon the singer in the wild-orange tree:

> *"Sweet bird! thy bow'r is ever green,*
> *Thy sky is ever clear;*
> *Thou hast no sorrow in thy song,*
> *No winter in thy year."*

That was quite perfect, she said to herself, and it suited the sanguillah perfectly. The Scotch boy's poem, though little known, had long been a favorite of hers; she preferred it, she decided drowsily, to Mr. Wordsworth's more recent and more celebrated ode. The sanguillah had moved to a twig nearer the window; she could hear, faintly, another bird answering it from the distant woods. It was much pleasanter, her thoughts wandered on, to be waked by sanguillahs pouring forth their April ecstasies than Zedekiah. Then she began to wonder why Zedekiah hadn't waked her this morning, as he nearly always did, and this question produced at once an acute anxiety as to the cause of Zedekiah's unwonted quietude.

It would be terrible, she reflected, still with closed eyes, if Sinkler had done what he had threatened. Satira would probably have hysterics. Her fondness for pets had long been something of a problem, and Zedekiah was the most exasperating pet of all. Only two days before Diane had overheard her brother talking to the cook.

"Look here, Satira," Sinkler Rowland had informed her, "I've put up with most of your nuisances; the coon you had last winter and that fawn that used to walk into the dining room and upset everything. But this damned goose yours is too much. The next time it wakes me at crack of dawn on a Sunday morning, I'm going to wring its neck."

Satira hadn't been impressed. As the autocrat of the Notteley kitchen, she was perfectly aware of her power. "Mas' Sinkler," she had informed him with an imperial dignity, "you ain't got no call to come cussin' 'roun' here in *my* kitchen. An' ef you tech a fedder ob dat goose Zedekiah what I raise from a little baby here in *dis* bosom, dey ain't gwine to be no mo' ob dat speshull spoonbread you crave so."

That, Diane reassured herself, had probably been decisive. Satira, a Rowland negro for fifty years, knew all the weaknesses of all the Rowlands; it was likely that Zedekiah, thanks to Sinkler's weakness for special spoonbread, still lived. This probability became at once a certainty: suddenly Zedekiah's clamant voice was heard, obliterating the liquid notes of the sanguillah, making the morning hideous. The sound began just under Sinkler's window; it was there, under the side-steps, that Zedekiah always slept. Diane heard muffled noises in her brother's room next to hers; she got out of bed and ran to the window.

Sinkler Rowland, a fair-haired, solidly built man of thirty-five was visible in his nightshirt at the window of his room. Below in the yard Satira was walking toward the house, her arms extended, and Zedekiah, his wings half-spread and his long neck outstretched, was rushing to meet Satira, screaming his morning welcome at the top of his lungs. He did not throw himself into his mistress's arms but ran round and round her, vociferating his delight, while she walked slowly on toward the kitchen door apparently oblivious of Sinkler Rowland leaning from his window.

Sinkler's face was red, but he controlled his rage. His voice trembled, yet his tone was courteous, almost courtly. "Satira," he said, "won't you as a special favor to me take that infernal goose home with you to-night and make him sleep under your house instead of mine?"

Satira looked up at him, an expression of deep gloom on her round black face. "Mas Sinkler," she replied, "I ain't got no time for talk 'bout dat now—not ef you 'speck me to mek dat spoonbread for yo' brekfuss." She swept majestically on, Zedekiah, marching behind her, around the corner of the house toward the kitchen.

Life, fortunately, had a good many things like that in it, Diane reflected; things like Satira and Zedekiah and Sinkler's spoonbread; small, more or less humorous things that forced themselves upon one's attention. She remained for some minutes at the window looking out. It occurred to her that this would be a good time to write to James—James Hail. He was in Alabama with Charles Gough at Barnwell Rhett's suggestion conferring with Senator Jefferson Davis, Robert Toombs of Georgia, W.L. Yancey and other political leaders; she hadn't answered his last letter and she mustn't wait another day. The view from the window however, still engaged her, and the letter faded from her mind.

It had rained during the night, but the day would be beautiful, April at its best. The sun had just risen. The willow-oaks beyond the plantation yard were vivid green with fresh young leaves and above them the tops of the taller pines were gilded by the slanting rays. She was just in time, she said to herself, to see the changing play of color in the tops of the pines as they gave themselves like brides to the morning light. She watched this with an intense, sensuous pleasure; until the gold was gone from the pines her attention was completely absorbed.

Now that Zedekiah's voice was stilled, bird-songs in, a various and increasing chorus filled the air, and, mingled with these, she heard the querulous conversation of gallinules and coots in the lush wampee beds fringing the river. She could not see the river from her window nor the sweep of the bordering rice-fields, but she did not always regret this; the voices coming from that invisible region were perhaps the more fascinating on that account. Sometimes at dawn she heard far off the tremulous love-bellowings of great bull-alligators haunting the lower river and its adjacent swamps; sometimes she heard the shrill screams of mating eagles and the deep croaks of giant herons, and often these wild voices meant more to her than the singing of the smaller birds in the trees of the plantation yard.

Her room, at the back of the house, overlooked the yard and, to the right, a corner of the garden, bright with star-hyacinth, larkspur and mignonette. Beyond the yard the first cabins of the negro Quarters were visible; as she stood at her window, she saw smoke curling from the chimneys of the cabins, but from the nearest of them, she noticed, no smoke arose.

That was the house of Sheba, Diane's maid, and she said to herself that Sheba was evidently sleeping late this morning: on Sundays there was an almost complete suspension of the plantation routine, and the house servants, except Satira the cook, were allowed to come in almost when they pleased. Sheba, moreover, was still an object of special sympathy because her husband had died only a week ago.

Diane wondered how long Sheba would do without a husband; she was young and comely, though very black, and there would be no lack of suitors. Sheba's celibacy, Diane decided, would probably last about a month. The thought was still in her mind when a figure emerged from the back door of Sheba's cabin, a negro man. He stood there for a moment, glancing quickly to right and left, then disappeared behind a clump of mulberry saplings. He did not reappear, and Diane knew that, keeping in the cover of the saplings, he had probably reached the woods unseen from any of the other cabins in the Quarters.

Sheba's celibacy, it was apparent, had not endured a week. In the thin morning light Diane had not certainly recognized the man, but he had been tall and a little stoop-shouldered like Sharpio, one of old Stepney's sons. Diane wondered, rather vaguely, what she ought to do. If Sheba was accused, she would have a good story ready: Sharpio had come to bring her something; he hadn't been in her house two minutes.

Diane frowned, confronted again by a familiar problem. Her mother expected to be informed whenever anything of this kind came to light: Belflowers, the overseer, had strict orders to report all instances that he discovered. Sinkler Rowland managed the plantation, but Mrs. Rowland was the moral guardian of the black hundreds whose bodies she owned. The task was discouraging, but she was seldom discouraged, and her discipline in serious cases was, stern. Sheba would be banished from the house, sent to work in the fields.

That, perhaps, Diane supposed, might be good for Sheba's soul, but it wouldn't change her. She wouldn't change they never did, until they "got religion," and she wasn't the kind to get religion while she was still young and handsome and attractive to the men. That could happen later when she was much older; religion would then become emotion stronger than any other, and then, as the old women expressed it, she would "put away sin." Meanwhile the only visible result of Sheba's banishment from the house to the fields would be the spoiling of her as a maid.

She was a good maid and Diane was fond of her. Field work would be hard on her; she had been a house-servant since she was a little girl. Besides, it was April, spring. Sheba, deprived by death, would find loneliness doubly hard in spring; and Sheba in Sharpio's arms last night had been no more conscious of evil than the sanguillah singing in the wild-orange. The same thing that made the sanguillah sing had made her let Sharpio in when he knocked on her door. It seemed to Diane a little unfair to praise the sanguillah and punish Sheba; what she was going to do about it she didn't know.

Below the window the plantation yard was still empty except for a hound or two and half a dozen game hens convoyed, with frequent interludes of gallantry, by a tall and arrogant red cock. The cock was Agamemnon, the pride of Ash Rowland's heart; there wasn't a bird in the parish that could beat him, Ash had boasted, and so far the boast had been sustained. Agamemnon—

the fact somehow seemed a further palliation of Sheba—was extremely attentive to the slim brown hens.

Three small black children came out of the cabin opposite Sheba's and began playing in the dirt, but no one else was yet visible, though Diane could hear Satira talking to Zedekiah in the kitchen. Breakfast was always a belated meal on Sunday. She could sleep an hour longer if she wanted to, or write her letter to James Hail; but, instead, she decided to dress, have a look at Roman's injured leg, and then pick some roses for the breakfast table.

Roman, she thought, as she slipped into her clothes, must have had a better night; he had been placed in a kennel in the yard away from the other dogs and she hadn't heard him whimpering. It would be pleasant in the garden—provided she didn't find Mr. Hemmerton there; sometimes he sat in the garden in the early mornings. It was going to be awkward about Mr. Hemmerton. Calvin Hemmerton, A.B., as he signed (defying the local preference for the nom de plume) the scientific articles that he occasionally wrote for the *Mercury* and the *Charleston Courier*. If she didn't encounter him in the garden, she would certainly see him at breakfast and his suffering was sure to be painful.

He had, she said to herself, an extraordinary capacity, a genius, for suffering visibly; an earnest and unbelievably literal young man from the Mount Zion School at Winnsborough, at present devoting his undeniable talents to the task of tutoring Mason, the oldest of Louise's three children. Louise Rowland—she was Mrs. Thomas de Lansac of Charleston, Diane's older sister—sending the children up from the city to spend March and April on the plantation, had naturally sent the tutor with them so that Mason's studies would not be interrupted. Mr. Hemmerton, however, had suffered a disastrous interruption at the hands of Sally Rowland, and as a climax Diane had found him Sally's feet in the gun-room the previous evening.

He had got up from his knees and fled from the room and Diane hadn't seen him since. She met him now, however in the lower hall, his hat on, his butterfly net—he had a marvelous collection of butterflies—in his hand. It was plain that he had slept little if at all, but she was totally unprepared for what he immediately told her without even the preliminary formality of a "Good morning."

"You thought I would mind," he said ferociously, "your seeing me there at her feet. You thought I would ashamed. Why, you—you don't know anything; you can't even guess how a man—you're as ignorant as—as hell! I'd like the whole world to see me kneeling to her. I want to be under her feet forever."

That left her speechless. He was out of the front door and down the steps before Diane had recovered. "Hell" on Mr. Hemmerton's lips, and to a lady! But even this wasn't as astonishing as the revelation of the state of Mr. Hemmerton's heart. Observing from day to day the progressive enslavement of the tutor, she had never suspected that it would have unusual results. But Sally must have discovered long ago that Hemmerton was inflammable material and she oughtn't to have gone on with it. Diane heard a slight noise behind her, and, turning, saw Sally standing on the stairs, a graceful, yellow-haired figure in a blue morning dress.

"That wretched Zedekiah woke me," Sally Rowland said, "and I couldn't go back to sleep. I heard what Calvin said. Did you ever hear such an incredible idiot?"

Diane informed her sister that she ought to be ashamed of herself, but Sally replied that she wasn't; she couldn't be, she added sweetly, seeing that she was Dee's sister and had observed her career for years. "Now, Sally," Diane began, but Sally was following her own thoughts.

The Hemmerton affair, she declared, had helped her to get through a very dull April during which she hadn't had a glimpse of Charles Gough. I don't like playing second fiddle to politics," she continued. "Charles and James Hail have been in Alabama for weeks now and you don't seem to mind. But I do. Charles has got to be more interested in me than in Barnwell Rhett's secession schemes. He's got to be just as mad about me as Calvin is."

Calvin, Diane remarked, appeared to be in the last stages, and Sally nodded.

"I've never had a man so absolutely helpless before," she said. "It's given me a delightful sensation of power. I envy you more than ever, Dee. And I'm beginning to think I'm getting more dangerous; though, of course, I'll never be completely fatal like you."

At any rate, Diane said, with a bluntness which she instantly regretted, there wasn't much glory in being fatal to Calvin Hemmerton; he was small game and Sally ought to have seen that he was the kind that could be badly hurt.

"Diane," Sally replied immediately, "if you insist on scolding me about Calvin, I'm going to have a lot to say about glass houses. You know, my darling, you can't afford to throw stones. I saw Mazÿck Marion in Pineland yesterday and of course he asked after you."

She yawned. "I had no business getting up so early," she added. "I suppose it will be hours before breakfast. I'm going to raid the pantry. Be a good girl, Dee, and forgive the dig about Mazÿck."

As a matter of fact, Diane said to herself, there wasn't anything to forgive Sally. It would be better, perhaps, if she didn't know about Mazÿck Marion, but she did know and apparently she understood. Diane went out on the piazza, stood there a moment looking over the river, then descended the steps. Walking across the yard toward Roman's kennel, she saw Belflowers, the overseer, ride through the gate. He turned, came toward her and lifted his hat.

"Miss Diane," he said, "Roan Mary's all right again. I looked her over carefully yestiddy an' I think you can ride her this mornin'. But I s'pose you'll be drivin' to church with your mother an' Miss Sally."

She nodded. "But I'll want a horse this afternoon. I'll look at Roan Mary after breakfast. I think a little exercise might help her, but I could use Santee instead."

Belflowers smiled: "You can handle him an' they ain't many ladies who could. But, if you take the Pineland road, mind that little slash at the foot of Hick'ry Hill. Santee always gits skittish just this side of it. There's sump'n there he don't like."

Probably, Diane told him, Santee saw a ghost. "Marion's men had a fight with the British there, you know. One of my Chantilly ancestors was killed, just at the foot of the hill."

She walked on, and Belflowers returned toward the gate. Diane could hear Roman's tail thumping the floor of his kennel as she drew near. She called and the big hound—he was an unusually large Redbone—came out on three legs. He had torn the bandage, of course, from the foot that the mule had mashed, but Diane, bending over him, saw that the foot was better. She touched the swollen paw with her finger, and Roman instantly howled as though he were being murdered.

"You bes' watch out, Miss Dee," Stepney, the yard man, came hurrying toward her, "dat houn' might bite you ef you squeeze he foot."

"Not Roman," Diane told him. "He loves me too much."

Stepney was frankly skeptical about that. A hound, he informed her, didn't know how to love. They weren't like bird-dogs or pet dogs or Newfoundlands; they had the debbil in them. "More-in-ober, Miss Dee," he went on, his tongue loosened for one of the philosophical discourses in which he delighted, "dis life so tricky you can't tell who lub you and who don't. De werry one what say he lub you is de one to stab you in de back."

She turned away abruptly and walked, without another word to Stepney, toward the garden gate.

Chapter II

Later (she had passed unheeding under the arbor with its tiny pink and white multiflora roses, delicate as Dresden china, and along the broad walk between the pomegranates and the Persian lilacs) she sat down wearily on a bench in a sun-splashed corner where flame-colored azaleas still blazed against the dark-green background of a wild-orange hedge. This, she said to herself, was the acme of grotesqueness. The wave—she always thought of it as a wave—had come again. The grotesque part was that Stepney had caused it: it had come this time because of what Stepney had said. Stepney, a black Gullah negro slave, even uglier than most; a pious old hypocrite who had children, and was still having them though he couldn't be less than sixty, in twenty cabins on the plantation. How could anything that Stepney said be of the slightest importance?

This passed through her mind in a flash; it was immediately submerged again in the emotion that possessed her. This was the way the thing generally happened, this wave—there was no other word for it—which from time to time engulfed her. It would come out of nothing or out of some utterly incongruous and unrelated circumstance: suddenly, sudden as light, the intoxication of that incredible night would return and a tide of longing would sweep over her—a blind, desperate longing for Richard Acton, followed by an overwhelming despair.

It had her now. It had come upon her as she stooped before Roman holding his paw and while Stepney was speaking. For one blinding instant she was in the summer-house in Richard Acton's arms; her heart, beating wildly, seemed to stop beating; then a sense of utter frustration, of profound self-pity, blackened the universe like a black cloud.

She had it under control almost at once: seated on the bench in the stillness and the fragrance of the garden, she drove it from her like some ugly and contaminating thing. She was able to do this now; the months that had elapsed since her pride was consumed to ashes had seen it rise from those ashes, renewed and pitilessly strong. Yet now, as always when the strange sudden wave of longing had swept her, its swift recession left her thoughts still entangled with the past. It clung to her, she sometimes felt, almost beseechingly—that bright illusion which had been so swiftly shattered—begging her to turn back and take it to her heart again.

Her thoughts returned now to the moment when it had died. It had not perished, she reflected, when, pressing her lips to his in an anguish of passion, she heard him whisper the name Jacqueline. For the moment she had been stunned. She had driven back to Notteley dazed, sunk in a despair worse even than the despair that clutched her when she had been told that he had been shot, probably mortally, in a duel with James Hail. But presently this had diminished, almost disappeared.

There might be, she had told herself desperately, a dozen explanations of the name that his fevered lips had uttered. "Jacqueline" might have been any one of a dozen associations whirled to the surface amid the shifting phantasmagoria of his delirium. She would have returned to him then if that had been possible, given herself to him again. But she could not see him; besides Doctor Skene, only Elizabeth and John Acton were permitted in his room. Later he had been removed to Charleston as the only hope of saving his life; and the day after that Sabina Slade had arrived.

Sabina—she had been Sabina Woodward of Beaufort, and Diane's most intimate friend—came to Notteley in early December, to spend a week that she had long ago promised. Her husband, Bowles Slade of Richmond, had been Secretary of Legation in Paris, and she had known Richard Acton there.

"It will be rather a pity if he dies," Sabina Slade had summed up her account of Richard Acton in Paris. "Something of a black sheep, as I've told you, but with a great deal of charm. And I couldn't blame him about the woman. When I met her, Dee, I really understood all about Thais and Ninon de L'Enclos and all the other disgraceful and delectable ladies. She was the most magnificent creature I have ever imagined. Probably she discarded him in the end and I suppose that's why he came home. I remember now her name was Jacqueline."

It was this that had ended it. Diane, listening to Sabina Slade, had known at once that it was ended. Sabina's words, she had recognized, were as final as a death-sentence. It hadn't mattered, of course, what Jacqueline was or what had become of her. She, not Diane, was in his heart: the perfection—and nothing short of that was tolerable—of the dream, was a lie. She had offered herself and naturally he had taken her—for the pleasure of a moment: the Carolinian women, he had probably said to himself, were surprisingly easy game…

That was nearly five months ago—early December. In January, because she knew that she must get away, she had gone to New Orleans to visit first the Beauregards and then the Delacourts, whom she had met two years before at the White Sulphur Springs. New Orleans was the gayest, the most foreign city in America; she was with Linda Delacourt at many brilliant parties; the young men of New Orleans, exquisite in speech and manner, were instantly at her disposal. They were connoisseurs of charm—none better; they couldn't see her heart. She had returned to Notteley in mid-March. Undoubtedly the homage of New Orleans had helped her. She was able now, she had told herself, to analyze her folly critically, to study it with an almost impersonal curiosity, as a physician studied a disease.

She had found the key to it in herself. Considering the familiar phenomena of her own experience, she understood with what seemed a sufficient clearness the nature of what had happened to her, what Richard Acton had done to her.

It was simple enough, she had concluded; there were no subtleties, no complexities. She had been able to make men forget everything else in a swift and unconditional surrender to some mysterious quality that she possessed, a charm that created in them an overpowering illusion of delight. There had been many such men: Adolphe LeClerc and Etienne Ramon of New Orleans, for recent examples, and, nearer home, Louis Treves and Mazÿck Marion. Mazÿck had been in love with her years ago when she had lived in Beaufort district; he had met her at a ball in Beaufort and had visited her at the Rowland plantation on the Combahee. Later, he had married and had become a planter at the Marion place, Deer Hall, near Charleston. Still later, when the Rowlands had removed from Beaufort, Diane had become his neighbor at Notteley; and suddenly, one moonlit evening here in the garden, she knew that Mazÿck was in the hollow of her hand.

What had happened to her at Richard Acton's hands was no more complex than—it was, she told herself, no different from—what she had done to Mazÿck Marion. There was something in Richard Acton that she could not at the time resist, and suddenly, completely, she had gone down before it. It was a madness, an illusion, just as the delight that men saw in her was an illusion. And its effect had been equally fatal. In the spell of an incredible infatuation, she had imagined a surrender as ecstatic and as complete in his heart. And all the while another woman was there, the woman whose name had come to his lips, whom his tortured soul had desired, when the fever of his wound had torn away his mask.

In the conclusions that she drew from all this, the ends to which her searchings led her, she was entirely ruthless with herself. She allowed no excuses for the disaster she had suffered. It was the kind of thing, she told herself, that happened to chambermaids, to negro wenches in the Quarters: her emotions had been entrapped in a net as common as that which customarily entangled theirs. The strange fact was that, seeing it all so clearly, she was still subject to such reactions as that which had just now assailed her as she listened to Stepney's talk; moments when the radiant mirage of that fantastic night returned and the longing for Richard Acton swept her like a wave.

Well, she concluded, she would probably never be able to prevent that altogether. And it wasn't, now, a thing to be afraid of or to worry about. She could control it if she couldn't prevent it, and no man or woman could entire elude the past. She had said to herself a while ago that Calvin Hemmerton, the victim of a ridiculous flirtation would never forget Sally; and she wasn't essentially different from Calvin Hemmerton. She, Diane Rowland, the victim of a stupid and common infatuation, could not easily forget the man who had made a fool of her for a night. He would return in memory from time to time to plague her, and perhaps there would always be a certain glamour about him, a glamour none the less actual because she knew that it was false.

But that, after all, didn't matter; Richard Acton could not harm her now; she had fought her battle and won. She had won it so completely that she had been able to burn, unopened, a letter that he had written her from Charleston just before her departure for New Orleans. She had done that impulsively, in a moment of extreme abasement, when her mind had been full of the wrong she had done James Hail. The next instant she had regretted it. Nevertheless, she saw clearly now that it had been the only thing to do. And it had been effective; he hadn't written again.

Soon or late, she knew, she would see him. His wound and the illness that had followed it had kept him in Charleston more than four months, but he might now at any time return to Avalon or to Sherborne, his own plantation, where, it was understood he intended to live. A meeting then would be inevitable, but she no longer feared it. It seemed to her that what she planned to do would wash a stain from her, cleanse her for the man whom she was to marry.

The man whom she was to marry. James Hail, of course, would never know what had happened in the summer-house. She reminded herself that she must write to James to-day; she had left his last letter too long unanswered.

James's letters from Montgomery had been hopeful; the signs were, he had written her, that if South Carolina seceded, Alabama and Mississippi would follow quickly, and that would mean the birth of a great Confederacy of the South, a new nation of glorious destiny. The presidential election next year, he believed with Barnwell Rhett, would bring the crisis: if a Black Republican was elected, the South must secede immediately or remain forever chained to the North's chariot-wheel.

Sometimes she almost felt that James loved South Carolina more than he loved her. That, she told herself for the hundredth time, was ridiculous. James had been in love with her almost as long as she could remember. She had told him that she would marry him in June.

Chapter III

THE CURRENT OF LIFE AT Notteley flowed steadily, strongly, smoothly. Sinkler Rowland contributed much to its steadiness and smoothness; Diane contributed something not briefly to be defined; Sally gave something to it, and it owed something of sparkle and grace to Ash. But that which above all else gave it impetus and direction was a small and delicate old lady of French Huguenot blood, Adèle Chantilly Rowland, the mother of these four.

They, with Louise, Sinkler's twin, who had married Thomas de Lansac of Charleston, were the survivors of ten children. After Louise's and Sinkler's birth, three brothers and two sisters had died in infancy, before Diane, the next child, was born. That fact, no less than the influence of the strong man she had married, had made Adèle Chantilly Rowland what she was.

There had been, deeply as she had loved him, a long conflict of wills between Robert Rowland and herself. Of an usual and seductive beauty, rich in her own right, a favorite of Charleston society despite, or perhaps because of, the daring originality of her moods, she would have preferred to make of Robert Rowland a mere dilettante planter, leaving the management of his lands to overseers and giving most of his time to entertaining in Charleston, enjoying the great northern resorts, or traveling in Europe. It was not only his quiet strength that had defeated her and changed her; it was the coming and the loss of child after child.

She had been bent, but not broken: bent to his way of life, his complete and contented acceptance of the career to which he had been born and which he would not have exchanged for any other. In the comparative isolation of the Rowland plantation on Combahee River, she had been for thirty years the teacher and the angel of a hundred, then two hundred, then four hundred slaves. But she was still Adéle Chantilly. Long before yellow fever, in one of its devastating descents upon the Carolina coast, struck Robert Rowland down at the beginning of his old age, he had been changed by her more than she had been changed by him. Her victory had been complete when he had consented to leave—though he still held and planted them—the fertile but lonely rice-lands on the Combahee, where he had made his fortune, and remove to Notteley, which, from the earliest days of Carolina, had been a Chantilly estate. He had been living there two years when he died.

The stamp of the Chantillys was upon Notteley. Their furniture filled its rooms; their portraits by Theus, Sully, Copley, Stuart and Güet of Paris, adorned its walls; the house-servants saw Chantilly ghosts on its mahogany stairs- at night. The name had come to Carolina with that René Chantilly, gentleman of Bretagne, who had arrived with the first Huguenots fleeing from the wrath of the Most Christian King and who, not forgetting that he was a gentleman, had labored with his hands until he had made with them the beginnings of a new fortune in the New World wilderness. He settled first, with most of the other French, in French Santee: but he built, before his marriage to Susanne Vervant, the first house at Notteley and gave it, because he liked the sound, its Cherokee Indian name. That first house still stood in the plantation yard, a cabin of rough-hewn timbers used now as a smoke-house, and legend said that the hatchet marks in its door had been made by the tomahawks of red men in the almost fatal war of 1715.

René Chantilly lay now in the plantation graveyard with Susanne Vervant and four of their seven sons and two of their three daughters; and, besides these, their virtues duly recorded upon stones increasing in size and dignity as the years increased, many others of the Chantilly name rested there, some of them men famous in Carolina history, together with other men of other Carolinian names that Chantilly women had married.

There had been, it seemed, a power in the Chantilly women; they were likely at the last to bring their husbands to Chantilly graveyards, at Notteley or Montauban or some other Chantilly plantation, to lie there through eternity. Thus it was not strange that Robert Rowland of the Beaufort Rowlands, themselves no mean clan, now lay in Notteley graveyard. It was his wish to lie there, but he wished it because Adéle Chantilly wished it. He had mastered her, with the help of the sorrows she had borne, and had made her over into the woman he wished her to be. But he would have gone to hell for her; and she made him a Chantilly in the end.

There had been, before her day, other Chantilly women for whom men would have gone to hell; some, perhaps, had sent men there; a few—one of these had become a countess in Rome—had possibly gone there themselves. The Chantillys had been a positive race; their men had been men, their women had been women. But in general their men had also been gentlemen, and their women, with all the dangerous potency of charm which many of them possessed, had been secure in that armor of chastity which Carolinian women of their class wore with so fine a grace that they became an American tradition.

The Chantilly men played their part in South Carolina. They mingled their blood early with the Carolinian English and with Scotch blood and Irish blood; there were dark-haired Chantillys with large Huguenot noses and fair-haired Chantillys whose eyes were blue or gray instead of black or brown. Some were obscure, some distinguished; some were worthless, others were steady, solid men. Generally they supported, often with notable devotion, the Anglican Church into which most of the Carolinian French Huguenots had been absorbed. Three out of every four Chantillys were planters, but some were soldiers, lawyers, politicians, merchants and physicians, and one of them was called a statesman. Some were poor, many were well to do; one of them owned two thousand slaves, thirteen plantations, and four town residences. They were individualists; they managed their own affairs; they upheld with fervor South Carolina's right to manage hers. With one exception, they fought against the British in the War for Independence, some with Marion the Swamp Fox, some with Sumter the Gamecock and some in the Continental line; and when, a half-century later, her right to nullify an obnoxious Federal rule was questioned, they were ready to fight for South Carolina again.

The Chantilly men were careful men; careful, that is, of certain things: the rights that made them men, the obligations that made them gentlemen. They were careful of their women; their women they regarded as the equals of any on earth. But the Susanne Chantilly who became a countess in Rome triumphed over even the Chantilly carefulness. It was the Chantilly law that women were either good or bad, and for the latter there was only oblivion. The Countess Susanne—and this was well known—had been no subscriber to that law, but she left behind her a legend of so transcendent a charm that oblivion could not engulf her and her name was still mentioned in Chantilly drawing-rooms, discreetly, yet with a certain homage. It was perhaps the same logic that enabled chaste Carolinian ladies to adore the fair Cyprians of Charles the Second's Court and abhor the coarse Roundheads.

There was no portrait of the Countess Susanne Falatresi among the pictures at Notteley or in any other Chantilly house; of what in reality her charm had consisted no one knew. One day in Rome—it happened to be her fifty-eighth birthday and she had been a widow two years—Adéle Chantilly Rowland, wandering alone through a small picture gallery there, came to a sudden stand before a stained and battered portrait of a young and lovely woman richly dressed. It bore no name, but for her no name was necessary. She stood for a long while gazing intently at the portrait, studying its every feature. She left it, however, before Diane, who had been dining with some friends, rejoined her; and she told Diane that there was nothing of interest in the gallery and that she had better not waste her time going through it.

Chapter IV

Diane came home one afternoon from a ride which had taken her to a cypress backwater about two miles from Notteley house. She went at once to her room. What she had seen possessed her; she could think of nothing else. Tethering Roan Mary at the edge of the backwater, she had paddled in a small flat-bottomed punt a quarter of a mile along a narrow water-lane winding among the tall moss-bannered cypresses; and coming presently to a small opening in the flooded forest, she had looked up and had seen perhaps a hundred white ibises circling above her. At first they had been far up under the blue sky, but gradually they had swung lower, descending in interweaving circles until they were no higher than the tops of the trees.

Now, in her room, her mind was still full of the wonder of that sight—those great, shining white birds with black-tipped wings and long curved orange-red bills wheeling and sailing above her in that wild solitary place; and now for the first time in months she was conscious of an imperious desire to put into words the beauty that she had seen. This was a feeling with which she had long been familiar; ever since childhood she had been subject to it; she could describe it to herself only as a need to praise beauty.

She was almost frightened by it sometimes, by the intensity of her feeling. It was pretty thoroughly pagan; it couldn't be fitted in at all with the Reverend Mr. Pallaye's quite liberally orthodox sermons at the parish church of St. Luke's, Berkeley, where every Sunday the wisdom, youth and beauty of all the parish plantations assembled in search of spiritual comfort in the little straight-backed pews and of social converse under the oaks outside. Sometimes her feeling came to this: that beauty alone mattered; it was beyond good and evil; there couldn't be evil where beauty was.

She smiled at the naïveté of that. A very convenient doctrine for all lovely ladies, Ash had remarked, studying her thoughtfully, when one day she had propounded it to him: a complete vindication of DuBarry, the Pompadour and the Countess Susanne. He seemed much interested in the latter speculation. "I wonder," he had suggested, "whether that doesn't explain our sprightly Falatresi relative. I've always thought there must have been some excuse for her... You'd better look out, Dee, old girl." She could generally make Ash understand things—he was closer to her than either Sinkler or Sally—but he hadn't understood her in this; obeying a subtle and defensive instinct, she never talked about it again. She kept secret, too—for this was a part of the other—the results of her longing to praise beauty; results which took the form of scribbled sheets of paper carefully locked away in a drawer of her desk.

She unlocked the drawer now, took out a pencil and tablet of paper, and began to write.

> *"We do not know [she wrote] what beauty is nor what it means nor why men seek it everywhere up and down the world from the tops of the highest mountains to the farthest islands of the sea and in poems and books and in shining stones dug from the earth and in the shapes and the colors of clouds. Today I saw white ibises soaring against the blue sky..."*

Thus far her pencil had moved rapidly. Now she paused, sat for some moments frowning, then with quick strokes of her pencil scratched out what she had written. She leaned back in her chair, her hands clasped behind her head. Abruptly what she had been doing had become useless, childish, a kind of mockery.

Something had happened in her, something of which she had been dimly aware for a long time, for months. Her thoughts went back to a day last spring on Edisto Island near Charleston. She was visiting Mary Gordon at Windy Hill Plantation on Edisto. Mary had been a classmate of hers at Madame Togno's French school in the city, and the Windy Hill visit was pleasant. There were no men; only the wide marshes of Edisto, the blue sea beyond the lonely yellow beaches, the wide blue sky of the sea-islands. It had been a delight to wander along the edges of the marshes then, where the winding creeks were abrim with the high spring tides, and watch the play of the afternoon sunlight on the plumage of the curlew flocks feeding or standing at gaze in the short grass of the lonely, seaside meadows within sight and sound of the surf.

Due perhaps to some effect of the slanting sun-rays, the birds appeared very large, much larger than they really were; and their long necks and legs, and long curved bills, as they stood motionless and erect, perhaps fifty or a hundred of them together, lent a fantastic touch to the picture which enhanced its wild beauty. But it was an even keener delight to watch them as they took wing and rose from the marsh in wide-spread ranks sweeping low above the tips of the marsh-grass. When the flock was in motion, the magic of the late sunlight was increased in power, and the rich color-tones of the beating wings and the moving bodies of the birds became even more varied and more lustrous. Yet, when this beauty of color was at its height, she was least aware of it, for suddenly there was something else that even more potently fascinated the eye—a beauty of movement wholly indescribable.

It was not that the flight of each bird was unusually graceful. Rather it was an effect produced by the flight of the whole flock rising together and flying straight away in wide close ranks just above the surface of the marsh. If the birds rose high, this effect was lost; but often the flock flew low, at about the height of her eyes, so that she saw plainly the up-and-down beat of the wings, their upper as well as their under surfaces. Sweeping onward side by side, in a crescent-shaped phalanx perhaps fifty yards in extent from flank to flank, the wing-tips of each bird almost touched those of the birds to right and left of it; and as those hundreds of long curved pinions rose and fell and rose and fell again and again and again, there was produced a shimmering effect of waviness, and the whole upper surface of the flock undulated with a rippling motion as of water ruffled by the wind. But to her this was more beautiful by far than any wind-ruffled water, because there was life in it, and a wealth of warm color never found in any sea or lake, and because of a strange, faint, golden mistiness that seemed to glorify those shimmering wings.

She could see it all still; the picture hadn't faded. But remembering how it had moved her, how its beauty had made her tremble, how she had felt, *known* that somehow in some incomprehensible way she was a part of it and it a part of her, she realized with an added sharpness that now all this was gone from her. Something, a kind of flame in her, seemed to have died. Riding homeward this morning from the backwater where she had seen the soaring ibises, she had been conscious again of the flame. But it hadn't lasted; soon it had flickered out.

Well, she said to herself impatiently, for one thing she was getting older; probably her enthusiasms were changing. And if she had lost something, probably it was just as well. She recalled with a little frown what Ash had said; perhaps Ash understood her better than she understood herself. She replaced the tablet in the drawer, closed and locked it carefully, removing the key.

She smiled faintly, sitting now by the window, her hands folded in her lap. She was thinking about what the locked drawer contained; it contained, she reflected, Diane Rowland. There were in it only a number of letters and in another corner some folded sheets of closely written paper. The latter were things she had scribbled in pencil—among them an attempt to describe the curlews at Edisto that day. The letters were from men; short notes, conventionally phrased, requesting the privilege of a visit or the pleasure of her company on some occasion. She had received hundreds like them, generally while in Charleston during the gay season or at the Springs or in New Orleans: these few—there were perhaps a dozen of them from as many different men—she had kept. They hadn't any obvious importance, yet she had kept them.

There was a tap on the door and Sheba, entering, handed her a letter. She saw that it was from James Hail.

"Sheba," Diane said, "when Sharpio knocks on your door at night..."

She stopped abruptly. "Never mind, Sheba," she added, "you can go."

She sat with half-closed eyes, holding the letter in her right hand. She was thinking that it was a peculiar thing she had been about to tell Sheba—a thought that suddenly, at sight of the girl, had sprung into her mind. She had been about to tell Sheba that when Sharpio knocked on her door at night, it was beauty; beauty somehow like that of the curlews winging away above the Edisto marshes. All beauty, she had been about to tell Sheba, was good if you gave yourself to it.

Sheba wouldn't have understood, of course; she herself didn't entirely understand, but she knew that she had always believed this, that this belief was at the bottom of her being. Now, though, she wasn't quite the same. Something had gone out of her; the fear smote her that she couldn't now give herself to beauty and that Sheba could. That was ridiculous, she recognized; the comparison was grotesque, repulsive; her thoughts were drifting into a fog of absurdities.

She realized, with a sudden hardening of her spirit, a swift rallying of her defenses, the dangerous undercurrent of her thoughts. She wouldn't allow that: that moment in the summer-house had left a scar but no irremediable hurt. It hadn't left her spirit dulled, insensitive, her perception of beauty blunted, her ability to give herself to beauty destroyed.

Her fingers tightened upon the letter in her hand. It was a relief to hear from James. He was still in Montgomery and she had not heard from him in five days; she had begun to worry a little. It was a thick letter; there would be a great deal in it about the secession movement. Probably it would be entirely that; the progress of his conferences with William L. Yancey and influential leaders of the Middle South and the Southwest. James shared with her all his hopes and fears for the South; he shared them with her more fully than with anyone else except Barnwell Rhett himself.

She rose suddenly and stood for some moments looking intently at her image (she was still in her riding habit, though she had laid aside her hat) in the mirror above her bureau; then she returned to her chair by the window. Strangely, her thoughts switched to Mazÿck Marion. She had seen him less often since the announcement of her engagement to James. But his eyes hadn't changed; there was the same light in them when he looked at her She was worried by it sometimes and yet she would miss it if it wasn't there; it was, in Mazÿck's eyes, at once beautiful and frightening. And somehow inevitable: a thing about which nothing could be or should be done: a thing to be accepted. And yet sometimes, because Mazÿck was what he was, a frightening thing. She hadn't feared it in the eyes of Adolphe LeClerc of New Orleans, in Etienne Ramon's eyes, in the eyes of Louis Treves.

A familiar thought returned to her, the frank thought that she had been put into the world to produce this look in the eyes of men. Always when she saw it she had a sense not merely of satisfaction but of fulfilment; a fulfilment of herself. Those notes in her drawer had been written by men in whose eyes she had seen that light. That was why she had kept them. She didn't hate the desire that she had awakened in those men; she rejoiced in it. It, too, was beauty. Beauty that she had made.

She said to herself that she was a strange being. She wondered how many of the others were secretly like herself: Sabina Slade, for instance, and Julie Chardon and Elizabeth Acton? No, not Elizabeth. She couldn't include Elizabeth. There was nothing—

well, indefensible—in Elizabeth. That was why Elizabeth didn't like her; that and the fact that John still did.

The shimmering wings of curlews, the shining whiteness of soaring ibises, the fires that she kindled in men's eyes. It was all there in her locked drawer. In herself. And it was all beauty, all the same thing really. Except in Richard Acton's eyes. For a moment that had been beauty, blinding, intoxicating beauty; then it had turned to ugliness. Beauty could do that—in an instant. It was treacherous, dangerous. Her lips, as she sat by the window, were compressed tightly. She had never seen those fires in James Hail's eyes. Perhaps that was why she was going to marry him. She opened his letter.

> "*Dearest* [the letter began] *I am more hopeful than ever. The long effort that we in South Carolina have made to save our beloved South by withdrawal from the Union is really bearing fruit. I had a long talk this morning with Mr. Toombs of Georgia, Mr. Yancey, Senator Wigfall of Texas, Senator Jefferson Davis...*"

Chapter V

SINKLER ROWLAND, FROM A DEEP chair in a corner of the dining-room, announced that the *Mercury* was waking up. It had been, he asserted, as conservative as the *Courier* of late, but now the Rhetts were striking their stride again. It was a Wednesday morning and Sinkler was in riding boots, his light trousers tucked in; he wore a loose jacket of tan linen over a white shirt open at the throat and secured by a narrow black scarf. Plainly he was ready for the field, but his attention at the moment was wholly concentrated upon the newspaper before him.

The others—Mrs. Rowland, Diane, Sally and Ash Rowland, young Mason de Lansac whose age was ten and Mr. Hemmerton, Mason's tutor—were seated around the table where breakfast was being served them by Andrew, the second dining-room man. Sinkler, as usual, had had his breakfast an hour earlier; except on Sundays, he was in his saddle and on his way to the rice-fields soon after sunrise. A hard shower, however, which had begun at dawn, was still falling; and, waiting for the rain to cease, he was in the dining-room reading the Charleston newspapers included in the previous day's mail when the other members of the household had come down.

His pronouncement as to the *Mercury* brought no immediate response. Ash Rowland had been relating some unconscious witticism of Thomas de Lansac, Jr., aged five years and some months, and the three women were plainly more interested in this than in the *Mercury's* renewed activity. As the laughter caused by Ash's story subsided however, Sinkler insisted upon having their attention. "This is well put," he declared. "It's young Rhett [the *Charleston Mercury*, Barnwell Rhett's organ, was edited by his son] at his best. You'll enjoy hearing it." In a somewhat sentacious tone he began to read:

> *"We beg leave to protest against the position of the New Orleans Bee that the Southern people are so cankered by prosperity as to be incapable of resisting the sectional domination of the North, and that the Union will be continued because of this prosperity. We think that the liberties of the South are not gauged by the price of negroes. She is capable of far higher motives and a nobler appreciation of her position and the duties it may involve. She can understand her rights under the Federal Government and maintain them simply because they are rights. She can cast off a government, as our fathers did before us, which, not only unconstitutionally through the taxing power compels us to pay tribute to the North but by its eternal agitations imperils the very existence of all property itself. She*

can comprehend what a national despotism established by Northern Abolitionists over us must produce not only in the loss of liberty and self-government but in its certain consummation of ruin and desolation over the South.'"

He finished with something of a flourish and looked triumphantly at his mother. "Good heavens, Sinkler," Sally said despairingly; "another secession argument before we've even finished breakfast. What a way—"

Mrs. Rowland, at the head of the table, pouring coffee from a great silver urn bearing the Chantilly crest, interrupted Sally.

"That is strongly written," she said, "though the statements are all general. Still, I think we can assume that the South isn't mercenary; what I'm afraid of is that it may lean too far in the other direction. Sinkler, I have a practical mind. I got it, I'm sure, from your father, for when I married him I had very little common sense. Our right to withdraw can't be questioned. But I'm not so sure as you are that it can be done peaceably. There's feeling in the North about the Union that we don't begin to understand. I remember Andrew Jackson. He was a southern man, a South Carolinian, but he would have made war to keep the Union and I think he would have hanged Mr. Calhoun. I also remember that two of my brothers fought for the flag in Mexico and I'm not eager to see my sons fighting against it. That may be mere sentiment, but it's not put on. And I'm afraid that even a successful war with the North would cost us more than it would be worth. If war came, I think it might do us a great deal of harm."

"It won't come." Sinkler Rowland said emphatically. "The North couldn't justify a policy of coercion and Andrew Jackson's been dead fourteen years. Besides, coercion's a practical impossibility. They couldn't coerce a united South and the South's getting together at last. Dee won't go into details, but she tells me James's letters are most encouraging, and Sally says Charles Gough is equally hopeful. It won't be South Carolina alone as it was in Jackson's day. I wouldn't approve of that a bit more than you would. Senator Hammond—he's the ablest man we have, by the way—is right in holding that, cooperation is absolutely necessary: I don't agree, as you know, with James Hail and the Rhett clique that South Carolina ought to secede independently; I think we ought to make sure first that we shall have support. But it's fairly evident now that we shall have it, and with all the cotton states back of us, we don't need Virginia. Even if she fails us, we'll have..."

He was interrupted by a commotion behind the closed door leading to the pantry, followed by the sudden irruption into the dining-room of Thomas de Lansac, Jr. He was in tears, his mouth was plentifully besmeared with egg, and close in his wake Amy Anne de Lansac, two years older than Thomas, also emerged from the pantry and began immediately a shrill explanation of the calamity that had befallen her brother.

"Bina had to go up-stairs for a minute," she said rapidly, "so I was fixing Thomas's egg for him an' he wouldn't let me an' that started it. Then he told me he saw a snake yesterday at the rice barn an' it was only a lizard 'cause I saw it too, an' I told him it was wrong to tell stories an' he tried to knock me with his spoon an' he missed me an' hit his own knee. That was terrible, an' so I told him if he wouldn't cry you would sing a song for him, Uncle Ash, but Bina came back an' said we mustn't come in the dining-room an' so Thomas cried an' we came in anyhow. You'll have to sing, Uncle Ash, because I said you would."

Ash Rowland rose and beckoned with his finger to Thomas, Jr. "Come here, young sprout," he commanded, and Thomas, his wrongs instantly forgotten, came at a run. Ash caught him up, carried him to the sofa against the north wall and seated himself there with Thomas facing him on his knee.

"This is outrageous, Thomas," he said sternly, "to make your unfortunate uncle try to sing before he has even finished his breakfast. But since Amy Anne promised, I s'pose it will have to be done. Amy Anne is a very great lady, a scion of an -illustrious race whose honor has hardly ever been tarnished. Did I ever tell you, Thomas, about that great-great-great-aunt of yours who became a countess and who was so beautiful that she found it hard to be very very good? Some day I'll tell you about that charming hussy, but it wouldn't be a good plan to tell you all about her. Your grandmother wouldn't approve and, besides, it isn't right to be disrespectful to countesses. Well, anyhow, Thomas, as I was saying, Amy Anne is a very grand lady and her promises must be kept though the walls of Jericho tumble and your Uncle Sinkler, who doesn't like singing at breakfast, has a conniption fit. But, Amy Anne, let me tell you now, my angel, if you make any more promises like this one, I shall undoubtedly give you a spanking on the tenderest part of your angelic anatomy. It's *very*, *very* inconvenient, Amy Anne."

Amy Anne opened her lips to speak, but Ash waved an admonitory finger. His deep baritone filled the room:

> *"When I was young I used to wait*
> *On Maussa's table, hand the plate,*
> *Pass the bottle when 'twas dry,*
> *And brush away the bluetail fly.*
>
> *"Do, Johnny Bigger, do!*
> *Do, Johnny Bigger, do!*
> *Do, Johnny Bigger—Oh!*
> *Can't you help a nigger—Oh!*
> *Do, Johnny Bigger, do!*
>
> *"When Maussa rode in the afternoon*
> *I followed him with a hick'ry broom;*
> *The pony, being very shy,*
> *Was bitten by the bluetail fly.*
>
> *"Do, Johnny Bigger, do!*
> *Do, Johnny Bigger, do!*
> *Do, Johnny Bigger—Oh!*
> *Can't you help a nigger—Oh!*
> *Do, Johnny Bigger, do!*

> *"The pony then began to pitch,*
> *He tumbled Maussa in the ditch;*
> *He died and the jury found Out why;*
> *The verdict was the bluetail fly.*
>
> *"Do, Johnny Bigger, do!*
> *Do, Johnny Bigger, do!*
> *Do, Johnny Bigger—Oh!*
> *Can't you help a nigger—Oh!*
> *Do, Johnny Bigger, do!"*

The song ended, but Ash Rowland's voice, resonant and extraordinarily sweet, seemed still to fill the room. Thomas de Lansac, Jr., on Ash's knee, continued to stare at his uncle with wide adoring eyes; Amy Anne, too, from a chair in the middle of the room, was gazing at him with mute adoration. Sinkler Rowland broke the silence.

"That was fine, Ash," he said, "I enjoyed it in spite of your remark about me. I'd give five hundred acres of prime rice-land for your voice." He moved to where his mother was sitting and kissed her on the forehead.

"Well," he went on, "the rain's stopped. I'm off." He half turned at the door. "I may not get back till late," he added. "We're flowing the south field today, the point flow, and I don't want to leave it to Belflowers. And there's a bad spot to be mended in one of the banks on Graveyard Creek; an alligator hole, I think. Look out for Roman for me, will you,

Dee? You might have Stepney put some more of that salve on his foot."

He went out. Through a south window opposite her place at the table, Diane saw him mount and ride through the yard toward the gate. She was conscious of a sudden swift affection for her older brother; it was especially nice of him, she thought, to say what he had said to Ash.

Sinkler's the best of us except mother, she said to herself, the least attractive but probably the best. He hadn't, for instance, a trace of jealousy because he lacked the magnetism that Ash so conspicuously possessed. Sinkler, fair-haired and rather deliberate, was completely and solidly English like his father. He was as much like Sally, in spite of Sally's animation, as she, Diane, was like Ash; in Ash Mrs. Rowland's French Huguenot blood gained added intensity from a fiery Irish strain that had been mingled early with the Rowland line.

Probably, Diane's thoughts continued, Sinkler would never marry. Rice-planting, aside from his typically Carolinian interests in politics, was his one passion, and he gave himself wholly to it, managing successfully not only Notteley but also the extensive Rowland holdings on the Combahee to which he made frequent visits, supervising closely the operations of the overseers there. In summer, when his mother and sisters visited the Virginia Springs, the North Carolina Mountains, New York or Newport or, under the protection of male cousins, traveled abroad, Sinkler generally remained at the Rowland summer cottage in Pineland village whence he could watch the Notteley harvest.

He worked hard, almost unceasingly, harder even than most other Carolinian planters who controlled thousands of acres and hundreds of slaves. It was really outrageous, Diane found herself reflecting, that Ash didn't work at all. Still, her thoughts ran on, that wasn't quite fair to Ash. He was the youngest of them, two years younger than Sally; he was just out of college—Princeton—and hadn't decided yet what he would do. Planting didn't attract him; he had shown no enthusiasm when Sinkler had suggested that he take over the management of one of the Combahee places.

He had stayed on at Notteley, reading a little law, hunting deer and foxes, attending every dance given in the neighborhood, making numerous trips to Charleston for Race Week, the St. Cecilia balls and other entertainments of the gay social season there. He drank about as much, Diane thought, as the average young Carolinian gentleman and had probably had, she supposed, the average number of love-affairs. He knew horses and dogs and sporting weapons and he had a passion for game chickens of the white-legged Lord Derby breed, and the poetry of Robert Burns. He had been involved so far in one affair of honour in which—thanks largely to Mazÿck Marion—no blood had been shed and he had lost more money than he could afford (though the same thing was true of nearly every planter on the river) when John Acton's English gelding, Avalon Prince, had been beaten by a nose on the Charleston track.

Ash was hardly more vain than was natural, Diane said to herself. The wonder was that he wasn't more so, for he couldn't help being aware of his own charm. He was above the middle height, straight, supple and strong; his hair was dark brown and a little curly, his nose was the large Huguenot nose of the Bretagne Chantillys, his eyes were the blue of the English-Irish Rowland strain. He was a little too fond, she admitted, of the sound of his own rich baritone, a little too loudly of the opinion—she suspected in this another kind of vanity—that *Charles O'Malley* and *Tom Jones* were the finest novels ever penned.

Nevertheless, most young men liked him. At Princeton, she recalled, he had been the most popular man in his class; returning to Carolina, he had been elected a lieutenant in the Pineland troop of cavalry ten days after he had joined the troop. If, in his own mind, he was another Charles O'Malley, on either Gray Arab or Santee he was well fitted for the role. In a country where nearly all men rode well, he rode better than most, more gracefully perhaps than any other. It was generally expected that he would win the tournament to be held at Pineland early next month; Diane reminded herself that she must begin work on his costume—he was to be the Knight of Alhambra.

"Uncle Ash," Amy Anne said suddenly, "it was nice of you to sing for us before you had finished your breakfast. I like you much better than Uncle Sinkler; I even like you better than Aunt Dee's Mr. Hail. I can't help it, Aunt Dee, I really do. I think Uncle Ash is the nicest and the most handsomest man in the whole world."

Chapter VI

On the piazza, after breakfast, Thomas de Lansac, Jr., standing in front of his grandmother's chair; returned to the matter of his breakfast egg. Amy Anne, he said, had tried to be smart. "Anyhow," he added proudly, pronouncing his words with a careful precision, "she hasn't ever been stung by a cattypillar and a half and I have."

Amy Anne explained this with a fine disdain:

"There were two of them and they came out from under a piece of board down by the landing. Yellowish and hairy, and Bina mashed one and it broke and the broken piece of that cattypillar was right along side the other cattypillar and Thomas put his hand down on them and they both stuck him. That's what he means by a cattypillar and a half, but it wasn't really a half—only a little piece of cattypillar. So Thomas is storying again."

No, Thomas wasn't, Ash told her: when you were stung by even one caterpillar it always felt as though it was at least a dozen. "Now," he went on, "you and Thomas have got to stop quarreling. When your Aunt Dee and Aunt Sally and I were little children we never quarreled or accused one another of storying. We were perfect little lambs. Or, at least, I was. Now that I stop to think, I seem to remember that your Aunt Sally and your Aunt Dee..."

Sally interrupted him. "Stop it, Ash," she exclaimed. "I won't have my character blackened before these children. They believe every word you tell them. If some of the girls of this parish knew that, they would have hysterics."

Ash smiled. "The girls of this parish, my dear sister," he said, "can take care of themselves against all comers. I've learned that to my cost; and I'm not the only one. If a certain gentleman from the up-country were here..."

He turned his head and pretended to discover for the first time Mr. Hemmerton, the tutor, standing beside the piazza banister gazing out over the river and the bordering rice-fields. Mr. Hemmerton, blushing furiously, continued silently to view the distant prospect, blowing clouds of smoke from his pipe. Obviously he was in an agony of self-consciousness, but Diane saw at once that, under this, he was angry. He turned suddenly toward Ash.

"Some of them can take care of themselves..." he began and stopped abruptly.

There was an awkward silence. Sally, in a rocking chair beyond Mrs. Rowland, was looking out over the rice-fields and Ash was lighting a cigar. The crimson was fading from Calvin Hemmerton's face, Diane noticed; his cheeks were almost white.

Young Mason de Lansac, an open book in his hand, appeared in the doorway.

"Can't we begin right now, Mr. Hemmerton?" he asked. "I want to get through early so I can go fishing with Under Ash. He's promised to take me." The tutor nodded and followed Mason into the hall. They heard him go upstairs with the boy to the room where Mason's studies were conducted.

"That wasn't very successful," Mrs. Rowland said. "Ash, I don't think you had better do it again."

Ash assured her feelingly that he wouldn't. "Good lord!" he exclaimed. "Did you ever see such an imbecile? Sally, why can't you teach him a little sense? And, for heaven's sake, teach him not to blush."

Sally begged Ash not to be more objectionable than he absolutely had to be. "Can't you see," she added serenely, "that Calvin has passed the stage where he can stand teasing about me. The truth is, you've all of you underestimated my destructive capabilities. I've really played the mischief with Calvin."

Ash grinned. "We know it now if we didn't know it before," he said. "It's an outrage, Sally. Calvin's not accustomed to this kind of thing, you know. They take life more seriously in the up-country."

"That was serious just now," Diane told him. "You didn't see him, Ash—you were lighting your cigar. He started to say something and stopped and turned deathly pale. You noticed it, Mother?"

Mrs. Rowland nodded and Ash laughed. "Nonsense, Dee," he said. "Old Calvin and I get along wonderfully. He wasn't angry—or if he was, he'll be over it in an hour. He's really a good fellow."

"He started to say something to you," Diane repeated. "Somehow I had a feeling that he was frightened by what he started to say."

Ash glanced at her quickly. "Tell you what I'll do," he said. "I'll take him with us when Mason and I go fishing and he can catch some trout. That'll soothe his ruffled feelings."

It wouldn't, however, Diane said to herself, relieve the situation that Sally had created. Perhaps, though, that wasn't entirely Sally's fault. Calvin Hemmerton's misadventure had been, after all, practically inevitable. Tutors from the North or from the up-country were notoriously unsafe in Low-Country houses. They came secretly scornful of Low-Country airs and graces, and they were likely to go away sadder if not wiser than they had been when they arrived. It was very ridiculous.

She wasn't sure, however, that this Hemmerton matter was entirely laughable: Sally ought to have stopped weeks ago. Calvin's condition was undoubtedly serious. He had been, momentarily at any rate, furious with Ash; and his sudden pallor had been strange. She couldn't rid herself of the feeling that he had been frightened by what he had started to say to Ash—he had broken his sentence off in the middle. She tried to remember what Hemmerton had said: it was something about some of the girls of the parish—he had emphasized the "some"—being able to take care of themselves.

That didn't on the face of it, appear very significant. Nevertheless, she saw now that it involved a plain implication: that others of the girls of the parish were not able to take care of themselves. Her eyes rested thoughtfully upon Ash. What had the boy been up to? And what did Calvin Hemmerton know about his affairs?

They were numerous, but she didn't think that any of them were serious; certainly none of the girls that Ash habitually flirted with was likely to take him too seriously. But to Calvin Hemmerton, the opposite of a flirt, Ash might well appear a Don Juan. Probably that was all there was in it: to Calvin of the austere up-country flirtation was sin. He had probably heard Ash whispering soft nonsense to somebody and in his anger just now he had almost accused him of trifling with somebody's heart.

Well, she said to herself, hearts in the Low-Country withstood a good deal of trifling, but Calvin Hemmerton's up-country heart was of a different kind. There would be an interesting situation when Charles Gough returned from Montgomery; probably Mr. Hemmerton's stay at Notteley would terminate then—she couldn't imagine him remaining with Charles monopolizing Sally before his eyes.

Mrs. Rowland rose. "Come, Sally," she said, "it's your turn, darling." She went into the house, Sally following her. Diane heard her mother giving directions to Marcus, the butler, in the hall, while Sally went on to the pantry to get the keys. There was first the matter of arranging the day's routine in the house, getting the numerous servants started at their tasks; then they would visit the Quarters of the yard servants, drive to the two other negro settlements, visit the hospital—the sick-house, the negroes called it. A long morning's work.

It was too much for her mother, Diane said to herself for the hundredth time; it was wearing her out. The two girls took turns in visiting the negro settlements and the sick—house with her, but she went every day. "Mother's looking badly," Diane said to Ash. "I wish we could persuade her to turn over the visiting entirely to Sally and me."

Ash nodded. "You can't, though," he replied. "She'll keep going until she drops. The spirit of a—of a gamecock. Diane, I took Agamemnon over to Mattesaw yesterday and tried him against that Tartar cock of Peter's. Just a sparring match; no gaffs. The Tartar didn't have a chance; if they'd had steel on, Agamemnon would have killed him in two minutes."

Amy Anne seated herself on Ash's knee. "If you had a elephant and a whale," she said, "and the elephant was on the shore and the whale was in the river, and you took a rope and tied one end of it to the elephant's tail and the other end of it to the whale's tail, and then made them pull, would the elephant pull the whale up on the shore, or would the whale pull the elephant in the river, Uncle Ash?"

Ash considered this with a complete solemnity. "I think," he said finally, "that I would bet on the whale." Amy Anne's triumph was immediately obvious; it was matched by the equally obvious chagrin of Thomas de Lansac, Jr., who had evidently favored the elephant. This, however, disappeared when Ash suggested a visit to the stables. They went off riotously together; Bina, the nurse, who had been waiting at the foot of the steps, called up to Diane.

"Dem chilluns don' need me, Miss Dee," she said. "All you got to do is tu'n um ober to Mas' Ash."

Chapter VII

Diane followed them presently; she was passionately devoted to horses, and a visit to the stables was a necessary part of her daily life at Notteley. Ash and the children, she saw, had been diverted; they had turned aside to the kennels where one of Ash's setters had recently brought seven black and white puppies into the world. The kennels were shaded by a gigantic live-oak, the largest in Notteley yard, and on a huge horizontal limb of this oak a bright red gamecock flapped his wings and crowed resoundingly.

It wasn't Agamemnon, she saw at a glance, but Bougre de Not, a fine young muffled cock of distinguished ancestry that Tom Elliott of Beaufort had sent Ash a week or so ago. No, it wasn't Bougre de Not; it was courage. Courage, courage, courage, she repeated. Courage flapping its wings and crowing in the face of the world. It was strange what idiotic things, what little things, kept reminding her of the need of that. A young gamecock crowing on an oak limb. The queer fact was that Bougre de Not was standing on the exact spot on the limb where, she had always been told, the rope had been tied—just where the limb began to curve downward.

She walked on, frowning a little, toward the stables. Cornwallis had established himself at Avalon and a detachment of British dragoons were occupying Notteley. The story was that Richard Acton had been captured near Goose Creek bridge; he was one of General Marion's scouts and the dragoons had kept him a prisoner at Notteley for several days. Possibly they had been drunk when they decided to hang him; at any rate, the rope had been slung across the limb where Bougre de Not was now crowing and the noose was around Richard Acton's neck. He had asked, so the story ran, to be allowed to smoke one more pipe, and just before he had finished it, a reprieve from Lord Cornwallis had arrived.

She said to herself that she knew better than any one else in the world how that Richard Acton had looked while he was smoking his pipe. She wondered what had become of the pipe. A small bowl of wood with a hollow stem. It had saved the life of one Richard Acton and, as a result, a long time after that, there was another Richard Acton and, as a result of that in turn, she, Diane Rowland, seeing a red cock crowing where the rope had been slung, had found herself envying Bougre de Not his courage. Well, it was a good plan to crow. She walked on humming:

> *"Out upon it, I have loved*
> *Three whole days together!*

And am like to love three more,
If it prove fair weather.

"'Time shall moult away his wings
Ere he shall discover
In the whole wide world again
Such a constant lover.'"

That was Herrick or Waller or Suckling, she wasn't quite sure which;—poets of a kind not always highly regarded in the Low-Country. Not, at least, as poets for the family library; it was felt that they weren't sufficiently mindful of a proper delicacy. She might never have discovered some of them but for Sabina Slade. What was that verse, from somebody else, that Sabina used to repeat?

"Like the Idalian queen,
Her hair about her eyne,
With neck and breast's ripe apples to be seen—"

That wouldn't do for the family library either, at least for most plantation family libraries, but it was a pretty thing; nothing so pretty should be forbidden. This brought her to the stables. There were only half a dozen horses in the stalls; the others, Roan Mary among them, were in the pasture, old Ned Scotland, the head stableman, informed her. Her attention was directed mainly to Gray Arab, the mare that Ash planned to ride in the Pineland tournament: a beautiful creature from the Wade Hampton stables at Millwood, the fine stock of which, unsurpassed in the South, had been further improved by Colonel Hampton's large purchases at the sale of the royal stud of William IV.

Ned Scotland conferred gravely with her regarding the feeding and exercising of Gray Arab; he didn't by any means approve of certain changes that Ash had ordered. "Dat boy t'ink he know eberyt'ing, Miss Dee," the old man grumbled. "Ef you an' me don' watch out, he ruin dat mare befo' de toonament." There was a new horse, a rather heavy but handsome bay gelding, in one of the end stalls, and here also Scotland found cause for misgiving; again his advice had been disregarded. "Mas' Sinkler *would* buy um," he said, "en he ain't wut. Enty you see he got t'ree white foot?

> "*One white foot, buy um;*
> *Two white foot, try um;*
> *T'ree white foot, doubt um;*
> *Fo' white foot, do widout um?'*

Miss Dee, dis creetur got t'ree white foot en I bet he got wuss'n dat eenside um. Tu'n roun', hoss, en' let Miss Dee see yer. She know t'ree time as much 'bout hoss as anybody else on dis plantation, cep'n only me."

This pleased her. She recalled that James had often told her the same thing. And Mazÿck. It was perhaps a part, a very small part, of the reason why James loved her. But it hadn't anything to do with the reason why Mazÿck—

"Miss Dee," Scotland asked abruptly, "when yo' lover comin'?" The question startled her momentarily; to Ned Scotland love was a very simple thing; it was in his case divided between two persons—James and herself. The old man walked with her to the stable door and she noticed again his difficulty with his left leg; undoubtedly his rheumatism was getting worse.

She must ask Doctor Roupell about it. Scotland, she said to herself, had been wise; he had been a freeman; but, with old age and rheumatism coming on, he had bound himself to James Hail to whose family his father had belonged; and later James had presented him to her. "Scotland," she asked him suddenly, "who would you rather belong to—Mr. James or me?"

Scotland grinned. "Miss Dee," he said, "I'd ruther b'long ter Mas' James dan anybody else een dis worl'. En' luck sho wid me— 'cause when you b'long ter him, I'll b'long ter him again too."

That meant, she reflected, that James and herself would have Scotland to feed and take care of until the end of his days—which, of course, was the reason why Scotland, getting old and infirm, had given up his freedom. It was rather strange, she thought, that such cases were not more common; yet she remembered, walking from the stables toward the house, how completely she had sympathized with Big Sam. It was true, as Sinkler had pointed out, that discipline was necessary on a plantation and that for the worst offenders only strong measures were effective. That was true not only on a plantation but everywhere. And Big Sam had been a trouble-maker, not only persistently insubordinate but, toward the last, dangerous. Yet when Big Sam had jumped into the river and drowned himself rather than submit to a whipping by one of the negro foremen under the overseer's eye, she had understood why he had done it. Big Sam, she said to herself, if he had been free, would have starved rather than surrender his freedom.

Big Sam's suicide had troubled her for a long time and her mother had been deeply troubled by it; nothing of the kind had ever happened before at Notteley. The Big Sams were the exceptions; but there ought to be some way of dealing with the exceptions. She remembered something that her cousin, old Captain William Chantilly of Montauban, had once said: that slavery, as it existed in Carolina and Virginia, was the best possible school for the negro race but that its great defect lay in the fact that no method was provided for the graduation of pupils who had completed the course.

That had impressed her. She had talked it over with James, she remembered. The deeper question, James had said, was whether the white race should continue to rule the South; in the end the problem before the white South was one of self-preservation. Outside the Union, it was conceivable that the South might, after a time, work out a method of emancipation, but within the Union that would be impossible; freedom for the negro would mean, before long, votes for the negro, and these, combined with the Republican votes of the North, would hold the white South in perpetual bondage. There was a buggy in the back yard and a negro man, whom she recognized as one of the Avalon foremen, was talking with Stepney. Sheba and a strange mulatto girl were busy at one of the flower-beds near the back steps.

Obviously Elizabeth Acton had sent over the Mexican seeds she had been promising Sally, and the girl had evidently been sent to attend to the proper planting of them. Diane walked on toward the front steps. She saw Ash and the children coming from the direction of the kennels; but Ash stopped suddenly, spoke to the children, then turned and walked toward the stables, with Amy Anne and Thomas following him.

The yellow girl stooping beside Sheba rose and, dropping her trowel, walked across the yard to a watering trough where she filled a bucket, returning with the bucket balanced on her head. She walked beautifully even with the bucket on her bead, Diane noticed—a smooth and rhythmical, almost a flowing, movement of her lithe body. A bandana handkerchief around her hair glowed a vivid scarlet in the bright sun.

Diane had planned to drive to Pineland with Sally in the afternoon; but Sally was carried off, rather unwillingly, for a horseback ride with Stephen Bevill and his sister, who had ridden over from Wisboo; and, Diane, after an hour in the sewing room, where two negro seamstresses needed supervision, rode, with only Roan Mary and Roman for company, through the pine savannas bordering the north field to a small wooded peninsula where James had made a rustic seat for her between the trunks of two young oaks. Sitting there, with Roan Mary tethered just behind her and Roman lying at her feet, she had the whole north field before her.

There was nothing, she said to herself, on Notteley Plantation more beautiful than the north field when the point flow had been let in—unless it was the north field in late summer when the tall rice was ready for harvesting. It lay before her now, a wide sheet of motionless shallow water above which the green tips of the rice blades were plainly visible; a shimmering silver-green expanse, the smooth sweep of it scarcely marred by the long low grass-grown banks or dikes subdividing the hundred-acre field into smaller areas. A full half-mile away, the main bank along the river-front interrupted her view; and at one point on this bank she could see half a dozen negroes working under the direction of Belflowers the overseer. They were evidently repairing one of the sluice-gates or trunk-docks through which the water was let in upon the fields or drawn off as occasion required; and for some minutes she watched them thoughtfully, trying to determine from their actions precisely what they were doing.

A flock of white herons, flying low above the surface of the water, diverted her attention. Their slowly beating wings were flashes of silver in the afternoon sunlight; but when, one by one, they came to rest in the shallow water, they were white as spots of snow; the whole north field was dotted with these white spots—herons or egrets feeding in the shallows or standing at rest along the edges of the deep canals. From the bench where she was sitting one of the canals extended straight across the width of the field; her eyes, roving along the narrow lane of clear water, saw here and there small dark knobs in pairs or threes—the exposed eyes and nostrils of small alligators watching her warily as they lay just beneath the surface. Slowly other and larger knobs appeared; and gradually three of these resolved themselves into the armored head and jagged back of a ten-foot saurian lying in the middle of the canal not more than thirty yards away, his ugly snout pointing directly at her.

She had no fear of the alligators which abounded in the rice-field canals and the cypress backwaters; they were seldom or never dangerous and there was a quality of mystery in them that fascinated her; their strangeness, as of prehistoric monsters, stirred her at times as deeply as the slender gracefulness of wading herons. Nevertheless, she spoke a word of warning to Roman lying at her feet. If the hound should get scent of a marsh rabbit in the wampee beds at the edge of the water and venture close to the muddy margin of the canal, the big 'gator yonder might enjoy the kind of dinner that he preferred above all others. There wasn't much fear of that, however; Roman long ago had learned his lesson. On his first deer hunt, when he was no more than a puppy, he had tried to swim across Crane Pond in pursuit of a fleeing buck, and an alligator had all but pulled him down.

It was Mazÿck Marion, she remembered, who had saved Roman on that occasion; he had shot the 'gator at the moment when it was about to seize the hound—fortunately the water was too shallow for the reptile to swim submerged. She owed Roman to Mazÿck and she owed Scotland to James; she didn't, she said to herself, owe Richard Acton anything—except the queer notion that Bougre de Not, crowing on that oak-limb, was courage; courage flapping its wings and crowing in the face of the world. She heard a shrill whistling in the air above the rice-field; an oak branch shut off her view and he moved quickly nearer the edge of the canal.

An osprey, holding a fish in its claws, was circling against the blue sky; she knew what the hawk's screams portended, but for some moments she couldn't see the eagle. Then he came into sight from behind the tall pines in the direction of Sherborne—a splendid white-crowned king of the air, driving onward with powerful strokes of his dark wings straight toward the screaming osprey. With shining eyes she watched the familiar drama, waiting eagerly for one moment—a moment of beauty and power.

The eagle was almost directly over the osprey when the smaller bird dropped its fish. Immediately the eagle plunged—a magnificent stoop—a feathered spearhead falling, falling like a meteor; she could hear, she imagined, the thin whine of the cloven wind against the hard edges of the eagle's half-closed wings. Twenty feet above the surface of the water he swerved in the air and, turning half over on his back, seized the falling fish. Her eyes followed his majestic flight as he beat slowly away toward the Sherborne woods, his booty clutched beneath him.

If only she could describe that, get it into words, all the splendidness and the terror and the eternal rightness of it—the triumph of beauty, of power. What she had just seen was not a rare sight above the Notteley rice-fields; she had witnessed the same thing many times and it was never merely an eagle robbing an osprey.

It was a thousand mighty and magnificent thoughts, mind-pictures. It was Rome and the eagles of Rome and the invincible legions of Rome; it was the soul of the emperor-god soaring from his funeral pyre to join the other gods on high Olympus; it was the splendor of Heliopolis, the ancient City of the Sun, whose emblem was the eagle; it was the barbaric pomp of Charlemagne, his eagle-standards tossing in the pass of Roncesvalles...

A pair of purple gallinules came out of the wampee growth at the edge of the water and walked with quick dainty steps over the lily pads, talking to each other incessantly, their rich purple-blue and olive-green plumage shining like iridescent armor; on a buttonwood twig just over their heads, a tiny orange-gold warbler, bright almost as a spark of living fire, was singing a shrill, clear song. Beyond, above the flooded rice-field, birds of various sizes and kinds moved in many directions and at many levels: vultures soaring so high that they were mere specks against the blue; long-necked fantastic water sailing round and round with scarcely a movement of their black wings; herons white and gray and parti-colored; summer ducks flying like the wind; a flock of great white and black wood ibises sailing southward in a long line like a squadron of stately ships.

She said to herself that they would pass, if they held their course, directly over the south field where Sinkler probably was with the main gang of field hands; but Sinkler would be too busy to see them. Well, that was the way to be; it was best to be busy with something all the time. Sinkler was letting the point flow into the south field to-day. The water would remain there about a week; it would be drawn off and for ten days or two weeks the field would be dry and the hands would be busy hoeing the weeds between the rows of the growing rice. Then would come the long flow, with Sinkler watching every detail, when, for two or three weeks, the field would remain under water, followed once more by a mighty hoeing. At last the lay-by flow would begin, continuing two or perhaps three months until the crop, shoulder-high and heavy with bending heads, was ready for harvest.

That was the wealth, the substance, of Notteley and of the Low-Country; along all the winding rivers of the Low-Country the shimmering fields would be alive with the swarms of the black sickle-men laying the tall rice low. The cut stalks would be gathered and stacked; then the threshing, the winnowing—the slow rivers dotted with the sails of the rice-sloops and schooners carrying the crop to the Charleston mills whence it would be shipped all over the world. Well, she would be married by then, she would be James's wife.

She got up suddenly from the bench between the two oaks, and Roman also rose and stretched lazily. Roan Mary, impatient to be gone, tossed her head and pawed the ground with her forefoot. Riding homeward through the pine-land, Diane was again aware of the golden color of the late light under the pines. The sunlight didn't come through the air, it seemed to hang suspended in the air; it was one of the loveliest, and most tragical, things at Notteley.

Tall sarracenias were blooming in the moist savannas, with here and there a clump of purple iris. There were blue harebells along the woods-edge, and white bay blossoms, but the best of the bloom was already over—there would be no more jessamine or Cherokee rose until next spring, and she wouldn't be at Notteley then. Seven white egrets in single file sailed slowly over the tops of the pines. Swamp robins and nonpareils were singing in the rose-tangles; near the gate a gray fox crossed her path and Roman, picking up the hot scent, went away in full cry.

The yard was empty except for two red roosters moving toward each other with the queer sidelong gait of game-cocks about to join battle. Some one, she realized, had let Agamemnon out of the pen in which he had been confined while Bougre de Not was given the run of the yard. The two cocks came together as she rode toward them; there was a swift, furious engagement, and then the young Bougre de Not, lamentably disheveled, was in ignominious flight. That, she said to herself, was what happened to courage—courage flapping its wings and crowing in the face of the world.

Chapter VIII

It threatened, Sally Rowland complained, to be the dullest week of a very dull spring. There had been fewer parties, she declared, than usual, only three fox hunts and not much visiting; except the Nesbits and the Dwights and the Pinckneys of Chetsworth and the Chantillys of Montauban, who were cousins, and now and then Ralph Cain and Mazÿck Marion and Julie Chardon and young Stephen Bevill, whom she loathed and despised, scarcely anybody (of course you couldn't count Doctor Roupell and Louis Treves) had called at Notteley in almost a month. Peter Delamott didn't count either; when he came he looked only at Ash's game chickens. And the men who came to talk with Sinkler about crops and politics didn't add to the gaiety of life. Now that the dance at Cranefield had been postponed because of mumps in the house, there seemed to be nothing ahead until the Pineland tournament. Unless, of course, Charles Gough and James Hail arrived from Montgomery in the meantime.

Sally was delivering these complaints while dressing in Diane's room on a morning when a thin rain was falling. Just now she was arranging her yellow hair, wavy and extraordinarily fine, before the tall mirror above the bureau. She was wearing a morning dress of pale blue, and Diane, dressed and sitting on the bed, noticed again how graceful she was, how slenderly symmetrical were her arms.

"Zedekiah woke me as usual," Sally continued, but this time I went back to sleep. It's really outrageous, Dee, the way Satira tyrannizes over us with that goose. You might think she owned us instead of our owning her. And she talks to Sinkler like a Dutch uncle. It amuses Calvin intensely. He says that, next to me, it's the most significant fact on this plantation. I don't know what he means exactly; something deep and philosophical, I suppose, connected with the slavery question. Anyhow, I'm glad he puts me first—that I'm even more significant than the way Satira talks to Sinkler. What am I going to do about Calvin, Dee, now that Charles is coming?"

That was something she would have to manage for herself, Diane informed her younger sister. "You'll remember, Sally," she added, "that when I spoke to you about it not so long ago, you told me to mind my own business. I've been minding it."

Sally continued apparently unperturbed:

"I've enjoyed Calvin, Diane; there's a great deal more in him than you realize. You called him small game, but he isn't really. Of course, he doesn't compare with Charles, but I don't think I'm ready to let him go yet. He's given me something this spring that I really needed—a kind of worship. I think it's something like what Mazÿck Marion, poor devil, gives you. Frankly, Dee, I'm not sure Charles has anything for me as real as that."

"The Hemmertons," Diane said reflectively, "are very good plain people from the up-country. I don't know them but I know what they are like. Presbyterians probably, though there are lots of Methodists and Baptists in the up-country too. They live there in little towns or on small farms. They haven't many negroes and they do most of their own work and they drink whisky instead of Madeira. What's happened to Calvin is clear enough. He's been transported to a different world and he's been dazzled by it and of course he's found a goddess in it. A goddess very different from the goddesses of the up-country. Why he chose you instead of me is a mystery, but there's no accounting for tastes. The goddess, having nothing else to do, has been willing enough to shine for him and naturally the disaster is complete. And now, with the goddess's god about to return, the situation threatens to become difficult. Undoubtedly, my love, it will lead to a duel."

She laughed. It was impossible without a smile to imagine Calvin Hemmerton fighting a duel. "Let's go down, Sally," she added, "it's my day with mother, and she doesn't like to be kept waiting." Sally turned away from the mirror.

"That reminds me," she said. "I met Lowndes—Lowndes Fenwick—while I was riding yesterday and it struck me suddenly that he hadn't been here since the affair between James and Richard Acton. Of course it's absurd for him to feel that way simply because he was the second of the man who was fighting James. Especially a quarrel about politics. I told him so—didn't mind being entirely frank with Lowndes—he promised to come. He said that Mr. Acton had completely recovered now and that he was expected at Avalon this week. I suppose he will be at the Pineland tournament with John and Elizabeth. Are you going to speak to him, Dee? I think you should. Of course, a duel is supposed to settle everything."

"Oh, yes," Diane answered after a brief pause. "I will speak to him, of course." She preceded Sally from the room. Going down the stairs, she was conscious of a difficulty in breathing. This lasted only for a moment, but for that moment it was as though her throat was tightly closed. It would happen, then, she would see him, at the tournament in Pineland. Unless she went away somewhere...Sabina Slade had asked her to come to Richmond for a month's visit...she could go there...she would write to Sabina after breakfast.

Her lips tightened. She wouldn't, of course. That idea was ridiculous. James would be coming soon from Alabama; she must wait for him. She wondered whether he would come before the tournament; whether she would see him, feel his arms around her, before she saw Richard Acton. But what difference would that make? James wouldn't have changed. He would be just what he had always been. She was going to be his wife. By the middle of June, she reminded herself, she would be James Hail's wife. His obedient, loving and faithful wife. His wife forever.

Chapter IX

THERE WAS A FOX HUNT at Montauban two days later—Stuart Chantilly had arranged it in honor of two young Rhode Islanders who had been classmates of his at Harvard—and the hunt, naturally, was followed by a dance. The Cranefield mumps having turned out to be a false alarm, the St. Juliens' entertainment also took place, so that the week was not, after all, so dull as Sally had feared. Diane, however, found herself lacking in enthusiasm for an invitation that arrived from Wisboo—an all-day boating party on the river.

Sinkler, of course, was too busy for mid-week frivolity, and Ash, too, contrary to what might have been expected, declined. This left only Calvin Hemmerton to go with Sally, and that was impossible, Sally said; it developed that she was just then engaged in punishing Calvin for some offense the nature of which she did not reveal. The result was that nobody went from Notteley to Wisboo, and Diane and Sally spent the morning in Diane's room working on Ash's tournament costume. Diane had decided to attend to this personally instead of turning the matter over to the plantation seamstresses.

She worked on it until long after midday—Sally's energy had flagged before then,—and, after dinner, she spent an hour in her room looking over a new *Edinburgh Review* and a new *Godey's Lady's Book*; subsequently the *Charleston Mercury* engaged her. There was an extract from the *Richmond Enquirer* asserting that the permanency of the Union rested wholly upon the issue of the approaching presidential canvass; a reply to Senator Seward's provocative speech at Rochester in which he had proclaimed an irrepressible conflict between North and South; a fashion letter from New York declaring that the coming season would be marked by a wide latitude in sleeves—the Odalisque and the Minetta continued to be favorites—and the renewed ascendency of the hoop-skirt.

Three columns of foreign news, brought by the steamer Arabia, concerned chiefly the rumors of war on the continent; the Earl of Clarendon, she read, had been interrogating the government as to the mission of Lord Cowley; but the Mercury's opinion seemed to be that it was all, in reality, an effort to depress the price of cotton. There was, too, a long reprint from the *New American Cyclopedia* which had just come from the presses.

"A large proportion of the population of Charleston," the *Cyclopedia* informed her, "consists of the gentry of the contiguous parishes, who, possessing large planting interests, are sufficiently opulent to maintain abodes in the city as well as on their plantations. Here they educate their children and hither they resort in mid-summer. This is the secret of something anomalous in the life of Charleston. The planters bring with them wealth and leisure and these naturally beget luxurious tastes and habits. These elevate the tone of society but tend to the disparagement of labor and industry." That, she said to herself, would make Sinkler foam at the mouth. The *Mercury* to-day consisted largely of advertisements; she noticed particularly an announcement of "Walton Female College Lottery, chartered by the State of Georgia, when prizes amounting to $212,000 will be distributed, the Capital Prize being $60,000."

She abandoned the newspaper finally for Charles Reade's new novel, *Love Me Little, Love Me Long*. This, too, however, failed to satisfy the restlessness of her mood, and she remembered with relief that she had an engagement with Sinkler. Sending Sheba to the stables with an order to have Roan Mary saddled and brought to the hitching post, she put on her riding clothes and went down-stairs. Mrs. Rowland was sitting at her small desk in the library looking over some letters; and Diane, coming softly into the room, saw that her mother's shoulders drooped and that her eyes were tired. The shoulders straightened when she saw Diane.

"Nothing's the matter, daughter," she said immediately. "I was only a little appalled at the idea of more negroes. We have so many already." In explanation of this she handed Diane one of the letters.

It was from Robertson, Blacklock and Company, Factors of Charleston, addressed to The Honble. Sikler Rowland. Diane read:

> *"Dear Sir: We duly received your favors of 2 and 5. inst. We wrote to Mr. Ames to know his prices, terms, etc., of the negroes he offered to sell you, mentioning you were willing to give 600 dollars round. But we have not as yet had any reply to our letter.*
>
> *"We bought to-day at Col. Conant's sale the bricklayer Brutus and his wife Minnie agreeably to your directions; we paid for them $750 ea, and have sent them to you by to-day's trip of the river steamer and will settle for them in accordance with the terms of sale i. e. one-third cash, balance in 1, 2, and 3 years with interest from the day of sale payable annually; secured by Bond and Mortgage of the property sold and approved personal security. Purchaser to pay for requisite papers, unless we hear from you to the contrary and in that event we beg your instructions in the premises. We are, dear sir, yours very truly, Robertson, Blacklock and Company."*

Diane finished and glanced at her mother. Mrs. Rowland's tired look had returned.

"The bricklayer will be a godsend," she said; "we've not had a good one on the plantation since Joseph's death. It's the ten new field-hands that appall me. They're needed, of course; Sinkler discussed the matter very thoroughly with me before he acted. If the new fields are to be opened, we must have more hands. But it adds ten more to the two hundred and ten I have to think of here and the four hundred on the Combahee places and I am too old now to welcome more responsibility and more work." She paused, then added: You've caught me in one of my rebellious moods, Dee, but I'll get over it. Here's another letter—from the Combahee. Stryke is a good overseer, at least Sinkler thinks so, but not at his best when he takes his pen in hand."

> *"Dear Sir* [the overseer's letter ran] *The People is over the sickness at both Places except a few Cases of Fever; not dangerous, the Children is again wonderful healthy. The crop will be I think the best we ever had altogether but afraid the oats will be sorry. Jason went with two of your sheep to D P last monday, came back yesterday and fecht two others and a yew and Ram lam which is a verry fine lam Ram indeed. We had a fine dinner last week at the Muster Field, aplenty of Brandy and Champaign which made Mr. Bethune and S C Raven Esq fall out with Col Barr for some language Mr. B used to the Col. he struck Mr. B for which had like to have given a good deal of trouble to hush up, I am not sure they are done with it yet. The neighbors is all well except Mr Black who the Dr says is quite sick. Capt Gregorie told me he was going to write to you some days ago, him and his family is well, my family and self is well, I am glad to here you and your family is well. Respctly T T Stryke."*

Diane smiled.

"What really interests you in all that," she said, "is 'The People is over the sickness' and 'the Children is again wonderful healthy.' So you can stop worrying about the Combahee negroes and go up-stairs and have a nap. Or read another chapter of *Eugene Aram* if you can find one you don't know by heart. I'll have Sheba take you some tea. I don't believe you've rested two minutes to-day."

Mrs. Rowland replied that she would have the tea but not up-stairs; Sheba could bring it to her in the library.

One of the women in the Middle Settlement is quite ill, Dee," she said. "You know her; Phibby—one of Stepney's daughters. I've sent to Pineland for Doctor Roupell, and I want to be there when he sees her."

Diane exclaimed in exasperation. "That means another two-mile drive to the Middle Settlement," she protested. "You saw Phibby this morning, Mama, and you spent at least three hours in the Quarters and the two other settlements. Why can't Sally and I meet Doctor Roupell?"

Her mother shook her head. "Phibby wants me," she replied. "I'll take Sally with me, but you mustn't disappoint Sinkler. He's expecting you. Where's Ash?"

"I saw him go out of the gate about an hour ago," Diane told her. "He was riding Santee. I suppose he has gone to Pineland; they're getting the muster-ground ready for the tournament."

Chapter X

SHE DISCOVERED ABOUT AN HOUR later that Ash had not gone to Pineland. Sinkler had told her the evening before of a colony of nesting egrets that he had found in the woods near one of the inland rice-fields. The field had not been cultivated in years, but this year he was having it planted; if she would meet him there in the afternoon, he would show her where the egrets were nesting. There was a little used road through the woods, by way of an abandoned farm known as Gilpin's, now part of the Avalon lands; and Diane on Roan Mary was following this track when a doe, walking slowly, crossed ahead of her apparently without scenting or seeing her.

The doe, she thought, might have a fawn hidden in the plum thickets toward which it had been moving; dismounting quickly, she walked perhaps fifty yards through the woods, her eyes searching the shrubbery ahead. This, she knew, was the site of the old Gilpin settlement, now thickly grown up in plum and myrtle; she remembered that one of the cabins was still standing; she could not see it, but she knew that it was directly ahead of her beyond the dense plum growth.

She was about to abandon her search for the deer when her eyes caught a spot of brown in the green of the plum foliage. Sure that she had found the doe, she moved forward again, careful to make no sound. The brown spot she discovered presently with amazement, was the flank of Santee, Ash's horse.

The horse was tethered within the farther edge of the plum thicket. Just beyond it and to the left stood the abandoned Gilpin cabin. Evidently, Ash was in the cabin. But why? Why was Santee hidden amid the plums? Diane had a sudden and swift conviction that something was wrong, that something had happened to Ash.

She moved quickly and noiselessly amid the plum bushes and across the small opening toward the tumbledown house. One of the two windows had been closed with rough planks, but the rotting shutter of the other stood open. Diane peered through this window into the dim room.

Again on Roan Mary, she did not at first realize that Mazÿck Marion was riding beside her. Whence or how he had come concerned her no more than, the blood dripping from her hand. She had gashed it deeply on a thorn as she fled through the plum thicket away from the Gilpin cabin; the sudden sharp pain had brought a cry to her lips, but she had choked back the cry. Ash mustn't know that she had been there, mustn't know that she knew.

That, during those first moments of her flight, was the only thought of which she was capable: Ash mustn't know that she knew. She was riding furiously, much faster than was safe, for the narrow woods-road was deep in grass and weeds. Marion had dropped back; the road, winding through a dense growth of young pines, was too narrow for two to ride abreast. She knew, however, that he was just behind her; above the rush of the wind she could hear the pounding of his horse's hoofs.

But was it Mazÿck? Could it be Ash? He might have seen her as she peered through the window into the cabin. Frozen with horror at the thought, she threw a swift terrified glance over her shoulder. It was Marion. She saw rather than heard him shout to her. Roan Mary stumbled in high grass and Diane swerved dangerously in her saddle. She recovered herself instantly, and, heedless of the evident danger, raced on.

She had no realization of what she was doing. It was as though a nightmare had her: thoughts half formed, visions inchoate and grotesque whirled and danced in her brain.

Why was Mazÿck here? Why was he pursuing her? It didn't matter; nothing mattered except the thing she had seen, the danger that Ash might discover that she knew.

She had a feeling that she was not moving, that the ground was slipping backward under Roan Mary's hurrying hoofs, that she was being carried back to the Gilpin cabin. There was a horrible thing in the cabin—a horrible unimaginable thing. Her mind was full of a sense of yellow. The thing in the Gilpin cabin was yellow; it assumed shape, a definite, a familiar form.

As she had peered through the window that form had come out of a shadowed corner of the cabin; an amber, almost a golden, woman, golden all over, moving slowly with a gliding rhythmic motion through the dim light of the little room.

A cry broke from her. Ash was there also in the Gilpin cabin. Ash! Ash! Ash who had sung for little Thomas, Ash whom Amy Anne had called the nicest man in the world. Ash had swung Amy Anne in his arms and kissed her. He had kissed Amy Anne! A thousand times he had kissed her, Diane. His lips against hers. Swiftly she drew her hands across her lips as though to wipe something from them. A stain—a yellow stain. She heard louder, nearer, the hoof beats of Mazÿck Marion's horse. The road was wider now; Marion was drawing slowly abreast of her. She realized dully that he was shouting to her.

The horses were racing neck and neck. Marion's was the faster; he was drawing slowly ahead and he was crowding her to the side of the road. She tried to ride into him, to force him out of the way, but the bulk of his powerful bay thoroughbred blocked Roan Mary. Suddenly, Marion had the mare by the bridle close to the bit. Roan Mary reared, but with his weight on the bridle he pulled her down. Gradually she came to a halt and stood trembling.

Diane, her hands on the horn of her saddle, sat staring at Mazÿck Marion. He was frowning, his dark, somewhat bony face was flushed. He did not say anything but took his handkerchief from his pocket and, leaning from his saddle, placed his hand gently upon her wrist. He drew it toward him and wrapped his handkerchief around her bleeding hand.

"You shouldn't have ridden like that," he told her. "You might have killed yourself."

She did not answer or give any sign that she had heard him. He sat his horse in silence for a few moments, frowning, biting his lip.

"Diane," he said finally, "I want you to come with me."

They rode on slowly side by side, neither of them speaking, and presently she realized that they were entering the Notteley yard. At the front steps, where a negro boy took charge of the horses, Marion dismounted and held out his hand to help her alight. They walked together up the stairs and into the hail. Marcus, the butler, appeared and Marion said to him: Marcus, please tell Mrs. Rowland that I should like to speak to her in the library."

In the library he nodded toward the sofa in front of the wide fireplace.

"You had better sit down," he suggested.

She obeyed mechanically. Marion remained standing in front of her, looking down at her, frowning, his lips twitching.

"This is hard," he began, "but there's nothing I can—Diane, I hope to God I'm doing the right thing."

He heard Mrs. Rowland enter the room and he turned.

"There is something," he said to her slowly, "that I will have to tell you. I'd rather have my tongue cut out, but I have to tell you because Diane needs you. Nobody is hurt or ill;

it isn't anything like that. I happened to be riding through Gilpin's when I saw a girl come out of the woods and go into the deserted cabin there. I recognized her—a quadroon wench named Vienna who works in the Avalon yard. In a moment Ash rode out of the woods on the other side, left his horse in the plum thicket and went into the cabin. I was leaving the place when I saw Diane. She had seen Ash's horse, I think, and was looking for Ash. She ran to the cabin and looked through one of the windows."

He had been watching Mrs. Rowland's face narrowly as he spoke, and what he saw there seemed to reassure him.

"You see," he continued, "it isn't anything very bad, but she"—he nodded toward Diane—"naturally, she needs your help. I hope I've done right in telling you like this. It wasn't easy, but it seemed the best thing to do."

Mrs. Rowland said quietly: "Thank you, Mazÿck. It was exactly the right thing."

Mazÿck Marion bowed gravely and left the room.

Alone with Diane, Mrs. Rowland remained for an interval standing exactly as Marion had left her, facing the door, her hands loosely clasped in front of her. Gradually the grip of her hands tightened until the interlaced fingers became bloodless and white. After a moment she turned, walked to the sofa and seated herself there.

Diane, at the other end of the sofa, had not moved. She was pale; her lips were parted slightly; her eyes, unnaturally large and bright, were fixed upon her mother's face. Mrs. Rowland was looking straight in front of her. Her voice was low, even, perfectly controlled.

"About twenty years ago," she said, "it must have been about 1837 or '38, I think, there was a meeting in Columbia of the Society for the Advancement of Learning in South Carolina. Your father was a member, he had just been elected, and we went up from the Combahee, so that he could attend the meeting. There were speeches and papers and the most important was by Chancellor Harper, one of our ablest and best men, on the subject of slavery. It was a very complete answer to the arguments of the abolitionists of that time and it made a great impression all over the South. Later it was printed and I read it and there was one part of it that I have never forgotten. Chancellor Harper said that the great purity of southern women of education and family was partly a result of slavery which provided an outlet for the passions which all men have and which some of them are unable to control."

She paused. She did not look at Diane. Her face, under her white lace cap, appeared very small, her hands, folded in her lap, were motionless. Diane watched her with bewildered eyes. She was conscious still of that hateful sense of yellow. It was a nausea permeating her whole consciousness, sickening her with a worse than physical sickness. Yet her thoughts were clear enough now to permit an increasing wonder at her mother's calmness, the irrelevancy of what she had been saying. A meeting in Columbia...Purity of women. Diane had a despairing conviction that her mother didn't understand what had happened, that she would have to tell her, describe what she had seen in the Gilpin cabin.

She couldn't do that. Outside in the hall she heard Sally calling for Daphne, her maid. Suppose Sally came in; what should she do? Sally mustn't know—Sally couldn't stand this. Ash stained—in this way. A yellow woman—a negro! Suddenly she saw it again with searing vividness. The woman's golden body had been lithe as a snake's. It had swayed, moved rhythmically, as if keeping time to barbaric music. In the profound silence the "tock—tock—tock" of the big clock in the hall became an endless reiteration of hammerstrokes in Diane's brain. She heard Daphne's voice, then Sally's giving the maid instructions; something about the curtains in Sally's room. Presently they went up-stairs together. Mrs. Rowland was speaking again in her low tranquil voice.

"What Chancellor Harper said shocked me. It seemed a hateful, degrading thing and I did not believe it. But I knew he was a man honored and respected throughout the South and a very able man, and when I thought carefully about what he had said I saw the truth that was in it. There is something very fine here in the South, a womanhood that has surely never been surpassed anywhere in the world; and there is another thing here that is ugly and terrible—this thing that Ash has done. I don't mean Ash alone, of course. I mean the many men like him who have lived here in the South and made it what it is and made us what we are. For it is our men that have made us—generations of our men—and now the Carolinian woman is famous the world over. It was a brave thing, Dee, that Chancellor Harper did when he said this was partly because of the conditions created by slavery—because there were always these other women, these women who could be had for the asking, like this girl that Ash met in the Gilpin cabin."

There was an interval of silence, broken only by the "tock—tock—tock" of the clock, a musical tinkle of glass as the prisms of the great chandelier in the hall moved in the breeze blowing through the open front door. Mrs. Rowland's hands, thin and blue-veined, moved restlessly in her lap. Her small slight form, enveloped in her voluminous black skirt and withdrawn into a corner of the sofa, seemed no larger than a child's; her face, as white as her lace cap, was pinched and small. Diane, at the end of the sofa, was motionless. There was no visible sign of her breathing; her eyes were wide, dark ovals in a totally colorless face. She heard her mother's voice again.

"You see I have thought about all this a great deal because I knew that some day I might have to face what has happened now. I've thought it out to the end and I am ready for it. I'm not defending anything or arguing anything—rights or wrongs or morals; I'm simply dealing with things as they are. Dee, our Notteley magnolias have grown out of black muck. You have just seen the muck. I'm not asking you to forget it, but I want to remind you of the white magnolia bloom. Because I think it is important, and because what Ash has done is a part of it all.

"We have to speak of facts, Dee. Our men aren't different from other men; life is strong in them too when they are young.

But our men have drawn a line and they have put us on one side of that line and there is no other country in the world where that line is crossed so seldom. That is a great thing, Dee, however it has come about. I think we have made a tradition here—that there will be a southern conception of what the word lady means, that will be a strength for generations. I oughtn't to say that we have done this, or that our men have done it: that is, I oughtn't to say that they have done it consciously and deliberately. It has simply happened; it has been the result, the absolutely natural result, of the conditions the South has lived under. It has cost us heavily—a heavy price. But at least, when we count the cost, we must not forget the gain; and when we have to pay the price, as you and I are paying it now when we think of Ash, we can remember...

She stopped abruptly. Her face, Diane realized suddenly, was that of a woman in agony. When she spoke again, her voice was shaking.

"I am sorry about Ash," she said. "I hoped he would be one of those who never stoop..."

Her words trailed off; she was silent for some moments, her hands moving in her lap. Suddenly she turned, looking at Diane for the first time.

"Diane," she said, her voice louder, almost defiant, "you mustn't blame our men. There are no better men anywhere. They have had a great responsibility and a great temptation and they haven't much to be ashamed of here in South Carolina. They have been strong men and they have done great things and they have done more here on these plantations for the negro race than all the missionaries sent to Africa by the churches of the North. But our men are only men. Even the saintly abolitionists of Massachusetts are only men, and if they were here instead of our selves, masters of thousands of women of another race, not only willing but nearly always eager, the results would not be different."

Mrs. Rowland rose quickly and, taking Diane's hands in hers, drew her to her feet.

"My throat's dry," she said. "I've preached a sermon, one that's not in the book." She paused, looking steadily into Diane's eyes.

"I'm not worried about you, Dee," she continued. "Women who are desired by men and are glad that they are desired understand more than the others." She smiled. "I suppose," she added, "that's a shocking thing for a Carolinian woman to say; an old Carolinian lady of one of the best families; a Chantilly." Mrs. Rowland stood silent for a moment, still holding Diane's hands.

"Diane," she said, "I am going to tell you something that I have never told you or any one before. There is a portrait in Rome of your great-great-aunt, Susanne Chantilly, the Countess Falatresi, and you are so like her that you might have sat for the portrait. That used to frighten me, but I think I am glad of it now. It's one reason why I know you will understand about Ash."

She moved with Diane, her hand on the girl's arm, toward the door leading to the hall. "You had better go up to your room and rest for a while," she said. "This hasn't been easy."

In the hall, at the foot of the steps, she stopped.

"There one thing more," she added. "When Ash kisses me this evening, my lips won't shrink from his. He is my dear son. I love him."

Sally had come once to the door of her room to ask why at that hour she was lying down, and Amy Anne had come once, complaining that she had nothing to do and would Aunt Dee come out and play croquet? Stretched on her bed, and still in her riding habit, she had had, except for these two interruptions, the whole late afternoon. She hadn't closed her eyes, she hadn't moved. Ash...Vienna...Richard Acton... Mazÿck Marion...herself. Herself and the Countess Susanne! When she had been lying thus for nearly two hours, she heard through the open window the voice of Amy Anne calling excitedly to Thomas: "Here he comes now. Hurry! Hurry!" She got up and walked to the window.

Ash was riding through the gate under the big magnolias. Amy Anne and Thomas were racing toward him, screaming with excitement. He waved his hand to them and halted, lounging in his saddle. She could see him laughing. "Run, you rascals," Diane heard him call to them. "The one that gets here first can ride in front."

Amy Anne won the race. Leaning far over, Ash lifted her and placed her on the pommel of his saddle. The negro yard boy, who had shut the gate, lifted Thomas to the horse's back behind Ash. "Hold tight, young sprout," she heard Ash tell him, "I'm going to make Santee fly."

To the accompaniment of screams of delight, the horse, began to move; one of Ash's arms was around Amy Anne; the other, flung behind him, reenforced the grip of arms. The pace increased to a trot; the screams of delight grew louder. Diane realized suddenly that Sally was standing beside her, looking out of the window.

"When Ash marries," Sally said reflectively, "I hope he'll have a dozen children. He'll be completely happy with all of them crawling over him." She paused, then added:

"He's an attractive young divvle, Dee, especially when he laughs. Aren't you glad you're so like him?"

Diane didn't answer.

Chapter XI

Mazÿck Marion, sitting midway of the long table, pushed back his chair and arose. The place was the dining-room at Notteley, the occasion one of the informal dinner-parties at which Sinkler Rowland, several times each season, entertained a selected circle of friends. The afternoon was now far advanced; the oil portraits on the cypress-paneled walls, adorned with mounted deer heads and polished antlers, were vagueley visible in the pale light entering through the tall recessed windows; the table, lengthened for the accommodation of some twenty gentlemen, had been cleared by two negro butlers of most evidences of the feast.

There remained, under a central bank of tall silver candlesticks running the length of the table, dishes of nuts and cakes and decanters of old Leacock Madeira and pale sherry. The dinner had been evidently a wholly masculine affair; the drinking had been in only one instance obviously excessive; the talk, ranging from the rice crop and the approaching tournament at Pineland to a recent attack in *Blackwood's* upon Lord Macauley, had been mainly political. Politics, the acute issue dividing North and South, was nearly always the principal theme at Sinkler's dinners. On this occasion it had absorbed the conversation to an even greater extent than usual due to the unexpected presence of Charles Gough and former Senator Barnwell Rhett of Charleston, the secessionist leader.

Gough had arrived in the forenoon, coming straight from Montgomery where James Hail was still detained; and Mr. Rhett, enjoying a week's rest at a neighboring plantation, had driven over to pay his respects to Mrs. Rowland, an old friend, and, finding the dinner about to begin, had accepted Sinkler's pressing invitation to join the party. He was the oldest and was accounted the most distinguished man present and he sat at the head of the long table, facing Sinkler Rowland. At his right had been placed Gilmore Simms, the novelist, a close friend of Sinkler's, who had come up from Charleston for the affair. Opposite Simms was Wade Hampton of Millwood, broad-shouldered and blond-bearded, reputed the best horseman in the South and one of the wealthiest planters in America. The other guests, with the exception of Doctor Roupell of Pineland, were planters of the neighborhood, men of about Sinkler's age or younger: Motte Nesbit of Wisboo, Stuart Chantilly of Montauban, Ralph Cain of Somerset, Huger Simons, Peter Delamott, Louis Treves and a number of others.

Mazÿck Marion's straight form, erect and expectant at his place midway of the table, commanded an immediate and surprised attention. "Silence, gentlemen!" Louis Treves rapped loudly with his nutcracker. "The gift of tongues has descended upon Mazÿck. An impressive proof of the virtue of old Leacock Madeira. Our usually taciturn neighbor is about to give birth to an oration. Fire away, Mazÿck."

Marion, in the ensuing silence, produced a folded paper from his pocket. "Gentlemen," he said, "Louis is right. I freely make my acknowledgments to the celebrated Mr. Leacock. He has given me courage to address you in this distinguished presence;" he inclined his head toward Barnwell Rhett. "But it isn't Sinkler's wine so much as Sinkler himself that moves me. We've heard him, and Wade Hampton too, counseling moderation. Gentlemen, I tell you there is no moderation, the time for moderation is past. Mr. Rhett has said that we must expect from the North continued and increasing aggression. It is worse than that, gentlemen; it is aggression accompanied by insolence and insult. I have here two articles clipped from newspapers; they were sent to me by a friend in New York, a southerner, as examples of Yankee courtesy and justice. I want to read them to you for your edification. The first, it is short and sweet, is from the *New York Independent* and it runs as follows:

"'The mass of the population of the Atlantic coast of the slave region of the South are descended from the transported convicts and outcasts of Great Britain. Oh, glorious chivalry and hereditary aristocracy of the South! Peerless first families of Virginia and Carolina! Progeny of the highwaymen and horse-thieves and sheep-stealers and pick pockets of Old England!'"

He paused, glancing from one to another of his auditors. "The question is, fellow-convicts," Louis Treves said, "which of us are the horse-thieves and which are the sheep-stealers. Now you, Mazÿck, from a certain sinister cast of your countenance..."

Sinkler Rowland interrupted him. "I don't believe," he said, "that that kind of venom represents the North, Mazÿck. I have friends there, northern men—we all have—who would be as much outraged by it as we are. The better class..."

He was himself cut short by Marion. "Sinkler, unfortunately you're wrong. Fatally wrong, and that's exactly what I'm getting at. The better class, as you call them, are our worst enemies. The most bitter and the most dangerous. I'll prove it to you in a minute. You remember the excitement over the North when Preston Brooks of Edgefield caned Charles Sumner of Massachusetts in the Senate Chamber—the mass meetings, the resolutions, the lies with which the northern papers were filled: lies which we knew were lies because we knew Preston Brooks. The provocation was ignored altogether: the merited punishment of a larger man by a smaller was pictured as a brutal and cowardly assault by a burly bully. In the general excitement so many things were said that I, for one, missed the choice bit that I am about to read to you. If you're already familiar with it, it won't do you any harm to hear it again, and I confess it was new to me until my friend sent me these clippings. There was a mass meeting in a certain New England town—I won't name the town just yet—and at this meeting one of the speakers said:

"'The events of the last few years and months and days have taught us the lesson of centuries. I do not see how a barbarous community'—mark the word barbarous—'and civilized community can constitute one State. I think we must get rid of slavery or get rid of freedom. Life has not parity of value'—please note that, gentlemen—'in the free state and in the slave state. In one it is adorned with education, with skilful labor, with arts, with long prospective interests, with sacred family ties, with honor and justice. In the other, life is a fever; man is animal'—an *animal*, gentlemen—'given to pleasure, frivolous, irritable, spending his days in hunting and practicing with deadly weapons to defend himself against his slaves and against his companions brought up in the same idle and dangerous way. Such people live for the moment, they have properly no future, and readily risk on every passion a life which is of small value to themselves or to others...Life and life are incommensurate. The whole State of South Carolina does not now offer one or any number of persons who are to be weighed for a moment in the scale with such a person as the meanest of them all has now struck down.'" Marion placed the paper on the table and addressed the company:

"That charming description, gentlemen, so profound, so reasonable and so accurate—a description of South Carolina, please observe—is not the work of some nameless abolitionist blatherskite or some foreign immigrant whose ignorance might excuse him. The meeting at which these gentle words were spoken took place at Concord, Massachusetts: and the man who uttered them was one who surely must be considered as belonging to what Sinkler calls the better class of the North: a man, in fact, whom the North magnifies as the greatest intellect, the greatest seeker after truth—truth, mind you, gentlemen—that this age has produced: Ralph Waldo Emerson."

A momentary silence followed. Charles Gough, in the act of lighting a cigar, glanced quickly at Barnwell Rhett. Rhett's blue-gray eyes were smoldering, his full-blooded face was flushed, his firm lips above his trimmed white beard were tightly compressed. There was a noise of a chair being pushed violently back and Peter Delamott was on his feet. His scarf was somewhat awry, his black eyes were blazing. "By God, gentlemen!" he shouted, "the damned, infernal—how long are we going to stand it, gentlemen? How long are we going to sit here and be called ruffians and barbarians and animals..."

Motte Nesbit's hand on Delamott's arm checked him. "Careful, Peter," Nesbit said. "There are ladies in the house."

Delamott glared furiously down at him, and Sinkler Rowland said quickly: "Peter, I feel—we all feel—just as you do. But you're out of order, old fellow. Mazÿck's broadside was fired at me. Because he thinks I'm too moderate. With your permission—"

Delamott hesitated, then bowed with an exaggerated gravity and resumed his seat. Sinkler continued:

"Mazÿck, you're becoming an orator. That was well done. Especially your point about the seeker after truth. If Mr. Emerson's knowledge of philosophy is on a par with his knowledge of South Carolina and its people..." He shrugged his shoulders and spread his hands.

"Of course," he continued, "that's the hopeless part of the whole business. The number of intelligent men in the North who really believe that we are monsters, fire-breathing desperadoes, working our negroes to death in the fields and beating them to death with whips and all the other 'Uncle Tom' nonsense. They form their whole conception from a few exceptional cases and they never consider their own factory workers ground down by tyranny and poverty and left to starve when they are too old to work. I can't explain the New England writers like Emerson, Lowell, Channing and the rest. I can understand their devotion to an idea, but I can't understand their blindness to facts. I can't understand their blindness to the cardinal fact of all—that no people in the world until the millennium arrives can be expected to ruin themselves for the sake of an abstraction in which they don't believe—which, in fact, they know to be false.

"All the same, Mazÿck, I stick to my contention. There is, there must be, a great mass of the better people of the North who know that these abolitionist lies are absurd. They must see our situation here in the South—that even if we wanted to abolish slavery, we can't do it now unless we are willing to commit suicide. In spite of Mr. Emerson, I count on their common sense. I rely on it not to preserve the Union—that's no longer possible or desirable—but to prevent war when the Union is dissolved.

"Confound it, Mazÿck, it's only when I hear you hot heads ranting that I preach moderation. I'm for secession. If a Black Republican is elected president next year, I think the South should secede at once. I'm as much for it in that case as Mr. Rhett is or Charles or yourself. But I don't think—and I know Wade Hampton agrees with me—I don't think we ought to act before then and I don't think we ought to act alone. We ought to be sure that the others are going out with us when we go out. And I think that all our acts, the acts and words of southern public men, ought to be moderate and reasonable, so that when the South does go out of the Union, the reasonable people of the North will refuse to be driven 'by their fanatics into making war on us."

"Sinkler," Stuart Chantilly was speaking, with one more glass of wine I'd call you an old woman. You're a secessionist, but, leave it to you and there'd be no secession. It's plain that if South Carolina doesn't take the lead, nobody else will. Secession's the South's only hope, you admit, but you don't want South Carolina to run the risk of starting it. And meanwhile we must swallow all kinds of insults and put up with all kinds of interference to keep the North from getting mad with us. Damned if you aren't the first Chantilly to preach that kind of submissionist doctrine.

"Well I'm with Peter and Mr. Rhett and Charles and Mazÿck and all the rest of us. I've had enough: enough insults and enough meddling and enough abolition and enough Yankee tariff. Goddamn it, man, for thirty years the North's been goading us into war, and I'm in favor of accommodating the self-made sons of what-d'you-call-its. I'm in favor of secession now and I'm in favor of South Carolina starting the ball rolling. That's where I want to see her; out in front, showing the others the way. If that means war, we needn't worry. We can take care of ourselves against the North and Europe's bound to be with us because it has to have our cotton. That's an old argument, of course, but it's sound; it's the reason we can't lose. Sinkler, you're a great fellow and your Madeira's wonderful. I'm proud to be your cousin. I know you're for secession, but your kind of secession is too damned slow for me."

Stuart Chantilly smiled, waving his cigar. The smile and the gesture conveyed his entire good humor. He addressed Barnwell Rhett: "I beg your pardon, sir, for my unparliamentary language. I had forgotten that you don't approve of swearing... What do you think of it, Charles?" he appealed to Charles Gough across the table. "Haven't I read old Sinkler's title clear?"

Gough nodded. "What Sinkler doesn't take into account," he said, "is the impossibility of getting the South to act completely as a unit. That's Senator Hammond's policy, of course—complete cooperation in advance—and he's made no progress with it. We're too much divided on minor questions, like the reopening of the slave trade, for instance. But what James Hail and I learned in Montgomery has been mainly encouraging. Encouraging, that is, to the belief that if South Carolina will take the lead in actual withdrawal from the Union, the others will follow. I think even Sinkler would be satisfied with the assurances we received."

Charles Gough paused, leaning back in his chair and tapping with his fingers on the table.

"There is a matter, gentlemen," he said, "that I think I ought to put before you. It concerns an individual whom you will soon have as a neighbor here on the river. It is personal, dangerously personal. I'll ask that you'll consider it as confidential."

There was an immediate focussing of attention upon Charles Gough.

Diane—the servants being occupied in other ways—had come softly down the stairs into the front hall and had entered the library, intending to light the lamps there. On the occasions when the dining-room was given to the wholly masculine gatherings over which Sinkler presided there was always a discreet absence of the female members of the household from the neighboring rooms. This was considered one of the merits of Sinkler's dinner-parties; it was possible to express one's self freely and, within reason, as emphatically as one wished without fear of offending feminine sensibilities in the vicinity. The door of the library stood diagonally across the hall from the open door of the dining-room, and Diane had intended to remain in the library no longer than the minute or two required for the lighting of the lamps.

She stopped just within the library door—in the dimming light the farther corners of the large room were already vague with shadow—and stood motionless, her muscles suddenly rigid. What was being said in the dining-room came to her with complete distinctness. It was Charles Gough's voice.

"Of course," he said, "I would not have made these statements about Mr. Richard Acton upon mere rumor. I am prepared to vouch for their correctness and if I have misrepresented him in any way I shall be ready to admit my responsibility. I've said what I have said because I think you gentlemen of this parish are entitled to know it when an abolitionist comes to live among you. Having said this, I think I ought to say more.

"It was generally understood, from certain utterances of his here last fall prior to his meeting with James Hail, that he was not in sympathy with the movement for secession. That in itself need not concern us; there are unfortunately more than a few of whom the same thing can be said. But the matter does not stop there. My information as to his activities came to me very directly in Montgomery; I am not at liberty to reveal the source, but I can assure you that it is completely trustworthy. The facts are, gentlemen, that Richard Acton is not only in favor of emancipation of the negroes but that he has been for weeks and months in constant communication with some of the principal leaders of the Black Republican party, including Philips Cordray of Boston and various others of the most radical abolitionist agitators of the North."

Gough ceased speaking. Diane's hands were clenched at her sides. She was conscious again of a difficulty in breathing. The shadows in the library became enormous; she had a sudden feeling that they were advancing upon her, surrounding her. She heard Charles Gough's voice continuing:

"These men with whom Richard Acton has been communicating are our enemies, they are our avowed and bitter enemies, they are among the most dangerous of those who are assailing and undermining the institutions and the prosperity of the South. Mr. Richard Acton is entitled to his opinions; but when one among us, himself an avowed abolitionist, is discovered to be in active communication with the enemies of our country, I feel that, within the confidence of this circle at any rate, the fact should be made known. I feel…"

The sound of Gough's voice was suddenly cut off and simultaneously the light in the hall behind Diane grew dim. Some one had come out of the dining-room and had closed the door behind him. Diane heard footsteps in the hall and instinctively she moved into the deeper shadow. A figure—in the dim light she did not immediately recognize Sinkler—appeared at the door of the library. Sinkler Rowland stood there for a moment looking into the dark room; then he returned to his guests.

Sinkler Rowland's dinner-parties, beginning in the afternoons, were generally over before dark, but on this occasion the discussion in the dining-room had continued beyond that hour. It was nearly nine o'clock—there had been a long and passionate speech by Gilmore Simms, a brief and dispassionate reply by Wade Hampton—when Stuart Chantilly rapped loudly on the table.

"With your permission, Sinkler," he said, I'm going to make a suggestion. We've all talked a great deal, and the distinguished statesman who is with us has contributed to our discussion. It would be, I think, an appropriate conclusion of an interesting evening if he would now at greater length set forth his views. Gentlemen, I give you the name of the Honorable Robert Barnwell Rhett, the most fearless and the most consistent Carolinian since Calhoun."

Rhett rose. He stood silent for a moment, his tall slight form erect, his blue-gray eyes moving quickly from one to another of the company, his small and beautifully formed hand caressing his close-cropped gray beard.

"Gentlemen," he said in a high clear voice, "the hour grows late; I shall be brief. The sectional majority of the North grows stronger every day. It is my judgment, as you know, that only by exercising its undoubted right, of withdrawal from the Union can the South avert the terrible dangers which now menace it. To remain within that Union, dominated as it will be henceforward by the populous states of the North, will make us mere tributaries, vassals, of an alien and antagonistic power whose interests are wholly different from ours. The impoverishment of the South by increased tariffs is only one of the perils that confront us. The very principle of liberty is at stake—a people's right to self-government, to self-preservation.

"We are contending for that right, gentlemen, and for the Constitution of our fathers. We do not admit that, at the whim of the North and to further the sectional interests of the North, a so-called higher law may be substituted for the Constitution and the whole nature and structure of the Union be changed for the advantage of one section and the ruin of another. We hold the solemn covenant of the Constitution—that Constitution which the abolitionists of the North have denounced as a 'covenant with death and an agreement with hell'—to be the highest law of all, and for ourselves we are resolved to preserve it.

"That is our ground and we shall stand firmly on it. Out watchword is still that of the great Calhoun: 'Justice Plighted Faith...the Constitution.' It is the question of the negro that now compels our action. The radical element in the North, controlling the Republican party, are determined to force upon us their solution of that question. It is a solution, gentlemen, which would bring with it not only financial ruin to the South but also that which the people of the South will never consent to suffer—social and political equality for the negro race.

"Therefore, my friends, I am for secession. Since there is no longer justice or safety for us within the Union which our forefathers helped to form; since we are no longer to be allowed to govern ourselves in our own way and to deal with our own problems as we think best; since the most sacred guarantees of the Constitution are to be violated as the North has already violated them again and again; since we are faced with the hard alternative of accepting the unjust and ruinous rule of a mad fanaticism persistently and wilfully ignorant of the people and the peculiar problems of the South; since not only grievous injury but reiterated insult is to be our portion and we are to be treated as a criminal people glorying in crime—since this is the prospect that confronts us within the Union, I say there is no choice for us but to leave that Union and form for ourselves a Confederacy of the South wherein, free from northern tariffs and northern tyranny, we may strike out our destiny.

"In that glorious consummation I hope that my own beloved South Carolina, so long the leader of the South, may have the leading and the chief part. She must lead if that great end is to be achieved and she must not too long postpone her action. I have served South Carolina, gentlemen, in the House and the Senate of the United States at fourteen sessions of Congress. Should the public regard, after I am gone, ever dwell upon my humble services, let it be remembered that, after twenty years of earnest effort to preserve the Union by arresting its fatal tendency to despotism, I turned at last to the salvation of my native land, the South, and did all that I could to dissolve her connection with the North and to establish for her a Southern Confederacy. And if this be considered treason, I have only to say what I have said before: I am born of Traitors; Traitors in England in the revolution in the middle of the seventeenth century, Traitors again in the revolution of 1720 and Traitors in the Revolution of 1776. I have been born of Traitors, but, thank God, they have ever been Traitors in the great cause of liberty, fighting against tyranny and oppression."

Barnwell Rhett bowed. He remained standing in a silence that continued for some moments unbroken. Mazÿck Marion's black eyes were shining; Stuart Chantilly's lips were quivering; Huger

Simons, leaning forward over the table, exclaimed, "Amen to that!" Peter Delamott was struggling to rise. He accomplished this with difficulty and stood precariously balanced, gazing at Barnwell Rhett, his glass lifted and tilting perilously. His lips moved, but no sound came from them; he proceeded, with great violence of gesticulation, to deliver an impassioned but wholly inaudible address. In the midst of it, undone by the momentum of an eloquent gesture, he was unable to regain his equilibrium; supported by Motte Nesbit, who sat next to him, he collapsed limply into his chair. Then, with profound and injured amazement stamped upon his face, he slid slowly out of sight under the table.

Chapter XII

Diane heard the clear call of a bugle—a slim bright sword of sound gleaming through the blue loveliness of the May morning. It came out of the woods at the northern end of the arena and flashed on above the open grassy expanse of the Pineland muster-ground to the gaily decorated grandstands built along the eastern side of the field.

The two grandstands, long open structures sheltering successive tiers of seats and adorned with banners and pennons, were crowded to their capacity. The Pineland tournament, an annual event, had been planned this year upon an even more elaborate scale than usual, and visitors had come not only from the plantations of the neighboring Low-Country parishes but from Charleston and the Middle Country. The Rowland party, arriving early, had found places near one of the aisles, and they had been joined immediately by Margaret Drayton and Louis Treves.

Louis was seated at Diane's left and Margaret Drayton at her right. In front of her, in the next tier of seats, Sally sat between

Charles Gough and Calvin Hemmerton and, next to Hemmerton, Mrs. Rowland and Sinkler. There had been an hour of pleasant talk with the Nesbits of Wisboo, the Cranefield St. Juliens and the McPhersons of Tranquil Vale on the tier above them; but now all eyes were fixed upon the woods at the northern end of the forty-acre arena whence the bugle call had sounded. There the road from Pineland entered the muster-ground; and the bugle call meant that the riders were coming.

In a moment Diane saw them. A spot of bright red appeared just within the fringe of the pine-wood at the upper end of the field; it resolved itself at once into four men dressed in scarlet jackets and riding knee to knee. Margaret Drayton exclaimed:

"There they come; the heralds and trumpeters. Buist Pringle and FitzSimons Bull and…" Her words were lost in an increasing babel of talk rising from the crowded tiers of the stands. Clear of the woods, the red-coated riders wheeled their horses and rode, two to the right and two to the left, some fifty yards along the woods-edge. They halted and faced toward the grandstands; two of them lifted bugles to their lips and blew in unison an exultant fanfaronnade.

Midway between them, where the road emerged from the forest, a horseman in black and gold appeared. He was mounted upon a magnificent white stallion; a plume of white heron feathers adorned his black velvet hat; in his right hand he carried a gilt baton.

"The King-at-Arms," Louis Treves announced in a loud sing-song; "the finest King-at-Arms in history, ladies; none other than our respected neighbor, Colonel Kit Bohun of Lancaster Plantation, hero of Chapultepec, husband of three wives (in succession, ladies) father of fifteen children and prince of two-bottle men." The black and gold horseman rode straight forward some twenty paces, then halted. Behind him, two other horsemen, one in blue, the other in white and silver, rode abreast out of the woods and took station in his rear—the Master of Horse and the Master of the Lists.

There was a brief pause. The King-at-Arms raised his baton. The trumpeters' bugles flashed in the sun. Before the ringing fanfare died away, other horsemen began riding two by two out of the woods. All were mounted on spirited blooded horses and most of them were elaborately dressed in costumes of various designs and hues. They carried long lances held perpendicularly, and, as they deployed in an extended rank behind the Master of Horse and the Master of the Lists, they made a glowing picture of many colors against the dark-green background of the woods.

"There's Ash," Sally said, "on Gray Arab, Margaret. The crimson jacket and white cape; you can't see the gold facing from here. Isn't he beautiful, Mother? If he doesn't win..."

A bugle call cut her short. At the signal the whole company began to move forward across the, field toward the grandstands; the King-at-Arms in front, behind him the Master of Horse and the Master of the Lists, and directly behind these the long rank of the knights, some twenty-seven in all, with the red-jacketed heralds and trumpeters on the flanks.

Charles Gough spoke over his shoulder to Diane sitting in the tier above him.

"Diane, I can't keep the secret any longer. James told me in Montgomery that he was going to do this if he could get away in time. He probably arrived in Pineland last night. You might as well get ready to be crowned Queen of Love and Beauty. Do you recognize the sixth man from the left end of the line?"

She saw at once that it was James Hail. In contrast with the others, he was simply dressed; buff riding breeches and white shirt, with a red sash probably borrowed in Pineland for the occasion. He was, as Charles said, the sixth man from the left end of the approaching rank of horsemen; she recognized the horse that he was riding—a powerful black gelding of Peter Delamott's. Probably he had spent the night with Peter whose home was only two miles from Pineland. He might, the thought flashed through her mind, as easily have ridden out to Notteley from the Rail Road depot; then he would have seen her hours sooner. But he had preferred to surprise her in this way; and, of course, if he won, he would crown her Queen of the tournament.

She did not answer Charles Gough immediately. She was gazing across the field at James Hail. The advancing horsemen were near at hand now. James was looking thin, she perceived, but well. He was holding a tight rein on Delamott's big black; not many men, she realized, could keep that horse under such perfect control. Suddenly she could no longer see James clearly; there was a film of moisture across her eyes; it was almost as though they had filled with tears.

Something, some strange compulsion, caused Diane to turn her head. At the left of the stands, where a fleet of carriages and buggies waited in charge of a swarm of negro coachmen and footmen, a red-wheeled two-seated phaeton was arriving. She recognized the two handsome boys at once. John Acton was driving and Elizabeth was with him on the front seat. Diane saw, with a sudden quickening of her breath, a swift confusion of her senses, that one of the two men on the rear seat of the phaeton was Richard Acton.

Chapter XIII

RICHARD ACTON HAD A FEELING, a swift and fatal conviction, that the world about him was rushing to destruction. The scene at which he was gazing assumed for him a darkly tragical significance; it was—the conception struck him like a blow—the final, the completely conclusive, proof that the South was doomed to perish.

It couldn't possibly survive, he said to himself: that, above all else, was the meaning of the spectacle before him. Knights and Kings-at-Arms and heralds, all the glittering paraphernalia of the age of chivalry, flung against the ruthless realism of the present. An anachronism as fatal as slavery itself. This thought, however, lingered in his mind only an instant. It passed at once, submerged in an excitement that had increased swiftly as the Acton carriage had approached the muster-ground.

He hadn't realized that it would be like this, that the prospect of seeing Diane Rowland would produce so strong an emotional reaction. The Acton party had been delayed in leaving Avalon by an illness which had attacked old Daddy Marony that morning; stopping at Elm Hill to pick up Lowndes Fenwick, they had reached the muster-ground too late to find seats in the crowded grandstands. They had, therefore, remained in their phaeton at the front of the fenced-in space reserved for vehicles and riding horses just to the left of the stands.

Richard Acton sat silent and withdrawn beside Lowndes Fenwick on the rear seat of the open phaeton. He had found himself wondering, as the carriage approached the field, where Diane was. She would be, of course, with the other Rowlands in one of the two grandstands, and his eyes had searched vainly among the hundreds of faces there. From the position which the carriage now occupied at the left of the stands he could see only the ends of the tiers of seats. He saw there a number of people whom he recognized: the Cains of Somerset, Harriott Keating with her mother and father, Eliza Stoney, the Chardons, Hutson Waight of Cypress Hall and his wife, and, in one of the boxes, Barnwell Rhett with a party of elderly ladies and gentlemen. The Rowlands, however, he could not discover; it was evident that they must be in the other grandstand or in the part of this one that he could not see.

He admitted to himself that it was as well that he couldn't see her now; it might not help matters to have her face actually before him during the progress of the tournament. Her beauty, at least, was real—real and formidable. It was, however, inevitable that he should see her, see her probably quite often. He couldn't live at Sherborne, a rice planter on the river, without seeing Diane Rowland from time to time. He would meet her at dances and other entertainments, at church, on deer hunts and fox hunts; and he would undoubtedly continue to see her even after her marriage to James Hail. He had heard that Hail intended, after his marriage, to remove from the Combahee and establish a residence on the river. And the river plantation community was closely knit. Everybody in it knew everybody else; isolation was impossible.

That, however, would come later. What he was facing now was the first shock, the first impact, and, inexplicably, the mere knowledge that she was there in one of the grand stands had excited him.

That, he told himself impatiently, was ridiculous, impossible. She couldn't excite him. A woman so cheap, so tawdry that on the night of her engagement she had left the side of the man whom she was to marry for the hot pleasure of a wanton moment with another man whose eyes had betrayed his passion! That this was the sum of it had, of course, become evident months ago. It had been hard to believe at first, but the facts were unescapable.

She hadn't come to him while he lay wounded—that fact in itself was sufficient. His mind for a time had retained a vision of her bending over him, but this evidently had been a mere phantasm of his delirium so obviously fantastic that he had never spoken of it. She had not written to him during the weeks while he lay critically ill in his brother's house in Charleston; she had not answered the letter he had written to her; she was going to marry James Hail in June. It was plain, nothing could be plainer, that what had happened in the summer-house had been for her merely an episode, and months ago he had accepted it as such. As for himself, his unbelievable innocence, his childish naïve conviction that she had miraculously fallen in love with him—that simply was one of those phenomena in a man's experience with women that couldn't be explained.

No, she couldn't excite him. A Carolinian cocotte who would have been at home in the resorts of the Place Pigal. The trouble with him now was that his nerves weren't yet what they ought to be; he hadn't fully recovered from the long illness that had followed his wound. Lowndes Fenwick and Elizabeth were talking, both at the same moment; the grandstands were mosaics of color, bright bonnets, flowered hoop-skirts and gay parasols glowing in the sun. There was a burst of applause; handkerchiefs fluttered, parasols waved and tossed in an exuberant confusion. With an effort of his will he forced himself to listen to what Elizabeth and Lowndes and John were saying, to realize the spectacle before him.

It was, the thought returned to him at once, a spectacle dark with meaning. But no one else would see it that way; no one else would perceive that all this foretold the end of South Carolina, of the South. The South playing at chivalry in a world that was done with lances and with Launcelots. The horsemen were ranged in a long rank before the grandstands, the King-at-Arms, the Master of Horse and the Master of the Lists in front. The Master of Horse—Richard Acton recognized Ralph Cain in a suit of blue merino faced with gold—spoke a command;

lances were couched and the grand salute was given. Richard admitted to himself the perfection of the illusion, an illusion of Templestowe, a page out of Walter Scott.

At either end of the line of horsemen were a herald and a trumpeter in their scarlet suits; the knights, their lances held high, were richly and beautifully dressed, their horses were gay with elaborately decorated housings. Near the right end of the line he recognized Mazÿck Marion on a beautiful chestnut gelding. Marion wore a blue velvet doublet with cloak of the same material trimmed with gold; his white trousers were confined within polished boots encircled by gold spurs. Stuart Chantilly, next to Marion, wore blue and silver with buff smallclothes and red boots adorned with lace around the knees; the blue and white housings of his spirited bay mare were fringed and tasseled with silver. Heyward Drayton, on a large and powerful roan, was dressed in the uniform of an officer of the Continental Army.

Elizabeth Acton was talking excitedly and continuously. She couldn't, she declared, look at the others because she was so overcome by the splendor of Colonel Kit Bohun, the King-at-Arms. "Cousin Kit's perfect," she exclaimed. "That black velvet sets off his white beard beautifully. He's something out of *Ivanhoe* and if Cousin Rosa made that costume for him she's a genius. The Knight Hospitaller's splendid too," she went on; "I like him better than the Templar. Do you recognize them all, Richard? Ball Moultrie is Master of the Lists and Ralph Cain Master of Horse. The Templar's Peter Delamott. That's young

Ash Rowland in the crimson and gold doublet with the leopard-skin housings. That lovely gray mare of his is pure Arabian. He's supposed to be the Knight of Alhambra and he'll probably win the tournament."

John Acton uttered an exclamation. "I didn't know James Hail was riding," he said. "I heard he was in Montgomery, but that's Hail as large as life in the white shirt and red sash. He's riding that black devil of Delamott's."

John turned and glanced at his brother. "Richard," he began, "of course the duel settled everything. There's no reason why you and Hail..." A bugle blast interrupted him. The King-at-Arms, in front of the long rank of horsemen, raised his gilt baton.

There was a sudden gasp from the grandstands. Directly behind the King-at-Arms, James Hail's black horse, frightened evidently by the bugle call, was standing on its hind legs. Hail was half out of his saddle; there was an evident and imminent danger that the horse would fall over backward. In a moment, however, Hail was firmly in his seat again and the horse, still plunging and rearing, was being brought under control.

A ripple of applause ran along the stands; Hail's handling of the powerful, animal under him was admirable, the unconscious grace of his bearing made the whole performance beautiful. As he wheeled the horse back into the line, a wave of handclapping swept the stands, and James Hail, in the act of patting the animal's black shoulder, bowed in acknowledgment.

The King-at-Arms again raised his baton. The gold chain across the black velvet of his doublet, the silver buckle of his blue satin scarf, the jeweled clasp binding the white heron plumes to his velvet cap flashed in the bright sun.

"Ladies and gentlemen," he cried; "fair daughters and loyal sons of our beloved South Carolina where, we are proud to believe, the spirit of chivalry still flourishes as of old: we are honored by your presence. I shall not weary you now with many words. Around us lies a land consecrated by the blood of heroes. In these woods Francis Marion, the Swamp Fox, rallied his men. From the plantations of these parishes he drew that band of warriors who kept the torch of liberty burning in those dark days when all seemed lost. His battle-fields are all about us. In these lists to-day will ride at least one, a gallant gentleman, who bears his honored name; we ourselves are many of us descendants of those brave and knightly men who fought for liberty under Marion's banner.

"It may be, ladies and gentlemen, that South Carolina ere long must fight for liberty again. Deliberat Roma, perit Saguntum: My friends, the day is near when our brave state, as ever in the van, must call the injured South to action.

"With that necessity in mind, let us keep alive the patriotic ardor of our fathers.. To-day we make use of our muster-ground for a kindred purpose. We go back to an earlier time, to the age of romance in the Old World, and we bring down to our own age and to our own land that spirit of ancient knighthood which we have tried, I think not vainly, to keep burning in our hearts. The world, they tell us, has moved on; the spirit of chivalry, the ideals of knighthood, are dead. They are not dead in South

Carolina; in this, our loved Low-Country, we cherish still those honorable traditions of the past. To-day, my friends, you shall see gallant knights strive in the lists as they strove in the days of Richard Coeur-de-Lion and Bertrand du Guesclin and the Black Prince—not for personal aggrandizement or glory but each for the honor of the fair lady upon whose brow he hopes, if victory shall be his, to place the crown which shall proclaim her Queen of Love and Beauty.

"Whoever the victor shall be, all honor to him. And for ourselves we welcome you to our jousting, and we thank especially those fair ones whom I see among you for deigning to bestow upon us the guerdon of their radiant and enchanting smiles."

He bowed low, sweeping off his plumed hat. Its white aigrettes were no whiter than his squarely trimmed beard sharply outlined against the lustrous black velvet of his coat; the jeweled hilt of a handsome rapier at his side sparkled in the light. A courtly and somewhat portly country gentlemen, rather too broad of beam and rather too ruddy of face, sitting his spirited snow-white stallion as though he had been born in the saddle; a typical Carolinian rice planter of the old Huguenot breed, believing himself just now a belted earl of Richard the Lion-Heart but, for all that, a good rice planter and very much of a man.

Richard Acton remembered Colonel Kit Bohun of Lancaster Plantation on the upper river; he had fought with the Palmetto Regiment in the Mexican War, where South Carolina's record had been second to none, and his wounds had been proof of his courage. Was there, Acton wondered, in all this pageantry something that he who had been away from Carolina so long had failed as yet to grasp? Some quality of the spirit more potent even than the vast forces that the South was rashly challenging? Some strength that could actually defy the tides that were sweeping the earth?

He found himself suddenly half convinced of this, half persuaded that his forebodings had been far-fetched, excessive. He was one of these people, these Carolinians, and he knew them. Whatever else it was, it wasn't mere childish masquerade, this mummery of make-believe knights and Kings-at-Arms riding in make-believe lists. These "knights" would be, if war came, perhaps the finest cavalry in the world. And whatever was wrong with South Carolina, whatever fate befell her, she wasn't decadent; the fact remained, and it was proof enough of her vigor, that for thirty years she had wielded, small as she was, an influence in the Union that no other state could rival. Lowndes Fenwick's voice interrupted his thoughts.

"Colonel Kit's good," Lowndes said, "but, as usual, long-winded. And I think he might have left out the politics." He paused. "Everybody's been expecting Ash Rowland to win," he added, "but we didn't know then that James Hail would be riding. He must have arrived unexpectedly. I've never seen Hail ride, but I've heard he's a good hand and he may beat Ash. Well, we couldn't have a lovelier Queen of Beauty than Diane Rowland."

John nodded, but Elizabeth shook her head. "Lowndes," she declared, "you and John infuriate me. Diane Rowland can do anything and you don't mind. She's like that Chantilly ancestress of hers that everybody knows about, the Countess Susanne Something-or-other who did just about everything. I'm through with Diane and it isn't just because John was in love with her before I married him. I didn't mind her making a fool of Louis Treves; that was to be expected. But this Mazÿck Marion affair is the last straw. If she is crowned Queen of the tournament..."

She left her sentence unfinished, and John turned and winked solemnly at Lowndes. Richard Acton remained silent. He recalled—it was a tradition on the river—the story of the Countess Susanne Falatresi, but he had not until now connected her with Diane Rowland. It was an interesting connection and it helped to explain certain things. And he hadn't until now known about Mazÿck Marion. So there were others besides himself. Suddenly he laughed.

"You can laugh, Richard," Elizabeth said quickly, "but it isn't just that I'm jealous."

"Of course not," he told her. "I didn't mean that at all. I was thinking—I can't explain exactly why it seemed amusing—of the Countess Susanne."

Chapter XIV

THE CEREMONIES IN FRONT OF the grandstands were proceeding; there was an evident and careful attention to punctilious detail; the Master of the Lists, in presenting the rules of the tournament to the judges, rode to the judges' stand bearing the paper on the point of his lance. The judges' stand, in front of the grandstands, was occupied by five gentlemen distinguished by yellow ribbons in their buttonholes; close to it stood a post with a cross-arm like that of a slender gallows. At the direction of the King-at-Arms, the Master of the Lists rode to this post and placed on a hook at the end of the cross-arm a small gilt ring. Resuming his place beside the King-at-Arms, he announced the opening of the tournament.

At the signal the long rank of waiting horsemen reformed in column of fours; under the command of the Master of Horse, they rode to a point some three hundred yards to the left of the grandstands, halted and stood at rest. The Master of the Lists, waiting with the King-at-Arms at the right of the judges' stand, raised his lance. A trumpeter in front of the grandstands blew a blast upon his bugle.

From the crowd of horsemen at the left end of the lists a man in blue rode forward some twenty paces, halted and waited motionless, his lance lifted. In a high clear voice that carried to the farthest tiers of seats a herald proclaimed: "Mr. Mazÿck Marion of Deer Hall. He rides as the Knight of St. Luke's. His motto is '*Animis Opibusque Parati.*'"

The bugle sounded a short call. Mazÿck Marion couched his lance. The grandstands hummed with suppressed excitement. Richard felt Lowndes Fenwick's hand suddenly gripping his knee. "Mazÿck's one of the best," Lowndes said. He won the tournament last year. I wonder..."

Marion's horse had leaped forward; he was racing at increasing speed down the lists. Richard glanced at the gilt ring hanging from the cross-arm. It seemed a tiny thing; it couldn't be as much as an inch and a half in diameter; to transfix it at the speed at which Marion was riding would need a sure eye, a steady hand. There was a burst of clapping from the stands, a confusion of tossing parasols and waving handkerchiefs. Mazÿck Marion, flashing past the post, bore the gilt ring on the end of his lance.

He brought his horse to a stand before the Master of the Lists and extended his lance. The Master of the Lists removed the ring and handed it to a herald, who replaced it on the hook of the cross-arm. Again the bugle sounded; from the company of knights at the farther end of the lists another horseman rode out, halted and waited with upraised lance. The herald in front of the grandstands proclaimed:

"Mr. Peter Delamott of Mattesaw. He rides as a Knight Templar. His motto is '*Nunquam non Paratus.*'"

Peter Delamott, riding at a speed noticeably less headlong than Marion's, missed the ring. He galloped on and took his place with Marion behind the King-at-Arms. Heyward Drayton, in his Continental uniform, announced by the herald as the Knight of '76, also failed. Stuart Chantilly of Montauban, in the character of Knight of the Lone Star, succeeded handsomely. In succession Rutledge Ravenel as a Knight Hospitaller, Huger Simons as the Knight of Berkeley and Frost Parker as the Knight of Chicora, rode vainly. Stephen Dwight as the Knight of Eutaw and Stevens Colcock as Edgar Ravenswood, restraining their high-mettled mounts, achieved better results. Ash Rowland, announced as the Knight of Alhambra and riding his gray Arabian at seemingly reckless speed, bore off the ring amid prolonged applause. His performance, Lowndes Fenwick exclaimed enthusiastically, had been even more dashing than Mazÿck Marion's.

"James Hail," Lowndes added, "can hardly beat that. Especially on a strange mount." At the farther end of the lists a white-shirted rider with a red sash about his waist waited motionless on a great black horse. The herald announced:

"Mr. James Hail of Beaufort. He rides as the Knight of the Liberated South. His motto is 'Constancy.'"

The bugle sounded. At once the black horse was in full career. Richard perceived that James Hail rode with a seeming carelessness that was the perfection of skill; there was no effect of strain, no evident concentration of his faculties upon the small gilt circle ahead of him. An uncontrollable and bitter anger flared suddenly in Richard Acton and with a tight mouth he damned James Hail to hell. Diane's lips would be parted slightly; her eyes would be like stars. He didn't see Hail at all—only Diane. In a dumb futile anguish he heard the storm of applause that proclaimed James Hail's victory.

Thereafter, while the remaining courses were being run, he sat silent and remote beside Lowndes Fenwick on the rear seat of the Acton phaeton watching with unseeing eyes the riders who flashed past beyond the rail bounding the lists. He had been subject for months to these fits of silence; they were believed to be an effect of the long illness following his wound; Lowndes and Elizabeth and John, absorbed in the events of the tournament, talked animatedly with one another, leaving him to his thoughts.

He could not see her, did not know exactly where she was; but he had a sense of her nearness, he could feel her presence. Watching James Hail ride past just now, he had known that her eyes, too, were fixed upon Hail; and suddenly he had hated Hail, hated him because he was going to possess Diane. It was incomprehensible, unbelievable, but it was true: in spite of what she was, what he knew her to be, he wanted her. Day after day, night after night, the thought of her in James Hail's arms would be a fresh, an unendurable agony.

That magic of hers—good God, there was nothing else like it under the sun! It was as potent now, as irresistible, as it had been when it had enthralled him, made a fool of him, in the summer-house. He was filled suddenly with a half sardonic, half exultant wonder at the power of women; only those men who had been destroyed by it really knew love. James Hail didn't know. But he knew and Mazÿck Marion—he remembered suddenly how Marion had looked that night at Notteley. And probably there were others. Yes, certainly there were others. He had heard that she had been recently in New Orleans and had made new conquests there. Who could say how many lovers...? How many kisses, how many embraces, in secret places where the moon was shining and perhaps a mockingbird was singing as that bird had sung beside the summer-house at Notteley?

A mere cheap cocotte like scores that he had known in Paris. Another Jacqueline Fleur, with the great difference that Jacqueline had loved him. Another Countess Susanne Falatresi whose amours had become a legend, masquerading as the type of that high and sensitive womanhood of which Carolina was so proud! And he, Richard Acton, loved her! If this torment of longing, which forgot everything except the magic of her, was love, he loved her. Here, now, at the Pineland tournament, before he had even seen her, the defenses that he had built up against her during the past four months had crumbled. The mere fact of her nearness had done that. What would happen when he saw her?

He had felt fairly sure of himself, sure that when the time came he could deal with her. But now his strength had turned to water. He longed to see her, the thought that he might soon see her made him tremble with an indescribable delight, but he feared the moment too, with a fear that was now utter panic. The Acton party were to spend the afternoon with the Hutson Waights following the tournament, and in the evening, concluding the festivities, there would be a ball at one of the Pineland houses. It was to be at the Bohun house, he remembered. Probably the moment would come then— unless he made some excuse to stay away. A sudden loud blast of a bugle broke through the veil of his abstraction, and Elizabeth, twisting around in her seat, took hold of his arm and shook it.

"Richard," she exclaimed, "you've been dreaming; you've been miles away, in Paris probably. But you've got to see, this. It's the climax: Ash Rowland against James Hail."

He didn't want to see it. Caught up in a wave of bitterness, of angry self-pity, he was about to tell her this when, fortunately, Lowndes interrupted. "The others have all been eliminated, Richard," he explained, "but the judges couldn't decide between Ash and Hail. They're to ride a course against each other. I'm for Ash. Our river against the Combahee."

Richard Acton stirred in his seat, leaning forward to obtain a wider view of the lists. He was for Ash too, he realized. Again that fierce hatred of Hail rose in him: he was, now and forever, for anybody or anything that opposed James Hail. His hand supporting his chin trembled with the intensity of his desire, his hope that James Hail would be beaten.

The other riders, twenty-five in all, were drawn up in line on the farther side of the lists facing the grandstands. Their lances were raised, the rich and varied colors of their costumes, the gay trappings of their restless, high-mettled horses flashed back the sun. At the nearer end of the line was the King-at-Arms; at the farther end, beyond the judges' stand, were the Master of the Lists and the Master of Horse.

Opposite them, the grandstands were in an obvious flutter of excitement; from the crowded tiers of seats, bright with bonnets, parasols and shawls, a continuous clatter of animated talk arose. At the lower end of the lists, three hundred yards away, Ash Rowland and James Hail waited, attended by a herald.

A bugle call sounded in front of the grandstands; a herald beside the trumpeter announced: "Mr. Ash Rowland of Notteley, the Knight of Alhambra. His motto is '*Spes*.'" Ash Rowland rode forward, halted and waited with raised lance.

The grandstands were silent now, breathless. There was a second short bugle blast. Ash Rowland lowered his lance, couched it, carefully, deliberately. "Ash is taking his time," Lowndes Fenwick whispered. "That's good. I was afraid he might be excited. He may..."

Lowndes's sentence ended in the middle, his hand on Richard Acton's knee tightened. Ash's horse had bounded forward. Richard saw that Ash Rowland was riding at the greatest speed of which his mare was capable. This greatly increased the difficulty of taking the ring, but it was, Richard realized, imperative; the speed at which the course was run might well, in so close a contest, be the determining factor in the judges' decision.

The gray Arabian flashed past. Ash Rowland, his white cape streaming in the wind, his crimson doublet open at the throat, was leaning forward in his saddle. Richard had a momentary impression of Ash's face, pale, frowning, tense. There was a burst of clapping from the stands; it died away suddenly, then began again as the spectators realized what had happened.

Ash Rowland had carried off the ring, but, barely caught upon the point of his lance, it had then fallen to the ground beneath his horse's hoofs. This was a partial victory, remarkable enough considering the headlong speed at which Ash had ridden. To surpass it, Hail, riding at the same furious pace, would have to make a perfect tilt.

"He can't do it at that speed," Lowndes Fenwick declared confidently. "I don't believe any man could. Not even this Launcelot from the Combahee. John, I'll lay you two to one on Ash."

The bugle had scarcely sounded when James Hail's horse was in motion. If, as John Acton exclaimed, the mettlesome black had started too soon, the fact apparently did not disconcert his rider; Hail couched his lance with the animal in full stride. Passing the rail in front of the Acton carriage, the great horse was fully extended. Much larger and more powerful than the gray Arabian, the black was probably as fast, and Hail had given him his head. James Hail was not riding carelessly this time.

He was bending forward in his saddle; his face, in the moment while Richard Acton saw it, was as intent, as strained, as Ash Rowland's had been. For an instant there was no sound except the drumming of the black's hoofs; then from the grandstands burst a salvo of applause.

Lowndes Fenwick brought his hand down on Richard's shoulder. "By Jupiter!" he exclaimed. "He's done it. Hail's won!"

Richard Acton's muscles were suddenly relaxed. He laughed.

Chapter XV

BY ELEVEN O'CLOCK—THE BALL had begun two hours earlier—the four-acre yard of Colonel Kit Bohun's summer residence in Pineland, the largest house in the village, was thronged with carriages and riding horses in charge of an army of negro servants; Bonfires of lightwood and pine-straw, tended by black boys armed with pitchforks, provided a fantastic illumination under the tall straight pines. The house, a rambling two-storied wooden structure like most of the summer dwellings of which the village was composed, was a blaze of light from piazza to attic. Laughter, the hum of animated voices, the music of banjos, harps and fiddles smote upon Richard Acton's ears in reiterated waves of sound

He wondered, as he helped Elizabeth from the phaeton at the foot of the front steps, whether she noticed the trembling of his hands. Inside, the dancing was in full swing. The Actons and Lowndes Fenwick had spent the afternoon quietly at the Waights, and after supper Elizabeth and Phoebe Waight had been in no hurry: Elizabeth, complaining of a headache, had been with some difficulty persuaded to begin her toilet for the dance at the Bohuns'. This, Richard understood, was in reality due to the fact that Diane Rowland, having been crowned Queen of the tournament, would naturally be the most conspicuous figure at the tournament ball.

One of the Bohun negroes took charge of the phaeton. They ascended the steps to the piazza where Colonel Bohun, still in his magnificent King-at-Arms costume, greeted them warmly. He was a cousin of Elizabeth, he declared, through a Huger who had married a Granville, and he warned her that he had had too much punch to be denied a cousinly kiss of welcome. "I didn't know that was possible, Cousin Kit," Elizabeth said sweetly and gave him her hand. Passing on into the hall, decorated with flowers and Spanish moss and hung with the vari-colored banners which had adorned the grandstands during the tournament, they saw momentarily through an arched doorway a large room filled with dancers, many of the men in costume, the women in evening dress.

A negro manservant, bowing obsequiously, conveyed with a wave of his hand the information that the dressing-rooms were up-stairs. Going up the stairs, Richard Acton was suddenly and deeply sorry that he had come; it was folly, he realized, to subject himself needlessly to the ordeal of seeing her. Alone with his brother and Lowndes Fenwick in the men's room, he said with a carefully managed casualness: "If you miss me don't worry. I think a very little dancing will be all that. I had better try; my legs aren't yet as strong as they used to be. If I get tired, I'll go out and take a nap in the carriage."

A drink would help him, Lowndes asserted cheerfully. "Why didn't you take some of Hutson Waight's Newton and Gordon? But Colonel Kit's punch is the best in the Low-Country. At any rate, the strongest. Wait here and I'll have them send you up a glass before you come down."

He went out, followed by John, and in a few minutes a servant appeared at the door of the dressing-room with a glass on a silver tray. Richard dismissed the man with a nod and emptied the glass at once.

It wasn't punch, he discovered immediately, but brandy—brandy of a very high degree of merit. He placed the glass on the mantelpiece and sat down in a chair near the door.

He wouldn't go down yet, he decided. He wasn't ready for the ordeal ahead of him; and unless some other belated guests arrived, he could have the dressing-room to himself. He sat listening to the sounds coming from below, a babel of voices, music, continuous laughter.

She was there, he felt certain; more than once he thought that he could distinguish her voice. She would be dancing with James Hail. Or perhaps with Mazÿck Marion or Louis Treves, her other fools. Marion, of course, would still be wearing the costume that he had worn in the tournament. So would all the others: Knights Templar and Knights Hospitaller and Knights of Alhambra and all the other mummery. It would be a gay picturesque scene; a kind of masque of the Middle Ages, the supposed age of Chivalry. And they were all dancing on the brink of a precipice and didn't know it.

Well, that didn't matter. It didn't concern him any longer. They could go over the precipice and he with them and be damned to them all. And the sooner the better. He was glad now that his correspondence with Philips Cordray and other northern Republican leaders had accomplished nothing. The abolitionists on one side and James Hail and the secessionists on the other could plunge the country into war as quickly as they pleased. He had been a fool not to understand months ago that war would be infinitely better for him than peace. "Peace!" He spoke the word aloud in bitter mockery. Peace—an endless succession of lonely interminable days at Sherborne, days of hopeless longing, nights of torment because she would be in James Hail's arms.

What an idiot he was, the thought struck him suddenly: a worse idiot than he had been that night in the summer-house; a worse idiot than when for her sake he had let Hail shoot at him. Surely he had had his fill of that kind of women—the kind she had turned out to be. James Hail's arms! James Hail's arms couldn't hold her. She had already betrayed him. The announcement of her engagement to Hail had hardly been uttered before she had given her lips to another man to soil. A woman not only loose but vulgarly loose. A damned potential harl—He couldn't, however, quite apply the word.

He got up suddenly, walked to the mantel and picked up the glass that he had placed there. It was entirely empty; damn it, damn it to hell, he couldn't squeeze another drop out of it. Why hadn't Lowndes sent up a bottle, a decanter? He needed a drink; a half-dozen drinks before he went down-stairs where she was—where he would see her—where her eyes would meet his.

He heard quick footsteps in the passage outside and he turned to face the door. The sound ceased; whoever it was had probably gone into another room nearer the stairs. He had better go down, he realized; if he didn't, Lowndes or John would be coming up to look for him. He left the room and walked along the passage toward the stairs.

There was a door at his left; it stood open and involuntarily he glanced into the room. He saw at once that it was a bedroom now utilized as a ladies' cloakroom; shawls, cloaks and veils were piled in seeming confusion on the four-poster bed and on tables and chairs. In the farthest corner of the room a woman was bending over a table. Her back was turned to him, but immediately he recognized Diane. He stepped quickly into the room, closed the door and turned the key.

She had evidently come up from the ballroom in search of something, her shawl perhaps, that she had left in the cloakroom. Hearing the door behind her close, she raised her head. She did not, however, turn immediately. There was a mirror over the table. Acton realized that she saw him in this mirror and that she was delaying deliberately, preparing what she would say to him.

He could not see her face in the mirror because her head was still bent slightly downward. Whatever emotions her face might have revealed were hidden from him. He knew, however, from the movement of her shoulders that her breath had quickened.

He stood with his back against the door; he was trembling and the blood pounded in his ears. She was in white; again there was a white rose in her hair; her shoulders were smoother than polished marble. She was the most beautiful woman that he had ever seen: his longing for her, his intolerable love, swept him. He took a step forward, his lips parted to cry out her name. Suddenly she turned and faced him.

She appeared entirely self-possessed. She was smiling—a faint amused smile—but her eyes were bright with a mocking laughter. Bright and hard. Her voice was low and perfectly cool.

"This is foolish," she said, "your coming in here. And horribly dangerous. You must go at once. You were very attractive that night in the summer-house. I enjoyed it. But I seldom kiss any man twice. Please open the door."

Richard Acton realized that this at last was fatal. He had known for months what she was, yet in his heart he hadn't really believed it. Now he had it from her own lips. He moved quickly toward her—By God, she shouldn't know what she had done to him! His arms enfolded her and she did not resist him. He pressed his lips to hers and kissed her fiercely, brutally, again and again. Her eyes were closed, her mouth was like that of a dead woman. Presently he released her. His voice was steady, cool, his tone scrupulously courteous.

"I am like you," he said. "I don't often kiss the same woman twice. But I was willing to make an exception for you and you don't seem to appreciate the honor."

He moved toward the door, then turned, his hand on the key.

"You'd better fix your hair," he said, with the same studied courtesy of intonation. "I'm afraid I disarranged it. James Hail wouldn't like that."

He bowed and went out. She heard his feet upon the stairs.

Part Three: Charleston

At last the hour of trial has come for Charleston—the hour of deliverance or destruction; for no one believes the other alternative, surrender, possible. The heart of the whole South yearns toward the beleaguered city with intense solicitude and yet with hope amounting to confidence. Charleston knows what is expected of her and what is due to her fame and to the relation she sustains to the cause. The devoted Beauregard is there and he, too, knows what is expected of him. We predict a Saragossa defence and that, if Charleston is taken, it will be only as a heap of ruins.

—*The Richmond Whig.*

Chapter I

At thirty minutes past two o'clock in the afternoon of April 7, 1863, the long-roll was sounded in Fort Sumter.

At that hour all doubt as to the intention of the enemy vanished from the mind of Colonel Alfred Rhett, commanding the fort. The meaning of the heavy concentration of Federal war-ships off Charleston bar during the past few days was at last entirely clear. The ironclads of Admiral DuPont's fleet were moving forward in line of battle.

In Fort Sumter, just within the mouth of the harbor, the movement of the ironclads had been observed from the beginning. By early afternoon the seriousness of DuPont's purpose was unmistakable. The great naval attack upon Charleston, elaborately prepared by the North and long expected by General Beauregard, the alert commander of the Department of South Carolina, Georgia and Florida, was about to begin.

Richard Acton, in the gray and red uniform of a private in Captain Mazÿck Marion's company of the First South Carolina

Artillery, perceived that flocks of white sea-birds were still wheeling in the air above the beach at Cummings Point. He had been watching the distant ironclads but now for a time the birds absorbed him: there was a grateful and familiar beauty in the swift intermittent flashing of silver wings in the sun. Nearer at hand, a few feet above the glassy surface of the harbor, a great blue heron passed with slow rhythmic wing-beats. His eyes followed the heron's deliberate flight; and suddenly he heard, faint and fine in the deep hush that hung over the fort and the calm blue waters of the bay, a golden tinkling of distant cow-bells.

The sound came, he said to himself, from the pastures of James Island; the wooded shore of James Island formed the southern boundary of the inner harbor, and in green meadows hidden by those woods the cows were grazing. He could not see them, yet his thoughts dwelt with a profound and tranquil pleasure upon the scene: the slowly moving cows, the fringes of the meadow blue with harebells, the April sorrel-grass rosy-crimson in the bright sunshine.

He smiled faintly. The cows whose bells he heard were grazing on James Island, but it wasn't a James Island meadow that his mind had pictured. It was the familiar pasture at Avalon; the big willow-oak that had stood there when he was a boy was still standing; he saw that the languid cows were all gathered within the shade of its boughs.

They vanished with the verdure, the rustic peace, that enwrapped them; he returned, with a stabbing momentary conviction that Avalon was forever lost to him, to the sharp reality of the present. His station, in the eastern parapet battery of Fort Sumter facing seaward, permitted an uninterrupted view in all directions; and Sumter, rising forty feet above the water almost in the middle of the harbor mouth, was the heart and center of the preparing drama. Standing close to the channel and commanding it, the fort must bear the brunt of the Federal assault. Upon its successful resistance the safety of Charleston, of Carolina, of the Confederate States depended.

Richard Acton was thrilled with an emotion unlike any other in his experience. The tremendous implications of Charleston these moments rushed upon him; they filled him with exultation and with something that was almost terror and yet had nothing to do with fear.

If he and these others failed, Charleston might be in flames by sunset, the chief city of Carolina would have fallen, the South would have suffered a staggering defeat. For months, while the Federal power at Washington prepared the most formidable naval armament ever used in war, not only America but Europe also had waited impatiently for the launching of the blow; and not since Bull Run had any undertaking enlisted so eagerly the sympathy and the sanguine anticipations of the northern people. At Fort Sumter two years ago South Carolina had begun the war that had split the nation; now at Fort Sumter, the newspapers of the North proclaimed, her crime must be expiated in blood. The proud and impetuous city where secession had been born, the bold and imperious commonwealth which, since Calhoun's day, had fixed the policy of the South and which at last had dared decree the dissolution of the Union, must reap the whirlwind they had sown.

Gazing seaward, Richard Acton saw that the line of the ironclads was perceptibly nearer. He no longer heard the golden tinkling of the cow-bells. They had ceased suddenly; he had a feeling that sound had ceased everywhere, that existence was suspended throughout the world. The trance, in which for the moment he was held, embraced, he was convinced, the whole earth. A complete and deathlike silence hung over the blue waters of the bay; in the fort itself, where, more than five hundred men stood ready at their posts, there was no movement, no sound.

Beside him some one coughed. The noise startled him like a gunshot. The tension of silence was broken and, like a man waking from long sleep, he became aware with a swiftly increasing sharpness of the panorama around him.

Beyond the low promontory of Cummings Point, at the south of the harbor entrance, he could see the whole line of the advancing fleet. The ships were moving slowly in single file, four long low turret ships of the Passaic type in the van, then the formidable bulk of the great *New Ironsides*, DuPont's flagship, then three more single-turreted monitors with a double-turreted ironclad, recognizable at once as the famous *Keokuk*, bringing up the rear.

They came on so slowly that they appeared scarcely to be moving at all—a grim parade of black, incredibly sinister shapes, grotesque as monsters from another planet. Seen thus in their long array, they seemed to fulfill the boasts of the northern newspapers that this was the mightiest war fleet ever launched: when it knocked at the gate of Charleston, those newspapers had predicted, the brick walls of Sumter would melt like snow in the sun. The battle in Hampton Road between Ericsson's *Monitor* and the *Virginia* had inaugurated the era of iron ships, and in the improved ironclads of DuPont's fleet the revolutionary possibilities of the monitor type had been skilfully developed.

The new monitors were said to be invulnerable; they were protected with no less than eleven inches of armor, and their turrets carried the heaviest cannon ever mounted upon ships of war. The *Keokuk*, a turtle-back ironclad of a new and mysterious design, was known to be less heavily armored, but to atone for this she had two turrets and a double hull which, it was believed, would render her proof against the severest gunfire. The *New Ironsides*, flying DuPont's flag, a three-decked armor-clad steam-frigate so recently launched that her masts had not yet been stepped, had been acclaimed enthusiastically as the most powerful offensive war vessel in the world.

Seaward, beyond the advancing column, the flotilla of gunboats and transports which had accompanied the heavy fighting ships were plainly visible. There, in accordance with arrangements made months in advance, the war correspondents of the northern newspapers waited: their glasses, Richard Acton knew, were now trained on the harbor entrance, their swift dispatch boats were ready to dash northward with the news that Sumter had been battered to pieces and the Union flag waved over Charleston.

That, he told himself quietly, might very well happen. He wondered what Beauregard expected; whether he was, as those close to him reported, confident of victory. It was hard to see how, with all his unquenchable enthusiasm, he could be completely sure. He faced a new and untried form of battle: ironclad ships, reported impenetrable, matched against walls of masonry and brick. He knew, too, that Union land forces threatened an advance across James Island where the Confederate lines of defense were weak and thinly manned.

Well, Acton reflected, Sumter had been Beauregard's lucky star. His fame had begun when, as the opening operation of the war, he had taken the fort from Major Anderson. To-day for the second time his hopes and fears were focused upon Sumter, a Confederate stronghold now, awaiting an assault by new engines of death believed by the North to be invincible. The Washington government needed badly the decisive victory which it believed Admiral DuPont was sure to win. In Virginia, where Hooker had succeeded Burnside, nothing had yet been gained to atone for the holocaust of Fredericksburg in December; in the West, Grant's tedious operations against Vicksburg had led so far to no tangible result; the autumn and spring elections in the North had reflected the growing discontent. If Charleston, the birthplace of secession, could be taken or destroyed, the determination of the northern people would be renewed, their hopes rekindled.

Richard Acton's gaze left the black line of the advancing ships. He turned and looked westward across the waters of the inner harbor toward the city that Sumter defended.

He perceived, with a sudden and swift abandonment of his habitual reserve, how beautiful it was. Three and a half miles distant from the ramparts of Sumter, the roofs and spires of Charleston rose seemingly from the blue waters of the bay; nearer at hand, within the line of log-booms and rope-nettings with which Beauregard had closed the inner channel, the Confederate rams *Chicora* and *Palmetto State* steamed slowly like pacing sentinels. Acton's eyes were fixed beyond the black squat shapes of the rams; the tranquil loveliness of Charleston possessed him; with a quick intake of his breath he realized that, next to Avalon, it was dearer to him than any other spot on earth.

Charleston wasn't wood and stone; it wasn't a place or a name; it was a symbol and a spirit. It was the heart, the capital of the plantations; all that Carolina was and had been from the beginning lived in it and gave it form and meaning. The thought came to him that now, as he viewed it from the walls of Sumter, with its steeples lit by the sun and its graceful sky-line clear against the April blue, there was a sweet dignity in its aspect that was completely feminine, and he found himself actually thinking of it as a woman, a woman of flesh and blood.

With this it seemed that in his mind a barrier went suddenly down, and his thoughts, like a torrent released by the breaking of a dam, surged tumultuously onward. She was there—Diane. Mazÿck Marion, returning to his post in Fort Sumter the day before, had told him that he had seen Diane Rowland in Charleston. She had come down from the plantation, she had told Marion, to be with Sally Hemmerton.

He stood, frowning and pale, seeing her clearly, seeing nothing else. He couldn't now drive her from him. He was conscious of no wish, no impulse, to do so; his pride it seemed, was dead and, yielding to her, he had, for the moment, no sense of self-contempt, no scorn of his weakness. This had happened to him before upon the eve of battle; it had happened in the bloody fight at Secessionville on James Island, his baptism of fire. Death had been very near to him then and in its presence he had surrendered to her. Equally she absorbed him now; he stood lost in the overwhelming realization of her power.

A hand closed on his arm; he saw that it was Louis Treves. Treves, an aide to Colonel Rhett, passed hurriedly on without speaking. He saluted Captain Marion, commanding the parapet battery, delivered a message and, returning, paused at Acton's side.

"Richard," he began—the crash of a cannon cut him short. Treves, facing the parade-ground, stood rigidly at attention. Richard Acton, turning his head, saw that the colors were being hoisted: the garrison flag of the Confederate States at the northern salient nearest the fleet, the blue flag of South Carolina, with its white palmetto and crescent, at the western angle of the gorge, the colors of the First Regiment at the eastern angle. He saw on the southeast parapet Colonel Rhett with Lieutenant-Colonel Yates and a group of aides. They were in full dress uniform and they stood erect and motionless, facing the Confederate flag slowly ascending its tall staff.

Another cannon roared; evidently Rhett had ordered a salute of thirteen guns, at once a tribute to the flag and a challenge to the grim line of ironclads silently advancing. Colonel Rhett, he reminded himself, was Barnwell Rhett's son—Barnwell Rhett, who, more than any other living man, was responsible for that secession of South Carolina which had brought on the war.

He had a sudden sense of helplessness in the face of fate. He, Richard Acton, was fighting for secession under Barnwell Rhett's son! Lowndes Fenwick was dead; he had been killed at Malvern Hill in Virginia; Hutson Waight was dead—dead because South Carolina had followed Barnwell Rhett and James Hail. Charleston might die to-day; under the guns of the invading fleet it might perish utterly.

Charleston where Diane was. It seemed to him that Diane and Charleston were one. Diane and Carolina. They had become one and the same thing. He frowned; that was a piece of damned soft idiotic nonsense! But his feeling, in defiance of his will, persisted and grew stronger.

He couldn't separate her from the country itself: the country, the soil, the trees, the fragrances, the songs, the memories for which he was going into battle. The green plantation woods, the shimmering rice-fields, the moss-draped oaks of Avalon, the high-walled streets of Charleston—in a little while now they would be gay with bignonia and sweet with honeysuckle—all these were Diane. It was in reality for her that he was about to offer his life. That was the absurd, the ironic truth. Why, in God's name, should he fight for her? What was there in her that was worth fighting for? He turned his back upon the city where she was and looked toward the east.

His eyes were fixed upon the oncoming ironclads, but he did not see them. He realized, with a strange mingling of something that was almost ecstasy and something that was almost despair, that he would never win free from her. She had bound him to her with chains that he couldn't break; she would possess him until the end of life. That was at once his happiness and his shame, his strength and his unforgivable weakness. Knowing her, he still loved her. He couldn't explain it or defend it, but it was true. All round him there was a sudden storm of cheering. On the ramparts of the fort, in sight and hearing of the enemy, the regimental band was playing *Dixie*.

Chapter II

At ten minutes before three o'clock the first ironclad in the line, the monitor *Weehawken*, having an Ericsson torpedo-searcher raft attached to her bow, was directly opposite Fort Moultrie at the northern entrance of the harbor. Richard Acton saw white smoke roll in a curling cloud above the parapet of Moultrie and the next moment the stillness of the bay was broken b a heavy detonation. The range was too great for Moultrie's smooth-bore columbiads; after a few rounds they suspended their fire. One shot from the *Passaic*, the second vessel in the line, was fired in contemptuous reply.

It was plain that the shore batteries on either side of the entrance were not seriously considered by Admiral DuPont. Fort Sumter, in the middle of the harbor mouth, was the lion in his path, and against it his effort was to be directed. The black ominous ships held steadily on their way, biding their time. But those opening guns had sent their message rolling above the calm waters of the inner bay. The roofs of Charleston and the long reach of the sea-wall promenade were thronged with thousands gathering to witness the battle upon which their fate depended.

At three minutes after three o'clock, the *Weehawken*, still leading the line, had approached within fourteen hundred yards of Fort Sumter. Two puffs of white smoke leaped from her turret, instantly merging to form a single snowy cloud. Richard heard the heavy report of the simultaneous discharges, he heard a humming sound increasing to a roar, followed immediately by the crash of a bursting shell, then silence.

The silence lengthened; he could hear the quick breathing of the men near him. A gunner behind him laughed nervously. There was another heavy report; the turret of the second ironclad was enveloped in smoke.

"Too high," a voice whispered hoarsely. "And one of 'em didn't burst. Look at that flag." Acton saw that there was a clean hole through the regimental colors flying above the gorge wall. "Rhett better come down," another voice said. "If that damned thing had been lower…"

Colonel Rhett and this aides were still standing on the southeast parapet fully exposed. Rhett, conspicuous in his parade uniform, was bending slightly forward. He was watching, the *Weehawken* intently. He hadn't, Acton realized, so much as turned his head when the shell burst.

Acton's gaze remained fixed upon the tall figure sharply outlined upon the parapet. He hadn't in the old days known Alfred Rhett well. In a duel in the second year of the war Rhett had killed Colonel Ransom Calhoun, at one time commander of

Fort Sumter, and later had succeeded to the post which Calhoun had held. The affair had caused bitter feeling—Calhoun had been exceedingly popular—but the prescriptions of the code had been followed strictly, and no one had questioned Rhett's fitness to command. He was fearless, a born soldier, a strict disciplinarian, and he had taught the Sumter artillerists how to shoot. Under his rigid training, the First South Carolina Regiment had become one of the best artillery commands in the Confederate service. A man at Richard Acton's elbow, a bearded private from the up-country, was muttering to himself.

"Why the hell don't he come down?" the man was saying. "I aim to kill him myself when the war's over on account o' Ransom Calhoun, and ef he stays. up thar, the Yanks'll kill him fust."

Richard Acton found himself wishing with an increasing intensity that Colonel Rhett would descend from the exposed parapet. The other officers with him didn't matter so much, but for the moment the whole fate of Fort Sumter and of Charleston seemed comprehended in the fate of Alfred Rhett. At any moment the next salvo from the ironclads might come. He saw that Rhett was still watching the *Weehawken* closely; he knew that the Sumter battery commanders had been ordered to withhold their fire until the leading Federal ship had reached a certain buoy.

A tall man, in the uniform of a cavalry colonel, his left arm supported in a sling, ran up the narrow brick stairway leading to the parapet where Rhett stood. He saluted the officers there and moved forward to Rhett's side. Richard recognized James

Hail. He was conscious of a sudden hot flare of resentment, anger. So that was why Diane was in Charleston. Evidently Hail had been wounded and had come home from Virginia on leave. He must have hurried down to Sumter from Charleston by boat to offer Rhett his services. Acton heard Captain Mazÿck Marion speaking in a low voice to the men of the battery.

"That's Colonel Hail, men," Marion said; "Hail of Wade Hampton's cavalry—we can't lose now."

There was a general craning of necks. In two years of war James Hail had become a legendary figure, one of those celebrated and romantic leaders in whose individual brilliance the passionately individualistic South found warrant for that faith which had dared challenge an adversary of three times its strength. There was the beginning of a cheer which Captain Marion quickly suppressed. Hail nodded, smiling; he lifted his unwounded arm in salute. Suddenly Richard saw Colonel Rhett raise his hand.

The *Weehawken* had reached the buoy upon which the eastern barbette guns of Sumter had previously been trained. With a deafening crash the whole front of the fort burst into flame. Crash followed crash; dense clouds of smoke rolled up above the rampart. Firing by battery, the guns of Sumter, combined at first upon the *Weehawken* and then upon the *Passaic*, ripped and churned the blue waters of the bay.

Richard Acton lost all knowledge, all consciousness, of what was happening beyond the sphere of his immediate action; his whole being was concentrated upon the swift and machine-like handling of the powder charges for the eight-inch gun to which he had been assigned.

He was filled with an exaltation, a happiness, surpassing anything he had ever known. It came somehow from Diane; she flashed in and out of his thoughts, but he had no clear vision of her. He saw, too—a momentary flash, as of lightning—the columns of Avalon far off through a shadowy vista of overarching oaks; he seemed to hear again a golden tinkling of cow-bells. But presently all this passed; the exaltation left him. Abruptly, as though until that moment he had been utterly deaf, he became aware of the infernal and intolerable din of the guns.

He couldn't stand it, he felt; it would drive him mad; the smoke in his nostrils and throat was strangling him. There was a heavy shock; the whole massive rampart of Fort Sumter rocked and trembled. He heard the crash of a falling wall, followed by screams and groans. The smoke around him cleared suddenly; beyond a space of blue water he saw the ironclads.

The funnel of one was black with a red band around the top—the *Weehawken*; another's funnel was gray with a green band; a third was enveloped in the smoke of her own guns. Out of that smoke he saw clearly a great black sphere, apparently as large as a flour barrel, burst suddenly. It sped in full view across the intervening space. He realized with an intense surprise that his eye had followed the shell as it bounded from the port of the monitor's turret to the wall of the fort, and in the same instant he felt another mighty shock and again the fort shook to its foundations.

He wondered whether Rhett and Hail were still on the exposed parapet; thick smoke now obscured the spot where they had been standing. He smiled faintly. James Hail had always excelled him, defeated him. He, Richard Acton, was one of five hundred private soldiers serving the guns of Fort Sumter; but Colonel James Hail, lustrous with the glory he had won in Virginia, was up there in the battle-smoke. Up there with Rhett on the highest parapet, the point of utmost danger. In front and near at hand he saw a waterspout rise from the surface of the bay. A mortar shell had exploded just beneath the water; a blue and white column heaved upward to twice the height of the fort and, breaking, deluged the rampart with spray. A man beside Acton cursed shrilly and snatched off his scarlet cap; he saw that the crown of the man's cap had been filled with water.

He laughed; the man's solicitude for his cap seemed indescribably humorous. A runner came racing up the spiral stairway leading to the parapet battery and spoke to Captain Marion. Acton heard Marion's voice, issuing an order; he couldn't distinguish the words.

The awful shocks, the more awful trembling of the fort, continued. The concussions were coming at shorter intervals; the Federal gunners were shooting more accurately. With a swift and horrible fear he realized presently that the firing of Sumter was perceptibly slower. The conviction came to him that the huge fifteen-inch guns of the turret ships were battering Fort Sumter to pieces.

He perceived in a moment, however, what had happened. Colonel Rhett had modified his plan of battle. The guns of Sumter were no longer firing by battery; they were firing piece by piece, searching out their moving targets with greater deliberation and certainty.

The *Weehawken* was backing. Evidently she had abandoned the design of breaking through the rope and boom obstructions of the inner harbor with the torpedo-defense raft brought for that purpose. She was firing vigorously; the *Passaic*, passing in front of her, fired and then moved backward in turn; the two other monitors of the first division, the *Patapsco* and the *Montauk*, were completely hidden in the smoke of their turret guns.

A heavy curtain of smoke surrounded the fort. It lifted slowly; he saw for the first time the complete panorama of the battle.

On both sides of the harbor mouth the Confederate shore batteries were firing at long range: Fort Moultrie and Batteries Bee and Beauregard on the northern shore and Battery Gregg at Cummings Point on Morris Island. As yet only the first division of the fleet was in action against Fort Sumter. The *New Ironsides*, leading the second division, had halted. She had the appearance of a ship becoming unmanageable from lack of headway; her uncertain movements threw into confusion the line of vessels behind her. She ran foul of two of them, got clear with difficulty; Richard saw that she was signaling. The ships of the second division moved forward past her. As though encouraged by their boldness, the *New Ironsides* swung round and advanced again.

Acton realized that within a few minutes the offensive power of the enemy actually engaged with Sumter would be more than doubled. The *Catskill*, *Nantucket* and *Nahant* of the second division, were monitors of the *Passaic* class, carrying fifteen-inch and eleven-inch guns; the *Keokuk*, with her double hull and her two sloping turrets, was an unknown quantity, while the *New Ironsides'* powerful broadside batteries of rapid-firing eleven-inch guns rendered her probably the most formidable unit of the fleet. Moultrie was firing upon the flag-ship at long range, and, although she was still twice as far distant as the first division monitors, there was for some minutes a concentration of fire upon her from the eight- and ten-inch columbiads of Sumter.

She halted and hung uncertainly in the tide. Undoubtedly she had been hit, but at that long range her armored sides could hardly have been pierced. Nevertheless, she held back; larger and more vulnerable than the monitors, she might have suffered severely in close battle with Fort Sumter, while her great size increased the hazard of maneuvering her within the arms of the bay. But the other ships of the second division were coming rapidly on. Already the first of them, the *Catskill*, was in action. Soon the *Nantucket* and the *Nahant* were hotly engaged.

The light breeze lulled; the smoke curtain shut down; it was denser than ever and it had a different smell. Again it lifted. He saw that the whole fleet was now in action. The *Nahant* and the *Keokuk*, last in the attacking line, had moved gallantly to the front. They were fighting at shorter range than any of the first division ships.

Richard Acton realized that the crisis of the battle had come; the entire force of the ironclad fleet except the flag-ship was concentrated against Fort Sumter.

The ceaseless and shocking uproar of the guns increased; more than a hundred of the heaviest cannon ever used in war were thundering together. The monitors were constantly in motion; each moved in an ellipse, and together they formed a wide half-circle in, front of the fort. The thick walls and arches of Sumter trembled under the impact of the great fifteen-inch and eleven-inch shells; when at the moment of impact the shells burst, deep craters were blasted in the brick walls of the fort. The smoke became so dense, its acrid smell so penetrating, that breathing was almost impossible. Richard realized suddenly that Fort Sumter was on fire.

If there was talk around him, he heard little of it. A voice with the accent of the up-country cursed the *New Ironsides* because she wouldn't come closer. "The god-damned old bitch!" he heard the man say. "The pot-bellied old—" The crash of an exploding shell obliterated the rest. A gunner beside him screamed and fell backward. He was coatless now, his face black with powder, his shirt half-torn from him. He saw faces, flitting forms, in the smoke: Mazÿck Marion, Louis Treves, runners with ammunition. One of these shouted that the fire was close to the magazine.

That, however, meant nothing to him. There was something else far more important, but he couldn't fix what it was. His hands, his body, ceaselessly engaged, seemed entirely separate from his mind. He realized vaguely that he was trying to think of Diane. But it was as though he couldn't think of her. She was near him and yet immeasurably remote; she eluded even his thoughts.

Well, she was worthless. Damn her, she was worthless! He knew her for what she was. Jacqueline had been worth ten of her. Jacqueline Fleur. How long ago that was! Paris...St. Petersburg. The cafés of the Boulevard Saint Michel. It was all ashes. She had consumed him. He saw her eyes; they looked as they had looked that night in the summer-house—they were lying now just as they had lied then.

A sudden and overwhelming sense of her enchantment, her magic, poured through him. The rampart under him shook. In front of him the parapet trembled, cracked; a section of it toppled over into the sea. Another fifteen-inch shell struck the wall of the fort below the breached parapet and exploded...

The concussion stunned him momentarily; he fell sideways against the chassis of the gun. He hung there dazed, only half-conscious. His mind groped blindly: James Hail's bullet, he imagined, had hit him; he was at Avalon—at Sherborne. Vienna was bringing him his supper. It was a hot night, but that wasn't why she had bared her amber shoulders. She moved as gracefully as a cat; she was watching him out of the corners of her eyes.

Diane, of course, had heard the talk about Vienna and himself. He wanted her to hear it. So that she wouldn't know... Ash Rowland, he remembered suddenly, was in the Army of

Northern Virginia. He looked a little like Diane—a great deal like her. Richard Acton pushed his hand through his hair; his head was pounding, black spheres revolved before his eyes.

He stood swaying, one hand clutching the gun-chassis, but presently, almost suddenly, his vision began to clear, the pounding in his head diminished, the revolving spheres disappeared. Through the breached parapet he could see the whole fleet, the whole battle. Except for the noise and the white jets leaping upward from the water where the shells struck, it was like a picture, a picture in a frame.

Most of the ships were hidden or half-hidden in smoke. One monitor—from her position he believed it was the *Passaic*—had retired to the eastward. Her pilot-house had been wrecked and a cloud of steam was issuing from her deck. The *Weehawken*, too, seemed to be in trouble; her funnel, painted black and red, was riddled; her side armor was cracked and split. The *Nahant* and the double-turreted *Keokuk* were sustaining the hottest fire of Sumter. All round them the water seethed with the rain of projectiles. Acton saw the *Nahant* struck three times in as many minutes; he could see the black fragments of solid shot falling back from her impenetrable turret.

It was impenetrable, but the heavy blows jammed it so that it could not revolve and her guns were rendered useless. Her steering gear apparently had also been disabled, for she was drifting helplessly...The *Keokuk* turned bow-on and headed straight for Sumter. Immediately she received the concentric fire of all the fort's guns that could be brought to bear. Spouts of foam and jets of spray flooded her turtle-backed decks; in front of her and on either side the water was churned white by a deluge of shells and balls.

Firing from her forward turret, she came bravely on. Richard could see that she was being hit repeatedly. Her eleven-inch bow-gun was silenced; a solid shot crashed into her forward turret; a bolt from a Brooke rifle ripped open her hull ten feet from her stem and barely above the water-line. Her headway slackened, then ceased; she drifted toward the fort under a hail of fire.

The guns of Sumter, served with almost perfect precision, were hammering her to death. Her sloping turrets were cracked and dented; her armored hull was torn and ripped, her funnel riddled. Slowly she gathered way again. With ninety wounds in her—all the high courage of her officers and crew made fruitless by the cool skill of Sumter's gunners—the *Keokuk*, mortally stricken, moved slowly out of the fight.

The fire in the fort bad been controlled; a squad under Lieutenant Inglesby had stopped its progress toward the magazines. The smoke cloud over Fort Sumter was less dense. Richard Acton saw the Confederate flag at the top of its tall staff. Through a thin white veil of drifting smoke it shone like a flame. There was a great hole through its red union with the stars of the Confederate States, but the blue flag of South Carolina at the western angle of the gorge was unscarred. Acton was conscious of a queer contraction of his throat; he was stirred strangely by the sight of the flags.

He laughed harshly. He wasn't a sentimentalist, he told himself. Flags were nothing but flags. A battle apparently was mainly a hellish noise, a bad smell and an aching head. Nevertheless, he realized presently that he was shouting, cheering. The men around him were cheering. Captain Marion was trying to stop it, but throughout the fort the consciousness of victory had overcome the rigidity of Rhett's discipline. The men of the other batteries were cheering also, waving their caps.

The half-circle of ironclads in front of the fort was shifting, breaking up. The battered *Nahant*, her steering gear repaired, was steaming slowly out of range. The other monitors, still firing sullenly, were retiring; he saw that signals were flying on the *New Ironsides*—the Admiral's order to withdraw from action.

A shirtless, powder-blackened man jigged up and down in front of Richard Acton. His grimed face was almost unrecognizable, but Acton saw in a moment that it was the up-countryman who had cursed the *New Ironsides*. He was singing in a high cracked voice:

> *"King Abraham is very sick,*
> *DuPont has got the measles,*
> *Old Sumter we have got it still.*
> *Pop goes the weasel."*

Another man joined him, two more,—half the battery. They were singing madly, waving their caps. But now it was *Dixie*:

"I wish I was in the land of cotton,
Old times dar am not forgotten;
Look away, look away, look away, Dixie-Land.
In Dixie-Land where I was born in,
Early on a frosty mornin';
Look away, look away, look away, Dixie-Land.

"Then I wish I was in Dixie;
Hooray! Hooray!
In Dixie-Land I'll take my stand
To live and die in Dixie..."

A salvo from the big casemate columbiads of one of the second-tier batteries came like a crash of applause. The garrison of Sumter, their outburst of joy over, had returned to the service of their guns; there had been, as a matter of fact, hardly more than a momentary slackening of their fire. A rumor ran from battery to battery that the ships would return, that Rhett expected another attack at once. It was known that, so far, casualties had been few and that the fort had suffered no irreparable damage; but the walls had been weakened, a renewal of the bombardment might have serious results. Rhett's order was to continue firing as rapidly as accuracy permitted. Until they had passed beyond extreme range, the retreating ironclads were pursued by the persistent Confederate shells.

They did not turn. Few, if any, of them could have survived another half-hour in the deadly fire-zone in front of Sumter.

They filed past the *New Ironsides* in slow and solemn procession, and when the last of them had passed, Admiral DuPont got his flag-ship under way and followed his broken and beaten fleet. He was wondering perhaps—Samuel F. DuPont was an old man with years of honorable service behind him—how Washington would receive the news that he had to give. Defeat instead of the victory that had seemed so sure. The invincible iron armada flung back from the gate of the hated city. The vaunted *Keokuk* sinking, four other ships disabled. The *"Rebel"* flag still flying over Sumter...

Richard Acton looked westward toward Charleston. He was alone on the western rampart; the stir and excitement following the victory had in large measure subsided. Over the bay—over the whole world, he thought—a profound and serene silence reigned. In the softened afternoon light the waters of the inner harbor, barely ruffled by the faint breeze, were a delicate and luminous blue. The sun was going down behind the roofs of Charleston. The tall steeples of St. Michael's and St. Philip's were sharply drawn against a golden sky.

Charleston, with the blue water in front of it and the splendor of the sunset above...

He felt again, suddenly, that contraction of his throat-muscles which the sight of the flag over Sumter had caused. Damn it, he wouldn't be an ass. Charleston was—Charleston. He, or at least his brother, had property there; the Acton town-house overlooked the sea-wall promenade.

It was safe. Charleston hadn't been captured; Fort Sumter had beaten back the enemy. That was all that needed to be said. So far as he was concerned, the chief result of the battle was a headache.

He saw Mazÿck Marion approaching. Thank heaven, there wouldn't be any heroics, any sentimental gush from Mazÿck There would be plenty of patriotic eloquence in the *Charleston Mercury* in the morning, but he wouldn't have to read it. Still, what had happened this day had gone some distance toward proving that the *Mercury* and Barnwell Rhett were right—that the South might win. God, he exclaimed to himself, if only that could happen! He had differed with Barnwell Rhett, after all, on only one, but the most essential, point—the practicability of secession; it was probably true, as Rhett believed, that the South would be better off outside the Union. He had opposed Rhett and secession solely because he hadn't believed that the South could win a war against the North. But now the South seemed to be winning.

He smiled. He had perhaps helped Barnwell Rhett win the revolution that Rhett had worked all his life to launch. After opposing Rhett's secession policy, he had helped establish it. But there was a sharper irony in the fact that he had helped defend Diane. He had fought for her; he had been conscious all the while that it was she he was fighting for. Well, he was a fool, that was all…Mazÿck Marion was standing at his elbow. Marion said simply, "Well, Richard," then stood silent, gazing across the calm blue water.

He saw that Marion was deeply moved. Mazÿck's dark eyes, fixed upon Charleston, were strangely bright; his tanned bony face was transformed by some inner radiance.

"We've saved it," he said in a low trembling tone. "Thank God, we've saved it."

He paused. Without looking at Acton, he went on, his voice steadier.

"I kept seeing her. I think I saw her the whole time. It was a strange thing, Richard, that all three of us were here. You and I and James Hail. All three of us here in Sumter and Diane yonder in Charleston..."

He stopped abruptly. Richard Acton, without realizing what he was saying, replied:

"Yes, that was very strange."

Chapter III

WHEN, AFTER SOME FURTHER AND casual talk, Mazÿck left him, he-remained on the parapet, a sardonic amusement flickering in his mind. He was thinking of what Marion had said: James Hail, Mazÿck Marion and himself—all three of them in Fort Sumter fighting for her. All three of her fools. Or rather, he amended this, three of her many fools. How many or who the others were didn't matter. Doubtless they were to be found in various places: in Charleston, in New Orleans, in Richmond, in Paris where she had spent the year preceding the war.

So Mazÿck knew about him—knew that he had been in love with Diane. Well, that didn't matter either, and perhaps it wasn't really surprising. Since the beginning of the war he had been thrown intimately with Marion, the captain of the company in which he had enlisted. He wondered, nevertheless, how Mazÿck had discovered his feeling; he hadn't, he was sure, given a hint of it in anything he had said. Perhaps there was some subtle and unconscious interchange among the men who loved her.

But that couldn't include James Hail. He had told James Hail in so many words—told him that first night at Notteley that he loved Diane.

He heard voices behind him. In the parade-ground he saw Hail with Colonel Rhett and a group of officers; they were inspecting the damage to the inner walls resulting from shells striking them in reverse. It was the first time—except that brief glimpse on the smoke-wreathed parapet of the fort a few hours before—that he had seen Hail since the war started; Hail had been continuously in Virginia with Wade Hampton's division of Stuart's cavalry. He was looking well, in spite of his wounded arm; he hadn't changed perceptibly, Acton reflected, since that day at the Pineland muster-ground when he had won the tournament.

Well, Hail was the greatest fool of them all, the greatest fool and the most incomprehensible enigma. How was it possible that Hail could still love her? Only the blindest ignorance of her could explain that. They were to have been married, Acton remembered, in the June of '59 but Mrs. Rowland's sudden death had intervened. Later Diane had accompanied Margaret Porcher and her husband to Europe. After her return, Sally Rowland's desperate illness and then the outbreak of the war had again postponed the marriage.

And James Hail was still engaged to her. He had never, Acton said to himself, seen through her. He hadn't in all these years discovered her—discovered what he, Richard Acton, had discovered that night in the summer-house. Or rather, he hadn't discovered it then. It wasn't until later, not until she had revealed herself with her own lips in the cloak-room at the tournament ball in Pineland, that he really knew her. The Countess Susanne Falatresi reborn in Diane Rowland.

Well, he wished James Hail joy of her. They were to be married, it was understood, as soon as the war was over. It would be a good thing for James Hail if the war could last forever. James Hail and the Countess Susanne! The beau ideal—he used the term in complete sincerity—of southern reverence for the antique tradition of woman married to Diane Rowland! A woman who could do to him what she had done in the summer-house at Notteley. Acton's somber eyes lingered on Hail, the center of the group of officers in the parade-ground below. By God, it was monstrous! Diane Rowland was—he knew her to be—her lips against his had proved it—the negation of all that James Hail held most sacred. If he knew her, he would never touch her again.

But he, Richard Acton, knew her and yet he loved her. She was able, in spite of his knowledge, to compel his love. Well, that was his weakness; he hadn't the strength to prevail against her; she, mysteriously, overwhelmed him. James Hail, he believed, was stronger; from the beginning, he had understood, as by a sort of intuition, the man's extraordinary fineness.

Richard's eyes still dwelt upon him; bronzed and tall, he was a commanding figure in his cavalry cape and polished boots adorned with silver spurs. The perfect pictorial conception, Acton said to himself, of that romantic ideal of aristocratic fineness and indestructible courage of which southern orators had declaimed too much—an ideal brought to earth and astonishingly realized in the more fortunate captains of the Confederacy. The young officers with Rhett were hanging on Colonel Hail's words; their eyes seldom strayed from him. It was obvious that even now, fresh from their own battle, their minds were full of the glamour of this man, the glory he had won in Virginia.

Richard turned abruptly away. He hated the man as he had never hated any other; yet, in the midst of it, he could recognize the singleness, the inadequate motive, of his feeling toward Hail, its significance as an evidence of Diane's power. He saw Mazÿck Marion come out of the post hospital and walk toward the center of the parade-ground. Louis Treves joined Marion and the two walked on more slowly, as though to attach themselves to the group of officers with Hail and Rhett. Acton remembered suddenly that Louis Treves also had once been in love with her; why couldn't the thing have passed from him as it had passed from Louis?

That thought, however, was not only ridiculous but somehow repellent; he didn't envy Louis his freedom. He was—and Mazÿck Marion also—infinitely happier than Louis Treves could ever be. Marion, if he should talk to him about it, would, of course, agree to that. It wasn't true, it was damnably untrue, and yet in a deeper sense it was completely true. But there would be no more talk between Mazÿck and himself about Diane. What Marion had said had been said in a moment of deep emotion, immediately after the battle. Mazÿck had never spoken of her in that way before. A way that confessed everything.

Mazÿck's case, he reflected, was as strange as his own; perhaps it was even stranger. Mazÿck knew her, he must know her; that which existed between them, which she permitted to exist, was in itself a sufficient revelation of her. Yet he too loved her. A strong man and a gentleman, married and the father of two children, he loved her. She was more potent, it seemed, than the most imperative obligations of honor—even the honor of such a man as Mazÿck...Well, there were forces, tremendous, irresistible forces...He turned away with a feeling of weariness; of helplessness in the face of unfathomable mystery, and looked across the water toward Charleston.

The colors of the sunset were fading; in the fine houses along the sea-wall promenade—the High Battery, it was always called—lights were beginning to twinkle; he thought that he could distinguish the lights in his own house. Actually, of course, it wasn't his but John's—his father's will had left the Acton townhouse to the older son—but Richard thought of it always as his also. Next to Avalon, it was his home; all his summers, before he had deserted Carolina for Europe, had been spent there. He was as much at home there now as he had ever been. In spite of all that had happened, his old room was always ready for him.

Elizabeth and the children were in Charleston now—they had moved down from the plantation earlier than usual—but John was in Richmond; as a member of the Confederate Congress, he was much of the time at the capital. Richard smiled grimly; John's secessionist views, never extreme, had not been intensified by his experience in the Confederate Congress; he hadn't always, to put it mildly, been able to agree with the policies of President Davis. Richard saw presently that a small steamer was approaching the fort from the direction of the city. He recognized it as a boat attached to the Department headquarters; probably General Beauregard was sending some officer of his staff to report on the condition of Sumter after the fight.

Well, Beauregard had been right; his confidence, whether real or assumed, had been justified; the ironclad fleet had been proved neither invincible nor invulnerable. Beauregard, with all his vanity, was able, undoubtedly one of the ablest of the Confederate commanders, but he wasn't a favorite of the Richmond government. John had said in one of his letters that the antagonism to Beauregard originated with the President himself. Richard Acton became aware again of the voices of the officers in the parade below: Hail's voice, Colonel Rhett's authoritative tones. Turning, he saw that Louis Treves had joined the group, but that Marion was not with them.

He wondered whether Marion shared his feeling toward Hail—because of Diane. He didn't think so. Marion's feeling—surely it couldn't help but exist—was of a different kind. He was conscious suddenly of his affection for Marion; Mazÿck had become, now that Lowndes Fenwick was dead, his closest friend. His feeling was something more than a natural development of his boyhood friendship; Diane, who had driven James Hail and himself apart, had somehow brought Mazÿck and himself together.

He felt all at once a cold anger rise in him, a sudden tightening of his sinews. James Hail, gazing upward at the rampart, was looking directly at him. His lips compressed, his eyes narrow and bright, he returned Hail's stare. For perhaps ten seconds this lasted; he felt rather than saw the contempt in James Hail's eyes. Contempt, he realized, not hatred: James Hail, damn him, didn't consider him worth hating! Colonel Rhett was pointing to a shell crater in the earth of the parade-ground and Hail turned away at once to resume his conversation with Rhett.

Richard Acton felt his tight muscles slowly relax; his mouth was twisted in a bitter smile. Some day he would kill the man. But to be despised by him now! Because of what had happened at Sherborne!

His thoughts, flung irresistibly back, dwelt somberly upon the days at Sherborne. They had begun, practically, on that night of the tournament ball in Pineland when, in the cloak-room of the Bohun house, he had taken Diane into his arms for the second time. The night that had revealed her finally, that had ended all hope. He had moved to Sherborne, defying the danger of summer fever, immediately afterward—he had to be alone—and had begun planting rice with the negroes that John had lent him.

There had been enough and too much of that—a long drawn torture. Diane before him always. At night the vision of Diane in James Hail's arms. That vision had persisted even after Mrs.

Rowland's death had caused postponement of the marriage. Or if not James Hail's arms, some other man's...There would be others; she had very practically told him that with her own lips...And the brandy at his elbow day and night, the brandy that brought dreams of Jacqueline and of Paris. And the girl Vienna coming in each evening to serve his supper and later to clear the table; moving noiselessly about the room, watching him expectantly as he sprawled in his big chair with the bottle beside him. Vienna inviting him with her hot eyes, her naked golden shoulders, her lithe body...

Well, he said to himself now, there had never been in reality any danger of that—that degradation. Not even when the brandy was most potent. Diane had made it doubly impossible. Diane, who had brought him low, had made it impossible for him to sink lower. Between Vienna and himself, Diane's face, her eyes, intervened. But the world didn't know that. The world knew only that he was living alone at Sherborne and that every evening there was a handsome yellow woman in his house.

Mazÿck Marion and Lowndes, he remembered, had told him plainly that he was doing a foolish thing; and John, when he had sent Vienna over from Avalon with the other negroes, evidently hadn't foreseen that Richard would use her as a house-servant—in the circumstances he would normally have had only menservants in the house. But the girl had seemed too slight and graceful for field work; and for the rest, he hadn't cared then what the neighborhood said or thought. They had thought, too, that he was an abolitionist—Charles Gough, he learned afterward, had spread that report. An abolitionist who kept a yellow mistress!

Yes, his visitors at Sherborne had been few. They were fewer still when it became evident that Vienna was going to have a child. Only Mazÿck Marion and Lowndes Fenwick and John. He had let them and the world in general think what they chose to think. He hadn't told any one what Vienna had told him.

Well, he had been a fool, an idiot. What that—his silence—had cost him had been incalculable. Perhaps, he thought cynically, the brandy more than anything else deserved the credit. Secession and the war had ended the Sherborne chapter; it had, at least, ended the brandy; in that sense, at any rate, he had recovered his manhood in Fort Sumter. He saw that the headquarters steamer had reached the wharf below the gorge of the fort. Captain Feilden, of Beauregard's staff, was standing on the forward deck. There were other officers in the cabin and he perceived with surprise that there were ladies also; he could see their dresses through the cabin windows.

Girls from Charleston evidently, friends of Beauregard's young aides, a-flutter with excitement at the prospect of visiting a fort which had just been the scene of a battle. Colonel Rhett, James Hail, Louis Treves and several other officers were hurrying through the sally-port and along the stone quay to meet the visitors about to land from the steamer. Richard turned and walked along the rampart, intending to descend to the parade and go to the barracks.

He lingered, however, some minutes on the rampart; he was again conscious of his headache and the breeze on his forehead was pleasant. Turning to go down the brick stairway to the parade, he heard voices, laughter. He halted, standing on the rampart at the top of the stairway.

Rhett, Feilden and the others were coming through the sally-port into the parade. Rhett and Feilden were talking earnestly; they were followed, more slowly, by Louis Treves and three young staff officers surrounding two young women. The evening light was fading, but he recognized Margaret Porcher and Julie Chardon. Then he saw James Hail and Diane emerge from the sally-port.

He grew cold. If he moved, she would see him on the rampart. He remained where he was, tense, trembling slightly. She was in white, with a white cape-like cloak, and her white hat was small, its felt brim caught up with a red cock's feather. James Hail was pointing out to her a scar made on the inner wall by a solid shot; he picked up and was showing to her a fragment of a fifteen-inch shell.

If only she would keep her eyes down! But it seemed to Richard Acton that her eyes were roving ceaselessly—once she seemed to be looking directly at him on the rampart. The light, however, was fading rapidly; there was a chance that he wouldn't be recognized. Suddenly the feeling came to him that if once his eyes could meet hers, though only for an instant, a miracle would happen. But something held him rigid; he remained through an eternity motionless except for the violent and uncontrollable shaking of his hands.

The others at last moved off across the parade. Margaret Porcher turned and called to Diane, "Aren't you and James coming? Louis has invited us to his quarters." Diane nodded. She moved slowly away at James Hail's side. So long as he could see her, Richard Acton's eyes followed her.

Chapter IV

At intervals, as the dawn lightened, compact swift-flying flocks of curlews, coming in from some offshore sandbar, burst through the curtain of mist with the suddenness of projectiles. It was a breathless morning in the July of '64, and Richard Acton, gazing seaward from the jagged parapet of Fort Sumter, said to himself that only in this portentous year could a fog so dense as this one shroud Charleston harbor in mid-summer. Charles Gough, turning to look eastward toward the invisible ironclads, moved his head quickly and uttered a sharp exclamation.

"I thought those birds were a shell," he explained, "coming right for us. One of those shells you see or think you see." He paused, then added, "I'll get used to this."

Richard Acton answered briefly, "Yes." Gough's explanation had hardly been necessary; his record in Micah Jenkins's Brigade in Virginia was known to have been more than creditable. The third man, an artillery corporal, spoke reassuringly to Gough:

"Yes, Cap'n," the man said, "you'll git used to it. You'll git used to a sight o' things if you stay in old Sumter long enough. An' them damn curlews bustin' out o' that fog is just like shells for a fact."

Gough made no comment; the discipline of Captain Thomas Huguenin, holding the battered remnant of Fort Sumter against the land and naval forces of the Union, permitted on informal occasions an easy intercourse between officers and men. Richard Acton tried to remember this fellow's name. Barr—Baines—Barnes—something of the kind; a corporal of artillery now but before that a private of Keitt's regiment from somewhere up the state. He had met him first in Battery Wagner; they had been through that hell together and he wasn't even sure of the man's name! That, however, wasn't remarkable. Outside of the Charleston Battalion, he hadn't known the names of a dozen privates in Wagner. There had been a constant shifting of the garrison through reliefs brought down from the city; no body of men had been able to stand the strain in Wagner for more than six successive days.

Charles Gough, staring fixedly into the fog, remained silent. Richard Acton, too, felt no inclination to talk. Unable to sleep in the hot and ill-ventilated bomb-proofs which had taken the place of the barracks long ago destroyed by the Federal siege guns, he had wandered rather aimlessly to the southeastern parapet facing the blockading fleet and the Union works on Morris Island, and he had been annoyed when the man Barnes and, a few minutes later, Charles Gough had joined him there.

Gough's presence disturbed him vaguely—he didn't at the moment ask himself why. Gough had arrived only the preceding evening at Sumter; he had been sent home from Virginia, he had said, on sick leave and, having now recovered, had requested a temporary assignment at the fort before rejoining his regiment in front of Richmond.

Well, he would learn soon enough what he had got into; his first night in Sumter had been one of the few quiet nights since the third great bombardment had begun. But the quiet wouldn't last much longer; the morning light was brightening and the fog was thinning; at any minute now the Yankee ships and batteries would become visible. Behind, in the obscurity of the empty amphitheater of the fort, the work details, busy since sundown in repairing the damage of the day before, were hurriedly completing their labors before the shelling was resumed. A glance over his shoulder into the parade showed Acton a dim file of men toiling across the torn and tumbled ground with bags of sand on their shoulders.

The fantastic and sinister grandeur of the scene took hold upon him. After three years of war, the whole interior of Sumter within the compass of its ruined walls was a vast crater cluttered with huge blocks of broken masonry, pitted with great holes and water-filled sinks blasted by exploding mortar shells, strewn with the wrecks of gun-platforms and gun-carriages and with dismounted cannon half buried in sand and mud.

He was conscious of a deep pride in the spectacle. Fort Sumter was known now from end to end of the civilized world;

the defense that had been made there would be famous through all the history of wars; it would be the glory of South Carolinians forever. It might be, the thought came to him, the dearest thing they had—a possession that no anguish of ultimate defeat could take from them. Charles Gough turned and looked down into the obscurity of the parade. "By thunder, Acton," he said, "you men have done well to hold on like this with the fort a ruin."

Acton nodded and the man Barnes said, "You're mighty right, Cap'n." He spat tobacco juice. "Anderson held this fort ag'in' us for two days," he drawled. "By God, we've held it ag'in' them for mor'n three years an' we're goin' to keep on a-holdin' it." He was silent a moment, staring into the fog, but almost at once he continued:

"When it's nice and quiet like this I remember how this damn thing started. Ef I'd a knowed as much then as I know now—but I reckon I'd a come anyhow. My brother and me was plowin' in a field about a quarter from the house. Father was peculiar; whenever he got excited, his face got white as a wad o' cotton. I seen him comin' from the house an' his face was white when he come up to us.

"'What's the matter, Father?' I ast him, an' he raised up his hand with his head cocked on one side. I could see he was listenin' too, an' I listened too, an' fer a minute I didn't hear nothin' except the birds a-singin'. It was April—April of '61, three years an' three months ago—an' the mockin'birds was kickin' up a racket. But I kep' on a-listenin' an' bimeby I heered it. I looked at father an' he said, 'Well, it's started.' Yes, sir, my home, where that field was, is in Aiken district; must be ninety miles in a straight line from Charleston. But we could hear them guns; we could hear old Beauregard givin' Anderson hell."

Richard Acton's sense of irritation increased. April of '61. Three years ago, Barnes had said. A thousand years ago! I was a mistake to go back to that time. At Sherborne the guns had been plainly audible. He had slept late—he had had too much brandy the night before—and Vienna, frightened by the far-off continuous rumbling, had come to the house to wake him. He had hurried to Charleston that day and enlisted as a private. John's influence could have obtained a staff appointment for him, but he had preferred to shoulder a musket.

He had never regretted that. He had opposed secession, but when secession came, he had very thoroughly accepted it. As a private,—a private in the ranks of the company that Mazÿck Marion had raised. They had served on James Island, including the Secessionvile fight, and then had been attached to the First South Carolina Artillery. That was how he had found himself in Sumter in time for the first attack by DuPont's fleet.

That—the fact seemed wholly incredible—was only a year and three months ago. April of '63 and this was July of '64. What had happened in Sumter between those dates had been enough, more than enough, to fill a lifetime. But those celebrated and tragic events engaged his thoughts only briefly; there was something in the stillness around him now that brought, suddenly, another and more poignant memory.

He had been standing, in the half-light of evening, on the western rampart. Diane, in the parade-ground below, had seemed to be looking directly at him; and abruptly the feeling had swept him that the barrier between them was unsubstantial, unreal—that if only their eyes could meet, the barrier would vanish. He had never known whether or not in the vague light she had recognized him on the rampart. He hadn't moved. Some inner compulsion of pride had held him rigid. And presently, answering Margaret Porcher's call, she had moved away.

He had never been able, in the months that had followed, to explain finally the feeling that had possessed him during those quivering moments—the sense of a miracle suspended, awaiting only the meeting of their eyes. It had had, while it lasted, the strength of complete conviction; yet it had been, of course, no more than a fantastic and ridiculous halucination. He was inclined to attribute it less to the strain of the battle he had just experienced than to Diane's power over him—power which again, in spite of all that he knew, had in those moments nearly overwhelmed him.

Well, thank God, he hadn't yielded to it. How fortunate that was had been made clear when next he had seen her. This—his next sight of her—was some four weeks later, in the buoyant springtime of Confederate triumph, when Chancellorsvile had been won in Virginia and often on the bright May afternoons Sumter was gay with Charleston's most charming girls, brought down to the fort by Rhett's and Beauregard's young officers to admire the perfection of the First Regiment's dress parade and dance in the evening to the music of the regimental band. She had come with three young officers in close attendance upon her: Lieutenants Ramon and LeClerc of New Orleans, temporarily attached to Beauregard's staff, and another whose name Richard hadn't learned. His eyes had met hers as he stood at attention in Captain Marion's company—and his eyes had been the first to turn away.

That, in a sense, had marked the end of a chapter; it had been a little easier thereafter to keep her at a distance, to confine her to the shadowy background of his mind. This last glimpse of her, the adored of Ramon and LeClerc, with James Hail again absent in Virginia, had been a reminder of what she was. A woman whose favors were so cheap that she seldom kissed any man twice—those, he remembered cynically, had been almost the last words he had heard her lips utter.

He had withdrawn after this farther into himself and yet, at the same time, had sought more actively Mazÿck Marion's companionship—his realization of a bond between Mazÿck and himself had grown steadily stronger. They never, of course, spoke of Diane; and Mazÿck's love for her remained for him inexplicable, a deeper mystery even than his own. He couldn't explain Mazÿck as simply another victim of her magic, despising her and yet compelled to love her. A heavy report in the direction of Morris Island interrupted his thoughts. The corporal, Barnes, said casually:

"Another one for Charleston. I kin tell by the sound."

Looking toward the city, where the fog bank had lifted, Acton saw the shell burst—a momentary flash low in the obscurity of the west. It had exploded apparently somewhere near the seawall promenade.

"I was in Charleston last week," Barnes continued calmly. "Didn't see twenty people this side o' Beaufain Street. The down-town streets had weeds in 'em high as my waist. That hotel—what's its name?—the Mills House—had eleven holes an' I seen plenty of other houses with roofs and walls busted in. A sight o' dead pigeons layin' 'round. A nigger told me they starved to death 'cause the shellin' scared 'em so they couldn't light an' eat."

He laughed and spat tobacco juice again. "I reckon that nigger was lyin'," he drawled. "Well, I ain't sorry if Charleston is feelin' this hyar war. She started it, an' it's right and fitten' for her to ketch some hell."

Charles Gough stared coldly at Barnes. Barnes grinned.

"No offense, Cap'n," he said. "I'll keep on a-fightin' as long as they's a Yankee with a gun in South Ca'lina. They ain't got no right hyar an' they got to git out. But I been shot at considerable and I done had one bullet in my guts an' I ain't as hot about this hyar war as I used to be. An' I come to find out all the sons of bitches ain't on the Yankee side. We got some too an' some of 'em is the double-j'inted kind an' meaner'n water rattlers. I'll keep on a-fightin' all right, but I kind of wish leetle old South Ca'lina hadn't of been so dog-gone brash back in '61."

Even Charles Gough, Acton said to himself with a grim inward smile, must share that wish. What had happened to Charleston and to Sumter since Gough's last visit to the fort—

he had spent a day there not long after the repulse of DuPont's squadron—was symbolical of what had happened to the whole Confederacy. The flush of victory hadn't lasted long; the girls, the dances, the parties, had ended suddenly. Their laughter had been drowned by the roar of cannon.

His thoughts swept back, with a bitter and exultant wonder, over the panorama of the past fifteen months, the desperate drama he had shared. By God, it was something to have been in Sumter during that time, to have had a part in what had been enacted there! For the moment this absorbed him and, forgetful of Charles Gough and Barnes on the parapet near him, he was thinking—a familiar habit of his memory—of the tournament at Pineland. No, it hadn't been only mummery, mere childish masquerade; the "knights" of the Pineland tournament had proved themselves men. On the battle-fields of Virginia and of the West and of Carolina and here in Sumter.

It was Sumter that concerned him. There was a tragic satisfaction, almost a happiness, strangely out of keeping with his accustomed cynicism, in thinking of what these, his countrymen, his Carolinians, had accomplished here. That it was vain, fruitless, doomed to ultimate failure took nothing from its glory—yes, he repeated, glory was the proper, the necessary word. It had begun, for him, with the repulse of DuPont's fleet; yet in reality that had been only the prelude. The ironclads had returned, after an interval, under a new commander, Dahlgren; Union land forces under Gillmore had effected a lodgment on Morris Island. He had been transferred temporarily to Battery

Wagner, Fort Sumter's principal outpost, and had been in the thick of the terrible fighting there.

That was in mid-July, a year ago. Motte Nesbit and David Ramsay of the Charleston Battalion had been killed then; he had seen Colonel Shaw of Boston killed on the Wagner rampart leading the great assault that had filled the moat with Union dead. Wagner had been held through fifty-eight desperate days and nights against the combined army and fleet, and meanwhile Gillmore's great siege guns, the most powerful ever used in war, had opened upon Sumter and upon Charleston itself.

That, the first of the great bombardments, had reduced Fort Sumter practically to a ruin and disabled all its cannon. Yet that first bombardment, lasting more than two weeks, was itself only a beginning. Colonel Rhett had been succeeded by Major Stephen Elliott—it was an odd fact, Richard reflected, that both Rhett and Elliott had been present at the dance at Notteley where he had met Diane. Elliott had scarcely taken command at Sumter when Morris Island had been evacuated and the heavy breaching batteries of the enemy were advanced to Cummings Point only fourteen hundred yards away. The total annihilation of Fort Sumter appeared inevitable. But Stephen Elliott, with Beauregard's approval and with a careful grammatical exactness, had answered Dahlgren's demand for surrender: "Inform Admiral Dahlgren that he may have Fort Sumter when he can take and hold it."

He had tried promptly to take it in a surprise attack at midnight by five columns of boats: the assault was beaten off with rifle-fire, hand-grenades, fireballs and brickbats. Especially brickbats, Richard recalled; his rifle disabled, he had fought the assaulting column with fragments of Sumter's crumbling walls. There had followed various engagements with the ironclads and the land batteries; and it was about this time, he thought, that the little cigar-boat *David*, designed by St. Julien Ravenel and built on his plantation near Avalon, had slipped out of the harbor with only her small stack showing and exploded a torpedo against the *New Ironsides*. A product of a Carolina plantation, he said to himself; the first submersible torpedo boat successfully used in war. Will Glassell had commanded her. A brave man—brave men all. But no braver than the men of the *Hundley* which had drowned four crews before George Dixon took her out with a fifth volunteer crew and sank the *Housatonic* and was himself drowned with all his men.

Was that before or after the second great bombardment of Sumter? It had lasted—the siege guns supported by the combined fire of the fleet—forty-one days and nights. Good God, the contrast between those days and nights and the pageantry at Pineland! But that perhaps was why they had kept the flag flying. A point of honor, a part of the old punctilio. They didn't really need a flag, but as fast as it was shot down from the shell-swept and disintegrating rampart they'd plant it there again. He had been wounded in the hand and shoulder; men had been struck down at his side; he had seen a whole detachment instantly killed by a collapsing wall. The worst blow had been the explosion of the magazine, killing and wounding more than fifty and setting the fort ablaze. That had happened, if he remembered correctly, not long before Christmas; and on Christmas Day the enemy had left Fort Sumter in peace. They had, however, thrown a hundred and fifty shells filled with Greek Fire into Charleston. The *Mercury* had announced sardonically that an old man, an old woman and a female negro slave had been killed.

All that was in '63—last year. It barely skimmed the surface; a thousand other things had happened; the *Weehawken*, he recalled, had been sunk; another boat attack had been repelled; Frank Harleston, Joe Huger, Stevens Colcock, among others, had been killed. The record of these first six months of '64 had not been greatly different. Fort Sumter, famous now all over Christendom, still held out, still blocked the water-gate to Charleston. But the shapely Fort Sumter of masonry and brick which had repulsed DuPont's fleet had vanished; what remained was a shapeless earthwork the sloping sides of which were formed by the fort's own ruin and by thousands of bags of sand brought in barges from the city at night.

That had been an enormous labor; the whole gorge front of Sumter facing the siege batteries had been converted into a massive redan of débris and sand. Lieutenant Johnson, the post engineer, had directed it and gangs of negroes had done most of the work under cover of darkness when ever the shelling lulled. When was it, his thoughts ran on, that Elliott had been called to Virginia and Mitchel had succeeded him? He couldn't, he found, remember dates or arrange events in their proper sequence. It was, at any rate, nearly three weeks ago, early July, that the third great bombardment had opened. General Foster had succeeded Gillmore on the Union side and he was determined, Union prisoners had reported, to obliterate Fort Sumter completely.

Yes, the past three weeks had probably been the worst. All day the great Parrott rifles on Morris Island thundered; at night, when the enemy's calcium lights at Cummings Point illumined the crumbling walls of the fort, a rain of mortar shells shook the bomb-proofs through an earth-covering seven feet thick. Mitchel had been killed and Tom Huguenin of Charleston had taken command...

His thoughts were halted suddenly by Barnes's hand closing on his arm.

"Look yonder," Barnes whispered.

The fog, still dense to the east and south, had thinned toward the landward side. Acton saw, for no more than a moment, the vague outline of a ship—low-hulled with short raking masts and two tall funnels. It vanished at once, melting into the fog; for an instant he almost doubted whether he had really seen anything. He knew, however, that he had: a blockade-runner putting to sea to run past the Union fleet guarding the harbor-mouth.

"Lordy, lordy," Barnes said, "I'm glad I ain't on her. I made one trip on a runner to Nassau an' back, an' that was enough. A foggy mornin' like this an' the damn fog lifted when we was right in the middle of 'em. Three Yankee ships slammed loose at us an' I was skeerder than I ever been before or since. Yes, sir, if I got to be shot at by Yankees, I want to be on the solid land. I don't want to feel no water gurglin' in my goozle when I'm a-dyin'."

He shook his head solemnly. "Reckon that's the *Banshee*. She come in last week from Nassau—I heard she brung in seven thousand rifles an' a lot o' uniforms. Now she's tryin' to run out again loaded to the gunn'ls with cotton that'll bring sixty cents a pound on the wharf at Nassau. Reckon that cargo of hers is wuth most every bit of half a million dollars. Well, she ought to make it if the fog holds. But, thank the lord, I ain't on her."

He yawned and stretched his arms. "I got to be goin'," he added. He took a plug from his pocket and bit off a piece of it.

"You-all better git down off this parapit," he continued. "It's nice and cool up here, but it ain't goin' to be healthy much longer. Them turret ships is liable to run in close on a mornin' like this an' lam loose at us the minute the fog lifts a leetle."

He made his way down the steep and uncertain slope of the mass of débris piled against the inner face of the gorge wall and disappeared behind a huge block of fallen masonry in the parade.

"A damned talkative nuisance," Charles Gough muttered.

Chapter V

Richard Acton said to himself that now Charles Gough would begin; he had had all along a feeling that Gough wanted to tell him something, that he had been waiting for Barnes to go. He didn't want to talk to Gough, or to anybody. The blessed peace, the quiet; that was what he wanted. He wanted to enjoy it undisturbed while it lasted; in a little while— any minute—the guns would open again.

They would begin as soon as the fog lifted. The huge mortar shells and the swift deadly shells from the Parrott guns. All day and perhaps all night and all day again. No peace, no safety except in the stifling bomb-proofs and the subterranean tunnels. Yes, Charles Gough would learn soon enough what he had got into. Richard Acton's thoughts jumped back to his first meeting with Gough. He could see him sitting on the piazza at Avalon with Louis Treves; they had come to bring him what was practically a challenge from James Hail. That, too, was because of Diane, because of what had occurred when he saw her for the first time in the pine-wood. Well, it was all fated, predestined from the beginning—all that had happened. It was at that moment in the pine-wood, the moment when he first saw her, that his conflict with Hail had begun.

Yes, all that had happened since then had been inevitable. Lowndes Fenwick was dead and Hutson Waight was dead. Dead in a war in which the South itself was perishing. He hadn't any doubt about that now, though there were still some who wouldn't see it; Mazÿck Marion, for instance. Mazÿck was as confident as ever that the Confederacy would be established; because he couldn't believe that a just cause could be lost. Well, Robert Shaw of Massachusetts, charging the rampart of Wagner at the head of his negro regiment and dying on the bloody parapet, had also believed that his cause was just.

He had met Shaw at Philips Cordray's house in Boston before the war and had liked him. Shaw was dead now, and Lowndes, Fenwick was dead. But William Lloyd Garrison the abolitionist and Barnwell Rhett the secessionist were alive. And Mrs. Stowe was alive—a good woman whose pen had killed more men than all of General Grant's cannon. Probably some of the other young Bostonians he had met at the Cordray's were dead in battle; half the men he had met at the Notteley party, half the men who had ridden in the tournament at Pineland, had been killed or crippled in the war. Stuart Chantilly, Buist Pringle, Ball Moultrie, Stevens Colcock. There were others; he couldn't always remember whether they had been killed or badly wounded. The last he had heard of was Ash Rowland; he had died of wounds received at Cold Harbor.

That, so far, was the hardest blow the war had dealt Diane. He knew that she had been devoted to Ash; perhaps it was because they were so like each other. In more ways than one, he added grimly. Well, at any rate, she had kept the memory of her brother unsoiled. His eyes rested on Charles Gough leaning upon a jagged remnant of the parapet gazing seaward into the fog. Why was it he didn't like Gough? A positive and practical man of more than common intelligence. Gough, he remembered suddenly, had spread the report that he was an abolitionist. But that wasn't the cause of his feeling—it was so far in the past that it no longer mattered. Probably, he admitted to himself, it was simply that Gough was associated in his mind with James Hail.

He saw that to seaward the fog, instead of lifting, had grown more dense. That ought to help the blockade-runner; he pictured her threading her way silently amid the watchful Federal ships. It was a dangerous game those fellows played, more dangerous than ever now. For a long while they had had it all their own way; the runners—light Clyde-built steamers, slim and colored like grey-hounds—were the fastest vessels afloat; they were equipped with telescopic funnels that in case of need could be lowered almost to the decks and their short masts carried no spars. But with the increasing efficiency of the blockade the perils of blockade running had increased; probably the *Banshee's* fate depended largely on the fog.

The thought was still in his mind when, away to the east, he heard the report of a cannon; then another and another. They had seen her, perhaps they had sunk her; the beaches on both sides of the harbor-mouth were dotted with the wrecks of runners which had been driven ashore to escape capture.

He heard another and heavier report—judging from the direction, another shell for Charleston. Evidently the guns that were trained on the city weren't waiting for the fog to lift. Diane was in Charleston, but he knew that she wasn't in danger. Only the lower half of the city was in range of the Federal shells and it was deserted. Diane was living in the house up-town that Sally Hemmerton and her husband occupied.

Sally Hemmerton! He glanced again quickly at Charles Gough. He had forgotten that Gough had been in love with Sally. They had been engaged to be married; James Hail was engaged to Diane, and Gough, Hail's closest friend, was engaged to Diane's sister. At the last moment Sally had thrown Gough over. There had been almost a scandal; Hemmerton, a tutor from the up-country, hadn't been regarded as Sally Rowland's social equal. He had turned out pretty well, however—Richard realized with annoyance that Gough was speaking.

"Acton," Gough said, "if we had listened to you, this wouldn't be happening."

He didn't immediately grasp Gough's meaning—his thoughts had been too far removed from the war; but his irritation was sharpened. He wanted desperately to enjoy the silence, the peace; it had been merely accentuated, made more sweet, by the distant cannon shots which held no menace for Sumter. It was worse than useless now to go back to the beginning. All that was irrevocable. He had opposed secession because he hadn't believed that it could succeed. It was clearer than ever now that he had been right. Charles Gough continued:

"Shells dropping in Charleston. Sherman before Atlanta. Joe Johnston superseded. The Mississippi lost. In Virginia—well, we're holding them in Virginia. Grant's lost more men since the Wilderness than Lee has in his whole army. By God, Acton, Lee is one of the great captains. But you were right: it's hopeless. I think it's been hopeless ever since Jackson died."

He paused but resumed quickly.

"Don't misunderstand me. I don't regret anything I did to bring this about. You remember I was one of Barnwell Rhett's supporters and he was the real head of the secession movement in South Carolina. He was right. Secession was the only course for us; it was independence or complete subservience—the South a mere appendage of the North, paying perpetual tribute. And it was true that liberty was at stake. There won't be any real liberty any more—liberty in our sense, the individual integrity of the states. What we'll have from now on in America will be central consolidated power with the North in the saddle. That, in reality, is what we've fought against. We ought to have been able to win, but we've botched it—not our soldiers but our politicians."

Richard Acton admitted briefly the justice of that; he had no desire to discuss anything, least of all the war, with Charles Gough, but it seemed necessary to say something. He had again a feeling that there was something else in Gough's mind, something that he found it difficult to come to. Gough, however, continued:

"By thunder, Acton, the men who made this revolution haven't been allowed to run it. Barnwell Rhett couldn't foresee, none of us could, the mistakes that have been made. I'll admit Mr. Davis's difficulties—Rhett and the *Mercury* and plenty of others have given him the devil—perhaps they've been too critical. But largely they've been justified.

"We've wasted our opportunities—just as at the beginning we wasted our cotton. Our best weapon. But it's the military side I'm thinking of. We ought to have concentrated our efforts and, instead, we diffused them. Lee's been too tractable—it's almost his one weakness. He ought to have taken things into his own hands; they haven't a man that can touch him and he could have won his war.

"Damn it, I think Beauregard might have won it; he had the concentration idea very clearly in his head, but of course they wouldn't listen to him in Richmond. Maybe they will now, after what he did at Petersburg last month, but I doubt it. Of course Early's invasion is nothing but a diversion; there isn't a chance of taking Washington. The worst thing yet is taking Joe Johnston out and putting in Hood to fight Sherman. Sherman's able—hard, but able—and Johnston was playing the only possible game. Obviously, the pressure on Davis was heavy with Johnston giving up half of Georgia—but, if Atlanta falls—"

He shrugged his shoulders and was silent for some moments. Presently he continued:

"What I mean, Acton, is this: we can't win this war in the field. We could have once, but we can't now. I talked with Wade Hampton just before his fight at Trevilian's. I think he agrees with me, but James Hail doesn't. He thinks the *Mercury* and Mr. Rhett are right in opposing any compromise peace—any peace short of complete independence. Well, damn it, they're wrong. The time's past for that; we can't have it now. The North's tired, ready to quit, but they'll go on if we force them to. If the Northern Democrats win the election, they'll make a peace offer and we ought to meet them half-way. I've come to that—"

He stopped with a gesture of annoyance. A figure, shadowy and vague in the mist, was climbing the steep slope from the parade-ground. It wasn't, however, Barnes returning but Mazÿck Marion. Captain Marion greeted them with a pleased surprise.

"I wanted a whiff of breeze," he explained, "before hell breaks loose again. I didn't know you two were here. Not intruding, am I?"

"I'm glad you came, Marion," Gough answered. There's something..." He paused for a moment reflecting.

"There's something," he went on, "I want to say to Acton and I'd like you to hear it. You remember a dinner at Notteley when you made a speech in favor of secession and Mr. Rhett also spoke? You'll remember, too, I announced that Acton was an abolitionist? We'd discovered that he had been writing to certain northern Republican leaders and we formed our conclusion from that.

"Well, we were mistaken. I won't go into details now. Acton, we captured Philips Cordray of Boston, in a skirmish on the Chickahominy. He was an infantry major and a nice fellow. I saw something of him while he was in our camp and I learned the facts from him—about those letters of yours. It was my fault that you were pretty generally, regarded as an abolitionist. I want to tell you now that I'm sorry."

Acton looked at him briefly, then nodded. What Charles Gough was talking about seemed to him very far away, utterly unimportant; and what he had tried to accomplish through Philips Cordray had been, he realized now, a pitiful futility. He had tried to sweep back the tide; he had tried to make the northern Republican leaders see that if they nominated Lincoln, southern secession would follow. A little later Samuel J. Tilden, of New York, had tried to do the same thing: he had warned his people, in an open letter which had attracted wide attention, that the election of Lincoln, a sectional candidate obnoxious to the South, would bring disruption of the Union. They had both failed—his own obscure effort had been as futile as Tilden's.

Well, it didn't matter now. That water had gone under the bridge long ago; and the fact that he had been regarded as an abolitionist had be the least part of his unhappiness at Sherborne. He stared into the fog hiding the Union batteries on Morris Island and the ironclads of Dahlgren's fleet. Unmistakably the fog was thinning; it wouldn't be safe to stay on the parapet too long. Joe Huger, he remembered, had done that and an unexpected shell had taken off his head. The low-lying monitors could see the bulk of Sumter before they themselves became visible. They might be lying close in, as Barnes had said, and when they opened, there wouldn't be any warning. Charles Gough was again speaking:

"There's another matter," Gough said. "You both knew, of course, that Ash Rowland had been killed. He was hit in the stomach in the last attack at Cold Harbor and he died late that night. I was with, him. He knew he was dying, and just before the end came he told me this:

"He said that he had had a child by that quadroon girl you had with you, Acton, as a house-servant at Sherborne. He said that all the talk about you and the woman was false, that he didn't believe you had ever touched her, that she had been his wench for months—they used to meet at the old Gilpin cabin, he said—and that her child was his. He asked me—damned if I know why—to tell Diane all this. He also asked..."

Richard Acton interrupted him.

"To tell Diane!" he said in a harsh angry voice. "You won't do that."

Gough glanced sharply at him.

"Ash made me swear," he replied, "on my honor..."

"Gough," Richard said, "to hell with your honor. If you tell Diane this, I'll kill you."

Mazÿck Marion grasped Acton's arm.

"Richard," he asked, "did you know this all the time? Did you know that child was Ash Rowland's?"

Richard stared at him in silence. Marion fell back a step and exclaimed:

"Good God, man, why didn't you tell us? Why did you let us all think..."

The sudden and heavy crash of a cannon cut him short. Simultaneously Acton saw for a fraction of a moment a red gleam in the fog to the eastward of the fort, like lightning flashing in a gray cloud. He was conscious of a humming sound that sharpened to a whine; it filled his ears; some thing passed him screaming. Behind, within the fort, there was a shattering detonation as the shell burst over the parade.

Mazÿck Marion leaped down from the parapet. Acton turned to pull Charles Gough down, but Gough wasn't there. Richard looked behind him and saw Gough lying on his back half-way down the rough slope.

Chapter VI

AT NIGHTFALL, WHEN THE SEVERITY of the day's bombardment had diminished, one of the quartermaster department steamers, with which communication between the city and Fort Sumter was regularly maintained under cover of darkness, approached within three hundred yards of the fort and sent her boat with mail and small supplies for the garrison. This boat, returning immediately to the steamer, carried Charles Gough's body and that of a private killed later in the day, together with several wounded men. News of these casualties had been included in the commanding officer's daily report sent to the city over the submarine telegraph connecting Fort Sumter with the headquarters in Charleston. It was expected that a military escort would be waiting for Captain Gough's body at the wharf. Mean while Captain Mazÿck Marion was in charge of it.

The escort was waiting—a guard of honor composed of cadets from the Citadel Military Academy. Mazÿck Marion, his immediate duty discharged, left the wharf and walked rapidly westward along Broad Street.

He saw by the light of the gas lamps that the shelling of the city by the long-range Federal guns was becoming an increasingly serious matter. Charleston, the lower part of it at least, had now been under direct fire for nearly a year. The firing was irregular yet persistent; on some nights no shells would be thrown, on other nights a hundred or more. Probably it was true, as the *Mercury* and the *Charleston Courier* indignantly asserted, that this desultory bombardment achieved no military advantage for the enemy. But the damage to buildings had now become considerable; the southern half of the city, including the finest residential section and the business district, had been virtually abandoned.

Broad Street was empty as he walked west toward Meeting; grass was growing in the street and in places the pavement was littered with fallen bricks and slates. He saw above him the shattered facade of a bank building and, near Church Street, he passed the ruins of two houses which had been totally destroyed.

At the corner of Meeting Street, with St. Michael's steeple looming above him in the faint moonlight, he turned north up Meeting. On his left he saw the dark mass of the Mills House, before the war a fashionable hotel, its high walls now riddled with shell-holes. Beyond this was desolation—the "burned district," a broad belt across the width of Charleston, swept by the great fire of 1861.

Here nothing remained except blackened chimneys and broken walls with now and again the stone or marble steps of what had once been the handsome town-house of some wealthy planter. On his right were the ruins of Institute Hall, where the Ordinance of Secession had been signed, and next to this the burnt-out shell of the Circular Church with its dismantled stately columns like an antique temple. The besieging guns had wrecked what the flames could not destroy; in the churchyard tombstones had been thrown down and shattered by exploding shells.

Meeting Street, except for a few prowling dogs, was as lifeless as Broad had been. The heavy and tragic stillness around him was broken only by the intermittent thunder of the guns on Morris Island. Apparently there would be no rest for old Sumter tonight, though, as usual, the firing had slackened since nightfall. He heard suddenly the familiar whining sound of a shell. It burst in the air perhaps a hundred and fifty yards to his right; he thought he saw in the momentary glare the tall outline of St. Philip's steeple.

He smiled grimly. John C. Calhoun was buried in St. Philip's graveyard. What would Calhoun have said if he could have known that fourteen years after his death Union shells filled with Greek Fire would be exploding over his grave?

Well, he wouldn't have wavered. And Charleston, thank God, wasn't wavering. She was bearing her long agony with a courage worthy of her past, a fortitude that her future generations couldn't forget. This was her dark hour, but she would rise from her ashes. He told himself that he had no more doubt now than he had had at the beginning; the cause of southern independence couldn't fail; no cause that was so completely just could be lost.

It was strange, he reflected, how remote his thoughts had been from what was now immediately ahead of him. That, however, was only partly true, and, in so far as it was true, it was due to a deliberate effort of his will. Diane, the consciousness that he was about to see Diane, had never been absent from him. For the rest—well, he had tried not to think about that, about what he was going to say to her.

Beyond Market Street he passed out of the burned district and, somewhat later, out of the bombarded area. The silence and desolation were now behind him. Much of the non-combatant population had left the city with the approval of the military authorities; those that remained were concentrated in these upper precincts which the enemy's shells could not reach. The houses here were open, bright with lights, the streets alive with people, most of them women and children with a few old men.

Marion turned to the right out of Meeting Street and rang the bell at Calvin Hemmerton's house. Hemmerton, a writer on the *Charleston Courier*, would hardly be at home at this hour, but, besides Diane, Sally would probably be there and, of course, her two children. He was admitted by a servant who greeted him with a respectful familiarity, and within a few minutes Diane joined him in the drawing-room.

She was, as he had expected, in white; wisely, he thought, she had decided not to wear black for Ash. She had told him this the first time he had seen her after Ash's death. Ash wouldn't have wanted it, she had said, and there was too much black already; nearly all the women of Charleston were in mourning. She greeted him warmly, holding out her hands to him with her old smile. She was pale and thinner, though not less lovely, than when he had seen her a month ago during his last leave of absence from Fort Sumter. Her beauty—it was always, for him, so much more than that—was tonight a stab in the heart. What he had made up his mind to say to her, he realized, had better be said quickly.

It would be cooler where they were, she suggested, than on the piazza, since the breeze was from the east. She sat among cushions on a sofa near a window. They spoke, first of Charles Gough; the morning papers, of course, had reported his death.

It had been a shock to Sally, Diane said—to all of them...it had brought back the old days at Notteley when they had seen so much of Charles...Sally wouldn't come down, she added, and Calvin was at the *Courier* office, the children in bed. Marion had, suddenly, an impression that there was something, something important, which she was about to tell him.

"Diane," he interrupted quickly, "I'll never change; I'll always feel about you exactly the same way. You know that, of course. You have always known everything about me. Everything that, for obvious reasons, I couldn't tell you."

She nodded gravely. Marion continued:

"I wanted to say that much. I felt that tonight I could say it. Perhaps when I'm through, you will see why."

He paused. She was looking at him expectantly.

"You'll have to let me talk for a while," he told her. "I have to talk about a disagreeable thing. I'm going to speak plainly because I can't do it any other way. It's about Ash and that girl Vienna."

She was silent for some moments; her eyes, he thought, had grown wider and her pallor had increased.

"You have to talk about that now, Mazÿck," she said slowly, "With Ash dead only two months?"

He nodded, frowning. She spread her hands in a helpless gesture.

"Very well," she said.

"You know part of it already," he continued. "You know that Ash and that girl—well, you'll remember the day I brought you home from the Gilpin cabin. What I have to tell you now is that it didn't end there. You remember that later on this girl, Vienna, was sent to Sherborne with the other negroes that John Acton lent Richard when he was starting his rice planting. Richard foolishly used her as a house-servant, had her in the house every evening, serving his supper and so forth. That was idiotic—the woman was too handsome to be safe and it was plain enough what she was.

"Naturally all kinds of rumors started—he was already under a cloud because he was supposed to be an abolitionist. I tried to make him see that he was ruining himself—that people wouldn't overlook so open a performance—but he didn't seem to care either about the abolitionist rumors or the talk about the woman and himself. He was in a curiously black mood at

Sherborne; at the time I didn't know why. He was so stubborn about the woman that there didn't seem to be any doubt, the situation seemed plain. I knew about Ash, of course, but I thought that was over and done. When Vienna had a baby, obviously by a white man, I believed, like everybody else, that it was Richard's. You believed that too, Diane. He never denied it. There wasn't anything else to believe."

She was looking at him intently. Her lips were parted slightly. Marion, trying to read her eyes, imagined, that he saw in them the birth of an incredible hope. He continued quickly:

"Diane, that wasn't true. I learned the truth from Charles Gough. Richard and I were with Charles on the parapet when he was killed. He had just finished telling us what I have to tell you now. He said that he was with Ash when Ash was dying. Just before the end came he told Charles that he, Ash, was the father of Vienna's child. He said that all the talk about Richard Acton had been false, that Richard had never touched the woman, that she had been continuously his, Ash's, wench. And, Diane, he made Charles swear that he would tell you this."

Watching Diane's face with a strained, almost a desperate, intentness, Marion was conscious suddenly of a loathing of himself. Good God, he had been mistaken after all; what he had told her didn't mean what he had hoped it would mean to her. All that he had accomplished was to hurt her cruelly, to hurt her unbelievably. He had made her see her dead brother as he really was: a coward, a liar, who had held his tongue while Richard

Acton had been damned. She hadn't known that Ash had done that, that he was that; she need never have known.

Mazÿck Marion turned miserably away. When he looked at her again her face had changed; what he saw in it amazed him. He hadn't destroyed her! He had given her life! He knew this instantly, knew it beyond all doubt. He rose and moved toward her. For a moment, however, he couldn't speak. Suddenly, looking down into her eyes, his longing for her overwhelmed him. The words came, at first, slowly:

"You see I had to tell you. Ash wanted it. I suppose it was a kind of atonement. There's another reason, Diane. I wanted you to know what Richard did, how tremendous it was. He knew the child was Ash's. I think Vienna told him; at any rate, he knew. But he never told anyone; not even John or Lowndes Fenwick or myself. He let us, everybody, believe that he was living openly with a yellow woman at Sherborne, having children by her.

"Good God, Diane, think what that cost him! He was practically ostracized, you remember. Only a few of us had anything to do with him. He went through hell. And at any minute he could have cleared himself; he could have made the truth known about Ash. Your brother, Diane. Remember, he didn't know that you knew anything about Ash and Vienna. Diane, don't you see why he kept silent? Why he let us, why he *made* us, think what we all thought? Why he deliberately took this thing upon himself?"

Marion, waiting breathlessly for her to answer, was suddenly frightened, afraid of something he couldn't name. Her hands were at her breast, her lips were parted, her eyes were very widely open. He saw with bewildered consternation that the life had gone out of her face; it had been succeeded by something that was like death. He couldn't look at her; the despair in her eyes stabbed him like a bayonet. He turned away and walked toward the closed fireplace.

He stood there, his back turned toward her, stupefied, utterly dismayed. After a long time he heard her voice; he had an impression of one groping in darkness.

"Mazÿck," she said, "you mean you think Richard Acton did this for me—so that I wouldn't know about Ash. I can hardly believe that. Because there are other things, things that I can't explain, that make it seem almost impossible. Things that have happened between Richard Acton and me. But, Mazÿck, I want to believe it, and if you are very sure of it I want you to thank him for me. I want you to tell him that I'll never forget it. But only if you are very sure, so sure that there can't be any mistake..."

She broke off abruptly, but he did not turn. He knew somehow that he must not see her face. She continued:

"I am going to be married to James day after tomorrow."

There was a long silence. Marion, staring down at the hearth at his feet, opened and shut his hands. He heard her voice again:

"James is here, in Charleston, now for the wedding. He has waited a long time and I decided three weeks ago that he needn't wait any longer. So he came home from Virginia yesterday. It will be very quiet, of course, because of Ash: only Sally and Calvin and Sinkler and, I hope, you. I wrote to you last night at the fort to ask you to come if you could. Look at me, Mazÿck."

He turned and looked at her. She held out her hands to him. She was smiling. It would have been less terrible, he realized, if she had wept. She held his hands tightly. He had a feeling that she was clinging to him, desperately clinging. But not to him really; to something he represented.

"That was fine of you," she said, her voice shaking; "your not looking at me when I was telling you that. You have always been fine, Mazÿck. And this thing you've tried to do for me now... Mazÿck so many things come too late."

He glanced at her quickly. He saw at once that she had not meant to admit what that implied. Her courage thrilled him.

"I don't know what I meant by that," she said immediately. "Not what you may have thought, Mazÿck. I am going to marry James because I love him. We are going to be very happy..."

He turned from her. The look on her face was destroying him; he couldn't bear it. He moved toward the door.

"You will remember to thank him?" she said brokenly. "You will remember..."

Chapter VII

GOING DOWN THE FRONT STEPS into the street, he stumbled and struck his knee against the iron side-railing. He was only momentarily conscious of the sharp pain. He walked rapidly to the corner of Meeting Street and turned south along Meeting. Later—he had passed unheeding through the desolation of the burned district, under the pillared portico of St. Michael's, and between rows of dark houses empty and scarred by shells—he found himself under the oaks of the Battery Park overlooking the harbor.

He loved her, he said to himself, as much as either of these others. Yes, he loved her as much as Richard loved her, as much as James loved her. Well, then, what was he going to do for her now?

There must be something—some way out. He couldn't stand idly by—let this happen. Not after what he had seen in her face. God, she hadn't known how tragically her face had refuted that proud and gallant lie!

Day after tomorrow. Damn it, there was no time. He walked on rapidly and turned east under the oaks of the park toward the sea-wall promenade. Far off down the harbor he saw a momentary flash in the darkness—a shell bursting over Sumter; another and another. The boom of the siege guns on Morris Island was an insistent menacing reiteration of heavy thumps against his eardrums. High in the air a thin fiery snake darted across the black heavens. He saw the fiery snake curve downward, heard the explosion as the shell struck perhaps half a mile up town beyond the City Hall.

Ahead of him he heard voices, men talking and laughing. In the vague light of the park gas lamps he saw the rounded dome of the mound battery built to command the inner harbor; just beyond this the sea-wall promenade, once the favorite resort of fashionable Charleston, bristled with ten-inch columbiads and a huge Blakely rifled gun. He saw in the dimness the shadowy forms of half a dozen artillerymen leaning against the railing of the southern sea-wall.

He turned and walked westward toward the middle of the park. Thank heaven, the place was deserted; since the city had come under fire the park was no longer thronged every evening. Most of the shells, however, passed north of it and fell among the houses. He could sit here and think in quiet and the breeze from the harbor would help. He didn't as a rule mind the summer heat, but now he felt as though a fever were raging in him. He took off the jacket of his uniform and with his handkerchief wiped the perspiration from his face.

There must be a way—some way. Suddenly tired, he wondered irritably what had become of all the benches; the Battery Park used to be full of them. He found one presently under one of the oaks in deep shadow beyond reach of the feeble gas lamps. Seated there, his unlighted pipe clenched between his teeth, the thumping of the siege guns in his ears, he tried to set his thoughts in order.

That, however, wasn't possible at once. He couldn't for a time think of anything except her face as he had just seen it. "Good God!" he exclaimed aloud. "Good God! Good God!" Day after tomorrow! The thing was on him. There was no time for thinking or planning. No time to talk with her again, to argue with her...

That would be useless anyhow. She could do nothing. It was too late. James was in Charleston to marry her. She couldn't stab James Hail's soul to death, kill him, murder him. That would be what it would amount to. He wouldn't die physically, but he would die, she would have murdered him. Because James was what he was. Mazÿck Marion saw with an increasing clearness that she couldn't save herself, that only he could save her because he alone knew. Well, he ask himself coolly, precisely what did he know?

One thing that mattered now—that she loved Richard Acton. He had staked everything that night upon his belief that she loved Richard. This belief had become almost a certainty when he learned that Ash had made Charles Gough swear to tell Diane the truth about Vienna. Ash and Diane had been very close to each other. Clearly Ash had known what was in her heart.

There was no vestige of doubt now: her face had revealed everything. Not only her face—her words. What she had said at the last had been practically an avowal. There was much, Marion told himself, that was still obscure, hidden from him. Something had held them apart, something that had happened before Richard had moved to Sherborne. He had a feeling, a feeling that almost frightened him, that in some strange fatal way Richard had failed to understand her. What Richard had done at Sherborne—the role he had deliberately adopted there— had driven them still further apart. And yet what Richard had done there he had done for her sake—a sacrifice, an enormous sacrifice, that a man could make only for a woman he loved.

That was clear, and something more than that was clear: Richard loved her, but he had no hope of her; for this very sacrifice that he had made for her had placed an impassable barrier between them. But now suddenly the barrier was down, and the sacrifice was revealed. He, Marion, had revealed it to her that night.

God, what that must have meant to her! The truth bursting upon her like that! She must have known then, in spite of what she had said, in spite of anything that had gone before, that Richard loved her. He thought of how her face had looked, how for a moment it had been transfigured. Then it had changed, changed so that he couldn't bear to look at it. She had told him then that she was going to marry James Hail.

Well, he told himself through tight lips, she wasn't! That wasn't going to happen. Christ, he wouldn't let it happen! There must be some escape, some way out. For a moment, a blind moment, it seemed to him that the way was plain. He would go and see James now, tonight, put the whole situation before him. James would be at the Merchants' Hotel; he always stayed there when he was in Charleston. He began to go over in his mind what he would tell James and at once he saw the impossibility of this plan. It would mean simply that he had caused Diane to murder James. She would have murdered him as truly as though her own lips had dealt the blow.

He saw that clearly. He couldn't, behind her back, make Diane do what she had already declined to do. She herself had realized that she couldn't by destroying James win happiness. Mazÿck Marion understood finally with an unescapable and tragic certainty that his problem was either beyond solution or else was very simple. That depended, for him, upon which of two alternatives would be better for Diane; and, as quietly, as calmly as he could, he began to consider these alternatives, to weigh them against each other with a minute and far-sighted and searching carefulness.

For an hour he struggled thus, his face, his whole body, bathed in sweat. A shell exploded at the entrance of Meeting Street no more than fifty yards away. He wasn't aware of it.

In the end his decision was clear, unshadowed by doubt. What that decision implied for him he accepted with a calmness that amazed him. That, he supposed, was partly the effect of war; but even before war had hardened him, he had never, he said to himself, shrunk from realities, necessities. He heard, without being conscious of the sound, the intermittent boom of the guns bombarding Sumter; again he saw a faint trail of fire in the air and heard the crash of a shell somewhere near St. Michael's Church. The thought came to him that four years ago that would have been incredible—shells bursting around St. Michael's, the heart of Charleston. Well, there were other things as incredible as that. This thing that he was going to do.

It was incredible and yet there was a cold logic in it from which there was no escape. If it was true—and it was—that he placed Diane before everything else, his course was plain. The price couldn't alter that—there were other things more important than life. Thus it was held in Carolina not merely permissible but imperative that an insult to a woman be answered with a challenge. To that principle, unquestioned in the circle in which he moved, he was, had always been, wholly committed. It was, in his view, necessary to the maintenance of the only kind of society that was worth maintaining; it was a part of that conception of individual responsibility and obligation which enabled men to be gentlemen.

If, then, he would have felt compelled to take upon himself the life of any man who offered insult to Diane, upon what ground of logic could he refuse the service to her that fate had forced upon him now? True, it wasn't her honor that was at stake; it was her happiness. But her happiness was not less dear to him, he admitted, than her honor; to make possible her happiness was, in any practical consideration, a more adequate reason for taking a man's life than a slight that could do her no real harm. And there was no other way in which that could be accomplished. If he stood aside, if he failed her...

He dismissed this impatiently—he had already been over it all in his mind. He wouldn't, he couldn't, fail her. No matter what the cost. Thence, inevitably, his thoughts turned to James Hail. He had known James since boyhood, they had slept in each other's homes, hunted deer together; he remembered that they had attended together their first St. Cecelia Ball. It was James who had introduced him to Diane long ago in Beaufort before the Rowlands had moved to Notteley. Even after it had happened to him, even with Diane standing between them, his admiration, his warm affection, for Hail had never been impaired.

That had been possible because he had recognized from the beginning that he could never have her. An obvious and immutable fact. He had put his love for her where it had to remain; what his name and tradition required of him he had fully performed. And now he alone could save her—at a cost to himself beyond all calculation, all repair. Well, Richard had done as much for her. But at once he realized, with a certain exaltation, that that wasn't true. Not even the thing that Richard had done was as difficult at this. James Hail! His friend!

He tried, summoning all his resolution, to foresee what would happen in James's room at the Merchants' Hotel. It would have to happen there and at once; obviously formalities, seconds and so forth would be impossible. In the strict sense it wouldn't be a duel at all. But there were precedents; such duels had been fought. He would stand against one wall, James against the other.

It was likely, he realized suddenly, that James would think him crazy; another case of insanity caused by the war. For a moment, overwhelmed by the unspeakable horror of what might in a certain case become necessary, he wondered whether this was true, whether his long ordeal at Sumter had affected his mind. He dismissed this conjecture at once, but his thoughts dwelt with a fearful and almost a terrified fascination upon what would confront him if James refused to fight. A duel, no matter how irregular, was one thing; a murder was another.

He couldn't face the thought of that. Yet he knew that all along that was what, he had been facing—the possibility, perhaps the probability, that he would have to abandon Diane in her extremity or kill James Hail in cold blood. "Oh, my God! My God!" he cried aloud; the words were a supplication upon his dry lips. He had a sudden and utterly desperate feeling that something, the universe, was crushing him, pressing upon him from all sides. He rose abruptly, put on the jacket of his uniform and looked at his watch.

It was nearly midnight; James would certainly have returned to the hotel. Walking up Meeting Street, he was strangely calm, acutely conscious of everything around him; he saw in the faint moonlight that the weeds and grass in the middle of the street were as high as his waist. Several of the fine houses near the Battery Park had been badly damaged by shells; the Scotch

Church had great breaches in its high brick walls. He turned west through Tradd, then northward again up King Street, seeing no sign of life except an occasional monstrous rat, gaunt jackal-like dogs and a squad of soldiers moving southward—reliefs evidently for the artillerymen at the guns mounted on the sea-wall promenade.

At Broad Street, glancing to the left, he saw, against a glimmer of heat lightning in the west, the jagged ruins of St. Finbar's Cathedral; near it stood the blackened remnant of St. Andrew's Hall where often he had danced at the St. Cecelia Balls. Midway of the burned district he heard and saw another shell coming. It burst in the air—a fuse shell evidently—five or six blocks ahead of him and to the east.

That, he thought, was a little too close to the Hemmerton house. Diane and the others would have to move farther up-town. Diane...A woman in whom dwelt a power beyond all comprehension, the power to create a love like this. But she had done, he reflected, an even greater thing: she had triumphed over what until then he had regarded as concepts eternally fixed. She was bound to another man, and he, married and James Hail's friend, was bound by an indissoluble tie; yet her acceptance of the fact of his love had taken nothing from her, had only revealed more clearly to him her knowledge of its quality, its power. In any other woman that attitude would have been fatal; his definition of it and of the woman would have been plain. But there wasn't a spot upon Diane, not one spot.

He wondered, with a sudden and almost angry impatience, whether Richard knew this, understood it. If he didn't, if he doubted her—but there wasn't time to deal with that question now. Walking rapidly, he was on upper King Street above the burned area; a few people were still moving about despite the lateness of the hour. He found himself suddenly at the corner of Society Street before the entrance of the Merchants' Hotel.

He stopped in the darkness outside to examine his pistol. He was perfectly steady; he satisfied himself that there wasn't the slightest tremor of his hands. For a moment his thoughts turned homeward, to Deer Hall. Well—if it came to that—he wouldn't be missed there. In the hotel the lobby was deserted; the sleepy clerk at the desk, answering his inquiry, expressed the belief that Colonel Hail was in his room. He hadn't seen him go out. The room, the clerk said, was number 33 on the third floor—turn left from the head of the stairs.

Going up the stairs, Mazÿck Marion saw her face before him, her face as he had seen it no more than two hours ago; her face and then James's. He had a moment of whirling blackness, of blind chaotic horror; then suddenly he was steady again. Turning left along the corridor, he examined in the flickering light of the gas-jets the numbers on the closed doors. In front of the door of number 33 he took his pistol from its holster. He rapped on the door.

There was no answer. He tried the door and found that it was not locked. Opening it gently, he saw that the room was dark. He struck a match and lit a gas-jet. No one was in the room, but evidently Hail was still occupying it. On the bureau a sheet of paper caught his eye. He saw—he couldn't help seeing—what was written on it:

> *"Dear Peter:*
>
> *"Sorry, but I've been called to Fort Sumter. Not sorry either because it will give me a chance to see Mazÿck—haven't seen him in months. And I can get the particulars about Charles's death. Will return tomorrow night. I'm leaving the door unlocked. Make yourself at home. You can sleep in my bed if you want to.*
>
> *"Yours*
"James H."

Marion walked slowly to the bed and sat down heavily upon it. He was shaking now like a man with ague; his hands shook so violently that he had difficulty in returning his pistol to the holster. It was all, suddenly, an incredible nightmare—what he had tried to do, what he had failed to do. A fantastic thing, an unbelievable thing. He would have done it—for her. Well, he had failed. He couldn't help her. There was nothing more.

He heard footsteps in the corridor outside. Peter Delamott, in uniform, appeared in the doorway.

"Hello, Mazÿck," Delamott said. "Didn't know you were up from the fort. I'm off duty too, for a couple of days. Came in from John's Island this morning."

Marion didn't answer and Delamott, coming into the room, said: "What's the matter with you, old fellow? You're white as a sheet. Feeling sick? Must be this devilish July heat. Where's James?"

"Gone to Fort Sumter," Marion said slowly. "There's a note for you on the bureau."

Chapter VIII

THE LATE RELIEFS WERE POSTED upon the parapet of Fort Sumter at midnight and at three o'clock; at the latter hour Richard Acton went on duty as a sentinel at the southeastern angle facing the Federal batteries on Morris Island.

The bombardment of the Fort, maintained with great violence throughout the day, had continued well into the night. The garrison, keeping under cover, had escaped further casualties with the exception of one sentinel struck down at his post. By sunset the flag had been shot down twice, the remaining casemates of the western front had been cracked and weakened; the crest of the gorge had been breached in two additional places.

Shortly before midnight a quartermaster department steamer from the city, anchoring in the darkness four hundred yards from the fort, had sent in her supplies in barges which were momentarily in danger of being sunk by the plunging fire of the ten-inch mortar shells. One of the barges had been struck, and an officer of high rank—Richard Acton hadn't heard the officer's name—visiting the fort for a conference with Captain Huguenin, had narrowly escaped death.

Then, an hour past midnight, the firing of the Union batteries had slackened and presently ceased altogether.

In this, Acton knew, there was no particular significance. Often the shelling continued throughout the night as well as all day, but on other nights the weary garrison of Sumter enjoyed brief interludes of peace due to the necessity imposed upon the Federal commander to limit somewhere the enormous quantity of ammunition expended in the effort to reduce Fort Sumter. The bombardment undoubtedly would be resumed at dawn; and meantime there was always the danger of another attempt to storm Sumter by means of a boat attack—a danger against which the sentinels were expected to guard with special vigilance whenever the bombardment lulled.

Richard Acton's post upon the parapet was protected by a breast-high earthwork enclosing the sentry-box. The night was hot and still; a breeze from the east had now died away; westward beyond Charleston he saw an intermittent glimmer of lightning. As though in answer to this, there was visible at long intervals, in the darkness shrouding Cummings Point, a flash of fire followed by a heavy report as one of the great Parrott guns trained upon Charleston sent another shell curving along its five-mile arc to crash downward amid the houses of the city.

This slow shelling of the city would probably continue all night. It was conducted now mainly from Cummings Point where one of the most effective of the long-range Parrotts was mounted; this one gun, according to the count kept at Sumter, had thrown more than four thousand shells into Charleston. That number, however, impressive as it sounded, meant little in comparison with Sumter's own experience.

The tide was ebb and at the base of the steeply sloping mass of sand and débris piled against the exterior of the gorge wall Richard could see in the dim moonlight a narrow strip of beach extending to the water's edge. The rubble covering this margin of beach was itself covered and hidden by a thick deposit of cannon balls and fragments of exploded shells. This enormous agglomeration of rusting iron, the weight of metal thrown against only one of the faces of Sumter, was, no less than the ruin of the fort itself, mute evidence of Sumter's long ordeal. Probably no other fortress in all the numberless wars of the world had with stood so terrible an iron hail.

This thought, however, left him unmoved. What he was doing in Sumter, helping to defend it, seemed tonight as futile as all the rest of his life had been. Curiously, he had been thinking about Wade Hampton—he had been reading in a month-old *Mercury* an account of Hampton's battle with Sheridan at Trevilan's Station.

He had met Wade Hampton at Notteley, he remembered, and had been strongly attracted by him; and now Hampton was lieutenant-general of cavalry, the successor of Jeb Stuart in the Army of Northern Virginia, the most celebrated officer that South Carolina had contributed to the war. James Hail was one of Hampton's colonels, a figure almost as famous as his chief. Most of the other men he had met at Notteley—those that were still alive—were officers. But he himself remained a private, a private in a cause sinking to defeat.

Well, that fact—his obscurity—was due primarily to his own feeling. A musket instead of a sword; that had been his deliberate choice. He had never regretted it, yet now the thought of it depressed him: it was symbolical of his own defeat, his own failure. From this mood he was presently released by the sudden effulgence of the enemy's calcium light at Battery Gregg on the nearest peninsula of Morris Island. The light blazed out like the glare of some soundless and sustained explosion; from a focus of intense brilliancy the long rays were flung like bright and dazzling lances over the dark waters of the bay. They illumined with a pale suffused radiance like that of the full moon the whole expanse of water between Fort Sumter and Cummings Point and threw into, bold relief the jagged and broken ramparts of the fort itself.

The illumination lasted for perhaps five minutes. It was part of the enemy's routine at Cummings Point—a precaution, apparently, against a possible boat attack upon his position there; often it was repeated at irregular intervals throughout the night. Richard Acton saw that none of the Federal ships now lay within the area reached by the calcium light; two monitors, the *Patapsco* and the *Nahant*, which had assisted the land batteries in the day's heavy bombardment, had withdrawn to their regular anchorages. It was a shot from the *Patapsco*, opening the day's shelling, that had killed Charles Gough.

That had happened not twenty feet from where he was now standing. It had solved one problem for him; it had sealed Gough's lips forever. Diane would never now know about Ash. It was ridiculous—pathetic, he said to himself, might be a better word—how important that seemed to him; his careful guarding of Ash's memory was the one thing he had been able to do for her. Gough had been killed, instantly; he had been dead when Mazÿck Marion bent over him; practically the shell had taken off his head. That, Acton thought grimly, had been the very definite and effectual end of what Charles Gough had done to bring about the secession of South Carolina.

He had done a good deal, Richard reflected. Gough and James Hail had been the most active of Barnwell Rhett's lieutenants. South Carolina's secession had been the work of no one man; it had represented the settled and deliberate conviction of a people. Nevertheless, Barnwell Rhett, for more than thirty years the champion of independence for the South, had been the aggressive leader who had done more than any other to make South Carolina's secession an accomplished fact. And it was South Carolina that had carried the rest of the South, led it into the great adventure that was bringing its ruin.

Well, Rhett had been right in every particular except one; he had believed that the South could win. It was plain enough now that it couldn't; even Charles Gough had admitted the impossibility of victory. What he, Richard Acton, had feared from the beginning was coming to pass: the South, with the millstone of slavery around its neck, was going down not merely to defeat but to obliteration. It was being destroyed not by the armies of the North but by a new age—an age of universal mass democracy disguised as universal equality and freedom. That dream could never come true, but the world dreamed it and those who would disturb its dream it would destroy. Later there would come an awakening, the shattering of that illusion, perhaps the cataclysmic collapse of a system founded upon an impossible vision. But meanwhile the South would have perished.

It would have perished, he told himself, completely. And, worse than that, it would be branded like most lost causes, not merely with failure but with guilt, with sin. Over its memory the convenient tar-brush of slavery would be drawn. What it had really been would be denied; a new picture of it, distorted and ugly, would be shown and would presently be accepted as the truth. Some day, he said to himself bitterly, *Uncle Tom's Cabin* might be read in the schools of Charleston—John C. Calhoun might be held a little man in the State House in Columbia— South Carolinians, remembering only that Barnwell Rhett had pointed a way that had led them to disaster, would forget, wouldn't even know, how clearly he had foreseen the South's vassalage, its slow death, if it feared to strike for the freedom it had the right to enjoy.

His thoughts lingered upon Rhett. He had foreseen the consequences of Rhett's policy; yet strangely, as the war had dragged on and its result had been more clearly foreshadowed, he had come more and more into sympathy with Rhett, with the movement that had led to secession. Secession was destroying the South, but it would have been strangled in any case—the rival civilization which had grown up in the industrial North would have tightened gradually its grip upon the South's throat. Better perhaps to go the way it was going than to disintegrate in a gradual and ignominious decay.

That, for thirty years, had been Barnwell Rhett's conviction; it had become, in the end, the conviction of South Carolina and of the South. Rhett, considered for the presidency of the Confederacy, had been judged too aggressive. Yet he was so far from the fire-eater he was often supposed to be that throughout his stormy life he had refused to recognize the duel; and as for his aggressiveness, it might have been better for the Confederacy, Acton reflected, if a more aggressive policy had prevailed at Richmond. There might have been, for instance, an advance after Manassas; there might have been—well, there were a thousand might-have-beens. Barnwell Rhett, pushed aside, had been ignored except in so far as the *Mercury* reflected his views in its outspoken criticisms of the policy of President Davis. It had been Rhett's fate to see the revolution he had launched sink slowly toward failure in the hands of others.

That, however, didn't complete his tragedy; his tragedy, like that of the South itself, went far beyond the fact of defeat. Something more important than the physical body of the South was perishing. It summed itself thus, in Acton's thoughts: The South was going to discover that it had never had any great men. This conviction was going to be burnt into it with fire, driven into it with bayonets. Men had labored for it, men whom the South had considered able, even great, and now all that they had striven for was being swept away. The South was going to be told, it was going to be made to believe, that those men had been little men, tainted men, men to be ashamed of.

They were going down into oblivion with the ideal they represented, the kind of liberty they believed in. Calhoun, Hayne, William Lowndes, Langdon Cheves, James Hammond, Barnwell Rhett—all that they had accomplished had been brought to nothing and so they would be brought to nothing. Their great love-it had been idolatry almost—of their state would be twisted into a false, a treasonable thing. Prophets of a defeated faith, they would be branded with error, with rebellion, and then, after a while, they would be forgotten. It would appear—it would appear even to the new generations of southerners—that the South for thirty years had been a sterile land where nothing worthy had grown, whence not one leader of stature had come. And the South of those thirty years preceding the war had been the South of South Carolina—the South, it might be said, that South Carolina had made.

Richard Acton, in the darkness upon the parapet of Fort Sumter, was lost in a dark contemplation of the fate that had overtaken his country. His mind turned inward now and then to himself and to the woman whom, strangely, he loved. Somehow there was a parallel between his own individual futility and the great futility that had been South Carolina. At least Fate, in fashioning both these things, had been in the same sardonic mood.

He had in a double sense given himself, his devotion, to ideals which, it seemed, had no right to existence. The Diane that he had once imagined didn't exist. The new generations of South Carolina, chastened by disaster, enlightened by bayonets, would learn that the South Carolina of their fathers had never, existed. They would come to believe that what had actually existed— yes, the bayonets and the successors of *Uncle Tom's Cabin* would drive this home—had been a South Carolina of error, of treason, of rebellion, of slave-driving, of oppression, of braggadocio and fire-eating, of ignorance and stupidity and iniquity. They would praise God that, thanks to Mr. Lincoln and the holier North, that iniquitous South Carolina had been destroyed.

His gorge rose at the thought.

Toward dawn Richard Acton became aware of a renewed activity in the enemy's siege works on Cummings Point. He could see nothing, hear nothing; the distance to Cummings Point was three-fourths of a mile and the faint moonlight had long ago been obliterated by a low curtain of cloud. His feeling, a slow excitement rising in him, was due, he decided, to nothing more than the virtual certainty that at dawn the bombardment of the fort would be resumed. His post upon the parapet, protected only by the sentry-box, would then become one of extreme danger. This, however, would not last long. As soon as daylight removed the possibility of a surprise attack in boats, he could retire behind the stouter barrier of the rampart itself.

Awaiting the first glimmer of dawn, he realized that his feeling of tension was increasing. He became possessed with the idea that a boat attack was impending, and this seemed the more probable because for the past hour or more the enemy had not employed his calcium light; the expanse of water between Cummings Point and the fort had remained veiled in a complete and sinister obscurity. Once he believed for an instant that he saw dark shapes in the night moving toward Sumter.

Not long after this, when a hint of day was just visible in the east, he heard a slight noise behind him. Turning quickly, he saw a vague figure ascending the rough slope of debris from the parade of the fort. A messenger, perhaps, or an officer making the round of the ramparts; he couldn't in the darkness distinguish whether the man was an officer or not. The figure climbed to the crest of the gorge and moved along the parapet toward the sentry-box. Suddenly Richard's blood turned to ice. He knew that the man was James Hail.

He knew this when Hail was still twenty feet from him, a mere darker blur in the darkness of the night. He knew also that his eyes hadn't told him; it was some deeper, deadlier sense. Something in his very blood; that was why his veins seemed to have congealed. He remembered suddenly that an officer, whose name he hadn't learned, had arrived at the fort on the quartermaster steamer that had landed supplies just before midnight. That evidently had been Hail. At home from Virginia again to see Diane. Probably he had come to Fort Sumter from her house. Her kiss upon his lips...

These thoughts raced through his mind, swifter than lightning flashes, yet they seemed to him deliberate; the moments moved slowly, more slowly than the tall figure advancing toward him. Hail wasn't ten feet from him now. The details of his uniform were dimly visible. He had discarded his sword; his double-breasted cavalry jacket was open; he was hatless, but his features were still obscure in the darkness. In a low voice he was humming a tune—*Lorena*.

Richard Acton was standing just outside the sentry-box. Hail halted and raised his hand to his forehead.

"Hello, sentry," he said easily. "I'm Colonel Hail. It's too hot to sleep in your funny old fort, so I thought I'd come up here and find a breeze."

Acton hadn't moved. What filled his mind now was the happiness in Hail's voice; it was alive, vibrant, with happiness. That, of course—the thought was like a knife—was Diane; he had just come from Diane and presently he would return to her. There was a sudden effulgence, a ghostly luminousness pale yet bright like that of the full moon—the long beams of the enemy's calcium light on Morris Island flung across the waters of the bay against the rampart of Sumter. In the white glare he saw Hail's face; and in the same instant Hail saw his and recognized him. They were facing each other and for a moment they stood thus motionless. What happened was entirely outside of any realized purpose that had then formed in Acton's mind. It was the contempt upon Hail's face that turned Richard's blood from ice to flame. Damn him, the man despised him! Because he had been whipped aside when he had dared think of Diane. Because of what had happened at Sherborne—Sherborne where he had destroyed himself to guard Diane's happiness. To James Hail he was a cur who had lived with a yellow woman.

This was plain upon Hail's face; it was as palpable, as explicit, as though Hail had flung the words in his teeth. He was a cur—that was all. Not worth a cursing. James Hail turned contemptuously away. Nothing that he might have said could have equaled the insult of his silence, his back.

In the instant and blinding blaze of his anger Richard's movement was involuntary, automatic. His hand reached out, grasped Hail's arm, whirled him round, so that again they were facing each other. Hail's response was almost instantaneous. He jerked his arm free and in the same moment his other arm shot forward. The flat of his open hand struck Richard's cheek.

This was over before either realized what was happening; it had been as swift, almost, as a flare of gunpowder, and as conclusive. There was now, Richard knew, no escape from what must follow.

A profound calmness, a sense of fate, descended upon him. His fury had gone; it had been succeeded by something deeper, more potent. Something that was in his blood as Diane was in his blood. He had never in his thoughts attempted to defend his hatred of Hail. That was both impossible and unnecessary. It was, simply, the inevitable reflex of his love. His love and, out of that, his hate; the one was as eternal as the other. His voice was steady.

"Hail," he said, "we'll end it now. Man against man. Are you ready?"

After a moment's pause, Hail said quietly, "Ready." Richard leaned his rifle carefully against the earth-wall of the sentry-box and sprang at James Hail's throat.

They swayed, locked in each other's arms, upon the parapet. The pallid glare of the calcium light faded as suddenly as it had appeared, and they fought in darkness and silence. Hail had been braced for the attack; other wise Richard's onset might have carried him over the parapet's edge. As it was, they toppled for a moment almost at the verge before Hail's straining muscles forced Acton back.

Hail was a little the taller; in weight and strength they were well matched; for several minutes they kept their footing, reeling back and forth in a blind and furious grapple which allowed no opportunity to strike. Then they went down, rolling over and over.

Somehow they struggled to their feet again and suddenly Acton wrenched himself free. They faced each other, half crouching and half naked, their uniforms ripped almost to tatters, their eyes blurred with sweat and blood. Richard Acton felt rather than saw a faint pink glow suffusing the east; at any moment, he knew, the Federal ships and batteries might open. Three feet behind Hail was the rim of the parapet. Richard plunged for him; they swayed drunkenly upon, the brink; then they went over the edge together.

Chapter IX

He realized presently that he was lying at the base of the steep declivity of sand and débris sloping down from the gorge wall of Sumter to the narrow strip of beach exposed at low tide. His feet were in the water; his bruised and half-naked body rested upon the uneven mass of rusted cannon balls and fragments of exploded shells covering the margin of beach. Evidently he had been stunned; it was now bright dawn; his ears were assailed by tremendous and reiterated crashes of sound. He saw a sudden and fountain-like upheaval of sand and bricks near the top of the redan above him where a Parrott shell buried itself and burst.

He raised himself slowly to a sitting posture and looked around him. James Hail was lying face downward six feet to his right. Hail's body, the arms fully extended, was sprawled upon the rubble of iron covering the beach. His head rested against a shapeless lump of rusted iron that had once been a cannon ball. His head, too, was shapeless; a rust of blood upon it.

Acton sat staring dully at it. Well, that, at least, was finished…fulfilled. He had no sense either of exultation or of horror, but his mind, heedless of the crashing shells, dwelt with wonder upon the strange fact that this ugly thing had come out of beauty. He didn't mean by that merely her visible loveliness; he was thinking of the whole inexplicable enchantment of her. That was why James Hail was lying there, his head crushed like an egg. Dead because of the charm, the power, of a woman; a woman unworthy to tie the laces of his boots.

Beauty and ugliness—love and hate. It seemed that they were necessary to each other, they created each other; it was a senseless, an idiotic, scheme of things. Well, he was as good as dead also— even if he lived to regain the parapet of the fort. He had killed James Hail, Colonel James Hail of Wade Hampton's cavalry, of General Lee's army. The result of that to him was sure; it would be better to be killed where he was by the enemy's shells.

He became suddenly and fully conscious of the scene before him, the havoc around him, the crashes of sound battering at his ears. Three ironclads, lying close in, and the entire armament of the land batteries were pouring their combined fire upon Fort Sumter. Shells were bursting incessantly above the fort. The sloping redan of the gorge face above him, pitted and plowed by a rain of projectiles, seemed to crawl and writhe before his eyes. In a dozen places its surface heaved upward as if in volcanic eruption where the Parrott shells dug into it and burst.

He got slowly to his feet. Vaguely at first, then more and more definitely, he realized that he must get back into the fort.

The shortest way, the only way, was up the shell-torn slope of the redan to the parapet. His knees and chest were bloody, but his plunge down 'the rough declivity had broken no bones. A mortar shell, bursting directly overhead, rained its deadly fragments all around him.

He began to struggle upward. He must get there! Damn it, he would get there. He wanted every one to know how Hail had been killed; he didn't want them to think that Hail had been killed by a shell. The concussions around him were almost continuous. Probably the gunners on Morris Island had seen him; to right and to left of him fountains of brick and sand leaped upward where the projectiles struck.

He was half-way up when he saw the flag on the parapet fall, its pole cut in half by a solid shot. Two men appeared near it, but a shell burst close above them and they vanished. A purpose formed and fixed itself in his mind; he forgot everything else.

Long after this, it seemed to him, he was running along the parapet toward the fallen flag. He stooped and lifted it. The broken stump of the staff had remained fixed in the parapet; holding the two sections of pole together, he tried to lash them fast with the halliards dangling from the flag. This was impossible; he couldn't with one hand hold the two lengths of pole against each other.

A man ran up the ladder from the parade to the parapet and joined him—Barnes, the artillery corporal. Amid the almost incessant crashing of the shells he heard Barnes cursing. "You goddam fool," Barnes screamed at him, "you're gonna be killed.

We're gonna be killed. We ain't got a chance." Barnes held the two poles together, and Acton, wrapping the halliards round and round them, lashed them fast.

Barnes leaped down from the wall, but Richard Acton looked up at the tattered flag fluttering above him. He saw it only for an instant; the blue southern cross with the stars against a red field. A shell burst directly over his head, and blackness fell on him.

Chapter X

He emerged from this much as a man wakes from a long sleep; as easily, with the same gradual, almost unwilling, resumption of conscious existence. A haziness over his mind cleared slowly away and he realized that he was lying on his back in a bed in the small bomb-proof chamber used as an emergency hospital. He remembered that he had raised the flag upon the parapet and that Barnes had been with him; what had happened before and after that wasn't clear. Evidently he had been hit, but he couldn't decide where his wound was; he was conscious of no pain, no difficulty in breathing.

He knew, however, that he was incapable of even the slightest movement of his limbs or body; his body, apparently, had ceased to exist as a part of him. Yet this discovery did not alarm him; it seemed entirely unimportant. What concerned him most was something quite apart from his physical state, something upon which he tried in vain to fix his mind.

It was something of great importance, but it eluded him. His thoughts, in spite of his will, slipped away. He was at Avalon... Faces and scenes at Avalon...His mother, the big oak at the head of the avenue, Marony whose grandfather had been an African king, white herons flying over the rice-fields, Lowndes and Eliza Fenwick and Motte Nesbit, lights twinkling on the river, Ringo his pet raccoon, Black Samson hallooing as a deer broke cover...

He said to himself that he had evidently fallen asleep again, but now his return to consciousness wasn't like the waking of a sleeper. Rather, he had a vague impression that he had been away and that he had come back for some definite and imperative purpose. He heard the familiar sound of a mortar shell exploding outside the bomb-proof; through the thick, earth-covered walls the noise came to him as a dull and heavy thud. He seemed to be alone, but then he couldn't turn his head or speak. Doctor Chardon, the post surgeon, or one of his attendants, might be sitting somewhere behind him.

The reiteration of the muffled explosions annoyed him. His thoughts were no longer consecutive; flashes of intense mental activity alternated with periods of drowsiness. He wondered irritably where he was, remembering only after an effort that he was in Fort Sumter. Then it was night under the magnolias at Notteley, and Diane, in white with a white rose in her hair, was standing in a pool of moonlight in front of him...

Sherman before Atlanta...it couldn't be true that Davis had taken the command from Joe Johnston and given it to Hood at the moment when Johnston was ready to strike—the ablest man the Confederacy had, after Lee...Ash Rowland was the Knight of Alhambra, Peter Delamott was a Knight Templar, and Mazÿck Marion was the Knight of St. Luke's. They ought to be able to beat James Hail. But they couldn't; Hail, on a great black horse, had beaten them all. They were charging massed batteries of Yankee cannon: Mazÿck and James Hail and Ash Rowland and Peter Delamott and hundreds and thousands more. They were mounted on splendid horses and they wore shining armor and plumes; they carried long lances and glittering swords and over them waved the Confederate flag. Fools! Didn't they know that the world had changed, that plumes and lances had passed forever, that feudalism and chivalry were dead?

Well, he had tried to make them see what would happen if the South seceded; and he had tried to make Philips Cordray see what would happen if the abolitionists lashed the South to madness. And now it was happening. Massed batteries of Yankee cannon were blowing the Pineland tournament into eternity. The swords and lances were broken in blood...The paneled rooms of Avalon were full of smoke; negroes in blue uniforms were in the front hail. The women—the women weren't safe, Diane wasn't safe...

Good God, those fanatics talked about equal rights, equal power, for the negroes! They didn't know or didn't care what that would mean for the whites, the whole white race. Black freemen, black men with guns and votes, ruling the South! Vienna was smiling at him, laughing at him. Her eyes burned like coals, but Black Samson's eyes were gentle, there was no hatred in old Marony's eyes. The negroes, in from the fields, were singing in their cabins, but their voices were drowned by cannon. The *Weehawken* had reached the buoy; the guns of Sumter crashed; the walls of Sumter rocked under the shock of the great fifteen-inch shells...

He had again an impression—a conviction, rather—that he had been away, wholly removed to a distant place, whence he had now returned. With this was the feeling that he had returned for some definite and important purpose; this purpose achieved, he would not return another time. He discovered suddenly that Mazÿck Marion was now stooping beside his bed. That was good; it was pleasant to see Mazÿck to hear his voice.

He understood perfectly what Mazÿck was saying—"Richard, can you hear me?" Marion repeated the question and waited, watching him anxiously. He tried with his eyes to reassure Mazÿck to tell him that he was listening. He knew presently that he had succeeded, for Marion nodded and bent closer to him.

"Richard," he said, "I want you to know that Diane loves you. I was with her last night and there is no doubt about it, Richard. No matter what may have happened between you, I swear that this is true."

Was it, he wondered, for this that he had returned? Was it this—this folly, this illusion of Mazÿck's—that had brought him back yet again from that shadowy country of forgetfulness and peace? Could a lie, an illusion, have that power? It couldn't! He knew this surely, with an immediate and everlasting certainty; and slowly, like the coming of dawn, the truth came to him.

Slowly at first like the coming of dawn, then swiftly like the noon sun blazing forth after a summer storm in sudden and overwhelming and incomprehensible glory.

This too—this miracle that now filled his mind—was incomprehensible. He did not try to understand it. He only knew—because no lie could have that power—that this was true. It made, perhaps because of his weakness, no ecstasy in him. There was no exaltation, only a sense of fulfilment. He lay with his eyes fixed steadily upon Mazÿck's. He was going away again now—he had found that which he had been seeking.

He waited, free from all pain, his brain active and clear. He was thinking—but, strangely, the thought had no power to assail his happiness—that he had failed her. Through some fault, some blindness, of his being, he had failed her. He hadn't caught the bright gleam of her, he had never really discovered her heart. That was why, in a sense that seemed to him now evanescent and unimportant, he had lost her. Mazÿck had never failed her, he had never doubted her. Yes, Mazÿck had been somehow stronger, had owned a finer faith. But this reflection, too, left his peace untroubled. She had forgiven him his great fault; it was he, Richard, that she loved.

That was enough. He was tired now; there were shadows, a slow confused shifting of scenes and familiar faces and thoughts. His father—Twis'foot Toby—Lowndes Fenwick—old Blue, the first dog he had ever owned. Barnwell Rhett was speaking to him; a brave, high, bitter man going down into darkness with the South he cherished. He saw the live-oaks of Avalon and then, suddenly, he was on the parapet of Fort Sumter. The tattered flag was up again, but the thunder of cannon had ceased. There was a faint sound of fiddles, and Diane was moving toward him through a soft enchantment of moonlight. The moment before his arms would have enfolded her, he died.

The End